C000084481

Return of the
Black Magician

Richard Raftery

**Grosvenor House
Publishing Limited**

This book is published by
Grosvenor House Publishing Ltd
Link House
140 The Broadway, Tolworth, Surrey, KT6 7HT.
www.grosvenorhousepublishing.co.uk

This book is a work of fiction. Any resemblance to
people or events, past or present, is purely coincidental.

A CIP record for this book
is available from the British Library

ISBN 978-1-78623-641-8

Preface

I began working on *The Return of the Black Magician* in August 1980. Having read many horror stories in my youth, and being avidly interested in politics, I thought it might be somewhat unusual, if not entirely unique, to write a comic-horror novel with a political dimension.

My original handwritten manuscripts were passed on to an old schoolfriend, **Vincent Rayner** who, as well as typing them up on his antiquated typewriter, would often draw from his own very substantial reservoir of knowledge on many matters to advise, as appropriate, on some contextual specifics. Vincent was an aficionado of both science-fiction and the macabre, both in film and print. It was possible to learn a great deal by simply sitting at a table in a pub and listening to him. Neither of us ever dabbled in actual witchcraft or black magic so a certain amount of research was necessary. There was a woodland a few miles from Ormskirk where it was rumoured that such things went on, but I did not undertake any personal investigation to establish the veracity of this.

I completed the first draft in 1985 and then life got in the way. I have visited it many times over the years, constantly editing and redrafting sections (all made much easier with the welcome advent of the word processor and the internet).

In March 2017 I received the sad news that Vincent had died suddenly. In many ways, this work is a tribute to him, as it would probably never have seen the light of day were it not for his support.

The story is centred around the town of Ormskirk and surrounding villages. However, the landscape is surreal and distorted. There is no intention to disparage either the people or the district itself as the story is an allegory (or something similar). Ormskirk is a fine town and has very much moved with the times.

The Stanley Arms does exist and can be traced back to the 17th Century, although it does not remotely resemble the establishment depicted in the novel. At the time of writing it is an outstanding (and award-winning) place to go and enjoy a beer and a pub lunch – it successfully eschews many of the trappings which make so many modern pubs inhospitable places in which to find solace. There are no fruit machines, jukeboxes or Sky TV. What it does have is a great selection of draught ales, as well as a whole variety of alternatives. The Ormskirk Gin is highly recommended.

The year in which the story is set is one prior to the advent of mobile phones, computers and other modern devices for communication and investigation. Probably the late 1970s is a reasonable approximation (with a shot of the 1670s for added ghastliness). However, some of the themes explored would seem to be disturbingly perennial.

The characters in the novel are entirely fictional. All are flawed – some deeply so. They frequently express preposterous and sometimes repulsive views, some of which may sound ominously familiar in the convulsive and turbulent political climate of today.

It goes without saying (or should do) that the views expressed by the characters are not (in most cases) those of the author.

We live in an age when some people are regularly offended, sometimes even outraged, by what they read. If you find anything in this novel offensive you are advised to employ the services of either (a) a homeopath (b) an astrologer or (c) a chiromancer. Take your pick; I guarantee they will all serve you equally well.

I am additionally indebted to the artist **Lorna Johnstone** for producing several illustrations for inclusion as well as designing the cover in the distinctly *pulp-horror* style which is a definite constituent of the novel.

Now read on . . .

Dedicado a

Liam Raftery

Tu estrella alumbró brillantemente pero muy
brevemente
Siempre estás conmigo donde quiera que vaya
Escucho tu voz y veo tu sonrisa
Cada noche estas en mis sueños

Siempre amado
Jamás olvidado

Devil on the Highway

The Devil's on the highway
He's coming to your town
The Devil's on the highway
And walking to your town
You'd better lock your front door
And keep your head well down

There's black magic stirrin'
Beneath the blood-red moon
There's effigies a-burnin'
Beneath the blood-red moon
You can hear the dogs a-howling
When the devil plays his tune

It's too late to start cryin'
When you fall beneath the spell
There's no use in complainin'
When you fall beneath the spell
And no amount of runnin'
Will get you out of hell

Now evil glides through darkness
Where no light will ever shine
Yes evil glides through darkness
Where no light can ever shine
And poison crawls through cobwebbed halls
Into unsuspecting minds

Nobody saw him coming
He never made a sound
No one ever saw him coming
He never made a sound
But he cast a long dark shadow
Right across our little town

Benny 'Bean picker' Barwise
(a.k.a. The Bickerstaffe Bluesman)

Chapter 1:

Throat Cut!

The Black Magician stumbled down the road to Ormskirk. His gait was clumsy, uneven; he weaved from side to side like a ship in a strong wind. His right hand was clasped tightly against his neck in a valiant attempt to stem the flow of blood that poured from a hideous wound. This was only partly successful; his black garments were soaking up considerable quantities of the red fluid and there was a zigzag trail of droplets on the road he had faltered along. His face had a ghastly white pallor, but his eyes flashed with rage and frustration.

A normal person would, long ago, have succumbed to the weakness that swept in waves over his body, but not the magician! His feet were leaden, and the coldness spreading slowly upwards through his body was enough, perhaps, to give ample warning that death was impending — yet he failed to surrender. His head was bent forward, his left arm hung at his side — but still he staggered on. Some instinct sustained him, and he turned off the road and down a dusty track towards a peasant's cottage. He lurched against the old wooden door, kicking it to get attention.

"Let me in," he croaked. "In the name of Beelzebub, let me in."

The door opened, the occupant leaping back as the senseless form of T'osh fell to the floor. Then he seemed to revive. He whispered:

"I will stay here . . . You will obey . . . I shall spend some days here. You will hold your tongue . . . Perhaps you will be rewarded . . ."

As soon as T'osh mentioned a reward the peasant dragged the magician inside, placing him in a comfortable bed. Bandages were produced so that while T'osh slept his wounds were tended. In due course, he wakened and was convinced to take a herbal remedy, a dose that was repeated whenever he regained consciousness, which, in those first few weeks, was an occasion neither frequent nor prolonged.

"Will he live?" asked the peasant's wife.

"I do not know," said the peasant.

"Who is he?"

"A man of some clout, judging by his garb."

"But the wound . . . has he been in trouble?"

"Methinks an assassination attempt."

And with that the conversation ended.

At this point it might be best to mention that the cotter was a fellow in his late twenties by the name of John Ambler. A stocky, unintelligent, stoic person, he lived with his wife, Adaline, and eked a steady if miserable existence from the land. In the back of his dull mind he suspected that his guest could possibly be the infamous Black Magician and, oblivious to the dangers of dealing with such an unscrupulous and evil creature, thought that his charitable deed might land him in good stead with T'osh.

* * *

Three weeks passed . . .

. . . and the magician could now sit up in bed and hold a monologue. He did not do this too often, but preferred to scribble madly upon pieces of paper, committing to ink his plans for *the perfect state*: a system that incorporated certain individualistic, and indeed idiosyncratic, economic and social theories. This book, when completed, would become, he hoped, the sole charter of his rule in the land. It would give the peasants an unfailing instruction book for their existence, an explanation of the universe and much, much more: in fact, it would be the only book allowed in the land, a sort of Bible, *Leviathan* and *Look and Learn Book of the Black Arts* — who could wish for more?

Apart from this scribbling T'osh did little else, other than gobbling down the basic fare as was reverently placed in front of him by the Amblers, but once or twice when he seemed to be thinking aloud and trying to put his thoughts into coherent sentences, he would stare into space and deliver a monologue in a gabbling, high pitched shriek.

"The essential nature of man: what it is. Man is a slave to various passions, and these can and must be channelled into the correct direction for the betterment of myself; or, as it shall hereafter be called, the State. Firstly, man is SUPERSTITIOUS: There is no doubt but that this can be forced into the correct direction. He can be controlled by his superstitions and they can be used to bring out certain innate qualities. He will bring gifts and unquestioning obedience to his Superior. To allay the dread of the unknown he will offer up some — nay,

nearly all — of his produce, and he will execute certain rituals to keep the demons of the dark from his hearthside. The coming state will utilize this to the full; the economic gain will be obvious to all who can consider the matter with intelligence.

"BIGOTRY: Man is by nature a slave to bigotry and prejudice of all kinds. Only scholarly fools believe otherwise; they shelter behind a smokescreen of detailed rationalizations. In the perfect state, it will be necessary to utilize this bigotry for the greater good of the state, for the bigoted man can and will hate all who live outside of this state, and he will despise and then destroy all who would seek to change things, desire for power, desire to dress differently, speak differently, walk differently — in short — any who would aspire to question any aspect of the perfect and eternal state. Man can be reduced to a seething foaming maniac when the objects of his hate are mentioned; he can be ever vigilant and ready to take up the pitchfork and the cudgel against any who would differ from the norm, seeing them as his sworn enemy, though they have done him no harm. He will despise any who would seek to enter the perfect state regardless of their talents and disposition, for he is easily persuaded that they are intent on pursuing an evil agenda.

"IGNORANCE: Man is by nature ignorant. He does not seek learning; he eschews it. He does not wish to become erudite, except, as a way of belonging to the peer group should society place learning as its desiderata; if he cannot achieve this learning, he will despise not only the most learned, but also the knowledge itself. Taught to read, man will only gravitate to the most lowly, trashy and dismal written words. He is much happier burning a *dissident at a stake, and he is of a melancholy nature when trying to absorb knowledge. He rejects advances and fears progress, believing that things were always better in the 'old days'. Education will be discussed in a later chapter, but it needs must be said at this point that man in the perfect state need only be taught in a very limited sense: to be able to read and write to the extent that he will be able to absorb the propaganda put forward by the rulers. There will be no place for books or learning other than these books already mentioned. Certainly, the new citizen will not be allowed to think, neither for himself nor anyone else. He will remain suspicious of any who appear to have expertise in any subject and is easily swayed into thinking that such people are charlatans and best ignored and to adopt instead a much more simplistic ideology reduced to a few basic mantras designed for endless repetition.*

"However, in each generation a few will be spawned who do desire learning. Such children will be identified and given instruction in the Black Arts and leadership; this being dealt with in a later chapter . . .

. . . ah, indeeeeeeeeeeeed, but the planning for the new state is no simple affair."

And so it went on. T'osh would scribble away for hours, sometimes breaking into speeches like the one above until, with eyes flashing and hands shaking, he would fall to the floor and roll upon the carpet, pounding with his fists some unseen adversary.

Meanwhile, the cotter and his wife went about their daily business, promising themselves that their end reward would justify their actions.

* * *

9

The weeks passed; now T'osh could walk with the aid of a blackthorn stick. He would walk down to a nearby pond and there consider his future return to the world. He would mutter to himself.

"No doubt they think me dead. Ha! Well, let the fools think this. I shall return. Indeeeeeeeed!"

Having so mused he would look around for a small animal, such as a rabbit or hedgehog, which he would proceed to beat with his stick, then drink the corpse's blood.

Though he was not aware of it, he was, on occasions, observed in his activities. A wide-eyed, haunted-looking, threadbare character would sometimes be crouched in the nearby ditch, either rubbing sticks together or cradling his cat and moaning softly to himself. This was the first time Noah Halfmoon had ever come across T'osh and he regarded him with a peculiar mixture of fascination and fear. Their paths would ultimately cross in a most spectacular manner, but for the moment his presence in this story is unremarkable, as indeed had been his entire life thus far.

*   *   *

On the border of Aughton and Melling there was sited a large house set deeply in the rural landscape. Its occupant was a man of science and learning named Quartus Poffle. He was small, pale and wore large spectacles, this insubstantial form containing a disposition and character that had ensured he pick up few friends upon the road of life. He was an intolerable bore, little more than a sack to contain his much-vaunted learning. He could not hold a conversation but that he would bring it around to subatomic particles, monads, or such subjects, or, what was worst, his physical deformity — ingrown toenails. In season he suffered from boils and heat-lumps; at such times these savoury subjects entered his talk, generally while he was eating a meal of corned beef or a dish of what he liked to pretend was ice cream (in reality it was a curious combination of ordinary cream which had been placed in his cellar for two days and then laced with sugar, yeast and dried elderflowers before being allowed to 'mature' for three more days).

"In truth," he would opine, "I am cursed by vese toenails, and can do nuffing to get rid of vem. I tell you, vey are a curse. Vey keep me awake at nights and distract me from my studies. I would sell my soul if I could spend ve rest of my life free from ingrown toenails, boils and heat lumps. I fink vat if ever a man was cursed by vese fings, it was me. I have been plagued by vese fings for years and it is absolutely terrible. You don't know how lucky you are not to have to suffer as I do from vese severe ailments. I warrant vat I suffer more van any man in vis country."

"But surely," asked a weary guest, "surely a man of your knowledge would be able to do something about these matters?"

"Do you not fink vat I have tried everyfing? I have spent nights looking frough every book I could and have even sunk to herbal remedies. But all to no avail! I am still sorely distracted; ve pain is perpetual and badgering. It is an evil manifestation vat a man such as I should suffer in vis way!"

"Why don't you try the services of the Black Magician?"

"Hah! You don't imagine vat I believe in vis kind of rubbish, do you? What do you fink I am? Do not forget vat I am a man of letters and learning."

"But there are those who are greatly influenced by him."

"Well — vey can be as stupid as vey like, but I tell you vat if he can cure me of my ailments ven he would be superior to any doctor, for I have tried everyfing. If he was to cure me I would greatly reward him, I can tell you. No man knows how I have suffered over ve years wiv vese fings."

"Do you mean that you would give him a try?"

"I would be willing to try anyfing once, vough I can't say I have much faif in vese fings. Why? Do you know him?"

"Er . . . vaguely."

It had better be pointed out that the companion was an employee of Poffle's, a labourer who tended the acres of the lands that Poffle had inherited from his ancestors. This man lived in a cottage some distance from the Poffle mansion, but he was often invited to dine with his employer. This the labourer did not relish, for every meal followed the same dreary pattern: a cup of lukewarm tea, a plate of corned beef, dry, stale bread, this followed by a dish of 'ice cream'. Bad though this was, the crowning horror was Poffle's reedy and never-ending voice talking of his complaints and his condition — a subject guaranteed to turn the strongest of stomachs even if the meal did not. Often the meal went on for hours, sometimes until after 9.30pm, thus leaving the labourer a scant hour in which to wash the taste out of his mouth with pints in the Stanley Arms. When he did manage to escape to the local, he would stand at the bar, passing many remarks about his employer's physical appearance, intelligence, parentage and various other topics — all of which tended to be markedly uncharitable.

But on the evening in question it was yet early. Time had passed since the magician had been mentioned and Poffle was holding forth on guns.

"You must always oil vem regularly or vey become very rusty very rapidly. If vey are well-oiled ven vey can be used wiv great accuracy. I fink vat if any man—"

"Tripe and trotters, that reminds me!" exclaimed the labourer. "I found a fox-hole this morning and, if I get out at once, I might be able to catch the scheming little vulpine before he gets at the chickens. If it's all right, I'd like to be excused."

Ten seconds later, leaving Poffle open-mouthed at the table, he was moving at quite a remarkable speed down the road which led to the Stanley Arms where he was soon to be found leaning against the bar in conversation with the curvaceous landlady, a certain Florinda Farrier.

"Do you know what became of the Black Magician T'osh?"

"Some say his throat was split by some *do-gooders* so that he was left for dead. Mind you, I don't think he died, not him."

She leant forward so that her low-cut dress revealed her not inconsiderable charms while she whispered into the labourer's ear. The information pleased the labourer and he bought Florinda a drink.

* * *

On the following night Poffle entertained guests for tea. Earlier he had played croquet with them, but now they were all hunched over plates of corned beef. Poffle's guests were two newcomers to the area who had just bought a tumbledown farmhouse up the road. They had readily accepted Poffle's invitation. He was their nearest neighbour and they were desirous of joining the local community — within reason, of course: Poffle was acceptable but the grimy labourers and farmers and artisans were not. Timothy and Cressida wanted to escape the rat-race of the city and sought a life of peace, tilling the land and living off its yield. Of course there was always her 'inheritance' to fall back on if all else failed.

Timothy was wearing his newest and least patched jeans, together with a kaftan, while Cressida wore what she supposed to be a peasant's smock, though it had cost Timothy a not inconsiderable sum when she had spotted it in an expensive bohemian shop in what was intended to be their final trip to London before they relocated to their rural idyll. She was holding forth on a subject dear to her heart and simple enough for her restricted thinking — astrology.

"Look at it this way, if the moon can influence the tides, then the stars themselves must influence us and determine our character. Do not forget that there are people who are influenced by the moon. It has always been so. Now if one casts a horoscope, its true readings will reveal one's hidden strengths and weaknesses. For myself, I have no head for logic, science or material things: I am one with the sphere of the arts, there can my spirit soar. Painting and music are my all, as indeed they must be, for they are the dominant qualities when Saturn is in trine with Mars and Sagittarius is in the house of Leo (*or some such gibberish — typist's note*), events which happened at my nativity.

"Yes, the position of the heavenly bodies at the time of one's birth is all that counts. Once this was shown to me, I found my strengths and depths. I have learned peace with myself. Now I meditate twice daily, live a simple life, forbearing to touch the charred flesh of innocent creatures wantonly and cruelly slain by man — thus I hope you understand my refusal of your corned beef. I would much prefer a cabbage or lettuce leaf, if you have them available."

"Well . . . er . . . I don't eat vegetables myself." (Poffle would soon be adding scurvy and vitamin deficiency to his many complaints.) "However, ver is a cactus in my window. Perhaps if I boil it up you will be able to eat vat, along wiv some of ve mushrooms which grow outside. I never eat fruit and vegetables myself; rarely anyfing but corned beef. To me ve taste of corned beef is ve most pleasant fing in ve world and for a moment takes my mind off my complaints." (Which, should this disproportionate corned-beef consumption have carried on, would have had a new number, protein poisoning.)

Having said this, he went to prepare the cactus and gather the mushrooms. When he returned, Cressida continued:

"Of course, one just doesn't have to rely on astrology; a glance at one's palm will usually confirm all these things. For example, Mr Poffle, I can see you are a practical man of science and learning, sceptical of these very real matters."

"Well, yes, I guess vat is true."

"With me," said Timothy, "it is all a matter of the community. I believe in the traditional village way of life and all its aspects. To me city life is alienation — that's how I would define it! The sound of traffic pollution, vandalism, the people themselves, oh how I detest it! I abhor it, I tell you! Give me the draughty and damp farmhouse any day. Ah, the smell of manure, cockcrow at break of dawn, windswept meadows and the rain in my face, the smell of real farmhouse cooking, the singalongs in the local tavern. That is the life for me. And for you? What is your preferred lifestyle?"

"Well . . . er . . . I don't really have much to do wiv ve actual running of ve farm, and as for taverns, well I am a tea drinker myself. Take my labourer, for example: he is always in ve tavern, drinking. In consequence, he cannot do more van ten hours work a day and always must have Sundays off. It makes him very lazy. Look at me vough, I am always at my books despite ve sorry state of my healf."

. . . and he proceeded to tell them about his boils, his heat-lumps, his ingrown toenail, at one point stripping his right foot and displaying it upon the table in order to convince his guests of the extent of his agony. Both turned greener than the cactus, and Timothy went so far as to rush from the room with his hand over his mouth.

"Why don't you see a faith healer or a herbalist?" asked the ill-looking Cressida.

"Well I have twice tried herbal remedies, but all to no avail. I don't believe in vose uvver fings."

"Ah yet, did I but suffer from the most appalling patch of dry skin on my left elbow until I went to a white witch, an old friend of mine. She had books on sorcery, alchemy and arcane lore, which showed that I was the victim of a hex. You see, I had tried everything to get rid of it, still every day I was troubled by this thing. But the white witch broke the spell and I was cured. You may well be the victim of such a thing; anyone have it in for you?"

"I don't fink so."

"Well, even so, if I were you, I'd be thinking about it. It'd be worth trying. Goodnight."

"Goodnight."

*　　*　　*

As Cressida began to walk home, she started to feel dizzy. She was quite alone; Timothy had left some time earlier to take some medication for his queasy innards. Without warning she fell on the dusty road, writhing, her hands crossed over her belly in a vain attempt to stop the pain.

"What ails ye, woman?" asked a gruff voice from the night; so was she introduced to Poffle's labourer as he careened home from the Stanley Arms.

"Oh, oh, oh! I feel as if I'm dying. Ah, help me, help me . . . please. Oh! Help me— aaaaahhhhhhh!"

Wasting no time, he picked her up with an easy sweep of his arms and brought her across the fields to his small cottage. He did not take her inside but put her on a bench. Then he went through the front door and emerged seconds later with a glass of murky green liquid.

"Drink this at once, for — if what I suspect is true — your life may depend upon it."

"Aaaahhhhhh . . . oh . . . but what is—"

"Never you mind! Drink it quickly, else I will be required to hold you and force it down your throat."

Cressida, never having been spoken to in such a manner, quaffed the drink exactly as she was bidden. For a time nothing happened. But then, with a scream, she fell into the dust. Convulsions followed, during which she moaned, retched and vomited. It was almost an hour before these tremors ceased but, when they had gone their way, Poffle's labourer led the shaken woman into his abode, where he sat her on the bed and produced a second, more pleasing draught.

"Oh," she said shortly afterwards, "I'm beginning to feel much better already. Do you know . . . can you guess what caused my illness?"

"I would say that it was caused by bad food. Where and when did you last eat?"

"I dined with a local landowner."

"Who? Tell me, woman, tell me at once."

"Mr Poffle— your expression! Do you know him?"

"Know Poffle? By the mark woman he is my employer, and I have often dined with him: but faith! I would eftsoons have supp'd with the Prince of Darkness, than feasted upon his infernal corned beef, food that is tunnelled by maggots and where mould makes impious claim."

"But I had no corned beef. I do not follow the habit of consuming the flesh of dead animals."

"But you must have eaten something! Anything in that house is tainted with corruption. Ere I dine at the house I fortify myself with draughts such as you have supp'd. Come leman, say what you did eat?"

"All I had was boiled cactus."

"And the rest — the rest!"

"Just some mushrooms gathered by Mr Poffle from his own garden."

"Mushrooms? Mushrooms! Woman, say you mushrooms? Don't you know that such wholesome growths flourish not in Poffle's gardens. Nay, he hath nought but a goodly crop of toadstools. Methinks thou ought give praise to thy maker for thy deliverance."

"What was in the drink?" asked Cressida, changing the subject.

"Plenty of salt, washing fluid, some ingredients of my own; of the nature of the second drink, ah well, that is my secret."

Sometime later Cressida returned home, where Timothy was seated, anxiously waiting for her.

"What gives?"

"Oh Timothy, I have been at death's door. I swear that I felt my soul begin to leave my body — Timothy, by now I could have been a ghost, traipsing along the astral plain!"

*　　*　　*

The next evening someone visited John Ambler's house. He was first made aware of it when the stout oak shuddered under someone's knock upon the door. Timidly, Ambler opened the door and saw two people standing there. One was small and bespectacled; the other taller and more workmanlike.

"We come to see T'osh," said the taller.

T'osh now occupied a small room upstairs; the strangers were directed there.

"This is the one," said the taller one to T'osh. "The one I was telling you about, the one who wishes to be cured of his ills."

"Indeeeeeeeed. I will be at the ruined chapel in the wood; you know where it is. Be there, both of you, thirty minutes short of midnight. Indeeeeeed."

*　　*　　*

About an hour after the meeting at John Ambler's, Poffle's labourer called upon Timothy and Cressida. Timothy was nowhere in sight, but Cressida sat cross-legged on the floor. She was in a state of dishabille; her silken attire was flimsy and revealing. Her eyes were closed. For the first time the labourer noticed the fullness of her décolletage.

He pulled himself away from the window and smote the door which was opened by Cressida some minutes later; she was now fully clothed.

"Good evening. You may remember me from the other night. My name is Wladek. I — I was passing and sought you out to enquire after your health."

"Oh. Well — thank you. I'm fine now. Thank you again for all you did. Won't you step inside? I'm afraid that Timothy isn't here at the moment: he's off visiting his father, something about a loan."

They went inside.

"Would you like a cup of nettle tea?" asked Cressida.

"Er . . . yes! Why not? I'd love a cup."

She disappeared for a few minutes then returned with two cups of nettle tea and some homemade buns liberally smeared with homemade butter and homemade marmalade. Wladek sat in silence, not passing comment on the tea or buns; after all he was an honest man and countless meals with Poffle had dulled his gastric senses.

The snack being over, they began to talk of many things. Cressida noticed for the first time Wladek's soothing, almost hypnotic voice tones, rough though his words were at times. He spoke with a heavy accent which Cressida could not identify and his speech was peppered with words and phrases which were archaic and, in some cases, virtually obsolete. She listened wide-eyed and enchanted as Wladek spoke about his life on the farm. There was something strange yet reassuring about the man: he seemed to be an integral part of the country, one with the hoary trees, one with the primal rocks, yet he was not more than forty years of age.

". . . and so," he was saying, "there I have lived for nigh on five years; five come Martinmas. I run the farm well and completely, for my employer cares nought for it — nor anything else but his books, his corned beef, his damned ingrown toenails." His face cracked into a smile of crafty triumph. "Because of this unworldliness, I have been able to fool him. He is passing mean, paying but a pittance for my services. Yet what he does not realise is that I also complete the books, and can, generally on market days or when traders call, generally salt away some of the profits. Do not look at me as if I were a common thief! I tell you that he pays but starvation wages. Anyway, he already has more money than is good for one soul, not to mention the rooms filled to the rafters with tins of corned beef, and the library and laboratory set up to cure him of boils, ingrown toenails and heat-lumps."

"Yes, but if that is the case, why work for him?"

"I have admitted that I make quite a bit of money out of my employ — and for all its ills 'tis better than some work that I have done. Besides, I find it difficult to find employ." Here he rolled up the left leg of his trousers.

"My God! How did that happen?"

"My leg is wood to the knee because one crazed and drunken hobbledehoy thought that I had placed the evil eye upon his soul. So, one moonless night he crept up to my bed and smote me with his axe! 'Twas luck that he was drunk and there was no moon, for he could not see which way I lay abed; had he struck the other end of the bed . . . well! But this reminds me: are you not interested in the occult?"

"That is so."

"Well then, you might care to go with me to convocation, not far from here, just prior to this very midnight. It is concerned with the Dark For— . . . occult arts I mean."

"Then I would love to come. I feel, I know that I am well equipped to deal with these matters. My palm and my stars show that I am a *Sensitive*. For example, when I am in an old building, I'm aware of many presences which I know—"

"Good," said Wladek, cutting her off, "I'll call for you betimes."

* * *

"I tell you it all happened," said Martyn, "not one word of a lie. All as I have said, down to the smallest event."

Time had passed, and the academic life of Martyn Hopkins was a thing of the past. He had been forced to take employment, much to his distaste. Work had its consolations though: here he was sitting in a pub in Maghull of an evening with his workmates. However, he could have wished for a more — gullible was a word that crossed his mind, but he substituted receptive — he could have wished for a more receptive audience than his still cynical workmates. He stared them out, failed, and said with the aggression of a cornered rat;

"Look, my friends can easily verify my words."

"Well . . . we don't see much of them, do we? Where are they, hiding in the lounge?" said the spokesman, the most voluble and the most cynical of his workmates.

"There's reasons for this. Frank Grogan has spent most of the time locked in a room since it all happened."

"Are the walls padded?"

"Very funny. No, he's been writing a book which, I am informed, will be no less than one thousand pages in length and will concern two hours in the life of a man in a coma — told from his point of view, naturally."

"And the others?"

"Dancing Jack has gone off once again on his travels; he may return one day. Red Joe has gone to ground, but I hear that he is writing a book on a political theme; this book is both provocative and stimulating, designed to undermine the stability of decadent capitalist society — well, that's what I got told at any rate."

"What of the Poblagryn? Does he still live?"

"Yes, and I can tell you where; he is in a nursing-home here in Maghull, still suffering from the after-effects of his injuries and a mental breakdown caused by his suffering at the hands of his henchmen. Ha! He was always giving such good instructions in torture, but he could not take it. Poetic justice indeed. I hope he never recovers."

"The Black Magician?"

"Of him I have not heard, though it would be a godsend indeed if he were dead. But, even if he is not, then I doubt we'll hear from him again."

"I'm sorry to say this, but I think that it's all a bit bloody implausible. Been on a bad trip, eh? Come on, admit it."

Martyn's face went the colour of dully glowing iron. "No way, man. It happened like I said."

"I still have my doubts about—"

"Why the frigging hell should I care about whether you believe me? Look, people used to think the world was flat — did that make it flat? People might believe in hobgoblins, bloody well die for that belief, but that's not going to make any appear at the bottom of your garden. I don't care if you believe me or not. These things happened, and it's your lookout if you don't believe me.

"But — and this is what I don't like one bloody bit —you seem to doubt my integrity: no man does this with impunity. I shall say just one more thing before I down my drink and take my leave of you, that, if this land is ever menaced again by the likes of the Black Magician or his henchmen, then you had better pray that there are the likes of Dancing Jack, Red Joe, Frank and myself abroad in this zone; people who are willing to use their wits, courage and strength in order to defend this land."

Having said this, he stormed to the door. Cool evening air poured through the open doorway. The sun was setting, but there was yet enough light to illumine the tracts of land: fertile fields, shady coppices, winding country roads, crofts, some with the first light lit, all were cast into an aspect of poignant beauty by the crepuscular light.

Martyn pointed to this panorama.

"I love this land; I would wish to live nowhere else."

He took a deep breath and stood himself erect. "If I must fall in honourable conflict against a dishonourable rogue, no matter what his rank or station; if my blood must one day stain the fair fields of Ormskirk, or Melling, or Maghull, then so be it! I welcome it! If I can save this land from evil or pestilence, at whatever cost, I will. I WILL!"

Tears rolled down Martyn's face, and his farewell was a choked sob as he went into the deepening twilight.

"Goodnight," muttered a few of Martyn's workmates.

"Dancing Jack, that's a funny name," said one.

"Who do you fancy in the 3.30 at Haydock?" asked another of the first.

"Dunno," said the first, "anyhow, who's getting the ale in then?"

* * *

It was now quite dark. Martyn turned up his collar at the unseasonable chill. Though the road was empty, there was a feeling of menace in the air, faint yet distinct.

Martyn shuddered and he knew not why.

Chapter 2:

The Magician Strikes Back

Cressida sat before the bedroom mirror taking more care than usual about her appearance: She was preparing for her nocturnal jaunt with Wladek. It was past nine in the evening and, after thoroughly washing herself in the tin bathtub, she dressed herself in a long black robe and dark stockings, putting on her feet flat, sensible shoes. She put on a pair of exotic silver earrings; each shaped like an octopus, and plaited her dark hair, finally donning a broad-brimmed, black hat.

Whilst she did this, her thoughts were on Wladek. She could not help but remember his handsome, weather-beaten face; his coarse silvery hair, his dark grey eyes, his firm shoulders. His hands! — She could picture them vividly: dark, strong and agile; how favourably they compared with Timothy's pink, small, clumsy hands with fingernails that were constantly breaking and skin that seemed ever ready to split.

"I'm being a blind fool," she said to the mirror. "I'm bewitched by a — a common farm labourer. Oh, if Daddy knew what nonsense was going through my mind, he would have another heart attack or drive the Daimler here himself to drag me back home and incarcerate me for my wanton thoughts. But it's so . . . so natural: in Wladek's cottage I felt something that Timothy could never give me. I felt at home. That man is part of the very meads and leas upon which he treads. I feel that he knows all about animals, nor any less about humans. The way he handles that Poffle!"

She stared into the mirror in silence.

"No!" she cried after a few moments. "I'll throw caution to the winds and embrace whatever this evening holds — come what may."

* * *

Quartus Poffle was seated at his typewriter having been commissioned to write an article under the title, "Could insects take over the world?" His toenails had been giving him so much bother that he had almost missed the deadline date given by the obscure scientific journal that commissioned the article. He was trying to make the article both interesting and crammed with relevant facts, but so far he had produced but a few scant lines.

"Insects, as most of us are aware, are all around us, yet we generally disregard them unless they anger us, when they will feel the crushing pressure of the shoe or the short, sharp shock of the rolled newspaper. Otherwise people give little thought to these creatures; they are easily forgotten or ignored. And yet, who has not paused, struck with wonder, at an ant struggling to transport some huge burden many times its size, totally occupied at the task, and rarely failing in its attempt?"

Suddenly Poffle realised the late hour. Hurriedly he dressed but, being the local magistrate, it behoved him to go in some sort of disguise to this strange gathering: so he dressed in a black suit with matching tri-corn hat and hid his eyes with an old pair of horn-rimmed National Health glasses. He picked up a stout walking stick then admired himself in the mirror.

"In truth, I look quite imposing," he chortled.

As the appointed hour was still some time in the future he returned to his work, but he was quickly disturbed by a knocking at the door.

"Who can vis be at vis hour?" he muttered testily.

He was surprised to see a stout, robustly built maiden in the porch, although he knew her immediately to be his sister, Miss Harmony Poffle, the local schoolteacher.

"Going to a fancy-dress party?"

"Er . . . no, not exactly, more a sort of ancient ritual; a bit like ve druids, I fink."

"Well then, I think I'll come along too. It sounds like it might be fun, there's precious little of it 'round here." She forced her way past Poffle.

"I'd better get disguised myself, hadn't I? You can never be too careful, can you? Come on, let's have a look."

In short time they had found a black veil and an old black cloak, the latter having belonged to Poffle's long-dead grandfather.

"Vese will do you, I fink.

"Yes Quartus, this is going to be fun."

* * *

The Black Magician rubbed his hands with glee as he thought of the notables and dignitaries who had been convinced, cajoled or, in some cases, bribed to attend.

"Indeeeeeeeeeeeeed," he hissed through clenched teeth. "The world shall soon shudder at the mention of my name. My return is nigh! Absolute power shall be mine! Yaaaaarrgghhh!"

He had given great consideration to the nature of the night's events. A black mass had been reluctantly discounted, since this could induce stark terror, or nausea, or both to the uninitiated. Instead of this, there would be a more understated display. With John Ambler's help he had procured a vast quantity of a mead like beverage, brewed from honey and very potent, known as melomel[1]. A few simple chants and incantations would be followed by a liberal imbibing of this melomel, after which T'osh would give a prepared speech. There would be other surprises too. All this should be enough to arouse interest in the black arts so that at least the same number would return

---

[1] **Melomel**
Melomel is a variety of the ancient beverage mead, in which honey forms an integral part of the fermentation process. This is a recipe for rhubarb melomel.
Ingredients for 1.5 gallons
   -1 gallon water
   -1 tsp yeast nutrient
   -3.5 cups of honey
   -6 cups of chopped rhubarb
   -yeast
Boil water. Add nutrient and honey and allow to dissolve. Bring back to boiling point then remove from heat and add rhubarb. Leave to cool in covered pan. Stir vigorously. Add yeast sediment. Rack after approximately one month. Bottle when clear.

A recipe for melomel

for the second meeting, hopefully bringing along their friends.

*   *   *

As the time came near, groups of strangely clothed people made their way along the country lanes of Melling. Their destination was a wooded area in which there was a ruined church. There was a full moon that night; the pilgrims had no need of artificial light. That they were nervous or highly strung there was no doubt: every time something stirred in the thicket, be it fox or other creature, they grasped or cried out in whimpering voices.

The church had been a Catholic church up to about the middle of the 19th century when it had been gutted by fire. Now only three crumbling walls survived, dimly discernible out of the moss and ivy. The altar too had survived, though up to this evening it had been buried in foliage.

At last the notables were all gathered in the silence, a silence that was broken when a number of sullen peasants, who had marched from Ormskirk, arrived.

The stone block, the last remnant of the altar, was still black in the silver moonlight when T'osh clambered to the top of it. His arms were akimbo as he surveyed the gathering. He made no sound.

Certain members of the throng were well versed in these affairs, so that when a gorilla-like giant stepped from the shadows to shout a chant, they knew what to respond.

"We are a people who seek guidance!"

"Beelzebub, we seek your guidance!" cried the 'plants' in the audience.

"We are a people who look for answers!"
"Baal, we need your answers!"
"We are a people who seek the truth!"
"Asmodeus, we seek your truth!"
And so on.

*　　*　　*

The chanting continued for a long time, ever increasing in volume as the uninitiated were drawn into the mystic net. A drum boomed in mighty rhythm from the trees, emphasising the beat of the chant. Soon all were caught up in the chant; even Poffle, the cynic, lost his reserve and became one with the multitude, his high-pitched voice enthusiastically bleating the responses.

The chanting ceased all at once; as if in response a great fire blazed up from behind the altar, silhouetting T'osh, so that he seemed like Satan himself emerging from the very gates of hell. Then drinks were passed around the crowd; the people being told to drink quickly and deeply; all the while fresh flagons of the brew were distributed.

This was the moment, T'osh thought. He spoke about his doctrine and new social order, emphasising those points which would appeal to the clods below.

". . . and so I say to you, my people, what has progress brought us? Machines! Technology! And from these what have we gained — what? Pollution, ill-health, both physical and mental, vandalism and apathy. We are forced — by law! — to suffer vandals and do-gooders and officials — unelected bureaucrats — of every degree, whose very employment is paid for by ourselves.

"Where is the freedom that once existed? Gone! Swept away like dead leaves. The farmers are told which crops to grow and must pay heavily for this privilege. Publicans are told when and what drinks to sell. Doctors which medicines to prescribe. Teachers what to teach — Satan, but I could go on all night. Our lives are controlled by rules which we have no say in.

"Yes, there are the signs for all to see, but what brought on this madness? *Progress*! That is the root cause of all these ills. We are becoming slaves, condemned to an utterly dismal existence: to me, progress and the dehumanisation of mankind are the same thing. Man will become the slave to the very machine he thinks he controls. He will live and die for the machines — but is there no better way? Is it not time to rid ourselves of the corrupt and insidious colonisation of our land by the merchants of development? Should we not restore our sovereignty by whatever means necessary?"

T'osh went on long and loud about progress and few in the audience were unimpressed. Although imprecise as to the dates he painted a vivid picture of an erstwhile golden age when people lived simple, wholesome and fulfilling lives, until these were swept away by the dreaded progress. When he had finished, the woods rang with the frenzied cries of his new converts. He climbed down from the altar, behind which the fire still blazed, its flames climbing higher still, now burning with a horrid greenish glow.

Then came the last part of T'osh's vile ceremony: he signalled two of his aides who brought into the light a barmaid from a tavern in Melling called the Goose and Goslings. She had been paid quite well by T'osh so her struggles and whimpers were quite realistic; they would have been more realistic had T'osh fully explained what was expected of her.

T'osh's eyes glowed green in the firelight as he pointed to the woman and shrieked, "Behold, an evil doer!"

The barmaid was stripped to her underwear by the henchmen and was commanded by the Magician to confess. This single word was taken up by the converts until it became almost a chant.

Zombie-like, the barmaid walked to the altar and turned to the multitude. "In the name of Beelzebub," she said, in a carefully prepared and well-rehearsed speech, "I, Celeste Phlegg, being of sound mind and body, do confess that on the second of August last year, knowingly and with malice aforethought, did seek to acquire excessive profits from the sale of whiskey; this being done by adding one penny to the rightful charge."

"What?" howled T'osh. "You admit your sin! Wicked woman, oh wicked woman, know you that our punishment be hard and not always limited to the temporal sphere?"

"No! Do not punish my soul. My body, if you must, not my soul, not that. I have rectified the loss of money — have I not atoned? It will not happen again. Surely you know that my tavern is the best for many miles. Torture me, defile me if you must, but do not use your dark forces to defile my very soul."

A whisper could be heard amongst the throng which steadily increased in volume. Soon the eerily rhythmic chant of "*Hang her high*!" echoed through the woodland. This continued for some time. Eventually T'osh spoke once more.

"Well then, since you have repented, five blows of the lash must suffice but, if you fail again—"

"I won't master, I won't!"

"So be it. Carry out the sentence."

The woman was dragged to a post to which she was tied. The gorilla-like person, now stripped down to a pair of bottle-green trousers, whipped her. She screamed. She screamed still as she was taken down from the post and into the shadows. She was no longer acting.

They began to talk amongst themselves in the crowd.

Said one, "She screams loudly; I do not think she will be other than honest in the future."

Said another, "His ways are cruel, yet does not the end justify the means?"

Said a third, "There is much truth in what he says: progress has a lot to answer for; has not the motor car killed more people than two world wars? Are we not slaves to crooked officials who seek to control us? We need to drain the quagmire. I blame outsiders."

Said a fourth, "I like his straight talking. He speaks my kind of language. We need to control our boundaries and make our own laws in this neck o' the woods."

Said a fifth, "She got exactly what she deserved. If you ask me this whole equality of women idea has gone too far. We do need to turn back the clock on a lot of stuff."

Said a sixth, "He's right you know."

*   *   *

If anyone had ventured to suggest that the supposed golden age is rarely seen as coinciding with the present age he or she would almost certainly have been on the receiving end of a vigorous pummelling. If anyone felt the urge to request some clarity as to what exactly this anti-progress *utopia* would look like in practice they would, on further reflection, probably have decided to shelve it for the time being.

The plan was beginning to work. The fire now blazed with many colours and the people were overwhelmed by the strange shades and odours. The melomel too was having the desired effect.

From out of the woodlands came the sound of pipes playing an ancient tune. It revived memories of days long gone, when life was simple and pleasant without care. Images were borne on the gusts of the music; none were unaffected by the tunes; first one, then two, then the whole assembly began to dance feverishly and primitively to the strains of the pagan melody.

And strange it certainly was, for it seemed at times to merge with the other sounds of the night, playing long, low refrains. Then it came to the front of the mind, hammering on the skulls of the dancers, making their feet move ever more wildly about the grass, about the trees.

Cressida found herself in the arms of Wladek — how had she got there? Not a word was said, but he picked her up with apparent ease and stole away to a quiet part of the wood, where he found shelter in the shade of an old oak. With his coat placed on the ground he positioned her upon it, kissing her passionately. Soon much of their clothing had been removed and Wladek slowly and gently caressed her until she thought she would explode with desire. She felt passion she had hitherto thought herself to be incapable of, and on a different scale from the more perfunctory carry-ons she had known with Timothy. This was down-to-earth sensuality in every sense of the word, she thought as she knelt on all fours, readying herself for *la position du*

Wladek and Cressida

chien and soon her cries of delight echoed across the woodland. Wladek continued his most pleasurable efforts almost until dawn. The pipes had long ceased to play. Eventually, just as the very earliest intimation of dawn was creeping into the darker sky, they fell asleep in each other's arms, their various clothes draped across them.

Noah Halfmoon sat on the trunk of a long-fallen oak tree. He had maintained a safe distance whilst studying the strange goings-on. After gnawing thoughtfully on a small hazel twig, he eventually allowed his thoughts to escape in the form of just one word.

"Ex . . . act . . . ly!" he said aloud to no one in particular.

"Ex . . . act . . . ly!" he repeated before rousing himself and making his meandering way back to the small hut which served as home for the time being.

In other parts of the area other bodies were sprawled upon the grass in deep, alcohol-induced slumber and covered with heavy dew. Many had clumsily removed some or all of their clothing, prior to engaging in all manner of physical excess, and the branches of many nearby trees resembled some form of surreal medieval jumble sale.

It was silent again.

* * *

Quartus Poffle was typing agitatedly. He wore his normal working spectacles. His horn-rimmed NHS spectacles had 'been mislaid' during the evening in the woods and he had been guided home by his sister Harmony. Their journey had taken some time as he had repeatedly stumbled and fallen into ditches and hedgerows due to a combination of myopia and the after-effects of alcoholic consumption.

He believed that the publication of his latest work would shake many of the fundamental structures of modern science. His ideas and outlook had changed in the past few weeks, and he was now determined that as many people as possible should come to accept his new ideology, not as a hypothesis, but as proven fact.

And so he wrote:

Only the blindest of fools could fail to perceive that so-called progress is nothing more than actual regression. Let us examine one facet of this progress, namely electricity: now we believe this to be necessary and beneficial but let me tell you that this benefit actually shortens many peoples' lives. Electric man suffers from cancer, heart disease, venereal disease, chickenpox, measles and ingrown toenails. Why? The answer is simple: continual contact with electricity is synonymous with ill health! Did the American Indians suffer from these ailments? Of course not! So, I say to you health seekers, lay down your light bulbs, your cookers, your gadgets; revert to the ways of old. The oil lamp, the wood stove, the candle, the night shirt: this is where the future of mankind must lie.

Beside him there stood a bottle that had been given him by T'osh. Poffle had been informed that it held a traditional herbal remedy for a variety of skin complaints and, after drinking considerable quantities of the beverage, he felt that it was doing no end of good to his spiritual and physical well-being. In fact, the drink was none other than melomel, the variety of mead referred to earlier, but Poffle, being wise neither in the field of alcoholic beverages nor herbal lore, remained blissfully unaware of this fact. Much of his writing was practised under the influence of this liquor, which might have explained why certain of his theories were of a slightly unusual slant — such as that rats could understand what people said should they but converse in Etruscan, or that a man would rise again from the dead were he but to consume three live house-spiders each day (this latter belief now feverishly carried out by Poffle himself).

* * *

Life continued much as normal at first. Poffle continued to sit each week on the bench of Ormskirk's Magistrate's Court. Nothing unusual was noticed until one day the lion and unicorn supporting the crown and coat of arms, that had been above the bench since time immemorial, was replaced by a skull from which still drooped some rotting rags of flesh. Then the sentences became somewhat more unusual: a 'gossip' was put in an iron mask; a thief was put in the stocks; a receiver of stolen goods was put in the pillory; and so on.

Radical though these changes were, there was no outcry, for the changes were gradual and subtle, so subtle that people did not notice them, but accepted the individual minor variation until it deposed the old method or belief in the mind.

All over the district were these minor adjustments taking place, such a tiny brick in the construction of a huge and fearful edifice. Poffle's articles appeared in the local press, a press that now depended on a hand operated mechanical printer rather than an electronic machine, and as a result of this series, machines that broke down were not replaced and, later, when more articles appeared, appliances were half unconsciously damaged or destroyed.

Candles and oil lamps now glowed in windows; water was drawn from the wells; meat was scorched on wood stoves.

Tractors no longer chugged over fields; lorries no longer drove through the towns and villages; both had been replaced, locally at least, by the horse.

Bookshops closed for want of business, and the library burnt down one sunny afternoon in mysterious circumstances, consuming not only the books but the librarian as well. No one was ever apprehended for this and other crimes of arson which had become increasingly commonplace, even though a certain Mr Noah Halfmoon was rumoured to have been in the vicinity at the time. Other bookshops opened, but those that stayed in business sold books of strange character, dealing in matters long-thought forgotten.

Yet what was worst was the shifting of the people. They had become blind to the subtle changes going on about them, yet more myopic still were they when it came to the changes in their own personalities. From being indifferent to strangers, they became actively hostile to anyone from beyond their pale. And strangers became far easier to spot, notwithstanding the examples of technology they carried about their person, for the locals now began to dress in austere manner, as if from some evil and ignorant age long past. Black or brown costumes were almost mandatory, together with a flowing cape and broad-brimmed hat. One merchant told an indifferent outside world of how he had been chased out of town by a frenzied mob because he tried to sell cheap electrical goods; another was stoned and had to be hospitalized after this or another mob had discovered him trying to sell 'frivolous' garments.

But by and large the outside world took no notice of such things. The town of Ormskirk and, to some extent, the surrounding villages had always been considered strange and backward places; though it must be said that because of their very isolation the outside world thought but little upon these localities. By indifference they had been let go their own way. Even when the stories began to percolate through to the outside world, these tales of violence, ignorance, hinted atrocity; the rest of the country bestirred itself to say an irritable "so what" before turning itself to the sports page. Then, when the stories, all stories, stopped coming from this strange region entirely, as if the district had been annihilated or an absolute censorship imposed, the world ignored the implications, satisfied that this, best forgotten, part of the world had returned to its customary anonymity. After all, was it not now embracing the very tenacious independence so beloved of certain politicians, journalists and literati in almost every region?

But one person *was* gravely affected by the news and that story is about to be told.

* * *

The Reverend Pedaiah Lock was a deeply worried man. As a local church minister he had seen the numbers of his flock dwindle in the previous months. He remembered those dear days, long gone, when the rafters of the church had vibrated with the thunder of the massed congregation's prayers and hymns. Now he could count his congregation on the fingers of his hands.

The lack of congregation also meant that there was less money coming in, and unless something happened soon, he would be forced to sell his investments — not to mention his vestments, though the former were more numerous than the latter.

The Reverend could not be described as a particularly generous or benevolent fellow: he had never been known to part with a penny if he could possibly help it, as his aged and partially unravelled duffle coat, worn and stained corduroys would testify. Indeed, there were some uncharitable souls who said that Lock's lifestyle would have put Malbecco[1] to shame in its frugality; some of

---

[1] In Book III of Edmund Spenser's The Faerie Queene, the knights Satyrane and Paridell seek shelter at a castle owned by suspicious

these unkind creatures had shortened his name to Padlock — out of his hearing, of course — for obvious reasons.

Padlock's appearance did not help to allay antipathy; he had ever an air of superciliousness. His pallor was unhealthy — or even unwholesome, with a gloss that turned the visage into a waxen mask. His domed forehead glowed with highlights. His hair was mousy and receding. Cold eyes were on either side of a long, knife-like nose, jutting far beyond his face and ending in a sharp point from which a dewdrop perpetually depended. Thin, colourless lips were pressed tightly into an abiding, arrogant smile.

*   *   *

One Saturday morning Padlock came down for his customary breakfast of bread and dripping. He had slept badly, though not because of the wind that had soughed in the trees, but because he had thought long and hard about his parishioners. Some evil force had ensnared them, he had decided: looking back he could see the small changes that had taken place in the people before they had abandoned the church and had been drawn to the conclusion that something had been warping the people for its own foul ends. Yet what was this evil force? How could he fight it? Could he oppose it, or was it so powerful that he would be destroyed by it; or worse, would it engulf him too like it had the parishioners? Be brave, he thought, looking at the pitifully few coins in the collection box.

---

old Malbecco, "a cancred crabbed Carle". His mind is set only on "mucky pelfe, / To hoord up heapes of evill gotten masse".

He left his house, determined to put his flock back on the straight and narrow path to salvation. First, he would speak to some of his ex-parishioners, to quantify the changes and perhaps discover the quality, the nature of the evil.

First, he called at the house of Quartus Poffle. Poffle opened the door himself and Padlock was told — rather curtly — that he could not be entertained that morning.

"You see," said Poffle, "I am right in ve middle of writing my book."

"Indeed."

"Yes. It is all about my feories and ve fings I believe in. I am of ve belief vat it is possible to live for several monfs wivout food, simply by closing one's eyes and refusing to accept ve need for food."

"Indeed, I say—"

Poffle's hand clutched at a spot some inches to the right of Padlock's shoulder, and it went to Poffle's mouth with a large spider. A look of delight crossed Poffle's face; then without warning he slammed the door to Padlock.

* * *

Padlock was still whispering "God, oh God", as he knocked on the door of a dilapidated farmhouse some minutes later.

"Hello," said Cressida. Pointing to her nightgown she said; "Sorry, but I'm right in the middle of my breakfast. But please, do come in!" (Cressida's breakfasts were not precisely timetabled but certainly they rarely happened before 10.30am.)

Padlock was shown to the kitchen, where he was invited to sit upon a cushion. This he did with some difficulty and discomfort. Cressida returned some minutes later with a bowl of brown rice and a cup of vegetable water. They had been talking some ten minutes when Cressida said, "Do you know, recently I have taken up writing poems — I'm writing a book of them."

"Indeed. Might I hear some of them? I have a passion for poetry." Cressida bought a large ledger and began to read:

oh yonder star from heaven
what pathways do you tread?
which strange circles of the universe
draw you towards them?
a magnetic overdose of light
is cast upon our shadows
and the blind must lead the blind
through history's dark ages

I shall look no more towards you
as the velvet coat of twilight
slips across our naked land
and leaves us all afraid
but when the trembling noonday sun
crashes like a fragile diamond towards the sea
then once more shall I gaze
towards your tender misty ways
and seek my destiny

"Oh, how absolutely marvellous!" cried Padlock. "Have you any more of that calibre?"

"Many more. But this one, this is my very latest: I haven't quite finished it though."

The black and the ancient robes
Hide a fire from bygone days
The cloak conceals a treasure trove
Of grim determination
And beneath the broad-brimmed hat
Perchance one sees a smile
From a mind as yet unequalled
By zealous imagination

For yes! It is the smile
That e'er leads me onward
And causes me to follow
Like a downtrodden slave
Into the paths of darkness
For therein lies my vision
And therein lies my future
E'en beyond the grave

"Interesting," said Padlock, "but pray tell what does it mean?"

Cressida suddenly hesitated, and a glazed look swept over her countenance.

"It means that the existence of he she or the old woman is both of consequence and insignificance that the living of life is the most notable yet pointless achievement the chosen appreciate the beauty of ugliness while the rejected can live out their lives and be swept away by the autumn leaves do I make myself clear?"

But Padlock had gone through the open door. No one observed him leaving the cottage as he made his way hurriedly along the lane.

*   *   *

As the Saturday afternoon progressed, villagers went about their business: some worked upon the farms; some baked bread or built sheds or prepared herbs; others preferred to while away the hours in the Stanley Arms.

Meanwhile Padlock sat at a rude table, holding his head in his hands.

"Madness! Madness! What has happened to the world that a rational man can spout nonsense? — And — ugh! — what he did to that spider! And the other one, that, that . . . Jezebel, what evil lies in those poems? God, give me the strength to combat this horror."

To one side lay a glass of water, whilst a half-eaten loaf lay by the cobwebbed window of the house. Padlock looked at the cobwebs and the husks of two dead flies that hung from strands.

His eyes blazed. "Truly, a web has been woven to entrap the village. A cat is needed to trap the spider ere the chance escapes us."

Padlock rose from the chair and left the house to the dust and silence and the two flies that swung like slow pendulums.

It was yet only early evening and time was on Padlock's side.

If he used it well.

If.

Chapter 3:

Martyn Takes A Stand

His bed was covered with well-thumbed news clippings, some with paragraphs underlined: Martyn was deeply troubled by these clippings, and by the accounts of the strange events that filtered out of Melling and Ormskirk — the whippings, the mob violence, random acts of pyromania, the abandonment of hygiene, these and all the other vague rumours of 'creepy carry-ons' in the woodlands, all had been talked about in Maghull, though usually in hushed whispers with frequent nervous glances over the shoulder, as if the teller feared for his safety.

Martyn knew that something had to be done, for he felt a sick certainty as to who was behind it all; yet how to act, that was the question. He knew full well that there would be no shortage of help when the talking and the verbal demands for feats of bravery were made, but there would be little support when the time for action came.

That evening, in his local tavern, he heard a conversation.

"It's the oddest place I ever set foot in, that's no lie."

"You keep saying that, but what do you mean exactly?"

"The place . . . well, it's like it was lost in time, if you get me. It's like going back hundreds of years. The people are positively primitive — and they're getting worse. God, you don't realise it but they're doing it themselves, regressing to feudal times. They haven't quite reinvented strip farming — but they're heading that way:

"Another thing, the speed at which it's all taken place: last year it was all normal — I can tell you that I wouldn't have bought a house there if it wasn't. But now it's a bloody race to wreck the machinery and go into horsepower and iron ploughs cast and forged in the local smithy. They've abandoned electricity; most of them use oil lamps, but some use candles."

"Come on now, it can't be as bad as all that?" There was little conviction in the words. "What about the outside world? Things can't be as bad as that, or they'd all be bankrupt."

"Don't you believe it? They've bloody well given up on the outside world. They ignore it — *ignore* it. Now I don't know this for sure, for they're a surly lot of coves, as like to gob you one as pass you by but, from what I can make out, they've got this closed economy, a sort of crude medieval version of protectionism I suppose; they produce enough for themselves, and that's it. No imports or exports, at least officially. Self-contained. Don't forget either that their tastes have become less and coarser, so that they are content with bitter ale and rough bread; they have abandoned material goods and refined tastes. God knows what the outcome of this will be."

"But what is your honest opinion of all this? I seem to remember that you were once a back to nature person, living off the land and all that. Setting your soul free, wasn't it?"

He gave a sick smile. "Yeah, I remember. Look, I still think that true happiness does not lie in the endless pursuit of material goods, but in seeking a more harmonious relationship with the eco-system, including one's neighbours and the community: only this path leads to oneself and inner knowledge. Ok, however high and mighty though that sounds, at least it's not completely lunatic. What they have there is utterly mad, and utterly evil; the people have no need to live a short and brutish life as a peasant. It's unwholesome and vile!"

The man paused for breath. When next he spoke, it was in a conspiratorial whisper that Martyn had to strain to hear. "It's like this; the whole thing is being run by one man. It is! He's always in the background, pulling strings; he's got some control over the people, God knows what, and he's not letting go. It's more than your life's worth to find out the details, but it seems that this is that person's second chance at control and he's not letting go this time. Seems that some time back he made his first try for power but was foiled by some enemies — I've heard that his head was nearly cut off. But now he's recovered, God help us all, for I fear that — what was that?"

"I — I'm sorry," said a white and trembling Martyn, "I've just gone and dropped my glass."

"Don't worry about it. Sorry about my friend, he's a bit nervous. Come on, finish what you were saying."

"Don't you see — he might be a spy!" (pointing at Martyn).

"Cobblers! And even if he was, you've told enough already to put you in a bad spot, assuming what you say is true."

"It is, and that's what got me worried. I think he plans world domination, don't laugh; this is all merely a try-out, or perhaps the first rung on the ladder. And if he wins here, I don't see much hope for the rest of it — this time next year we could all be behind a plough, or worse. You don't know what it's like."

"Is this the cause of the recent difficulty between you and—"

"I wish I knew. Lately our relationship hasn't been quite so . . . ongoing. She spends her time daydreaming or writing poetry. And she disappears for long periods of time; she won't even tell me where she's been. Something's wrong, but I can't fathom it out yet. But I will, and then . . . well . . ."

The man drank deep, and Martyn looked directly at this pitiable figure. In his late twenties, with longish hair and scanty beard, he was dressed in what seemed to be intentionally coarse and ill-fitting clothes, yet he emanated a sort of aura that was screaming for the body to be wrapped in a blue suit; a pair of NHS wire-rimmed spectacles dangled from a point dangerously near the end of his nose. He never finished his last sentence, but stormed out, closely followed by his friend.

With their departure, the mantle of gloom, fear and yes, say it — despair, settled over him once again, despite his hopes, yet bitterly in accord with the facts, his suppositions had been borne out; the Black Magician was back, and with him was his train of evil. Already it seemed he had made a beachhead for his unenlightened and intolerant feudal state based on the virtues of ignorance, fear, bigotry and lack of running water. Something had to be done, done damn soon, too — or, and he choked with fear at the thought — or was it already too late?

*   *   *

Martyn was striding determinedly towards Ormskirk. He had done so many times, though never with so heavy a heart. The December wind was bitter chill as it challenged his hair and jacket.

The gloom of the previous night had faded slightly; at least now he had a plan to carry out, nor would he be swayed from completing his mission. As he walked on, he saw fewer and fewer people, then, reaching the town, he saw great crowds at the Saturday market, searching for cheap oil lamps, ploughs, candles, harnesses, poultices, all the *modern* conveniences. Martyn wisely avoided this dour throng of pale, dour, oafish faces half-hidden by broad-brimmed hats, and went down a side street, but was nonetheless obstructed in his progress by two rather well-built peasants who grinned menacingly. Martyn noted that their teeth were cracked and yellow, indicating a lack of access to dental care at even a basic level. They most probably have discarded their toothbrushes he mused, whilst awaiting their next move.

"What brings thee 'ere, with tha fancy pants an' sissy 'airdo?"

"Aye, we don' lahk people lahk thee round these parts."

"I've no intention of staying long. Now let me pass."

"It's good tha's not staying long — unless th'art fond o' whips."

Chortling, the thugs moved on. Martyn just gritted his teeth; come on, he thought, you have more important things to worry about and, after all, those louts are but deluded tools of that Arch-Evil. Even so, the obvious local distaste for anything which hinted at 'foreign' or 'outsider' sent a shudder running through him. Bigotry was clearly an instinctive philosophy in this brave new republic.

*　　*　　*

By midday he had reached the gates of Frank Grogan's dwelling and, in no time, was in Frank's room. Though Frank lived on the edge of Ormskirk, it seemed that the madness had not reached the household: the conversion of the garage into a barn seemed but a cosmetic effect, designed to avoid the wrath of the madness' more fanatical followers. Yet, and here Martyn quailed, why had Frank not noticed the change in the land, done something about it, or at the very least alerted his comrades to the resurgence of the Evil Power?

When Martyn entered the room, Frank was lying on the bed, staring at the ceiling. He was quite motionless, but did not seem to be dead, though sometimes it was hard to tell the difference.

"Er . . . hello," began Martyn, "I thought it was high time I paid you a visit."

"—"

"You see, I think there's trouble brewing."

"—"

"Men of action are needed."

"—"

"Are you feeling ok?"

Then, very slowly, Frank turned his head away from Martyn and looked towards the window.

"You are all so trivial," he droned, "but you fail to realise it. Your antics are as spectacular as, and far less significant than, the dropping of a feather into the ocean. It is all a pointless exercise. I am the centre of my universe and, as for you, you are nought but nought. Why am I wasting my breath on you? 'Tis but the wind in the trees, but this knowledge is the key to total fulfilment."

Martyn sighed: It was going to be an uphill task, but at least this explained why Frank had not rung the alarm bell to signal the re-emergence of the Magician.

"I did hear you were writing a book," he said.

With quite alarming speed, Frank dived under the bed, scrambling out with a huge wad of paper.

"Read it," said Frank, thrusting the manuscript at him. It was not a request. Martyn read:

Chapter One: Prisoners of Thought

Nivek walked down the corridor. A door closed behind him. He lit a cigarette. Nervously. The match fell to the floor. Dead. Cigarette ash followed. One step. Two steps. Nivek coughed. Three steps. It was a weary cough. Four steps. It was a tired cough. Five steps. He stared at the floor. White tiles. Black tiles. Miles of tiles to make you smile. But Nivek frowned. And coughed again. Six steps. Seven steps. Eight steps. He turned to see. Nothing.

The key. The key in his pocket. The key in his left-hand jacket pocket. He found it in his handkerchief. So cold. Colourless. The room confronted him. A lion growling in silence. The seats. The visual aids. The black curtains. The brown floor. The grey projector.

The desk. The silver pen. The waste bin. Always the room. This room. Always coming back. Here. Where? Why? He coughed again. A globe of spittle fell to his lapel. The room. Always the Room. The Room drew him like a prostitute. A wrinkled whore. Old.

Was there no escape? A virgin screamed. No. The bell. It was wringing, ringing. Wringingringing. He frowned. He turned. Footsteps. Heavy footsteps. Heavy footsteps coming near. Clump! In the doorway. A figure. Nivek stood. Stared. His eyes widened. His yellow eyes widened. His haunted, yellow eyes widened. Knarf. He stood still. Looked back at Nivek. He was in the room. Decayed.

Nivek offered the corpse Knarf a cigarette. Knarf took it. Went across the room. Drew back the curtains. Light. Nivek groaned. Light. Nivek moaned. Light. Nivek's sins exposed. Two o' clock. Bells proclaimed the time. The corridor would melt with noise. The noise of youth. Untroubled youth. Heavy breathing. Light footsteps. Noise. Foolish noise. Foolish unnecessary noise, foolish unnecessary naive noise. Hellish naive unnecessary noise. Foolish. Why? Why me? Why only me? Accursed. Truly accursed. All is lost. Gone. Surely.

Nivek walked. To the back of the room. He sat down. Knarf followed. Sat down. looked at Nivek. Something intruded. The door. Someone at the door. A girl. At the door. Staring at Nivek. A girl. At the door. Staring at Knarf. Knarf caressed her. With his eyes. Slender. Breasts. All hid. Vest. Jeans. Jacket. She looked back. No one spoke. The silence screamed. A siren colouring our fears yellow. Febrile. There is no hope. Nowhere.

* * *

This went on in the same vein for several more pages. Martyn managed to finish the first chapter. Then he turned to Frank and said, in his best-ever acting role;

"Why this is excellent literature, quite the finest thing I've read in many a day. I don't think you'll have any problem with the publishers, even if the novel is, well, a bit avant-garde and intellectual. Even after reading it for the first time, I can tell you what it is about. It is obviously the story of a group of people battling against the system. Am I not right in this?"

"No. Not at all."

"Oh, then would you care to enlighten and elucidate?"

"Well, it tells the story of a small but enlightened group of youthful intellectuals who are trapped, as it were, in an institution of a certain type. I speak of an academic institution. They are aware of the oppression and, at first, they are overwhelmed by it. Then they fight back: they begin a resistance movement, but, in the end, they are corrupted and emasculated by the dominant values; bought off as it were. The story is based on my own experiences. Do I make myself clear?"

Frank paused, took a deep breath, then continued.

"Obviously the book is not as straightforward, or as easily readable, or as shallow as the pabulum that the publishers seem to prefer. In fact, though I say it myself, the concept behind the book is a re-examination of several of the themes found in the various works of Kafka, Joyce, Dos Passos and Borges. But I will not be compromised by these so-called market-forces. I refuse to prostitute my *art* for the sake of a few shillings. If needs be, I'll spend the rest of my life living in a garret. There can be no going back. Recognition is immaterial. Are you of sufficient intelligence to grasp this fact?"

"Certainly," said Martyn, who had had just about as much as he could take, "and I daresay your parents will see to it that you don't starve to death."

Frank turned his head to scan the dank garden.

"Frank, I'd better tell you the real reason for my visit. You know about the strange goings on in these parts?"

"No."

"Remember the Black Magician?"

"Vaguely: of what weight is this, anyway?"

"Bloody hell! Remember the last time you saw the magician, he was staggering down the road, leaving a trail of blood!"

"So. Just so."

"Well he's back. He's up to his old tricks again. Ormskirk and the surrounding districts are in his power."

"And?"

"Well it seems to me that maybe this land, maybe the world, is in a bit of danger."

"But what is this to me?"

Martyn remained very calm. "If you would care to cast your mind back, you played a not inconsiderable part in our previous dealings with the Enemy, and I thought that you would certainly wish to combat the resurgence of this scoundrel. I do not doubt that we will be victorious — if we pull together."

Frank laughed, a truncated sound like the final croak of an expiring frog.

"Oh, but this is impossible, ridiculous," he gasped between croaks. He calmed down. "Even were it to be possible to leave my work — my life's work — I would not do so."

"Why?" wailed Martyn.

"For the simple reason that whatever will happen, will happen regardless of any individual.

"Let me expound my wisdom. All events are the results of one or more causal factors, which are themselves past events caused by earlier factors, and so on. Let us assume that a leaf falls to the ground, solely because of the wind. Well where does this wind come if not from some other event, some other cause? For an event to happen there must be a cause, you see?"

"Certainly; but what has all this got to do with—?"

"Everything! If you follow it through to its logical conclusion, then one can, so to speak, adopt a causal explanation for everything that happens in the universe.

"Now with every day that passes science is able to tell us more about the causes of things, the factors that make things happen as they do. It follows — does it not? — that this must include the actions of human beings as much as physical phenomena. We are just as much a part of the universe as the sun. Further, so far as the psychological sciences go, we know more than ever about what makes people behave as they do. I am not arguing that stones have free will, but that humans do not. Free will? Superstition! We know far more today than ever before about peoples' genetics, environment, heredity; we know the laws of how people behave, all the factors that make people behave as they do. As our knowledge increases, so too does the similarity between men and stones as far as matters of free will are concerned. He may imagine he is free, but he has no more free-will than a piece of seaweed cast upon a beach. The forces are more complex, but they are just the same.

"To conclude, anyone who had a complete knowledge of his state and the forces at work at any given moment, would be able to predict his future actions."

"You are saying that we are not masters of our fate, that we can do nothing?"

"I am not. I am no fatalist, no determinist — they are fruitless and futile doctrines. If they were so then we might as well do nothing, since it will happen anyway, regardless of what we might do. My point is that we might well take actions, and that these actions, once taken, will influence the outcome of events, but our decision to take such an action, or not, as the case might be, is itself influenced by a variety of factors beyond our control.

"Take T'osh for instance. Now his decision to set up a state in which Black Magic held sway might seem to be an example of the exercise of free will. But I would say that this freedom is illusory, and that his desire for this state can be traced back to some unusual childhood experience, his ungainly appearance, the way his brain was formed — any of countless factors."

"No! I will not have it. I cannot accept that people cannot decide themselves upon some course of action — we are greater than a rock. Look, when has a sociologist proved something, made empirical generalisations if you like, comparable to those of the physical sciences?"

"It is only a matter of time."

"If we accept this, then whole areas of language, attitudes to each other, morals, history, society will have to be profoundly altered."

"Why? You are not making much sense."

"If you are right, then praise and blame, innocence and guilt, individual responsibility would be rendered worthless. For myself, I think this philosophy springs from a need to shuffle off moral burdens and minimize individual responsibility, transferring them to individual cosmic forces. It is nothing but a shabby, transparent alibi."

"You use emotive language; you do not disprove my philosophy. You seem to think that a society could not be built upon such a foundation. A feudal lord would have great difficulty in imagining modern capitalism.

"Then again, even in the current society, the concept of free will is not so deeply rooted. Whole peoples have been described as lazy, stupid and barbarous, with the implication that they can do nothing about it because of their 'bad blood' or because they are inherently evil.

"I think that I have made my point. I will not join in this series of causes and effects. Goodbye."

Martyn's long sigh carried with it bitter defeat and despair. Frank turned to the window and the dank garden. He sat motionless.

* * *

Outside, evening was falling, bringing with it a thin mist. Though it was a Saturday, Martyn found that the streets were nearly empty. A warm yellow glow did show that one shop at least was open. The cheap soda glass was far from clear, and the candles in the window smoked abominably, but Martyn could discern that it was a clothes shop, dealing mainly with the rough garments favoured by the rustics. Remembering his encounter with the thugs earlier, and with some half-formed plans in his mind, he entered the shop. He bought a coarse pair of trousers, boots, a cape, and a broad-brimmed hat, which would not only keep off the rain but also at least partly hide his face, should possible recognition become a danger. When he tried to pay for the goods, the proprietor snarled at his money. Luckily, he bartered his old trousers and boots, together with, of all things, a packet of paper tissues. So far as the odious shopkeeper gave the information, the tissue was to be recycled to become a rough parchment upon which some arcane magical treatise could be written. None of the peasants, it seemed, knew how to make paper.

*   *   *

Letting his instinct and intuition have free rein, Martyn found himself treading a familiar path; one which he and Frank had gone in youthful innocence. He was seemingly driven to the Stanley Arms, and when he arrived and saw the sullen sign swing in the gelid night, it was as if no time had passed.

Inside the décor remained from former years; even the few peasants hunched miserably over their leather mugs could have been the same ones who were there all that time ago. The buxom barmaid was there too, still as alluring as ever, he thought. She seemed, in her apparel at least, to have made few concessions to the new regime. Neither was her sparkling demeanour at all synonymous with the notions of the demure and submissive role for women which appeared to be the expectation of the *Perfect State*. She went to Martyn, asking him for his order. With his hat pulled low over his face, he hoped he would not be recognised. The barmaid did not seem to know him but gave him his drink with a cheerful smile, happily accepting cash payment, which seemed curiously at odds with the strictures of the new administration; he went to a dusty corner, pint of stout in hand. The time for intuition was past; now was the time for careful planning and violent action, should it prove to be necessary, which Martyn felt was a certainty!

Chapter 4:

The Forces of Evil

Timothy returned home to find Cressida in a strange mood, secretive, holding something to herself. She was seated by the fire, scribbling into a notepad. She acknowledged Timothy's presence only by hunching still more over the notepad.

"We are financially secure at last," Timothy announced, "for a while at least."

"Good."

"I've managed to get a loan that will see us through until we start to make a profit."

"Good."

"You know, we might even be able to get the roof fixed; make the place a bit warmer, just like the house we wanted."

"Good."

"Damn it, Cressida, is that all you can say?"

"Can't you see I'm busy?"

"Hellfire, woman! You call that busy? I'm working myself to a physical standstill every bloody day, and what do you do? Drink that blasted nettle tea and scribble inane poems."

"Inane? I'll have you know–"

"Be quiet, you fey, featherheaded giglet. I'm the one who works, and I've had as much as I can take of this nonsense." (Timothy had, at some point prior to his uprooting from the city to the country, immersed himself in a book which detailed all manner of regional colloquialisms which he felt, if allowed to pepper his discourse, would be commensurate with rustic dwelling.)

All Timothy's doubts and frustrations in the previous months seemed to focus themselves at this moment. With a violence that was alien to him he abruptly seized the notepad from Cressida and threw it into the fire.

"How dare you," hissed Cressida, her face distorted by rage and hatred. "Clown! Stupid, brutish, Neanderthal clown. Do you think that I give a damn for your work? Are you so cloddish that you fail to see that the material world is secondary to the spiritual world? Well, are you?" She studied Timothy for a moment. "Yes, yes, you are — damn, why didn't I see this long ago? I'm going to a better place than you could ever imagine, much less be a part of!"

Timothy's face collapsed into ruins of despair as he realised what he had done and what Cressida had said.

"Cressida, don't — for God's sake don't go. Cressida, I love you."

*   *   *

But Cressida was gone, striding over the fields with a definite sense of purpose. Timothy fell to his knees in front of the fire where black flakes, the fragments of a notepad, swirled in the hot convection currents.

Timothy sobbed uncontrollably, his tears plopping into the grate.

*　　*　　*

As usual Quartus Poffle was seated at his desk. He was preparing his weekly column for the local newspaper, this time detailing a certain cure for deafness by anointing the defective organ with the blood of a rat, the toenails of a witch, the entrails of a sow and the innards of the horse-fly, all whipped into a paste with a quantity of pond slime collected some time previously beneath a full moon.

Downstairs his sister was preparing his evening meal, after which they would prepare themselves for a trip to the woods.

As he worked Poffle would take sips from an earthenware bottle, the contents of which worked to create a reverie in his mind; he became highly pleased with himself as he remembered how his esteem in the community had grown in the last few months: how he was now a person of substance: how people dared not cross him: how his opinions carried weight. But — damn the man! — there was ever a fly in the ointment. Common labourer or man of mystery — whatever you are, damn you Wladek. He drank too much, talked too little — and that wooden leg! Even if he wasn't an overt troublemaker, and none could doubt that he did his work well, there was still that insolent attitude: really, he acted and spoke as if he were an equal! Always that air of dissent. The bounder simply didn't know his place. Still, in the future, and not necessarily the distant future, he could be shown which lowly rung on the ladder he was destined to occupy . . .

*　　*　　*

Isn't life strange? Martyn mused, cradling his glass of ale. The pub was now filling up as the evening advanced. He looked around the room. At the bar a man in his late thirties was whispering something to a delectable younger girl whose peasant clothes did nothing to disguise her affluent origins. It was weird; though the man was whispering in the girl's ear, he was thumping the bar for emphasis. In an inglenook lurked a thin, unhealthy looking individual with tattered duffle coat and corduroy trousers. The warm light from the fire did nothing to lessen the waxen pallor of the shiny skin, and it accentuated the long sharp nose, the dewdrop glistening at its end. A half pint of mild ale was untouched in his hand. At another inglenook, the brutish oaf that had related to Martyn his life story so long ago, then had thrashed Frank. Martyn shuddered, thankful for his disguise. Then he was reminded of *Prisoners of Thought*. Perhaps the oaf had been too gentle to Frank that day. Behind the bar; the barmaid of old, nowadays clearly the licensee or whatever equivalent they now had in this strange alternative region. Florinda Farrier was the name above the bar. Despite her elevated status her clothing was as revealing as ever. Martyn had no doubt that she was in league with the Dark One. Time passed and drinks were downed. One drunken workhand began to sing.

> *Satanic spells across our land*
> *Devour our nation and bring us light*
> *A manifesto stained with blood*
> *To further sacrificial rites*

How thou art fallen from Heaven
O darkest son of the morning
Unto our welcome homeland
A valley e'er yearning

Cast your shadows o'er us
Satisfy our longing
The altar of your vision
Must ever be our warning

Cloak us with your blackened cloak
Cloud us with the morning dew
Point out our direction
Satan's chosen few

Lead us through the darkness
Into the promised land
Let us see your wisdom
My sword is in my hand

"What brings you here so late, then?"

Martyn looked up and saw the emaciated person from the inglenook. The dewdrop still shone from the end of his nose, the skin was as waxen as ever, his coat was still covered with what seemed at first glance to be cement dust, but on closer inspection was mildew, his shoes were still cracked and scuffed.

"I'm . . . er . . . just having a drink," said Martyn warily, aware that this distasteful skeleton had been staring at him when the labourer had been singing. Martyn thought that the mind behind the mask was sharp, penetrating, though perhaps only in certain subjects.

"Allow me to join you then, for I am doing the same. I'll have a pint of mild. My name is Pedaiah Lock; to that name appends the title Reverend. Let me tell you something about yourself." He gazed at Martyn, smiling superciliously. "I know that you are not from these parts, and I am sure that you are on some sort of . . . clandestine, shall we say — mission?"

"Nonsense. What makes you say that?"

"You are unaccompanied; your clothes are too new; your actions and responses are not merely different from those of these clods but show an active dislike . . . loathing of it all. Further, beneath all this disguise your hands are not calloused with work, nor do your soft, well-fed features tell me but that you have been blessed, or cursed, with a student's face. Come, out with it!"

Martyn paled. He thought, cursed luck! Discovered by an agent of the magician already.

Padlock gave a dry, wheezing cough. "Oh, I see! A natural mistake. Before we go any further, let me say that I do not like what I now see about me; call me a native nonconformist. I've looked at these miserable peasants. Are they not mice? Are they not downtrodden slaves? What future have they? I tell you that I have decided to become their saviour or liberator — damn the consequences!"

Truth or lies? thought Martyn. Liberator or thought policeman? Nonchalantly he enquired; "What are your plans?"

"They are still being prepared, but I intend to bring down this barbaric regime. Then, when accomplished, become a leader of sorts to lead these miserables into the light. Ah, what a society then! One loosely based on the great humanitarian principles of liberty, equality, justice, perhaps others . . . as designed by myself. I shall deal with any major problems as they arise; a latter-day King Solomon. Trade unions would not, of course, feature prominently and, indeed, would be actively discouraged by a series of laws restricting the rights of workers to organise and protest."

"But I would imagine that you must have planned for freedom of thought: to let free speech rule."

"Not one jot of it. Opponents will be destroyed, though in the most humane manner, of course. For the *Lord* has shown me this: I am a vessel in his hands."

"Then you will succeed?"

"Succeed! We must! It is written: It is foretold. I am the last of the great prophets, come to embark on his mission to lead these people out of the wilderness and into the Promised Land. So be it."

A strange being, but Martyn sensed that he was telling the truth, and that certainly put paid to the idea that he was a tool of T'osh: they would have been at each other's throats in seconds. In his own way he was as bad as the Magician, with equally illiberal views apparently, but Martyn thought it was best to humour him, for — who knows? — he could prove useful.

He was buying the round when the door opened and Frank Grogan entered, dressed in an ill-fitting, light-grey suit and an absurd and unseasonal straw hat.

"Mine's a pint of mild," Frank said to Martyn.

"So's mine," said Padlock.

"What brings you here?" said Martyn coldly; he had not forgotten their last conversation.

"Well truth to tell, I began working again on my novel but found that the words would not flow. I need adventure. I need danger. I need stimulation. Here I am. Your mission is already well on the road to success."

"What mission is this?" whispered Padlock, his body trembling so much that his dewdrop fell into the ale, though it was quickly replaced at the end of his nose by another, even larger globule.

"Why," said Frank, "we are planning to bring about the downfall of this most backward regime and replace it with a free self-governing republic in which there shall not be either wage-slavery or exploitation of man by man; private enterprise will have no place in key industries, and state subsidies will favour co-operative projects as the most socially desirable; security against arbitrary arrest and detention will be guaranteed; and all citizens regardless of sex, age or religious convictions will have equal rights." He looked at Padlock. "By the way, who might you be, my skeletal confidant?"

"A friend, fear not," said Padlock. "You are in luck, for they are also my aims, sort of; though of course *I* will become the leader of the people."

"Well, I think we can shelve that for the moment," interjected Martyn, "But tell me Frank, do you sense an expectancy in the air, something is going to happen?"

Frank nodded, "I think we shall stay here awhile, although judging by some of the malevolent glares I have been receiving, I suppose a change of apparel must be a priority."

*　*　*

They stayed until closing time, with Frank and Martyn paying for the drinks, Padlock having muttered something about having lost his wallet. Eventually, closing time approached, then, as a one, all the drinkers left their drinks to go outside. Martyn and the others followed into the chilly, moonlit night. The horde of locals could be seen on the road to Melling itself.

"Look," gasped Padlock, pointing over the moonlit fields and roads. They could see, here and there, moving figures, hundreds of them, all striking for Melling.

Padlock fell to his knees, "Oh *Lord*, help me, a sinner."

"Get to your feet," demanded Martyn, "there's devilry afoot tonight. Let us follow this crowd to discover its foul secrets."

They followed and were soon lost in the mass of people. Some few miles further on they left the road to follow a rudimentary path. Though soon ankle-deep in mud they pressed on undaunted.

* * *

Having executed a large bottle of elderberry wine, Timothy decided that action of some sort was called for and damn the consequences. As he put on his tweed jacket, succeeding at the third attempt, he tried to think of what action he could take, and failed.

Blind rage engulfed him and when next aware of his surroundings, he found that he was well on his way to the Stanley Arms. And why not, he thought.

It was as he was approaching the tavern that he noticed how many people were about at such a late hour: strange too that they were all headed in the same direction.

And then, as he was being carried along by the mass of bodies, he caught sight of the mysterious Wladek, arm in arm with his beloved Cressida. Stifling a sob, he jostled his way out of the mainstream, falling into the grass verge. Savage self-pity set in. "I suppose their astrological signs are compatible," he whined. "Look at me, a year ago I was all set to take my accountancy exams, my future was secure, and then Cressida, Cressida . . . she led me . . . led me away from security — and now, you gull-catcher, look what you've done. It's all your fault — I'll get you for this. Flax wench!"

He staggered up and began to follow the last stragglers of the multitude.

*   *   *

Martyn and the rest of his band separated themselves from the mass as soon as it had become evident that the clearing in the woods was the intended destination of the horde. Now the three of them were standing at the edge of the wood watching the villagers light candles and fires, and moving about in a purposeful, if mysterious, fashion.

Martyn gasped as a hand touched his shoulder. Turning, he saw a weak, bespectacled face that he knew from somewhere.

"Hullo! My name's Timothy. Doing the same as me, havin' a gander at what's going on here? I hear it gets pretty wild."

The man's blind drunk, thought Martyn. "Well we're here for the same purpose, more or less."

"Good, thash— that's good. Let's have a look," he said, tripping over a branch; "whoops . . . weyhey . . . gerroff . . . I'll 'ave the lot a yer!"

Ten minutes later nothing had changed. Even Timothy, who no one trusted, was still on the ground, whimpering.

"By the powers," gasped Padlock, "this man is weeping. What sort of weakling do we have here? On your feet, sir, are we dealing with a man or a worm? Now sirrah, pray inform us why you were sitting in such a dejected manner, blubbering like some kind of *woman*." This last word was spoken with cold and profound venom. Timothy sat up suddenly.

"It's because of . . . Cressida. Look, I have deep misgivings about what will happen here. My girlfriend has taken up with these people and her behaviour has become odd to say the least. And as for that bastard! — If ever I get a chance to see him then I'll get him from behind kick him to the ground and start kicking his teeth in one by one then I'd get a knife and start cutting his fingers off then he'd be screaming by now then I'd start on his innards and gizzard tear and wrench blood blood—"

"All this for a *woman*," muttered Padlock whilst the others grappled with Timothy.

"Quiet!" hissed Frank, "Do you wish to be discovered? Stay calm, historical determination is on our side."

In the clearing, a stone slab was evidently going to be used as an altar, for a black cloth now covered it and it was surrounded by six black candles and an inverted crucifix was suspended at one end. Below the crucifix was a clay image of the Horned One.

A gong sounded. Utter silence fell. From out of the darkness a naked woman was led by an acolyte. She spread-eagled herself on the altar and black candles were put in her hands.

There was a stench of pitch that sickened Martyn, together with other rank smells. A profound revulsion rose like bile. All the same he could not help noting that the woman on the altar was generously proportioned and wondered if she had been chosen for that precise reason: a crowd-pleasing move no doubt.

"To what depths have these people sunk? Is that hussy on the altar behind it all?" whispered Padlock as he gazed long and hard at the naked woman.

Frank said nothing.

Judging by his costume, the man who now entered the light must have been the main priest. If nothing else, he seemed bored to death with the whole thing. He stood in front of the naked woman and removed his hat. It was not T'osh.

With a vast and cool ennui, the priest began the rites. The first rite was the acclamation of the nodes, but to Martyn it was some of the curious and vaguely naughty things that people got up to in certain types of *specialist magazine*. After further rites that might have been arousing had not a chill and damp wind been blowing from the east, the principal rite began. It turned out to be nothing more than saying prayers and portions of the Catholic mass backwards. After the initial strangeness and, after nothing horned and smoking had appeared, Martyn found it all rather childish: an active anodyne to his earlier moods. At points he felt like an extra in a low-budget horror film. We've seen the customary gratuitous nudity, he thought, I wonder when we'll get the obligatory violent scene. Martyn would not have to wait long.

The others were affected too. Padlock had stumbled off into the shadows. Frank was staring at the rapt audience, his mouth opening and shutting. Timothy was lost in thought, for he had recognised the priest. It was

Quartus Poffle, and his appearance had raised all sorts of questions in his mind.

* * *

Poffle wished he was home. He was cold, he was tired, he felt ill. The words of the chants came mechanically. He placed a chalice full of reeking liquid on the makeshift altar. His innards were queasy, his bowels water; he must have eaten that dubious looking corned beef hours before, yet still it was affecting him. Placing his soft pink hands on the woman's sturdy thighs he began to advance closer to her. He did not plan anything other than a few simulated grunts and moans — he did not feel well, after all – and was not a man consumed by base desires. Indeed, his life of semi-isolation precluded anything which might be loosely defined as 'hanky-panky' certainly so far as females were concerned. But the act of congress was mandatory by T'osh's act of congress, as it were, and the audience had to be amused. He picked up the chalice, pouring the libation over the woman's torso, then attempted to act his role with as much counterfeit zeal as he could muster, all things considered.

In the woods a dog howled.

* * *

Martyn was cast to the floor by a crazed Timothy. His cry for silence was choked by a boot aimed at the groin, which fortunately hit Martyn's upper thigh instead. Then Timothy howled again, now on all fours like a dog, now crashing through the thicket and into the clearing, a jagged rock in his hand.

"Interesting," said Frank, "an indeterminate has entered the matrix of the dialectic."

"Shut up," said Martyn massaging his injured leg.

In those few moments Timothy was temporarily insane. He had taken too much for nothing to snap. Invested with the strength of ten men, he pushed startled celebrants aside, using his rock to pulp the faces of the ones who did not move as quickly as his deranged mind wished. Nearer the altar and nearer the startled Poffle, Timothy hurled the rock, bouncing it off Poffle's head. He jumped over the dazed priest and embraced the naked woman on the altar.

"Cressida," he cried, "Cressida — what has —"

Then he heard the growing tumult behind. "Come with me, away from these maniacs."

"No! Leave me alone. I don't ever want to see you again. Go away!"

"God Almighty! Come with me, now!"

"No!"

* * *

Cressida had not readily volunteered for the position of *woman on altar*. She had been persuaded by a deputation of T'osh's 'administrators' that she was ideally suited to the part. T'osh, she was informed, knew of and liked her poetry; was impressed by her in-depth knowledge of herbal lore and had indeed said there *could* well be a position of power and influence in the *Perfect State* in a role to be specified at a later date. Susceptible to the flattery she had also been assured that the High Priest, Quartus Poffle, would not make much actual physical contact; the whole charade was a floor show designed to entertain the throng and once the cosmetic exercise had been completed she would be safe and held in even higher regard than previously. Had she known in advance the strange twist which the evening would take, it seems almost certain that she would have declined the proposal without much hesitation.

* * *

She tore away from Timothy and fled into the crowd where she was forced to run a gauntlet of lecherous, groping participants. One squat fellow in particular, grinning widely and displaying an incomplete set of crooked, yellow teeth, sought to block her way. He stood in front of her, eyes glazed over, drooling, arms outstretched.

"Ah lahks the look of thee ah do! Come into t' woods wi' me and— nnnnngggg!"

The last syllable was uttered as he fell to the ground, knocked senseless by a stout wooden branch applied, with considerable force and precision, to the side of his head by Wladek, who led Cressida to safety and a warm cloak.

* * *

Timothy turned from the altar to gaze upon the dark-robed celebrants milling about. Doubt and confusion were on their faces. Was this part of the ceremony or not? A calmer Timothy felt very small and cold. The darkness of the woods was very, very distant. Still, if he walked slowly and calmly through the mob, he might be—

"A heretic! A non-believer!" cried a terrible figure in black and Timothy knew he was doomed.

He leapt onto the altar, grasping one of the long candlesticks. He began to talk; anything to stay alive a moment longer.

"Yes, I'm an outsider and glad of it. Glad! You are all a disgrace to humanity and this entire pantomime is an obscene outrage. When I came to this dismal backwater it was to find peace of mind, to soothe troubled waters, calm the storms of torment that raged across my soul. And what do I find? Savages who pride themselves on being filthily backward; ignorant and bigoted serfs; People who treat their neighbour with distrust; People who worship some kind of anti-Christ and indulge and wallow in some pagan filth."

He paused for breath. The mob surged forward. Talk, for God's sake talk.

"Damn you all! I've lost the one person dear to me. She's placed herself in your hands. Damn you, for making her go to the devil himself. I've been betrayed and abused. But I'll be telling the world about you bast—"

But now the web of words broke, one worshipper, bolder than the rest, eyes ablaze with rage, leapt onto the altar. A blow from the candle sent her crashing into the bubbling cauldron behind the altar. The cauldron toppled over, pouring blazing liquid onto the grass behind Timothy.

Though he was safe to the rear, hordes of worshippers were now trying to clutch Timothy and there seemed no end of them. As soon as the boot or candlestick dispatched one frenzied face, two more seemed to replace it. Yet he was not doing badly, for some bodies were sprawled on the grass. He stomped the face of an aged loon with his boot, then swung the candlestick in a wide arc, braining a man and a woman who were trying to come at him from one side, and clumped a howling teenager intent on clawing Timothy's eyes. A further shove dropped him into the mob. Insanely he was enjoying this; not only were all the frustrations and humiliations of the past few days being paid for, why, here he was, last survivor of the Little Big Horn, warding off five thousand Sioux warriors; a pirate of the Caribbean swashbuckling with the best of them. It was quite romantic in a peculiar sort of way.

Then the mob moved away and became very quiet.

*   *   *

Into the flickering garish light stepped a brute of a man, a hulking monstrosity with a twisted lip. He smelt — of all things — of spearmint and stale beer. He was dressed in little but bottle-green trousers and a pair of homemade moccasins. Muscles like subterranean snakes slid under the skin. The hulking figure advanced to the altar.

Timothy swung the candlestick onto the creature's head, a blow that should have killed him, for it bent the metal and the vibration shook it from Timothy's hand. The ogre reached up and grasped Timothy's shirt with one hand, and with the other delivered a blow that nearly ripped head from shoulders. He was about to throw the senseless figure into the fire when an evil voice crackled through the night.

"Wait! Are we not indeeeeeeeeeeeeeeeed a lawful land?"

"The Black Magician!"

"Sub-human dolts, must we not observe due process of law before we inflict the final agonies upon this feeble wretch? Bind this man tightly, constrain him somewhere until such time as we can try him and devise a . . . meet punishment for this—" T'osh's voice broke, "*piece of maggot infested decaying meat*!" He wiped spittle from his lips. "But now, why not continue with your revels? Indeeeeeeeeeeed why not? Am I not a benign dictator?"

Despite the destruction and injury, T'osh was taken at his word, and before long the remainder of the mob, bar those still nursing injuries inflicted by Timothy, were virtually naked and infused with primitive lust, swilling down vast quantities of drink and indulging in every form of promiscuity and perversion that their limited minds could conceive.

T'osh sat on the altar aloof. His peons had been trained well. He smiled coldly and vindictively.

"The fool, the bloody fool," gasped Martyn as he saw Timothy battle the hordes. "What can we do?"

"Nothing," said Padlock, white-faced, "come away. Do you want to join that man?"

"But—"

"There is nothing any one of us can do, unless you can afford to buy a machine-gun." Padlock's face changed, "Say, do you have that sort of money?"

"Let's go," said Martyn, sadly. He hadn't liked Timothy, but . . . "Damn, damn, damn, everything I've done has been useless — for that matter, what have I done?" Suddenly a new enthusiasm entered his voice. "Enough of this cowardice, Pedaiah, your house is nearest; we shall repair there—"

"But it's a cold night, the fuel bill—"

"And you shall give us some wholesome fare—"

"But the expense—"

"And we shall plan before you give us a place to sleep; though in view of the late hour, mayhap sleep first."

"But — but —"

"Come!"

*   *   *

"Here we are," said Padlock at his front gate. "Let us hope we will be safe behind walls, lest Satan pay us a visit."

"Hardly likely," said Frank.

"What do you mean?"

"The fact of his non-existence could be a small impediment."

"Balderdash, sirrah. Anyway, how do you know?"

"It is obvious that there can be no supernatural beings. There is neither a logical imperative nor a physical theory to create or explain these beings. Therefore, they do not exist. It is only the devious ways of men that create and continue the illusion of such laughable fantasies. Only a simpleton would think otherwise."

"Bah! Such nonsense I have never heard in many a long day. Hah, explain this away, sirrah, if you can. If Satan does not exist, then tell me why Eve broke God's law and ate of the fruit? The idea was not her idea, but was presented to her by the Evil One in the guise of the Serpent, that spirit creature, identified in the good book as—"

"Excuse me," said Martyn, "but as it is past three o'clock in the morning, might it not be a good idea to continue the argument inside, out of the cold?"

They waited whilst the clergyman removed the various wards and bolts from the front door. Martyn had decided to put off discussing plans until the morrow. He was cold, downcast and dog-tired.

* * *

Padlock's house was as seedy and mildewed as its owner. Neglect and breadboard makeshifts were the first impression. Though the room was dirty, the furniture, what there was of it, seemed to be so ancient as to have centuries ago collected a permanent skin of ingrained filth, and it seemed that nothing could remove that adamantine layer.

"Er, you must excuse the dust," said Padlock by way of explanation, "I broke my broom some years — some time ago, and I have not been able to find another — ahem, I mean, buy another."

Frank and Padlock returned to their, at times eschatological, at times ontological argument. Martyn ignored them, looking for some food. At length he found the pantry and unlocked it with a hairpin which he carried in his pocket. It was stocked with thousands of tins of baked beans and spaghetti. Taking two cans of each, and adding some pieces of meat in the saucepan, he made a fragrant if unusual stew."

They were still in discussion when Martyn returned with three steaming plates, but talk soon ceased, and even Frank tucked in with gusto.

"I say," said Padlock, wiping up the fragrant sauce with a piece of hard crust, "it was uncommonly decent of you to find some all-night cafe and bring us three meals."

"Oh, I didn't. I used four of your cans, some meat, and cooked them on your stove. I'm sure you don't mind."

"Oh," said Padlock, "Oh no! Ohhhh noooooo noooooo!"

Padlock went upstairs to bed. As the others lay on the threadbare carpet, they tried not to hear the shrieks and piteous wailing that came from the upper storey of the house.

But even this cacophony was less of a distraction than Martyn's fears. Long into that drear night he lay awake, managing to doze only when the dawn was beginning to shine.

His army: Frank Grogan, at best someone who could cure insomnia by launching into a monologue on any subject, but who was otherwise fairly useless; Padlock, (and here Martyn winced), had anyone ever been cursed with such a fantastical fool? His obsession with religion, his desire for power, his warped political outlook and apparent disdain for women, the almost psychopathic inability to give financial or physical support — all these facts rendered him perhaps more useless than Frank.

But who else was there? Timothy had at least shown himself to be capable of action, but also of taking that action at the worst possible time. Did that man have a brain at all? Oh, for the likes of Dancing Jack or Red Joe, stalwarts who would throw down the gates of hell to fight and die for a cause they believed in. Oh, for such men.

"Moooooo! Moooooo!" articulated Frank in his sleep, apparently experiencing a bovine dimension to his dreams.

And worst of all, pondered Martyn, his enemy, more powerful than ever, growing all the more dominant, bringing together all his old cronies. The last time it had been damnably difficult to defeat him, now it might be impossible. Whilst he had been wasting his time in futile activities, had the power increased so much that the only reason Martyn had not been crushed was that he was too insignificant to bother about? And what of the civil authorities, why had they not acted? Were they dupes or part now of the Darkness? And here he was, insignificant gnat in ignorance and gloom, about to do battle against a largely unknown enemy with pathetically little might.

Damn it all, he thought, damn it all.

His sleep was made frightful with nightmares.

Chapter 5:

The Vanguard Takes Action

Padlock said that he would make breakfast the following morning, much to the others' amazement; though this feeling was somewhat assuaged when the meal in question turned out to be a few slices of hard bread, grey in colour, made slightly more (or less) palatable by thin streaks of dripping; this collation all being washed down by a small cup of weak, lukewarm and sugarless tea.

Though dawn had broken, the sullen landscape was fitfully lit by a thick grey light and it was necessary to light a candle; its glow shone on three grim faces.

"I say that we must plan carefully to take account of all possibilities," argued Martyn. "I fear that Timothy may be forced, perhaps by torture, into revealing the existence of our movement, little though he knows of it and its aims. We must be ever vigilant and ready for spontaneous action. We must be ready to take action ourselves, on the basis of the information at our disposal."

"And what information might that be?" sneered Frank, disgruntled and horrified at getting up at such an unearthly hour.

"I have pondered on this. Last night I was in despair, thinking that we had done nothing, yet when I think about it now, in the light of day — such as it is — I find that we have found out much about T'osh's organisation which would not be the case had we instead charged blindly into battle at the outset, in which case we would have been crushed as ants underfoot." He turned to Padlock. "My good curate, you have resided in this village for some time and must be familiar with many of the inhabitants, perhaps you could give me the names of influential people in the district; we should be able to obtain some useful information from these quarters. If we cannot gain direct interview, then observation should be made on their premises. Why? Surely it is obvious; this regime would collapse or be crushed without their tacit support at least."

Padlock nodded his head in what he hoped was a sage manner.

"You are right. I have been thinking of what my reaction would be were I to be rich and have all the luxuries of life, should some base upstart unite the peasants in such a medieval manner that would put at risk my possessions *and* my money. No, you are quite right. I am thinking of one person who, though her financial position is not in actuality very secure, she has all the airs and graces of one of the moneyed classes not to mention quite a fair local reputation. Further, you saw her last night; she was the strumpet on the altar."

"What? Why didn't you tell me this last night?"

"Precisely because of your present reaction. After all, the matter could wait until tomorrow, but I did not judge that sleep could."

Martyn made a further note to be wary of the curate's slyness in future, also to try and wheedle out of him all relevant facts; really! The half-wit clutched facts as well as money to his chill bosom.

*　*　*

The thick grey light stiffly lay over the frozen landscape, leeching everything of colour; grey earth, grey bare trees, grey bare hills fading into grey convoluted sky. Cressida's cottage, white painted, was a dirty grey. Padlock knocked on the stout oaken door, but no sounds came from the interior. Padlock knocked again, a stout thump that should have aroused the dead.

"Look!" cried Martyn, pointing to a crack between door and jamb, "The door isn't even fastened, much less locked."

They went into the house and found that, though there was little furniture, there was no lack of relevant objects to gaze upon; upset and empty bottles of elderflower wine; scattered books on such diverse subjects as yoga, astrology, Zen, palmistry, kirlian photography, the tarot, macrobiotics, fortune telling, real ale, organic farming, veganism, home baking, folk medicine, herbs, the I Ching, the Buddha, transcendental meditation, music appreciation, demonology, human sacrifice, torture, harp playing, traditional village life, Satan and black magic, folksong, chants and incantations and witchcraft. In one corner lay a heap of clothes, mainly expensive, peasant style garments, but also a black robe and some leather articles, the function of which the company was at a loss to explain! Then there was a Bible, some candles and jars of dry herbs.

Martyn had been examining a pile of papers and notebooks. "Look at this — poems by the thousand. Listen to this one:

> *Your hands can lure all manner of living things*
> *into your strange orbit*
> *as you circle through life*
> *controlled by none*
> *controller of many*
> *master of your own destiny*
> *man of the soil*
>
> *Only in your presence do I come alive*
> *my violent passions*
> *I cannot quell*
> *but when the tide of darkness*
> *slips across the land once more*
> *I will arise and follow*
> *with the tolling of the bell."*

"This piffle is the worst writing I have ever come across," declared Frank.

"Haven't you been reading *Prisoners of Thought* lately?" muttered Martyn.

"Eh? What did you say?" asked Frank.

"Nothing. Nothing. Still, just what is this poem about?"

"Me, I expect," a rough, fierce and most unfriendly voice behind the companions growled.

* * *

Despite the inclemency of the day, Wladek had risen early and, despite the excesses of the night before, dressed hurriedly and without confusion. Cressida was still sleeping in the bed, and Wladek noted that the look of haughty arrogance that seemed to be implanted in the genes of the idle rich was still embossed upon her face, despite her experiences in the recent past. He growled under his breath.

He went to the window to stare over the ghastly landscape. I wonder what she plans to do with her inheritance, he thought, probably set up business in homeopathy, herbal medicine or palmistry. In truth! These folks are amazing — is there nothing a bag of gold will not obtain?

Still, she had thrown herself — literally — into his bed, and she seemed to think that this would be a permanent thing, dependent solely on his acceptance of her unlimited company. This morning he had decided to let the situation subsist, for the time being.

He left the cottage to go to Cressida's former abode, there to pick up her few remaining possessions. Though the light was bad there was no hint of mist, so he could easily see the three figures at Cressida's door. He saw them stand at the door for some time, then go into the empty building. "Damned landlopers," he growled, setting off over the fields at a brisk, if irregular, run. But his anger changed to puzzlement as he reached the cottage; there seemed to be a poetry reading going on.

* * *

"It will be of no interest to me, I feel sure, but who might you be?" drawled Frank with exquisite indifference, for he had sized up the stranger, marking him down as a cloddish farmhand, no match for him intellectually — nor physically, if the uneven gait of the man was anything to go by.

Wladek did not answer at first, but looked slowly around the room and its occupants, finally transfixing Frank with his eyes, eyes that seemed pits of infinite depth.

"I am Wladek. I live and work upon yonder farm. I have done so for five years. Now tell me, who might you be and what brings you to this dwelling, which you would seem to have no right to be in?"

"I . . . well . . ." stammered Frank, feeling as if Wladek had torn his soul from out his body, and found it wanting. "We, that is, my friends and I, we — I know the circumstances look bad — well we came to this house to make certain enquiries of the occupant of this house, we believe that she might be able to help," he finished lamely.

"And what is the nature of these enquiries?"

Frank felt himself compelled to tell the truth. "We intend to overthrow the brutal regime that holds sway over this land; it is unjust and unlawful; it is illogical and flies in the teeth of social justice and progress. Men are regressing and the superstructure, as defined by the economic base, is undergoing an ongoing and retroactive decay of the infrastructure, which can only result in the mega-death of both structural and hardware or software scenarios, which in turn—"

"Silence! I have heard enough of this blather and have understood enough to suggest that we sit and talk awhiles. Ah, here is some wine."

They found seats and the unmarked bottle of wine was passed around. The first gulp had an unfortunate effect on Frank; he began to feel bolder and in urgent need of intellectual debate — why not? After all, was he not a writer? And certainly, mused Frank, he would surely get some piquant amusement by running intellectual rings around that lout. Frank felt sure that whilst he might be a master of things chthonic, the rest of his field of knowledge was untilled and arid.

"My friend Martyn here, he thinks many odd thoughts: to be precise he refuses to accept the causal theory as governing the universe and man and Pedaiah, he really believes in the existence of Satan. How misguided!"

"No more than yourself."

"What?"

"I accept nothing, or to put it in a less nihilistic or solipsistic fashion, I deny the possibility of nothing; anything may be true. Can you disprove the existence of Satan?"

"Yes, of course!"

"Can you prove the existence of the causal theory?"

"Yes, of course!"

"How simple you are. To finally disprove the existence of Satan you would not merely have to search every inch of the plenum — not merely the universe, the plenum mind — but to have examined every inch at every moment of recorded time and unrecorded time, from the first cause to the unguessable final end of the plenum, and then you could only say with fair certainty that there is no Satan, for someone will surely say that you saw Satan and did not recognise him; another will point to physical quantum theory and raise many doubts about times and locations, whilst the ghost of Heisenberg and the shade of Schrodinger chuckle in the wings. And, with your acceptance of the causal theory, I say prove it to me. Show me that every action of any sort at any time was the reaction to an earlier action, show me that the first ever action in the beginning of the universe was a reaction, show me that and show me what it was a reaction to. You are an ignoramus and your knowledge of science is nil, else you would not parade your ignorance that the causal theory is accepted as proven by today's science, you would know that causality is thought of as a rule of thumb approximation suitable only for Newtonian mechanics and entirely useless for relativistics or the quantum scholium.

"And why do you follow this ludicrous philosophy? It is because you are afraid of life, you want everything to be in its nice little peg, a mechanical universe populated by pre-programmed robots — yes, for if life and the universe frighten you, people and personalities make you want to scream and wet yourself. You hide from people behind your intellectuality — if that's the word I'm groping for. Why, it wouldn't surprise me to learn that you wrote crappy experimental novels or poems that no publisher would touch with a bargepole and whose very existence sullies this planet and you sit in your room wondering why the grasping publishers and dullard public do not accept your genius."

Frank gave what he hoped was a sneering smile and took a long drink on the wine.

"What plans to overthrow T'osh have you come up with?"

"Er . . . none," said Martyn.

"That's brilliant, though I might have expected it with *him* in your gang." (*Him* being Frank.) "I thought as much, though, since you are in great ignorance of what is going on. Don't you know that I am supposed to be in league with T'osh? Don't worry. I'm as anxious as you to see his downfall. I hate that evil-minded man and all he stands for. A vile megalomaniac, I will see him fall! And shortly, for I intend to leave this village as soon as my work is done."

"Work, what work?" asked Padlock, images of pay packets and banknotes floating into his mind.

"Do not ask."

"As you seem to be incapable of formulating any plans on your own, here's what you do. Split up, partly to avoid detection, for your fool of a friend will talk under torture, and partly because it will facilitate the gathering of further information. Martyn, you will take up residence in the Stanley arms: stay alert and ready for action. Pedaiah, you will take up residence in the Goose and Goslings tavern in Melling — no, I will not pay for your board. Frank, you shall call upon a certain Mr Quartus Poffle, for he is of great local importance and his tongue is easily loosed when the subject of himself crops up. Arrange a regular meeting place to exchange information; this cottage should fit the bill. Then act. Should you need explosives or barrels of black tar, I am your man. Now I must go. Good luck."

*　*　*

Martyn trudged through a thin, cold drizzle. Like the land, his mind was in a grey obscurity with scrambled thoughts and half-hatched ideas appearing like trees and low, stone walls out of the murk. Was everything going as it should? Was he a fool to trust, or at least follow, Wladek's advice? After all he readily admitted being a crony of T'osh. And then, what was the mysterious work he was so cagey about? For once Martyn longed for physical action; nothing less would stop these horrible thoughts.

But this was not to be, for he found no problems in booking a room, dusty, poorly furnished and with carpet and wallpaper that had seen better days though it was, and he sat on the end of the bed, listening to the silence, looking into the cracked mirror, his hateful thoughts his only company.

The light was rapidly fading when he summoned himself to action. He would stay in the tavern for a week or two and in the daytime would discover as much as he could outside the tavern, whilst in the evenings he would mix with the locals — his garb would not betray him — and attempt to draw whatever knowledge they had from their slow and simple brains. He had eaten little in the last few days and considered that it was better to fill his belly with beer than with nothing at all. He went downstairs and ordered a pint of strong ale.

*   *   *

Padlock, having made his way to the Goose and Goslings tavern, and after securing his room, went into the bar. He was served by a certain Celeste Phlegg, the barmaid who had been persuaded to make a full 'confession' on the altar at the first of T'osh's woodland extravaganzas some time ago. She seemed to have recovered from the injuries inflicted as punishment physically at least, though her face still bore a slightly pained expression and she did not make eye contact with those customers she did not know. To Padlock, of course, she was but a mere woman and therefore not worthy of consideration, as long as his ale was well topped up. It was dark outside and bitter chill; but inside a blaze was crackling inside a huge grate. A number of locals, including a plump, pink-faced woman in her late twenties, were seated around the blaze. Padlock joined them.

Said one: "I'll tell ye now that the quality of life these days is better than ever before."

Said a second: "Aye, you never see any theft here, and we'd know how to deal with a mugger."

Said a third: "That we would. That we would. Our children are respectful to their elders and betters."

"How right you are, sir," said Padlock. "Verily 'tis a rank and gross thing that the world does not follow the example shown."

The aforementioned woman looked at Padlock with respect. In the past, someone had given her some books on human genetics. It had been a bad decision. Whenever she could she dropped names and terms into the conversation without any respect for their meaning; words like protein, nucleotides, deoxyribonucleic acid, ribonucleic acid, thiamine, adenine, guanine, cytosine, random mutation, gene-pool, chromosome shift, dominants and recessives, all these terms and more were flung higgledy-piggledy into her speech as if out of a shotgun and, as for name dropping, one would think that she met Crick and Watson; Urey and Miller; and Gregor Mendel in the pub of an evening.

Knowing this it comes as no surprise to learn that her actual knowledge and understanding of the subject was on a level with a chimp's awareness of Shakespeare, and that her bias on the subject of race and heredity was somewhere to the right of Goebbels.

Also, her name was Harmony Poffle.

"A gentleman of learning," she said to Padlock.

"I am well read in theological issues, ma'am, and though I do say it myself, can hold my own in most matters."

"Would you care to join me at yonder table?"

"That I would ma'am. Mine's a pint of mild."

When seated, Harmony asked, "What say you of the local peasantry? Are they not different — well — inferior?"

"I am at a loss to refute you."

"Are they not backwards in many ways?"

"True, and I would venture to suggest that insanity, loose morals and intemperance in both the areas of drink and – ah . . . matters of physical . . . ah . . ."

"Sex, you mean."

"Well . . . yes."

"I thought so. You have researched this matter."

"Indeed yes, ma'am. Look at Bartram Boodle in Dudley's work. By 1720 this fisherman of ill repute had sired five daughters on several base harlots. By the end of the last century there were upwards of 2100 of the vile fruit of the loins, of whom 346 had been paupers, and had spent more than 2300 years collectively in workhouses. More than 546 were prostitutes, some 1600 had drink problems, seven were murderers and almost all had at some time brushed with the law. Some £3 000 000 would have been spent on them from state moneys.

"But — in 1854 a young Quaker of middle-class family named Michael Crumblehome begat a foul spawn off a slow-witted girl named Ada Springwell. Of their descendants, fully four-fifths were feeble-minded, epileptic or were criminals, and all of the women prostitutes. Now listen to this; at a later date, he married a staid Quaker of respectable background, and though the resulting progeny might not have all been moral paragons, their improbity related only to minor matters — you can be certain no criminals were begat and, certain as anything in this life can be, that none were feeble-minded. It might be pointed out that there are some eight times as many offspring from that first birth than from the eight children that Crumblehome begat with his lawful wife.

"It is the same here. No doubt these degenerates had ancestors with the traits associated with noble English yeoman, stoicism and endurance mainly, but through inbreeding and moral decadence and turpitude the more unpleasant traits arose, and the stoicism and endurance became this stupidity and animal placidity that allows a cruel leader to do the most frightful things. And here also, find the dull, repressed violence of the animal that knows his condition should be better but knows not how to rise above the cesspool."

As the evening fell into night, Harmony, entranced by Padlock, bought him drink after drink until the reverend was no longer steady on his feet. She guided him to his room where he fell upon the bed and was instantly asleep. Drunk and snoring, Padlock was oblivious to Harmony's visit. In a way, this was good; awake, he would have asked her how much she was charging to perform this service.

*   *   *

Frank was seated at a long table with an untouched plate of crumbling corned beef flanked by a flask of an interesting looking sauce. On the other side of the plate was a generous glass of the variety of mead called melomel.

"Well ven, we may as well tuck in," said Poffle; and from that end of the table came a horrible symphony of slurpings, gnashings, crunchings and gulpings with, towards the end, a scherzo of belchings. Frank ate with less enthusiasm: the beef was foul, though it was palatable with the strange sauce on it. The conversation was somewhat one-sided.

"I must say vat it is a surprise to see a strange face such as yours in vese parts. I can see vat you, like me, are a man of learning and verefore I must request vat you remain here for a few days so vat you can read and study my feories. I am used to rather low company, lacking in education and intelligence, and I seek stimulation. I fink vat you must know vat . . ."

And so on. Poffle rambled off into a lengthy, windy and discursive speech about all sorts of tendentious nonsense, repeatedly returning to the subjects of ingrown toenails, boils and the lacklustre attitude of the labouring classes.

"And another fing. Vis very morning I caught a fellow sleeping in my barn where I store my corned beef. He didn't seem to know wevver it was Wednesday or Fursday. His name he did know vough. It was Noah Halfmoon. I told him he could sleep anover night in ve barn if he managed to bring me ve bodies of 20 rats. He is out in the field now wiv his beloved cat looking for vem. He will bring me ve bodies so vat I can use vem. I have some interesting uses for vose fings. For a start off, when I am seeking a cure for chilblains I . . ."

At very great length he concluded, "Well ven, what did you fink of vat?"

"Er — delicious. Perhaps you could enlighten me as to the contents of that most unusual but tasty sauce."

"Certainly: I made it myself by boiling ve bowels of several rats, adding to vis a mixture of dead spiders and stewed crab-apples."

Frank rapidly left the room, heading for the sink. He returned some minutes later looking white and haggard. He quaffed the melomel and asked for more.

Their conversation roamed over a gamut of tedious subjects, that is, subjects tedious to Frank, which made them inducers of a near fatal boredom. Frank began to doubt his host's sanity as the buffoon prattled on about electricity, flies, washing with soap ("an unhealthy and futile exercise"), tooth extraction, diet and physical exertion. Eventually Frank managed to enter the conversation.

"Tell me, what do you know of the Black Magician — T'osh as he is known to his close confederates?"

"Well, I might describe him as a close friend. He is indebted to me on many counts. I might say vat I am his advisor in many spheres. I know him very well indeed."

"Where does he live?"

"Just across yonder fields. In a peasant's cottage."

"What can you tell me of his movements?"

"Vis is all getting rather serious. Are you a friend of his?"

"A very old acquaintance."

"Good. Ven I shall give you all ve information you require — tomorrow. Important fings tonight. Did you know vat broad-brimmed hats can prevent heart disease? It has been proved . . ."

*　*　*

Frank could have counted himself lucky that night. Timothy would have given blood to be with Poffle.

In a dank and gelid room below the streets of Ormskirk, lit only by a spluttering torch that sparked fitfully as if it too were poisoned by the noxious exhalations, Timothy etched the eleventh line on the wall. Eleven days — or so he thought, for he had lost all track of time in this filthy sty, and there was no way he could measure its passing; even the foul food, the slops they threw on the floor, came in no measurable rota. He could have been in this oubliette eleven hours or eleven weeks or eleven days.

His body was damaged, but his mind had taken further damage and his condition had been further exacerbated by the time of imprisonment. The room was so bare as to be a sort of primitive sensory deprivation tank, and his mind had grabbed at that possibility, so that now some part of his brain was trying to hold on to reality, but most of his personality had fled into some warm, dark place.

He was waiting on the crest of a sand dune whilst a fresh March breeze rode in from the sea. Apart from the soughing of the sand and the cry of some sea birds, all was silence.

Then Cressida kept her tryst; she was on the sand-dune with him, linking her left arm in his right, they started walking along the sand. She smiled warmly up at him. Life was perfect.

That was odd! Cressida had been on his right side, but when he looked to his left, there was Cressida. He looked again to his right; there was Cressida. He looked again to his left; there was Cressida. He leaned closer to this Cressida and it seemed that a mask split; there was a snarling, brutish face with snaggled teeth leering at him. He smelt the stench of the breath and vomited down his front and legs. Oh God, he thought between spasms, I'm being dragged down a corridor by two black-clad monsters.

"Nononononononononononononononooo!" he shrieked, "Let me alone!"

He was dragged into a large, well-lit room, where the brilliance dazzled his eyes. After a few moments, he began to recover and noticed two things. The room was filled with people, hulking and antagonistic, and at one end of the room there was a sort of judicial bench, almost entirely in darkness, the only lit area being over the high chair where a grotesque motif of a goat's head surmounted by a rotting human skull — real — was highlighted. And was there . . . was there a figure in that chair? Yes, there was, but Timothy could only distinguish a vague shape.

"What is happening?" asked Timothy. "Are you all part of my dream?"

The figure in darkness shifted forward, and his eyes by some trick were brought into light.

"Oh this is no dream," it said, "you are on trial."

"Oh, God, No! No! Nooooooooooooooooooooooooh!"

Timothy's action had not been caused by the words, but when he looked into those eyes, he saw limitless pits of cold and infinite malice.

Timothy shrieked and shrieked: and shrieked.

Chapter 6:

A Time for Every Purpose

The three agitators were heading for their planned rendezvous at the cottage. Martyn was despondent; he feared that little of what he had learned would have any value in formulating a plan of action. He had absorbed a frightening amount of gossip, half-truths, slander and outright lies, and all when standing at the bar of the Stanley Arms . . . but all would count for little against the forces of darkness. He felt impotent.

Padlock was as near elation as he ever let himself become. He had spent some time in the company of a certain female who had been entertained by his curious perspectives on life in general; was not the world his oyster? As he walked down the road his manner was dangerously jaunty. A supercilious grin was pasted to his pallid features as he thought about the finer points of his discourse the previous evening. Being of a puritanical and Calvinistic nature, he wholeheartedly embraced the entire doctrine of predestination and before a small audience, including Miss Harmony Poffle, had pointed out that people who led austere lifestyles, (of which his was, of course, the model) were certain of a first-class reservation in the Kingdom of Heaven. They were chosen ones.

Padlock was sagely nodding his head, thinking about his eloquence and forcefulness, when a mighty blow to his back sent him sprawling amid the dust and cinders of the highway. Looking up he saw Frank towering over him like an oil-derrick grinning broadly. This had been Frank's preferred method of announcing his arrival. Padlock said nothing, made a mental note that this man was in dire need of mortification, then climbed back to his feet. He dusted his mildewed clothes and the pair walked in silence to the building that had lately been Cressida's home.

*   *   *

Soon the three were seated upon the cottage floor and making free with the flagon of celery wine, discussing the situation.

"I must admit," said Martyn, "that I fear that I have not made much progress."

"Yes," said Padlock, "I think that we might have expected little progress from you. As for myself, progress has been satisfactory. Most satisfactory."

"What is this progress, Pedaiah?" asked Martyn when the silence had gone on too long.

"I am not going to tell you."

"Well it seems as if it all comes down to me to tell of real progress," said Frank, haughtily. He paused for dramatic effect. "I have found out the address of the Black Magician."

Came a gruff voice; "I could have told you that, fool, if you had but asked, though I doubt that such knowledge would be of use to you; he is well protected."

"But surely—"

"Quiet, dolt. Whilst you gibber like a fool your friend Timothy is on trial. I know not — though I fear greatly — what the outcome will be. You must rescue him by whatever means you can bring to hand, though the contents of this satchel will be of help. Here are bombs made by my hand; it is well to step quickly away once the fuse has been lit.

"Now go! Do not fail or we are all doomed."

"Well, Frank, Pedaiah, we had best do as we have been told."

"But we might be *killed*!" shrieked Padlock.

"Put your courage to the sticking post," growled Wladek and left.

"Excellent! We can now blow up the magician's cottage."

"No, Frank!" responded Martyn abruptly. "Our mission must be to rescue Timothy from his durance vile. We cannot delay. But look, we have bombs, and I have obtained a long knife and copious quantities of rope. What more do we need to win?"

* * *

Cressida heard of the forthcoming trial with interest, anticipation and perhaps a twinge of conscience. The great day came; Cressida was so excited that she felt she must attend or go out of her mind. She disguised herself and looked neither to the left or right, but only at the ground, as she headed towards Ormskirk; had she been more attentive she might have seen three characters upon the same road, whispering conspiratorially.

She found the court, outside of which an ebon eidolon of T'osh had recently been erected, and joined the throng entering the public benches.

The trial had started when she arrived. Timothy had finished shrieking and was standing all a-tremble in the centre of the court. Cressida gasped as she saw the befouled and emaciated figure of Timothy. Was this her lover, this skeleton who had lost touch with reality and seemed ever to be retreating into some new hallucination?

Everyone knew that Timothy would be found guilty. The judge, who doubled for the prosecuting officer (the defending officer was the defendant himself) read out a list of offences which included assault, sacrilege, blasphemy, abduction, defamation of character, desecrating a place of religious worship, being in league with anti-Satanic forces, white witchcraft, attempted murder and riotous assembly. He was asked if he had anything to say; he mumbled something about doing what had to be done. The jury, twelve ne'er do wells dragged at short notice from the streets, retired to consider their verdict and to quaff massive amounts of the local 'cock ale', this drink being provided by the prosecution. It was called cock ale because somewhere in the mashing process some several cockerels were introduced into the potation.[1]

---

[1] Cock Ale - A traditional recipe from a fifteenth century Scottish manuscript:

Take ten gallons of ale and a large cock, the older the better; parboil the cock, flay him and stamp him in a stone mortar until his bones are broken (you must gut him when you flaw him). Then, put the cock into two quarts of sack, and put it to five pounds of raisins of the sun - stoned; some blades of mace, and

Martyn and the others were in the dusty darkness at the back of the court. Martyn was staring out through a tiny window, looking at the winter chill's effect on the cloddish peasantry of this God-forlorn place.

Timothy was guilty, said the foreman of the jury when he and the other eleven returned; they were all unsteady on their feet. Further, they thought that Timothy's attitude at the time of the offence was both flippant and licentious; this should certainly be considered in sentencing. He and all his companions respectfully requested that Timothy be executed, though they disagreed as to the method of execution, one saying that his entrails be wound out before him, another suggested flailing with red-hot barbed wire, a third that molten bitumen be pumped into Timothy's bowels.

These suggestions were greeted with wild cheers, which for some time disrupted court proceedings. Finally, the judge, his face hidden in the shadow of a black tricorn, spoke in a whining voice these words:

"Vis fellow has indeed committed a very serious offence. I must be extremely grave in my punishment, for he must be made an example of. I verefore recommend vat he be subjected to ve following set of punishments:

"Two days in ve stocks;

"To be marched around Ormskirk, chained to a horse-drawn cart, wiv an iron collar;

"Two days in ve pillory; Not less van eight years in ve dungeons; Judgement is passed."

---

a few cloves. Put all these into a canvas bag, and a little before you find the ale has been working, put the bag and ale together in vessel. In a week or nine days bottle it up, fill the bottle just above the neck and give it the same time to ripen as other ale.

Though there were mutterings about the leniency of the sentence there was no rioting, only a sullen disappointment. However, Quartus Poffle (who indeed was the judge) had felt somewhat sorry for wretched Timothy and had thought that years in the vile cells with corned beef and dead flies for food would do more good than death.

As Timothy was being dragged back to the cells, Frank went over to the judge, just heading down a corridor on the other side of the court.

Padlock looked bewildered.

Martyn had turned to a weeping girl to his left. "You knew him?"

"Yes. . ."

"You knew him well, perhaps?"

"At one time . . . there was an ongoing relationship."

"You lived together?"

"Who are you? What gives you the right—?"

"Hush! My name is Martyn Hopkins. I am a stranger who might need your help."

"Why should I help you?"

"You have no choice," he said, opening his jacket to reveal the long knife. This terrified Cressida so much that she did not see Martyn's trembling hand (Martyn was not as well acquainted with violence as he liked to pretend), and she rose to the occasion by gasping.

"No more! No more, lest I swoon in panting terror. I am of a spiritual disposition, highly-strung and easily excitable. I have no choice but to do your bidding. Whate'er you want, do it!"

Though Martyn was somewhat taken aback with this gusher, he managed to say, "You know the prisoner — gain access to him. I will be there too. Fail . . . and you die; tell anyone of my plan . . . and you will die . . . very slowly."

*   *   *

Frank caught up with the luminary of jurisprudence.

"I say, I didn't know you were a magistrate."

"Oh yes. I am a man of very many parts."

"Perhaps you can help me. I'd like to see this prisoner, see his foulness for myself, close up. Could you arrange this?"

"Very easily. Come."

No one stopped them as they went their way; after all, he was the magistrate.

"By ve way. What is your real reason for seeing ve prisoner?"

Frank laughed nervously. "Er — oh, you've found me out. It's just that the bugger owes me money. Very astute."

"Why do you fink I am a magistrate? But I doubt if he will be able to pay his debt — tee-hee."

Without warning the two were cast to the ground by a shock wave that arrived just before two distinct explosions cracked in their ears. As they climbed to their feet, they saw a billowing cloud of dust coming towards them. They could hear objects falling, men shouting, somewhere a bell ringing.

"Ve cells!" shrieked Poffle.

Turning the corner, they could see the wreck of the cell, a gaping hole leading into the town square was all that remained of one wall. Three figures, dusty and dishevelled, were climbing through the rubble to the empty town square.

"Quick! Vey must not escape!" cried Poffle as the pair ran into the square — and into insanity.

As soon as they gained the outside, the pair were cast to the cobbles by a third explosion which shattered the statue of T'osh into a million fragments and made Cressida, Martyn and Timothy take cover. Disregarding the fallen rubble, a prancing idiot ran to the base of the shattered plinth and stood pointing at the wreckage with a supercilious grin upon his pallid face, like a two-year-old who had learnt to use the potty all by himself. Entreaties would not move Padlock, and Martyn had to drag the fool into the back of the cart parked at one corner of the square. Poffle got on without a word; he seemed to be dazed.

The cart was propelled by a spavined bay which Martyn prodded into its modest interpretation of a gallop by flicking the flanks of the aged beast with a whip; this was just as well, for a mob was beginning to form; a mob that would not be satisfied with anything less than blood; anybody's blood.

But the mob, such as it was, was left behind by the time they had reached the clock tower, though Martyn knew that a well-organised, much more dangerous posse would soon be formed.

Martyn turned to Cressida and said, "We have no further need of your services. You should return to your partner."

"You know about—"

"I know many things. 'Tis best not to question. Go now."

Cressida jumped off the cart and left. Timothy looked more crestfallen than ever, weeping in the rear of the wagon.

But what of Poffle? Why had they dragged him along? When they had discovered who the magistrate was to be, they had decided to take him too. He could be an asset, either as a hostage or, as a source of information. As to the former, they doubted that T'osh would do anything in the way of ransom and would instead send a few interesting methods of painful death to try upon Poffle. They had more hope for him as a source of information; they thought the prospect of red-hot needles in front of Poffle's eyes would be a fine inducement to conversation. As it was, Poffle was currently no problem; he seemed to have gone into a state of shock and was looking about him with the innocent wonder of a child.

"We shall hide in Poffle's house; that's the last place they'll think of looking," said Martyn, taking the reins.

Frank went white at the prospect of another meal at the residence, but he was distracted from his anxiety by a madly excited Padlock who, for some reason, decided that it was time to start gibbering.

"Did you see it, my fellow-me-lads? Did you see it? How I destroyed the statue; see it shiver into thousands of shards; the smoke; the dust; *the flames*! Oh, my dear friend, it is a day of glory — he is now running scared — that magician, that foul whelp, spawn of Satan, now he runs with his ragged tail between his foul legs; soon the fiery sword of Calvin will destroy him utterly. How sweet it is that verily I am the chosen one."

"Chosen for what and by whom?" interjected Frank

"Chosen by God, of course; but soon, heathens, by the peasants who now cower under the filthy shadow of T'osh. They need and will welcome strong, stable government, sympathetic to their needs but ever aware of hoi polloi's limitations. They need the food and drink of the Word; they need the old ways, the hard work and clean simple living. They need to be told of evil, to have a wise but firm hand at the helm; a man who will be ready to clamp down on dissent or any attempt to collectivise disputes or seek trade union recognition agreements. They need me! My fine fellow, what else can they do?"

Frank, who disliked being called 'my fine fellow' and was some-ways incensed by Padlock's ravings, was going to blaze away at the parsimonious parson, but Martyn spoke up, "Hold it — we are nearly at Poffle's house. I vote that we let the horse wander whither he wilt; that way our trail might be hidden."

"Good idea, you stout fellow," responded the ebullient cleric.

"Yes, my fellow," muttered Frank.

Frank and Padlock escorted the slowly recovering Poffle into his own home whilst Martyn rode the cart perhaps a mile up the road, then, loading the cart with dung, he let the horse wander. It is not entirely certain what eventually became of the creature, though it is generally accepted that a certain Mr Noah Halfmoon had at least some dealings with it before it became erased entirely from local knowledge. Halfmoon's rudimentary skills with livestock may well have inspired the animal to wander as far away from the area as his somewhat plodding bearing would permit.

"Now back to the revolutionaries' camp," Martyn muttered, as he trotted back.

* * *

Corned beef had effected a complete cure in Poffle.

"It strikes me vat your views are base, narrow-minded and old fashioned. Vese people go to Satan and are guided by him. Vey know and serve no uvver master; he provides vem wiv all ve fings vey need."

"How mistaken you are," whined Padlock. "Do you know not that these people are damned to hell for all eternity for their sins? Their flesh will burn and melt; they will scream for mercy and forgiveness, yet it will be far too late. Now is the time for repentance."

"But what harm do vey do?"

"Harm! *Harm*! My good fellow, they are bringing the wrath of the Lord down upon the land. Everywhere I see signs of what is to come when the Lord doth show his vengeance — then there shall be much wailing and gnashing of teeth; stone upon stone will be piled onto you – *It is so writ!* Why, was not the destruction of that image of Dagon in the town square this morning a sign of the wrath that is to come?"

"But you blew it up yourself . . ." chimed Frank.

"Exactly! Am I not the agent of the *Lord*, committed—"

"You should be," snapped Frank.

"To the light of goodness?" whooped Padlock

"Wouldn't have thought it," said Frank.

"Pah! My way of life is such that there can be no disputing my assertion. I am a prophet and a martyr. In my life there is a good austerity. Hard work and self-denial are everything."

(Martyn thought to himself that Padlock's self-denial was at its strongest when it involved not merely himself but other people, especially when it came to money. But he said nothing yet thought, once again, that if a revolution was ever lacking in sturdy reliable types, men of courage and vision, this was the one.)

"Look at this coat; it has seen many winters, many storms has it weathered. I acquired it twelve winters ago from one of my flock when he was on his death bed; stout fellow!"

"How frugal," murmured Frank.

"But what does it prove?" queried Poffle.

Hideously, Padlock broke into song, a sound like metal scraped on glass.

The pillars of the earth are the Lord's
He hath set the world upon them
He will keep firm the feet of his saints
And the wicked shall be silent in darkness
And by strength shall no men prevail
The adversaries of the Lord shall be broken to pieces
Out of heaven shall there be thunder about them
The Lord shall judge the ends of the earth

"I take it then," sneered Frank, "that the ten plagues of Egypt shall be visited upon the Black Magician."

"Blasphemer! How dare thou blaspheme? 'Twill be a plague descending upon your arrogant shoulders, I fear."

"Allow me to interrupt," said Martyn, "doubtlessly this discussion is of frightful significance, but might I point out that by this time the horse and cart will surely have been found; and though this place may be not quite on the list of priorities for searching, someone will be along sooner or later. I think that we might make a plan, or two, for moving. *Like right now!*"

"I don't . . . want to go to . . . to—to—to—to jail again," whimpered Timothy.

"I suggest that we repair to Timothy's old cottage. It is set away from the road and amid trees. We may well escape detection altogether. If not, there is plenty of cover in the trees. We must move quickly; this house now pleases me ill; I regret having suggested it and fear that I might have brought terrible doom to us all. Come; let us go now. We will be nearer our friend with the bombs."

Before they left, they bound and gagged Poffle (the latter more for peace of mind than for security). Discounting the risk, they searched the house for any useful objects — the corned beef was ignored. This search turned up several bottles of melomel, a large map of the area, a lucky rabbit's foot, and a double-barrelled shotgun with two boxes of cartridges — this last cheered them no end.

There was a knock upon the door.

The shotgun was forgotten as total panic fell upon everyone.

The knock sounded again.

Martyn discovered the presence of mind to whip out his knife and brandish it about.

"May I come in?" boomed a deep but female voice. Without any reply being given, the door was thrown open and Harmony Poffle marched in.

"Do come in; make yourself at home," said Martyn for want of anything better to say. A smug grin crawled over Padlock's face.

"Certainly, but what is going on here?"

Said Padlock, "Well myself and my subordinates, we are going to overthrow that tyrannical despot known as T'osh. We use whatever methods suit the hour: bombing, kidnapping, torture, bribery — though I must admit no one has tried to bribe me yet — and slitting throats with long knives. I am not a man to be crossed; why, only today in Ormskirk I risked life and limb in order to rescue an innocent prisoner from foul dungeons and oubliettes. And yet, milady, did I care a jot for my safety, for as soon as we were outside again, I further risked my life by demolishing a statue of T'osh with an infernal device."

Harmony glowed with admiration. "Clearly you are one of the valiant of life. Yet must I warn you that T'osh is after your blood; he has vowed to roast your eyeballs on a stick before the month is out."

Padlock shuddered, and Frank went white. Martyn broke the silence. "We must move now; and you, my good woman, you must come with us — as a prisoner, of course."

"Oh yes. And which of you is going to bind my firm young body with stout rope and threaten to whip me if I misbehave?" She turned to Padlock. "You look like the man for the job."

Padlock made no reply.

*   *   *

Soon they were all safely within the cottage, the two prisoners having been firmly bound and put into a cool and dark cellar. One had been placated with the promise of all the corned beef he could absorb, the other with promises of visits by Padlock at least six times a day. In one corner Timothy was stuffing himself with his first substantial meal in some time, whilst by the window Martyn was keeping a weather eye to the, so-far, empty fields and studying the map. Padlock (what else?) was arguing with Frank.

"But surely," said Frank, "you cannot accept this idiotic notion of predestination? Who could think it anything but fanciful nonsense?"

"My young friend, you are clearly not wise to the ways of the *Lord*. It is axiomatic that only certain chosen ones will be fit to enter the Kingdom of Heaven. There will be no place for sinners; they shall be cast aside, condemned to the blazing pitch of Hell for all eternity, never knowing the slightest respite from their agony no matter how many million years pass. Yet shall others gain access to heaven, and it follows that these people must have led a good life ere shuffling off their mortal coil, eschewing laziness, greed, hedonism, pride and all the sins of the flesh."

"Yeah, but where does this lead us?"

"Now it must be that God knows everything, and is well aware, long before a person is put onto the earth, whether that person is destined for eternal salvation; thus, people are chosen. It follows then, that the chosen have led simple, austere, hardworking lives; the rest are damned."

Timothy had finished his meal and was listening intently. Fortified by a glass of strong ale he seemed to be successfully reacquainting himself with reality.

He said, "Excuse me, but could you clarify a few points. Are you saying that no one has any choice in the matter, that whether they are damned or not is out of their control? In other words, free will is nothing but a figment of the imagination — if we have an imagination, that is?"

"That is more or less true."

"Does this mean that Calvinism and deterministic theories of the universe are irretrievably interlocked?" said Frank.

"I wouldn't know."

"Are you also saying," continued Timothy, "that only those people who lead austere lives, foregoing alcohol, fleeing from tobacco and sex, saying prayers fifty times a day, dressing in ragged clothes, bathing in shadowy, unlit rooms, sleeping on hard wooden beds, working hard at their calling, but not spending a farthing if they can possibly avoid it, are these the ones who are saved?"

"That is near the truth."

"So, you are saying that only these people can cross the pearly gates? People such as yourself?"

"Yes!"

"Then I put it to you that this damn kingdom will be so full of mealy-mouthed, sanctimonious, pompous, fun-less, sober-thinking, self-satisfied charlatans that no person in their right mind would care to be there for a single second. As for myself, were I ever unfortunate enough to turn up at that hellish place, the first thing I would do would be to seek out a few of those miserable characters and give them a damn good kick up the arse."

The thunders that crackle and race across the vast cloud surface of the planet Jupiter were no match for the tempests that now rolled upon Padlock's pallid face. He turned his back upon the company and strode down to the cellar. Came a clamorous female voice from the cellar, "I tried to escape — honestly. Are you going to punish me? Please."

Chapter 7:

The Sabotage Continues

T'osh was pacing up and down the cottage, a crumpled piece of parchment in his claw-like hand. His face was red, his eyes yellow, his lips cyanotic. Cowering in one corner were John Ambler and his wife, Adaline; they listened in terror to T'osh's rantings.

"Cannot anyone tell me what is going on? Do I have nothing but buffoons and dolts under me? Tell me, oh mighty Asmodeus, what is going on?

"One of my trusted judges is kidnapped in broad daylight; then a schoolmistress vanishes. My statue – *my statue*! is — is — is *assassinated*. And now, now this foul newssheet tells me what my lieutenants told me of in the chill of yester-night, a bridge blown up, a school burnt down and one of my most trustworthy aids beaten to a pulp.

"By the paps of Arienhod I will catch this filth. Throats shall I slit, intestines shall I pull apart, brains shall I eat: I will have the culprits by the end of the month — depend upon it — no matter what Satan-forsaken part of Ormskirk they hail from; or even if they come from outside—". He stopped suddenly and fingered the ragged scar on his throat. He seemed to pale for a moment. "No, they are not here; it is not them. I shall not fail this time.

"You! Ambler, sickening sycophant, go at once to Wladek the labourer. I will see him. Tell him to come at once. Go! Run to it."

He turned to Adaline Ambler. "Bring me the head of a calf. At once, for it will be nigh on three days since last I ate."

"It will take some time sir. The cleaning and the cooking—"

"What do I want for cleanliness and cooking? Bring me the head. At once, I say. Yaaaaaarrgghhh!"

*　　*　　*

Sometime later, Martyn was seated cross-legged in the corner of the cottage's main room thinking about the events of the days before. The biggest piece of luck, which had befallen them, was due to Timothy who, apparently fully recovered, had found a rusting printing press in an abandoned barn. They had cleaned it and repaired it as best they could and, surprisingly, the machine still worked. The printer's pie was quite extensive, though sometimes they had to use different typefaces for some of the more common letters. The lack of ink had been a concern, but Poffle had been the unexpected solver of that problem. He knew of a country method of stewing various barks and plants to make dyes. The resultant liquid had been profoundly black but too thin to make good ink. Timothy had mentioned that since flour and water make a simple paste, would not flour prove to be a thickening agent to the ink? It had been tried — and it had worked, not wholly successfully, but certainly well enough for an underground newssheet to go into production.

At least that was what had been thought — until Frank had asked, with contempt, what about paper? They did not wish to leave the area of T'osh's influence, for travel across the border was actively discouraged by the tyranny and enforced by a hidden legion of guards. However, there seemed to be no other course open to them but to go to more normal parts of the world for paper (T'osh having banned the sale of this commodity within Ormskirk to all but the authorised few), when, on a raid to Poffle's cottage — supplies having run so low that they were faced with the grim inevitability of eating the corned beef — a room was discovered that contained several tons of paper.

The only problem now was one of distribution, since anyone who was caught on the streets of Ormskirk distributing the leaflets would, *tout suite*, find himself deprived of eyes, ears, nose and tongue and be surprised to note that his body was now decorated with a wide assortment of knives. They had prepared a long statement attacking T'osh and denouncing him as a tyrant, a miser and a despot. His grandiose schemes were nothing less than plans for the subduing and enslavement of the human race *in toto*, forever. Martyn guessed that the disapproved of habit of reading was not quite extinct and that the leaflet, which also gave T'osh's past track record, would have no small effect.

But until some means of safe and relatively risk-free distribution could be found, the notices were gathering dust. Their first attempt, a simple newssheet printed in an excess of euphoria, their opening effort in the propaganda war, said nothing much more than that T'osh is a reeky horn-beast and giving details of the mayhem achieved the night before, had been a one-off event. It was not to be repeated; Martyn remembered a few close shaves as they had crawled through the pre-dawn streets of Ormskirk, showering sheets upon the road.

But — *the night before*! What a night of glory, thought Martyn. Soon after dark Martyn, Padlock, Timothy and Frank had left the cottage, Padlock with explosives to destroy the bridge between Melling and Ormskirk, the rest to burn the schoolhouse. They had synchronised watches, and both acts of sabotage were to happen at 10.30pm, when the vast majority of the locals would be sleeping or drinking their ale in a pub.

They reached their objective and Martyn and Timothy stood guard in the road while Frank sloshed paper and wood with copious amounts of petrol. With one room drenched in petrol, Frank threw a lighted sheet of paper into the schoolhouse. There was a mighty fireball and within minutes the whole ground floor was ablaze. By the time Frank re-joined the others the glass in the upper storey had shattered and questing flames were in every room, but Frank was not happy.

"Damn the maggot," he said, "it's a certainty that he's messed it up."

"Who, what?" asked Timothy.

"Pedaiah, of course, who else?"

"What do you mean?"

"What time is it?"

"10.40. But—"

"Right, Pedaiah was supposed to blow up the bridge ten minutes ago. Have you heard any explosion?"

"Hush," whispered Martyn, "list, what do you hear?"

They all heard it now; someone was fast approaching along the road. By the light of the fire its burly, wallowing lineaments could be made out as it waddled like a stranded whale towards the blazing building.

"Ballbags," it gasped between breaths, "gettin' me out o' the pub before the towels go up. Bollockbrains." Clearly it was not kindly disposed to any who crossed his path.

"Arrrrrrn'rrrrrrgh," it said as it fell across the cunningly hidden tripwire and toppled to the cobbles. For a moment its ghastly face was clear in the light from the fire.

"You," gasped Timothy, grasping a stout stick and running towards the prone figure; he had last seen this man in bottle-green trousers at the ceremony.

"It's him," said Frank, grasping his stout stick and recognising the man who had trounced him so long ago in the Stanley Arms during their previous adventure.

Timothy and Frank started to kick and beat the man mercilessly. Martyn stood some distance away; the man's shrieks he could stand, it was those other noises, the cracking of bone, the pulping and splitting of flesh that were so disturbing. After a time the shrieks stopped; the other noises did not for some time.

"Did you kill him?"

"No," said Timothy, "not quite."

"Can he actually *be* killed?" asked Frank.

*　*　*

They set off back along the fields. When they reached a point perhaps a mile from the site of the arson, Martyn could see that the place would be entirely gutted, though the flames were still dancing in the sky. Another disadvantage of the way of life under the regulation of T'osh was that there was, of course, no fire brigade. This was denounced as an extravagant waste of money which could be put to better use, although there was a notable lack of detail about what exactly that 'better use' might be. Concerned peasant 'volunteers' were simply expected to lend a hand, as they saw fit, in the event of a conflagration.

Needless to say, *the perfect state* did not seem disposed to provide much in the way of equipment. Predictably there had been a significant increase in the number of house fires in the recent past and a suspicion that the decline in health and safety provision generally (unsurprisingly castigated by T'osh as an unnecessary bureaucratic evil) had delivered an opportunity for scores to be settled.

To Martyn's right there was a sudden flash of light, followed by its reflection on the low clouds. Then a low resonating detonation rolled over the fields.

"Pedaiah's done it," said Martyn.

"Pah, half an hour late," said Frank, "'tis to be hoped that he managed to blow both the bridge and his miserable self to bits at the same time."

When they returned, they found Padlock already at the cottage. As he was in one of his moods they ignored him and went to print the newssheet, whilst Padlock examined with love the design of the halfpenny coin.

* * *

Wladek received the urgent message from T'osh and went to the pub — let the swivel-eyed miscreant wait, he thought to himself. Leaving Cressida in a self-induced trance he went to the Stanley Arms and drank deep. The ever-voluptuous Florinda Farrier tried to converse with him — and even laid her hand on his, but to no avail — Wladek was deep in thought, his brown brow furrowed.

It was well past closing time when he left the pub, and though his unsteadiness of step could have been partly due to a loose strap on his prosthesis, the probable cause was the amount of alcohol he had consumed that night.

He reached the Ambler's humble dwelling and knocked with such force that the door shook and rattled in its rusty hinges. Ambler eventually opened the door and without speaking a word led Wladek into the main room where, lit by the guttering glow of a reeking candle, T'osh sat at a table, scribbling into a huge tome with manic force.

T'osh looked up from the book, his eyes ghastly in the light from the candle. He spat in the general direction of Wladek and said, sarcastically, "So, you are here. Glad you could make it."

"Aye! Well I run my day by no man's schedules but my own. Why should I be a slave to any man's whims?"

"No matter. I summonsed you because of these outrageous incidents — you know what I mean?"

"Oh yes."

"They undermine *my* authority, and I fear greatly that people will shortly begin to question my power — *this must not happen*! My spies tell me that there has already been some smouldering unrest; these atrocities can only fan the flames. Why, but a few hours ago a man was found chanting in the streets, *no taxation without representation*, and though this swine did not chant for long I can foresee the time when there shall be talk of elected representatives. It's blasphemous and must be stopped. But what to do? What to do?"

"Simple; you re-assert your authority."

"Indeed. And how do you suggest I go about that?"

"Well, I would imagine that with your . . . er . . . shall we say, heavy handed methods and discharge of burdensome infrastructure you have salted away quite a bit of money."

"Perhaps. What of it? Come, out with it, lewdster."

"Yes, well, is this money readily available?"

"What has that to do with you? Men have died for saying less."

"Answer me, please. I am here to help you, am I not?"

T'osh did not answer for a moment.

"You may be right — but remember; your life is in my hands.

"If you must know, since currency was abolished and barter reintroduced, I have confiscated all notes and coins, both in private hands and in banks and industry. This is all hidden in and near this house and, as you can imagine, I am a very wealthy man." As he said this, he rubbed his hands in turgid glee.

"You must use this money carefully and wisely. Put on a show of strength."

"Indeed?"

"Put on a show of strength, I say. Use some of your wealth. Go to outside sources—"

"Indeeeeeeeeeeeeeeeeeed you speak heresy!" T'osh shrieked as he fell howling to the floor. "Never, never, never, never, never," he wailed whilst rolling on the threadbare carpet, "I have no contact with the outside, Satanless world."

"You lie."

"Yaaaaaaaaaaaaaarrrrrrggggghhhhhhhhhhhh!"

"You cannot fool me with your act; I know. I know all about the little luxuries; I know all about the sophisticated equipment and drugs in some of those rooms you care to call dungeons, though operating theatres and advanced interrogation centres would be more to the point. I know all about the bribes, the hand-outs, the slush-money you use to stop anyone outside really looking into this set-up. So, to put it bluntly, let's cut the crap and get on with it.

"As I say, go out and about to buy equipment to put on a massive display of some kind — use your imagination. Re-build the statue — do it one Friday night so that the people who come to market the next day will think it some marvel. Use your intelligence for Satan's sake!

"One further thing: a warning. There are people abroad in this land who know of your vast wealth and who would do their uttermost to acquire it. Perhaps you should give a large proportion of this wealth to me — I shall secrete it away and guard it with my life and soul; there is a sturdy cellar to my abode. 'Twould be safe there until such time as you would need it."

"Perhaps you are right. This fellow Ambler, stupid though he is, might try to plunder my riches, or, more probably, lead other, more rapacious men to it. Yes, I will leave three-quarters of it with you; the rest shall I keep."

"Good," said Wladek, "I shall bring a horse and cart tomorrow in order to collect this wealth."

* * *

Days passed; the tense calm continued. T'osh attended to his plans. Wladek kept himself occupied, sometimes with his normal work on the farm, other times with strange nocturnal comings and goings. This last might have bothered Cressida at any other time, but now she was infatuated with vampires and spent most of the time pondering upon such matters and consulting ancient legends.

Quartus and Harmony Poffle were still imprisoned in the cellar, and though they would probably have preferred more congenial surroundings, both were contented, though for differing reasons; Quartus had been given some of the paper found at his cottage, together with a quill pen, and was now expanding upon some ludicrous theory concerning the origins of the universe, meaningful communications with sycamore trees, and the possibility of methane-based life forms on Saturn's moon, Titan. Harmony had other reasons for contentment. In addition, Wladek was a frequent visitor and gave them bottles of melomel, culled from Poffle's own pantry, whilst telling them that he was doing the utmost to get them released as soon as was humanely possible.

Harmony's comfort was Padlock; she had become besotted with him and lived only for his visits. When he did call for the promised visits now, Padlock was truly grateful for the iron bars that separated him from Harmony. Yet ever did she speak of him in nothing but the most glowing terms, making it clear that she would not turn down the offer of becoming a clergyman's spouse.

Through all of this did Padlock go with his usual air of scornful smugness, seemingly indifferent to the feelings he managed to arouse in the trio of protagonists. In conference and away from Padlock these three often wished that the ground would open and swallow up the Reverend, that he would ascend into his own version of heaven, that Harmony would really get her clutches on him, or that he would simply clear off. But then, he knew too much already, and this fact necessitated his continued stay at the cottage.

Martyn had discovered a kindred soul in Timothy. Both expressed their desire to see materialism, selfishness and devastation of the countryside fade away and both firmly believed in the need of every individual to seek self-expression through the acoustic guitar, real ale and the legalisation of cannabis. Martyn was able to outline in detail how this could be grown in an attic if the correct temperature could be maintained although he remained vague as to whether he had actually partaken of the herb in question.

Frank had restarted work on his novel and would sit in a corner for hours, writing with fingers that seemed mechanical. His face would be impassive, his eyes glazed. He said to Timothy that the recent scrapes had revived his literary aspirations.

"Well then," said Timothy, "perhaps you would allow me to digest some of your outpourings."

"Yes . . . I think I will allow you the great honour. This chapter is based on a personal experience of mine, occasioned some years ago. It is both thought-provoking yet abstract, distinctly humorous, yet at the same time shudderingly ominous. Pray honour yourself and read."

Chapter 79: Expressions of oppression

Nivek frowned. The window. The window was. Is. And forever shall be. The window beckoned. Beckoned.

Light a cigarette. Smoke rose. E'en unto heaven. Smoke on glass. Curdling. Strands of grey in clear liquid

Out of the window. Look. He looked. Buildings. Were they druid stones? Accursed druids so many years out of time.

An ant. Crawling. Crawling ant. On the checkerboard of floor, mandarin's dream. Who is dreaming who? Ant. crawling. Shell like smoked glass. Shell? Exoskeleton. Get it right. Precision. Pigeonhole it. Be exact. Forever. Foregone willow tree weeping peeping leaping seeping into darkness alone and dead.

Knarf enters. Nivek smiled. Before. Was his smile the cause of Knarf's entrance? Always questions.

The ant still moved. Over obstacles. Always over obstacles. Like Nivek. Like Knarf. More like Knarf. THE WORLD HAD IGNORED KNARF'S MANY TALENTS. Like the ant. He would overcome the obstacles. They had gone. Gone forever.

Overcome all obstacles. Knarf.

(*Outside observer looking in. At Knarf. at Nivek. Both thought and fought: (disguised). Both thought same thought. At the same time. Disguised though. Hide. Look at it in open. Hidden thought. Both looked at the ant.. Ant was free. Not us. No. No. We are srenosirp. Do not hide it. Bring it out. Open the diseased limb. Show the gangrene. We are srenosirp! No. Face it. Bring it out. We — we are — Prisoners!*)

Learning hides the prison walls.

Rekaorc enters. cigarette in mouth. sees ant. Peers at ant. On Earth all creatures that do dwell. Draws on. Cigarette ash fell to the ground. Flakes sough off. Ant under ash. Ashant collided. Survives. Rekaorc scowls, twisted countenance of malevolence.

—break window; Knarf. Command? Request? Statement of Action?

—go ahead; Nivek. Matrix of probability gels — gelled. Knarf did nothing. Waits. Waits. A dry sea of dead time.

—What's going on here? You're standing around like a pair of statues — waiting for something to happen? Rekaorc. Criticism. Criticism of Knarf. Punishment is due. Rekaorc must pay. Pays. Slips. Falls through window... window diamond fragments. Laced. With blood. Like rubies. Wrists, face . . . can't take any more. Rekaorc isn't bleeding.

I'm bleeding dying is this the end of Rekaorc you bastards do something do something before I bleed to death get up and away from these maniacs rot in hell bastards god I need a cigarette these there the door out through the door bleeding not too bad got eight pints.

—always showing off that Rekaorc: Nivek

—glad he's gone; Knarf.

Into the past. Glass shattering. Stalactites of frozen infinity. Jewels. Crashing, bashing, gnashing, flashing. Sharp boulders. Asteroids. Worlds of crystal. Seeing fragments fall. Fall and shatter. All miss. Rekaorc gone. Leaving blood and memories. Red blood. Will he survive? Who knows? Cares. Tatters of flesh. Gobbets of gore. Blood. All Rekaorc's. Not Nivek's. Not Knarf's. Laugh. Laugh at the blood, the other person's blood.

Rekaorc returns. Blood. Falls to floor. Moans. Misses ant. Sounds. Other footsteps. Pounding. Echoing. Echoing. Urgent. Nivek lights cigarette.

Offered one to Rekaorc. No reply. Giving them up? Dead? Sounds near. Match falls to floor. Same time as Knarf pulls beard. New groan. Blood everywhere.

Door opens. Man, in uniform. Blue. It screamed. Authority. Blood. dripping, dropping, oozing, throbbing, pulsating. Blue man looked at window. Hatred. The window. The window laughed.

—we are all guilty; Knarf. point at Rekaorc. Nivek looks. Looks away. Reach for cigarette. No cigarette. Packet empty. Not like his head. Oh that it could be? Get rid of pain. Pain; pane. Smash it. Like the window. No. Not so easy. Guilty. One. All. You. Me. Him. Her. Guilty. Doomed. Forever. Despair. Despair.

the

despair

of

Prisoners

Rekaorc led away. Man shakes head —despondency breeds misery and defeat; Knarf.

Nivek closes his eyes. The pain. Pain. Like engines pounding. For ever and ever. Nivek opened his eyes. Reads Sartre. Some ease. Don't let me look at blood. Blood. Blood — all is surely not yet lost can we not draw some slight sustenance from the faith that maybe god does dwell in every blade of grass and that even the ant that crawls upon the floor has some element of the godhead of its carapace body?:

Knarf.—yes Nivek.

Rekaorc in chains. Led off. Blue man follows, hears Knarf. Hears the hope. Forbidden hope. No for these PRISONERS OF THOUGHT. Ant crawls. Onward. Blue man hears Knarf. Boot descends. Moves on.

(the ant is dead the ant is dead the ant is dead the ant is dead the ant is dead the ant is dead the ant is dead.)

What is dead? Anyone know? (Or care? Really?) Dead is the ant! Well dead. (Or is it, really? Prove it.)

(hope, hope no shattered like glass gone, gone like the ant now dead, dead of hope empty away oh that we could escape from this hell of eternity where how long and where what is the meaning the reality what is outside where is it why, why am I always denied it why was I put here and what is this outside of which I know/ no nothing/everything what has been done to me my mind feel like a character in a book horrible but what a masterpiece it would be if I could write it but not live it yet here I am forever imprisoned for no crime but think of other subjects better, think of better subject yes. I resolve to so do.

The ant is dead. Rekaorc lives on, for the moment. Inaccessible. Secluded.

*   *   *

"Well," said Frank, "do you not think that this is a work of considerable genius? Do you not think that I am destined to become part of the literary heritage one way or the other?"

"You may well be right," said Timothy, "one way or another."

"My style, would you not certainly call it excellent?"

"Well, it is certainly unique. I assume that you are a follower of the stream of consciousness movement and esteem most highly the works of Joyce?"

"Who?"

"Joyce."

"Joyce who?"

"James Joyce, the émigré Irish novelist — Ulysses, Finnegan's Wake and all that."

"Why do you assume that I have read him, or even ought to? My style is my own; no one could come close to equalling it."

"That may well be true."

Frank did not like the tone of the last remark, and he became somewhat heated. "Normal conventions — pah! I spit upon them. I break down boundaries and explore new frontiers, forging literary pathways through cultural deserts. An outlaw and a brigand, I respect no one. My art is everything. I would die before I changed one word of that work, that masterpiece, which you have had the rare honour to peruse."

"Just the same, a little more attention to a few minor literary rules—"

"Such as?"

"Characterisation, motive, clarity, sincerity, coherence, logic, tense, grammar, punc—"

"Pah! It just goes to show how little you know about the art of writing. No! I will not have another word spoken. Joyce indeed."

Frank went for a sulk in the corner. He positioned himself on a stool facing the corner, focussing on a spider's web long since abandoned.

Martyn had entered, catching the latter half of the conversation, thinking it strange that Frank was now claiming never to have heard of Joyce when, as Martyn's memory firmly attested, Frank had earlier said that *Prisoners of Thought* was a re-examination of certain themes found in the works of Kafka, Dos Borges and Joyce himself. Perhaps some eminent literary critic had recently denounced Joyce as a callow imposter and pseudo intellectual; Frank, ever one to take such matters to extremes, would claim up and down that he had never heard of Joyce, let alone have gone to the dubious extreme of soiling his eyes by glancing at one of his inferior works. Martyn said nothing however, but inwardly smiled.

*　　*　　*

On the following day Martyn and Frank, suitably disguised, set off for Ormskirk to obtain some food and see what information could be obtained for the cause and perhaps gauge the current mood of the peasants. Also, they were leaving the company of Padlock for a few hours; they were thoroughly sick of him and any absence was to be prayed for, the more so when it was considered that Padlock played with his explosive device when left alone. (Please God, an accident; only a small one.)

Timothy was risking a flogging (and much worse were he to be recognised) by the border guards should he be caught, but he had, nonetheless, gone to Maghull, where the doctrines of T'osh held no sway, to pick up supplies and equipment not available in benighted Ormskirk.

Martyn was feeling quite light-hearted. The day was clear and cold, with frost crackling under their feet and a brisk wind ruffling their cloaks. The fields were all bare, but the tints of the browns could be easily made out in the wonderfully clear air. In the distance the branches, nearly even the twigs, of the bare trees could be individually identified. The day had so worked its way with Martyn that he felt he could even face a conversation with Frank.

"In truth, much leather has this road worn off our feet as we have gone along it over the years, ever in search of justice and routing out oppression."

"There may be some truth in what you say," said Frank.

"Come what may, it always seems that we must return to this winding road, on a mission against the forces of darkness and repression; perhaps fate conspires to make it so?"

"Perhaps."

"Feasibly we are in hell, our own private hell. Everyday ordinary life is imaginary — a respite or mere digression. The reality is, was, and ever shall be that we are on a journey without beginning or end."

"Doubtlessly."

"A journey on which we meet wicked foemen and strive to overcome their evil. Always on the point of victory, yet always failing, for they, their henchmen, or evildoers from other parts return or make an appearance. This road, this long, winding, tortuous, painful road, can be seen as a — an allegory of man's journey through the ages, for is not mankind ultimately flawed and therefore doomed?"

"No."

"What? You are an optimist, an apologist for man's perversity and ignorance?"

"No."

"Then what are you saying?"

"Very little. You are doing most of the talking."

Martyn wondered what had come over Frank; he had never displayed this mood before. The pleasure Martyn had felt in the day had evaporated; the wind was now icy rather than bracing; the clear sky now being covered by a blanket of black clouds coming from the west. He thought for a moment about what to say next.

"Somewhat uncharacteristically you seem to be in a reflective rather than argumentative mood. However, I will press my assertion and seek a response. Thereby I may get a partial explanation of what has got into you today.

"Do you not accept that mankind is flawed and that only a handful of rules, conventions and customs stop every person on this planet from leading a life that is nasty, brutish and short?"

"What?"

"I mean that we have far more in common with head-hunting savages than we like to think about; that the axe carrying vandal is far closer to the surface of the mind than most people will admit."

"An interesting, if trite notion. However, as I have said before, I am the centre of my own universe."

Martyn interpreted Frank's silence as an attempt on his part to marshal the next part of the argument and so did not break the quiet. He did increase his pace and was thankful that Frank, though still distracted looking, did the same; the clouds were banking up in the sky and the far western horizon seemed blurred and indistinct, as if seen through a rain shadow. He did not wish to be caught in the open and there was some distance yet to travel on the road.

Frank's silence continued as they came to a small crossroads. Martyn cried out in horror and disgust at the gibbet in the roadside, for a green and decaying corpse was hanging in tatters from the chains. He did not think it was anyone he knew, but it was rather hard to judge; the eyes had gone, pecked by birds, and the puffed features were almost unrecognisable.

Frank looked at the lynch, said nothing, ignored it.

"Would you care to enlarge upon your last statement?" said Martyn at last.

"No; there is nothing to expand upon. My destiny is in my own hands, more or less . . . I think. Anyway, it is all no concern of mine."

What has happened to Frank, thought Martyn, is he ill? Never had the man been so unresponsive: so unwilling to take a definite and pedantic stand: so lacking in even a spark of argument. He seemed to be mulling over something that was troubling him. Martyn's first thought was that it was something to do with the book.

"How's your novel coming along? I hear that you've been working on it again."

"Yes."

"I'm sure it will attract much attention when it is completed."

"I doubt it."

"But surely you believe in yourself?"

Frank sighed wearily. "It is not a case of what I believe but what the unwashed and unenlightened masses choose to believe."

The silence built up again. Finally, Martyn saw no other course of action. "Frank, what's the matter with you?"

"Nothing is the matter with me."

"Don't try to fool me, you've been acting funny all day — don't deny it."

Frank sighed, "This Pedaiah fellow, Padlock."

Martyn laughed, the nickname was so apt, "What about him?"

"Is he insane?"

"Possibly."

"I do not think that we are doing our cause any good by keeping in with him."

"What would you suggest?"

"Braining him."

"Eh?"

"Splitting his head wide open so that his small amount of brain dribbles on to his mildewed jacket. It could easily be done: a hammer, a chisel, a pick would do the job; we have no need of extravagance. For example, a broad bladed chisel, placed slightly above ear-level at the temple, could be struck with a three-pound hammer; the force would be sufficient to impel the brain from its pan and lift off the cranium, which, like the following cerebral organ, would land where it would on the countryside. Or, facing him, propel a meat-cleaver down his contemptuous features, so that one side of his head falls upon one shoulder and the other side upon the other shoulder. There are many methods. It is only the finer details to be made out."

Martyn made no reply.

The long-augured rain began to fall.

Chapter 8:

The Fly In The Ointment

The day was cold and massive banks of rain-bearing clouds were fast piling in the west. John Ambler was indifferent to this; he was indifferent to most things now, for his hard life had been made all the tougher by the ban on all but the most primitive of tools and farm machinery. The backbreaking drudgery had driven Ambler's mind into itself, and in the dark convolutions were great, grim thoughts.

He had shielded the Black Magician for quite some time; but as T'osh's power had increased, Ambler's importance had diminished until he became little more than waiter and errand boy. Now he could consider himself fortunate indeed if T'osh acknowledged his existence with more than a grunt. And it was so unfair, for had he not saved the very life of T'osh and nursed him back to health? Was he not the path upon which T'osh had trod when he began his return to power? But where was his reward? T'osh had given him nothing, not so much as a single penny.

But what could he do? He could not physically harm T'osh, for he had at least two bodyguards with him night and day, nor could he sneak off with any of

T'osh's riches; he might get past the guards, but he would not escape the pack of night-black hounds that howled and slavered about the cottage. Indeed, he could not leave his own home at night, for the hellhounds would have ripped out his throat before he had gone ten yards.

No, T'osh was safe, securely ensconced in the second floor and attic of the cottage, which he had converted into a study, library and laboratory for delving into his foul and arcane lore. In this room were strange markings upon the floor that disturbed Ambler, and on certain nights, to the frenzied howling of the dogs outside, Ambler could hear grunting chants and ecstatic shrieks fall from that fearsome chamber as T'osh invoked some hideous presence.

He was brought back to present reality when his body told him that the job in question was now completed and his memory told him to hie to Ormskirk for it was market day. He plodded back to the cottage and loaded his handcart with goods for barter.

His muscles ached; he coughed and wheezed. Yet still he pushed his cart through the frigid air. Ah, he mused for the thousandth time, had anyone benefited from the advent of the Black Magician? Yes! But not he, Ambler, nor any of his ilk — they were worse off. He thought back on the first speech in the woods, when everything had been so cosily outlined by T'osh and a life of bucolic rural simplicity had seemed to be the sweetest thing on earth. Of course, it had been warm then, the trees in leaf, and everyone still sleek and fat from easy living. But he should have known that the sweetest apple is the first to rot. All this black magic and what had it brought? — Famine, rickets, infant mortality, pain and much, much more; the future was the only thing bleaker than the past few months. Ambler was a simple man; Ambler was a slow man . . . but Ambler knew the difference between good and evil.

He was drawn out of his pit of reverie by the conversation of two fellow travellers. So far as could be made out it concerned driving a chisel into some unfortunate's skull.

"Hallo, these sound a lively couple a' tha'."

He went towards them, impelled by some unknown instinct. "Good day, kind sirs. Mind if I join you on this foul, wet day?"

"No, not at all," said Martyn, pulling his broad-brimmed hat lower over his face.

"If you must," muttered Frank with scant civility.

"And 'ow do you find yourselves, all things being as they be?"

"Good enough," responded Martyn.

"Things being as they be," mumbled Frank.

"My but these be strange times we be living through, say you not?"

"Says who?" said Frank irritably.

"Why now there's them as says that folks 'ave become as queer as folks can become in these parts. Well, with all this black magic stuff and 'ounds of 'ell back ont' farm, and all this stuff, it do frighten me out of my skin some nights."

A weird fellow this, thought Martyn; he seemed as dull as a rusty E-string on a bass guitar, but he seemed desperate to tell some secret or other.

"Hounds of Hell?"

"Oh aye, a 'ole pack o' them, bayin' an' 'owlin', waking me most nights. Course, weren't like tha' 'fore

T'osh came. Aye it's 'is 'ounds and 'is guards and hell-damned chaunterin'. Fair drives me up pole it do."

Martyn was amazed that he had come across such a close confidant of the magician; why, he seemed to live in the same house. He remembered something Wladek had said about a cotter's kindness to T'osh after the magician had almost been decapitated by a character called Red Joe. This must be the man! Certainly he did not seem to be a willing agent of the Dark One. Martyn prompted; "Er . . . well, has anything special been going on of late?"

"Well, all I know is tha' 'e is very annoyed as to what's bin 'appenin' lately — them things as you'll 'a' 'eard. An' 'e's plannin' summat special like in a week or two. Summat as 'll show people what's what, 'oo's boss like. This've been planned for a while now. 'E wants to put down these rebels, like, them as've bin blowin' up 'is statue."

Like a conspirator, the labourer lowered his voice, went close to Martyn's ear, cupped his hand, and said, "Mind you, I wish 'e were done away with. I'm fair flummoxed wi' 'im, 'e makes me fair sick 'e does. Done nowt for the likes o' me. 'E just makes sure 'e's a'right." He raised his voice. "You sir, you 'oo was doin' all the talkin' abou' chisels and 'eads; why not do in T'osh's? 'Twould be a fair deed bravely done, though not the first, if I'm judgin' 'is scar right."

Martyn could see the clock tower of Ormskirk in the distance; soon they would have to leave this downtrodden, but not entirely diminished, drudge.

"Do you come here every Thursday?"

"Aye. Since I were a lad. There's always been Amblers in Ormskirk. Pray God there always will be."

"Good. We'll see you again sometime."

"Aye, if luck be with us." So saying, John Ambler gave a knowing wink and trudged off down some side street.

"Well now, T'osh planning something special."

"I wonder what that might be," sneered Frank, "Bringing on the four horsemen of the Apocalypse, maybe?"

"Doubtless Padlock would say so."

They went into a tavern called the Goat's Head.

* * *

Padlock was seated in Cressida's cottage, reading the Book of Revelations; he was wondering what the Great Beast 666 might have in common with T'osh.

Indeed, he scribbled on a piece of parchment, *contemplation of T'osh only magnifies his evil deeds, I do not doubt that he is the emissary of Satan, doing his utmost to ensure the ultimate supremacy of evil. This must not happen.*

His face became twisted and his hands clenched into fists. For a long time he stayed motionless, then he began to pace about the empty room muttering to himself.

"What buffoonery we have here. What idiocy. I am besieged with fools, incompetents, ne'er do wells. They have held me in check for many weeks; and worse still, they doubt the word of the Lord God and Myself. They whimper about revolution, whine about liberty, wail about equality, and all the while Satan is gaining power and establishing his dominion upon the earth. These fools could be limbs of Satan for all the use they are to me. They are like . . . like . . . like . . . *women.*

"Over thousands of years the dominance of evil has become more pronounced, but here we have the very beachhead of Hell itself . . . but, and I must believe this e'en though the flesh would shrivel from my bones, is not the hour of the Lord also at hand? Is not the coming of God imminent, till that day is but scant hours from completion? O happy day! O joyful day, when all the earth is cleansed of filth and rot and mould by the scourging tongues of flame. I have seen it. Then . . . then what shall I do to ensure that my actions now doubly ensure that I am with the happy band?

"In a nutshell, T'osh is Satan's final desperate attempt to grasp the earth to his scaly bosom. He is playing his last, most treacherous card; he is showing his final hand, yet we fail to see it for what it most manifestly is. T'osh must be prevented; then the world will be cleansed of sin.

"I am the man for the job."

Having talked himself into a manic rage, Padlock made his plans. Whilst doing this, he fortified his courage with liberal quantities of red wine of a certain vintage — this alone showing how aberrant was his mood. Then he dressed hurriedly, donning his clerical garb and mildewed duffle coat. He collected three long knives, candle and matches, a clove of garlic, a Bible, a large, wooden crucifix and a bottle of water blessed by himself.

Having pocketed all this he swigged the last of the zymurgic contents of the bottle to stagger out of the cottage and along the path that Frank assured him would lead to the House of Evil.

* * *

He cut a strange figure amid the bare branches of the winter landscape. His skeletal frame, hunched shoulders and mildewed clothing gave him the appearance of a perambulating scarecrow, and once, when his body was obscured by undergrowth and only his shining face was visible, it seemed as if a new and strange moon was riding the wintry sky.

Why Padlock had suddenly decided to act in such an uncharacteristic manner is a difficult question to answer. Perhaps it was that bravery which had its roots in cowardice and Padlock had been forced by his deceiving ego to act at this juncture rather than admit to himself that he was a coward. Perhaps Padlock's religious convictions, having vied long and hard with his more pragmatic views, finally won. Perhaps he might have gleaned an inkling of T'osh's vast fortune. Perhaps he went mad — rather, madder than he already was. Certainly the drink helped in fortifying his course of action.

Night had fallen. The rain had stopped and the only sound in the menacing woods was the drip of water from branch to mulch. The only sound made by Padlock, the squelching of his sodden shoes.

Yet all was not well, for the silence was too intense. Padlock felt that he was being watched. He drew the tattered remnants of his clothes to his chill chest and clutched the crucifix closer to him, but still he felt watched and the pallid skin of the small of his back crawled.

His fear was now the fear of a bad nightmare with none of the hope of waking up. Everything exuded menace, every shadow hid something foul. He wished

Padlock cut a strange figure

that the moon would appear; then fervently prayed that it would not, for what horrors might it reveal?

"I believe, O Lord, help me my unbelief," he wailed, forgetting for a moment that such a sound would doubtless bring any foul menace that happened to be within earshot.

"Deliver us from evil— oh!"

To his left something crashed through the brush — then another to his right — then a third. He peered through the darkness but saw only shadows move into shadows. Running may or may not have done any good, but Padlock was frozen with fear, his right hand holding the crucifix stretched ahead of him.

Then three nightmare shapes were circling him, huge animals that looked like massive dogs, but which must have been spawned within the gates of hell. Black as sable, they were the size of ponies. Great fangs gleamed in the starlight; skeins of hydrophobic spittle dripped from slavering jaws.

Acting as a pack they moved in on Padlock, their bodies low to the ground, mouths half-open. Slowly at first, then ever more rapidly, they closed for the kill.

Padlock was in an ecstasy of terror. Whatever rationality he might have possessed had fled ragged and screaming to the four winds. He started a whining shriek that modulated itself into a falsetto rendition of the Lord's Prayer.

At first the dogs came on; but as he began the rendition of the prayer, they stopped dead. Perhaps it was the power of the entreaty that sent them away after a few seconds indecision, but more likely it was the timely appearance of the moon from behind a scudding cloud that caused the rout.

For the first time the dogs could see the unwhole-someness of their intended prey; the alabaster skin glowing like china in the *clair de lune*; the lack of beef beneath the taut skin stretched over calcium deficient bones; the general air of mould and corruption that surrounded Padlock, as if he were a four day corpse brought back to tectonic motion, and it is certain that these dogs were not scavengers. Then too, there was the look and very appearance of Padlock's face which, dis-torted by his own terror would probably have seemed nonhuman from the dogs' viewpoint — certainly the dewdrop on the end of his nose, distorting the moon-beams and sending out rays of prismatic light would have been alien enough for most mastiffs, let alone the other aspects of the singular man. Then again, the high-pitched tone in which Padlock's utterances were delivered may have served to cause discomfort to the creatures.

But having said all that, Padlock found himself alone on the midnight path. He uttered aloud, "Praise the Lord, for he is mighty indeed," and strode through the now exorcised woods with a new determination in his stride.

*   *   *

Cressida sat at breakfast. The meal was one of her own making, consisting of home-baked beans, celery juice, raw mushrooms, sprout extract and home-baked bread. Wladek sat silently at the other end of the table.

He could rarely stomach any of Cressida's meals and to do so meant eschewing as much conversation as pos-sible whilst shovelling as much food as could be digested as quickly as possible. Often, when she was out of the house, or upstairs meditating, he would surreptitiously supplement his diet by cooking rabbits, squirrels or other small creatures on the hearth and devouring them before she resurfaced.

The morning post had brought a letter for Cressida. For unknown reasons, some post got through T'osh's blockade; this letter was one of the lucky ones. It was thought that either a very determined (or foolhardy) postman (or postwoman) ignored the signs and verbal warnings and adhered resolutely to the route which had been assigned pre-T'osh. The letter was from her father and gave details of certain (considerable) sums of money. She was due to come into her inheritance, though the condition of inheritance was not one of achieving a certain age, but of achieving a suitable match. Her grandfather, an irascible old gentleman, who had made out the will, had also stipulated a deadline for the happy event, a day not long in the future.

Cressida read the letter several times; each time she read it she became more excited.

"What ails ye, woman?" growled Wladek.

"Nothing . . . nothing."

"I said, what ails ye, woman?"

"Nothing . . . well . . . what is your opinion of marriage?"

"A waste of time, money, effort. An outdated construct."

"Oh! Oh!"

"Why do you ask?"

"Well, if I make a suitable match in the near future, under the terms of my late grandfather's will, a wily old cove with a somewhat archaic outlook, determined to see me settled before coming into what is rightfully mine — as I say, under the terms of my grandfather's will — Wladek, why are you staring at me like that?"

"I was just looking into the translucent beauty of your eyes; at the way your tresses fall — and I have been thinking that maybe we have been living in sin too long."

"But Wlad—"

"Not another word 'pon it. By my faith, we shall be wed ere the month is out,"

"But—"

"No more! I insist 'pon it."

"But Wladek, how can I be certain that you are not marrying me merely for my money?"

"Hah! Nonsense! Whatever gave you that idea? But I must go my love, for the farm calls. Ah, think of it; one day we might own our own."

Cressida remained seated at the table. Tears of joy ran down her cheeks and her face was suffused with delight.

"What a strange man," she said, "but — oh! — how I love him. He is far more of a man than that wretched Timothy — far more."

* * *

Timothy returned from Maghull to find the cottage in utter disarray. He was halfway through tidying up the mess before he thought of Padlock's absence from the scene but understood that he should not look a gift horse in the mouth. Later still he saw a Bible upon the floor, opened at a page in Revelations. A note had been written in pencil in the margin;

I finally understand the terrible
truth of it all. Have gone to meet
T'osh and be his executioner.
It is the will of the Lord.
Evil must be banished.
Rev. Pedaiah Lock

"Oh my God, that maniac will be the death of us all. Why don't people ever think before acting?" he bellowed. The room was otherwise empty, which meant that there was no one who might have reminded Timothy of his own recent shortcomings in that respect which had resulted in his incarceration.

He rushed down to the cellar with food for the prisoners and whilst the captives were eating their strange fare Timothy quizzed them about Padlock's disappearance.

"What? — what? — what?" wailed Harmony, "My Pedaiah gone? My dear Pedaiah, my dear, sweet Pedaiah gone into the teeth of death? Oh no, no, no, no, it isn't so. I want him back. Bring him back to me, bring him back."

Quartus was more phlegmatic; "Oh. In truth he would have done well to seek some advice from me. He is doomed. Vat is for certain."

Timothy left Harmony wailing and rolling about the floor and Quartus staring into space; a peculiar pair, he thought

Before long, just as the wintry sun was setting, Frank and Martyn returned from their short trip to Ormskirk. They were eager to tell of what they had learnt, but a distraught Timothy confronted them in the hall.

"What gives man?" drawled Frank.

"It's that bloody fool, Padlock — he's gone to execute the Magician."

"That blasted cleric!" roared Martyn. "He's bound to be caught and tortured. He'll tell them everything he knows – he'll tell them all our plans."

"I should've carried out my plan vis-a-vis the chisel sooner," muttered Frank.

"What?" asked Timothy.

"Oh, never mind that," interrupted Martyn, "we must think of something — but what in heaven's name can we do?"

"A difficult conundrum and no mistake," said Frank.

"I'll make fragments of that bastard when I catch up with him," uttered Martyn darkly.

* * *

As Padlock neared the cottage his spirits began to fail again, he wiped cold sweat from his glistening features and muttered, "Oh Lord give me strength."

And then he was through the last break of trees and facing the cottage which glowed faintly in the fitful moonlight. He took a deep breath and stumbled towards the door. He hammered on the door with all his limited strength and croaked in a voice that cracked with ill-concealed terror,

"Open up in the name of all that is hallowed; thy hour of retribution is at hand."

"I beg pardon, sir."

Padlock shrieked in unmitigated fright, turning in abject terror to where the speaker stood. What horror the distempered mind of Padlock imagined to be standing there must remain a mystery; but the speaker was a frail and worn peasant-woman of perhaps twenty-seven years who was staring at Padlock with a somewhat bewildered look.

She repeated her enquiry.

"I am searching for T'osh, ma'am, the Black Magician as he likes to call himself, though I would far better dub him father of all that is evil and unwholesome, sordid and rotten, disgusting and degrading, rotten and maggot-infested. He is the Beast whose number is 666 as is described in the Book of Revelations."

Padlock, now that peril had gone, or had been postponed to some future date, was now working up a shocking head of religious fervour. "Yea, list to me, you leman, he is the Beast, and it is my task to eradicate him. It is written, *'And I saw an angel come down from heaven, having the key of the bottomless pit and a great chain in his hand. And he laid hold on the dragon, that old serpent, which is the Devil, and Satan; and bound him a thousand years; and cast him into the bottomless pit; and shut him up; and set a seal upon him, so that he should deceive the nation no more, until the thousand years should be fulfilled; and after that, he must be loosed a little season.'* So where is he?"

Adaline Ambler looked nervously. "But he's out," she said finally.

"WHAT?"

"He's not here; he's gone away for a few days, something about urgent business that needed to be attended to."

"Well then Ma'am. I will and must examine the abode of T'osh."

"But—"

"Waste not my time, strumpet, ere you feel the taste of the scourge or the ministrations of the torturers. Let me past; I am on the Lord's business."

Padlock, as even the moderately astute would easily discern, had a somewhat low estimation of women generally. He roughly pushed the woman aside and in time found T'osh's inner sanctum. Studiously avoiding the arcane and recondite markings on the floor, he examined the masses of equipment and objects that were piled about the chamber. Of these, he understood the use or purpose of but few, yet knew instinctively that only foulness would come of the usages. Book titles caught his eye; *Sorcery in Medieval Britain, The Egyptian Technique, Alchemy and the Druids, Black Masses for Beginners, Teach yourself Voodoo*, plus myriad other tomes, some with foreign titles and alphabets. One tome exuded such a menacing aura that he could not approach nearer than a few feet.

Then he found T'osh's own *The Perfect State*. Opening it at random, he read;

CRIME AND PUNISHMENT
What it is. For every crime there must be a suitable punishment and in this punishment justice must be seen to be done. The needs of the onlookers cannot be ignored, so then the visual punishments (stocks, pillory, ducking stool etc., to name but the punishments for the most trifling possessions) have many advantages over the 'progressive', 'modern' techniques such as suspended sentences (other than it is suspended by the neck until dead). They are more enjoyable to all concerned - except to the wrongdoer and that is to be wished. Here then are a number of the more common punishments

that the Perfect State shall employ, together with a list of crimes for which this punishment is suitable;

AMPUTATION: The removal of limbs without any attempt being made to reduce suffering. Fingers are suitable objects for removal for first and minor offences, then onwards to whole limbs and culminating with the head, dependent upon the seriousness of further turpitude and recidivism.

BIRCHING: The stout and noble birch rod can and must be used as often as possible, preferably in conjunction with other disciplinary methods, meet according to time and circumstances. It is indisputable that . . .

. . . and so on. As the moon climbed to its zenith and as it went towards the horizon, Padlock ploughed through *The Perfect State*. He found himself agreeing with the book in many secular aspects, especially those concerning punishment.

He was brought out of his contemplation when he barked his shin against an object located against the leg of the table. It was a leaden chest fastened with a padlock that was but cheaply made. As might have been guessed, the Reverend was an expert upon such mechanisms. He brought two pieces of wire, one thin, the other thicker, from out of his coat pocket. With the thin wire poked into the keyhole he obtained the shape of the lock's tumblers, and when this was done, he duplicated the pattern on the stouter wire which he then inserted into the lock. The lock opened without difficulty. Inside the box was a large dagger, its pommel of silver, with a large ruby at the base, its hilt and blade of fine steel, the latter damasked with strange curlicues and cuneiforms which Padlock did not recognise as any writing he knew, though a partly destroyed stele in one corner of the chamber was adorned with similar characters. Padlock merely touched the left blade and was shocked to discover his blood was dripping onto the black velvet setting of the box.

Then, looking again at the damasking, Padlock gasped in amazement. "No, it can't be," he gabbled to the air. "I thought it all legend . . . but the engraving . . . it must be! This is the dagger of Ormr."

Padlock's awe was justifiable, for the Dagger of Ormr was a treasure of the first water. Snorri Thorsfensson, the founder of the town of Ormskirk over a millennium before, had been one of the most adventurous of all the Vikings, starting off with raids into Russia and Teutonic Germany, and progressing in his mid-twenties to Gunnarsson the Fair's raids in the Mediterranean. The details of Gunnarsson's last adventure were scant — not surprising since Snorri Thorsfensson had been the teller and, in all likelihood, had butchered Gunnarsson on that last voyage. The dagger had been the property of an Arab mage who had been murdered for it by a Berber, who in turn was murdered for it by Gunnarsson, and, in ghastly rote, Gunnarsson was killed by Snorri Thorsfensson.

Snorri Thorsfensson next turns up in Ybor — York — in the company of Eric Bloodaxe and Harold Hairybreaks. At first things went well, but in the end, Snorri Thorsfensson had to leave Ybor — he got away with the dagger and his life — the last only barely.

Snorri Thorsfensson then founded the garth of Ormskirk. He knew that the dagger had supposed magic powers and he promised to the citizens of

Ormskirk that the dagger and its latent power would always vanquish any latent menace to the town.

Early on it proved its power, for Ormskirk never became a fiefdom for Normandy but remained an independent mini-kingdom, and throughout the ensuing centuries the dagger, kept in rote by several families, ensured a placid time for Ormskirk in that horrible time — assuming that the dagger had some power, that is.

There the matter rested until 1608 when Dr John Dee, the astrologer to the late Queen, now living in obscurity as Warden of Manchester College, heard about the dagger. He was granted a sight of it, drew a fair copy of it and departed back for Manchester. In the following year, it was discovered that the dagger had been stolen and a cheap though effective copy had supplanted it. Suspicion fell upon Dee and a party hied to Manchester where they discovered that Dee had had the audacity to die the year before. No dagger turned up in the effects.

Later on in the century John Aubrey had been fishing around Dee's papers and saw the good doctor's fair copy drawing. Magpie that he was, he drew his own copy, dug up the story and wrote it up in Vol. III of his works.

The dagger never resurfaced, but the basic question was never answered; had Dee substituted the fake and disposed of the real one, or, did the custodian families, hearing of Dee's death and fearing for the safety of the dagger in its new-found publicity, make Dee the fall-guy, substitute the fake and hide the real one themselves?

The question had never been answered - until Padlock had opened the box.

Padlock gloated over the dagger. "No wonder he kept this well-hidden, for it can surely be used against him

— but then, does he even know the peril of the dagger, or does he keep this merely as a valuable artefact?"

Refastening the padlock and replacing the box in its original site, he placed the dagger in a niche in the torn lining of his coat. Madam Adaline Ambler was impressed by Padlock to make no mention of his visit to anyone; else all manner of unpleasantness would befall her. He then went into the chill night.

But not back to the cottage! He shook a thin and pallid fist in the direction of his erstwhile comrades. "A pox on you unenlightened buffoons!" he said, giving this valedictory malediction to the stilly night.

He strode towards the Stanley Arms, a hostelry that was seemingly open at all hours since the coming of T'osh, there to make plans.

He had the dagger. He was invincible.

* * *

"There is only one thing for it," said Martyn.

"What's that?" asked Timothy.

"We must make our way to the Magician's cottage and endeavour to discover what has befallen our comrade Padlock."

"Huh! Not if I could lie down and die first," mumbled Frank. "Come to that, going to T'osh's den seems to be about the same thing with more effort."

"For once your unworldly friend is correct," said Wladek, "for to go would be to fight folly with absurdity. Padlock is hardly a great loss to your mission and, as I am on first name terms with T'osh, I can easily discover whether he has been captured and what fate awaits him.

"I think it best, however, if you move house and thus I suggest that you all move into my cottage for a few days."

"But what of Cressida?" asked Timothy, whose memory was not as short as some might have believed.

"Not to mention our two prisoners," interjected Martyn.

"Some of you will need to accept that bygones are bygones and what is done is well done, and an end to it. As for the prisoners, you can either let them die in their cells or turn them loose; they are of no significance. Wait . . . having said that, I have an idea. Set them loose but make no mention of your plans to either."

"Although there will no doubt be problems," said Martyn, "your suggestion is by far the best. We must certainly make good our exit from this place. We must pack our bags and keep a low profile for the next few days. Yes, I am sure that the prisoners can be left to their own devices and, so far as Quartus is concerned, he rarely leaves whatever room he happens to be in, as long as corned beef is in close proximity. Yes, I accept your offer." Martyn shook Wladek's hand.

*   *   *

Later, about the time Padlock was taking the dagger, Martyn was staring over the gloomy fields from the doorway of Wladek's cottage. They had finished the move; it was late, yet Martyn did not feel sleepy. He had a glass of melomel in his hand, which he hoped would drive away the insomnia.

Suddenly the moon appeared from behind a cloud, pouring liquid silver over the landscape. The land was barren and dead, now it was winter, but the moonlight gave it a gentle lambent beauty. For the first time, it looked as if there would be another spring, however distant that time.

There and then Martyn identified the feeling of exultation. At some point during the night his subconscious mind had decided, after weighing all the factors, that T'osh was likely to be defeated — not certainly, but it was more likely than not. True, there were dolts like Padlock who could still bring defeat to Martyn, but with luck those idiots could be weathered. T'osh would fall!

He drained his melomel and went inside.

The stars looked down.

Chapter 9:

A Meeting of Minds

Padlock sat huddled in the corner of the Stanley Arms, his pallid hand thrust deep into his coat, clutching the sacred dagger. It was now the following day. Late the previous night Padlock had finally been cast out of the pub, and how he had spent the rest of the hours of darkness he could not recall; all that remained was a hazy phantasmagoria of icy panoramas seemingly frozen in time. His first coherent memory was of staggering through the door of the Stanley Arms in the full light of a chill day. He could only surmise that he had wandered through the country, still bemused by the awesomeness of the dagger.

His general oddness, but more acutely his recent bizarre behaviour, had caused the woman behind the bar, Florinda Farrier, to stare at him long and hard. At one point, she was distracted from her observations of Padlock only when an impatient customer had slammed his wealth — 5 lbs of potatoes — hard onto the bar.

"A pint for 'ee as well deserves it."

"Eh? — Oh yes, of course," said Padlock automatically. He saw standing before him a rough, rude, windswept person, but if this chap was standing the round, who was he to argue?

"Ah saw what 'ee did."

"What are you saying exactly? Speak up sirrah."

"Last night, comin' 'ome from market, after bein' detained as you might care to say. There was ah, 'id in bushes, not able like to get inside m'own cottage, when ah saw them 'ounds pounce, them self-same 'ounds of 'ell as kept me out. Thought you were done for — but the way thou tackled them 'ounds . . . well, good it were, good — and ah'd say that to any man livin'. Tell me, 'owd thou do it?"

"Those who walk in the sight of the *Lord* need never know fear."

"Aye, that might be right true. But what of this Black Magician? The wizard like; what 'ee do 'bout 'im? 'Im as needs fixin'."

"The *Lord* will destroy him as He did the idolatrous eidolon in the market square."

"But 'ow'll this come to pass?"

"I am the agent of the Lord; my task cannot fail. All is foretold in the great prophetic books of the Bible. What else is there to know or be told? Oh, by the way, my glass is empty."

After purchasing more drinks, Ambler continued, "Well, all ah say is that 'im who can banish 'ounds of 'ell can do anythin' else 'ee might be pleasin' to claim. An' ah say tha' ah wish to join 'ee mas'er, e'er that Black Wizard ruins me an' mine. Say what you will, an' ah'll like to be doin' my best to carry yon out."

"A fine goodly man you are sirrah. I see within you the red and undiluted blood of true yeomanry, the stalwart expression of the bravery and honesty of the true Englishman, unsullied by the taint of trades unions whose only interest is money and collectivising disputes. Join with me and follow exultantly until we find the end of the rainbow, where long breezes blow upon the dewy swards of pleasing ridges. If I succeed, and succeed I must, then you are guaranteed a high post in my enlightened government. Yea, I see it in your eyes, the generosity of a saint . . . and another drink would not go amiss."

And so, the long hours passed.

*   *   *

Sometime after midnight Melling was visited by a strange apparition. There was Ambler, outlined in the moonbeams, pushing a creaking cart upon which was sprawled Padlock, as unsightly as a cast-off coat, seemingly as boneless as a jellyfish. He was croaking in the manner of a frog with a severe throat disorder the following psalm, as amended by the Reverend himself

> *Come, behold the works of the Lord!*
> *What desolations he hath made in the world;*
> *He maketh wars to cease, unto the ends of the*
>   *earth:*
> *He breaketh the bow and shatters the spear*
>   *asunder:*
> *He blasteth the statue in Ormskirk,*
> *Leaving no stone unturned and upright.*
> *Be still, and know that I am Pedaiah Lock,*
> *Glad recipient of the dagger.*
> *The Lord's arrows are sharp*
> *In the heart of the King's enemies;*

For the Lord most high is terrible indeed,
And even Frank will be vanquished,
Amen.

In the ditch, viewing furtively, the shadowy figure of Noah Halfmoon struggled to make sense of this ostensibly nocturnal hallucination. Clutching tightly the body of the small rabbit which would constitute his supper he found himself strangely drawn to the verses as they rolled out of the gullet of the parsimonious parson. Though he could not place much in the way of meaning upon what he heard, nonetheless he felt that they encapsulated his inner mood in a way he could never have articulated.

"Van . . . quish . . . ed! Ex . . . act . . . ly," he repeated to himself several times as he scrambled out of the ditch and made his way back to the crumbling outhouse he thought of as home.

* * *

Quartus and Harmony Poffle, upon regaining their freedom, immediately returned to their cottage, where a sumptuous feast was lain on in celebration. The meal, mainly corned beef, was declared by Poffle to be "even better van ever," and, as a result of this repast, he waxed ecstatic about the elations that could befall a man who ate corned beef from tins.

Harmony, however, was preoccupied with the disappearance of Padlock and had little time for the brown fibrous meat or the grey globules of fat; instead she often drew out a damp handkerchief and told the world of her sorrow by a wail of total despair.

"Oh, my Padlock. My brave Padlock, will I ever see you again? Woe is me — will I never see my beloved again?"

"But isn't he rahver an odd fellow?"

"What do you mean?"

"He does go on rahver a lot."

"The words pot and kettle spring to mind."

"I also hear vat he never spends money."

"So what? Is that not his right? It is his religion; he condemns it as frivolous and futile; austerity is his aim. He will not squander the money which he acquires. He puts it to one side."

"Don't you mean he's tight-fisted? Tee-hee."

"How dare you!"

"Anyway, he's against the Magician."

"I don't care! If he is against the Magician, then so am I! I would throw in my lot with Padlock and follow him to the ends of the Earth. What good, what earthly good has the Magician brought you?"

"My ingrown toenails, my boils, vey are cured."

"Bah! Anyone could have done likewise with his fine words. And your medicinal drink —'tis nothing but an alcoholic drink, widely available."

"Well, I am not doing too badly – nor are you."

"I stand by what I said."

Poffle did not reply for a few minutes, pausing to shovel a nauseating quantity of corned beef in his jaws and deciding that further argument with his sister was futile.

"I will not betray your secret," he said solemnly, "and, trufe to tell, his overfrow would not bovver me too greatly. I have a good brain and currently I am working on a new book."

"What about? Corned beef?"

"Very funny. It is about leading a healfy existence wivout bovvering about vitamins, exercise, or any of ve trappings of modern existence. It is called: Ve guide to healf and happiness. Here is an extract."

Why Strain Yourself?
Each day the supposedly advanced Western world contains millions of people who strive for physical fitness. They run, walk, swim, play squash, basketball, football, do press-ups, sit-ups, bend, stretch and go to all manner of extraordinary lengths in the name of this chimera, fitness.

LOOK at the animals: Do they play games or run around if they can avoid it? Of course not; yet many animals live for much longer than man. The tortoise, to pick one animal at random, has a lifespan that can exceed two centuries. And why? Just look at their lifestyles. They spend more time in meditation than indulging in futile sports. An alligator in a swamp will spend its time in silent contemplation, only moving when food comes within very easy reach . . .
Read then, the recipes for a healthy life:
i MUD: a useful source of health and strength. Fill your bath not with unwholesome clear water but with plenty of thick, rich mud. Lie in it for at least two hours each day. One point: the temperature in the room should be considerable.

ii GRASS: any who would eat grass are guaranteed one hundred years upon the earth. It is rich in protein and very good and best eaten when rolling around in the bath of mud, together with any flies you manage to catch.

iii MOTHS: these are useful beca—

"Enough. Do you really believe this crap?" asked Harmony.

"It is all very true."

"Bah!"

She departed upstairs to her slumbers, though she did not think that she would get much repose. Surprisingly she slept deeply, but her dreams were haunted by a gaunt and pale figure that called her name but vanished when she approached.

*   *   *

T'osh had not been informed of Padlock's visit and, as all the objects in the chamber, especially the dagger's box, had not been disturbed or had been replaced in their correct locations, he suspected nothing.

It was a day or two after Padlock's visit and T'osh was scribbling in his commonplace book.

They will see at last what I am capable of. The equipment is ready or ordered; there shall be a display in Ormskirk that will still be spoken of in one thousand years. How the peasants will cower as they see the attendant majesty of him. A sight indeed: music and religion and execution and Satanic ceremony.

Indeeeeeeed all is set for the Coming of T'osh; I shall reign supreme. Yet there still remains the problem of the rebels. But they shall be smoked out — I fear too that there is a traitor in my midst. Small matter; he too shall pay. A new and golden age is coming.

"Drink," croaked T'osh. "I need a drink. I need a drink. Damn you, Ambler, get me a drink of ale."

The door opened and a troubled woman entered.

"Ale! At once."

"Yes sir."

"Why are you here? Why not your man?"

"I — I —"

"Speak up dolt, where is your man?"

"I don't know where John is, your Mightiness; he has gone off."

"Gone off, indeeeeeeeeeeeeeeeeeeeeeeeeeeeeeed?"

"Yes sir."

"Well, he had better return shortly or he has signed his own death-warrant; I will personally slit his throat." And here T'osh paused, nervously tracing the contours of the hideous scar on his neck. "Well, what are you waiting for? Get me my ale."

T'osh put away his commonplace book and put a huge pile of papers on his desk. His latest project, *The Perfect State*, *vol ii*, which, together with preparations for the special event, which he had noted in his scribblings as being the second coming, though without further clarification, had taken up most of his time of late.

The book was, in large part, his reaction to the present situation. It was true that he had radically altered the quality and style of life in Ormskirk, but, as other leaders had discovered in the past, once the *coup d'état* had succeeded the momentum was lost. Not merely did the people suffer from a lack of future goals, the initial grip that the new regime had on the populace had weakened to the extent that in some ways it was in a state of palsied feebleness: black mass attendance was down; witch hunts were less frequent, and, where they were held, though the culprit lost his or her hoarded machines and conveniences to the bonfire, they almost always escaped with their lives; and, to cap it all, where strangers and travellers had entered the land, the mob had not always thrashed them. Indeed, in two terrible cases, people had been allowed to travel unmolested. There was even talk of letters being delivered to houses near the border and people using some form of currency in institutions such as taverns. The border guards were reported to be lazy and susceptible to bribes especially if these were presented in the form of alcoholic beverages.

He could see the reason for it: innate conservatism paradoxically enough. The people had become inured to the conveniences of the modern world, and though they often talked of how much better the simple life would be, this was simply a middle-class buzzword without support of factual knowledge.

Oh, how readily they had embraced his vision of a rustic age in which notions of tradition and deft pastoral metaphors had been carefully wafted in front of an all-too-willing populace. His artfully constructed 'sound-bites' such as *seizing control* and *planning our own destiny* had proved very seductive indeed. The susceptible townsfolk had railed against *outside interference* and *foreigners* without any in-depth consideration of what this actually would mean in practice, especially the unintended negative consequences, of which there were many.

When the great change had come, it had indeed been great for a while, but as the year declined, so too did the enthusiasm, until at last the conservatism, that vast and implacable inertia, was almost all that remained; that and terror of the new State. Some people actually thought that the old way was better than this feudal state and said as much, T'osh reflected with shock and disbelief.

He looked over at a report from one of his lieutenants, concerning the gossip current in the state. It was worrying, for people were cheering such outrages as the destruction of the statue, the escape of Timothy; others spoke — though shortly before they were silenced — of the impending collapse of T'oshism and of enormous caches of hidden wealth secreted away by the leader, implying that the pared down lifestyle which he advocated was for the masses only. The report also mentioned something about a mystic artefact, a sort of Sacred Grail, that would re-appear and destroy T'osh, but the compiler had been unable to clarify what this talk referred to.

*　　*　　*

The first days in Wladek's cottage were strange and strained. Most notable in all the oddity was Timothy, who spent much of his time brooding in one corner, though he seemed suddenly animated when Cressida entered the room, and Frank, who spent the days and most of the night engaged in frantic scribblings.

The owner of the cottage spent most of his time in the fields except when he went off on one of his mysterious missions. Cressida stayed mostly within the house, though upstairs in the bedroom where she spent considerable time attempting to communicate with the spirit of her dead great, great grandmother; a project that had, so far, apparently met with scant success.

One morning the rebels found that both Cressida and Wladek had left at an early hour without giving notice of their destination or reason for departure, though there was much muttering as to plausible cause, little of it kindly.

"They've probably gone to turn us in to the Magician for some reward money," muttered Timothy, forebodingly.

"Or gone to look for ghosts and ghouls," sneered Frank, "though in truth I suspect that they are seeking temporary refuge from a being of superior intellect, by which I mean, of course, myself. Permit me to read you an extract of the latest outpourings of my genius, Chapter 34 of my matchless novel."

Of Corridors and Dungeons (Molten Truncheons)

Nivek. Nivek ran. Jumping. Over objects. There? There? No. Where? Nowhere. Nowhere ever. Entropy. Screams. Screams.

(*Rekaorc bloodbloodbloodblood with this bloody place build with bricks of blood cannot think if you have no blood Rekaorc had plenty sacrifice to the walls of hell and burying bodies under bridges ceremonies*)

Wait— Nivek saw. What did Nivek see? Knarf. Alone? Yes. Naked? No. Clothed in oppressive garments. Is this symbolic of the institute? Yes. Does Knarf have anything in his hand? Yes. A clock. An alarm clock. Is this clock working? Yes. How do you know? It has hands. That is not sufficient. It ticks. Nor is that. Still it works. No. The ticking could be synchronistic not causal. It works. How do you know? Whilst we have been talking the hands have moved. Good. Do you want to know what time it is? That is irrelevant. Nor do you ask questions.

This was my grandfather's. It's still working; you can hear the ticking; — Shows teeth. White teeth. Feral white teeth. It's a bomb, or at least the beginnings of one; we only need the explosives, then we can blow this place to hell and avenge Rekaorc: — Nothing but the gun and the bomb can set us free. They are prerequisites to deal with parasites. Bloodsucking leeches will be banished or killed. It is the way of truth and enlightenment. Forward. Onward. Destroy. Whippet-like. Smooth. Catastrophe. Knarf moves through the fog. Knarf is truly omniscient.

* * *

When Frank had begun his reading, he had mentioned that it was nothing if not thought-provoking. Timothy had taken him at his word and settled for nothing by leaving. Martyn suddenly remembered that he had to print some leaflets. Breaking only to whine that he was not the first, nor probably the last genius to suffer rejection at the hands of an ignorant public, Frank continued reading to the bare walls, As his tale of oppression and injustice, coherent only to him and perhaps to some of those people who impart their wisdom in the streets to a largely unappreciative and uncomprehending audience, was shouted to the air, Frank became more and more agitated as the list of indignities suffered by himself — or rather Knarf, grew lengthier. He put the pages on a table so that he could wave his arms about for emphasis. By accident one of his wild gestures spilled the contents of a large inkbottle over his manuscript.

"My life's work. *Ruined*!" he screeched, picking up the soggy pages and hurling them onto the glowing coals of the fire.

He paced the room several times.

"That Padlock. I should have brained him. What a sight! Blood. Brains. Screaming for mercy that never came. Blood on his dusty, dirty coat, brain tatters on his stained old dog-collar. Art. *Art*! That is the direction of true art. What a piece of work that would be. Performance art in the purest sense imaginable."

A strange, unwholesome expression crossed his face.

* * *

Cressida and Wladek returned later that evening; both were flushed of countenance and seemed blessed for once with a shared, excessive, sunny disposition. Even Wladek had lost some of his taciturnity, though he was still a closed book in many aspects.

He produced a number of bottles from some Levantine vineyard and suggested that they employ themselves in polishing off their contents, together with the copious — and, for once, edible — comestibles that Cressida was busily laying on the table.

Although history has not recorded the details of the vintage, or the chateau of origin of the bottles, suffice it to say that it seemed to be rather strong and that, before very long, even Timothy and Frank, who had been rather reluctant to enter the celebrations, were drinking with alacrity and celerity.

"By the way," said Martyn, "what are we celebrating? I mean, is T'osh dead, or what?"

"Chance'd be a fine thing," said Timothy.

"Aye, and Padlock as well," muttered Frank, darkly.

"Perhaps they killed each other!" laughed Martyn, realising for the first time just how long it had been since he had been drinking in happy company and in security, however fragile.

"I can just see it," said Timothy, "Padlock denouncing T'osh as the anti-Christ and driving a stake through his damned foul heart, *sirrah*, while T'osh sticks a hand grenade into the pocket of that mildewed duffle coat."

"Blood and brains everywhere," muttered Frank in a voice reeking of an unhallowed lust.

"I rather imagine, though," continued Timothy, "that comrade Padlock would, even at the outset, be more concerned over the destruction of the duffle-coat than any trifle of personal injury. After all, life comes free and death comes cheaply, but duffle-coats, well . . . they are a different bucket of crabs entirely."

"If it's damaged, I'm sure that Harmony Poffle will sew it together in time for the funeral," opined Martyn.

"Saves the cost of a shroud," said Timothy.

Added Martyn; "So when, or in some cases here if, you get to heaven, watch out for the angel with the duffle-coat, dew drop and second-hand harp."

"And wrap the harp around his neck," suggested Frank.

Though he had smiled at several jests Wladek had said little during the latter part of the carousing. Now he banged his fists on the table and boomed out;

"Cressida and myself are this day wed! From this point onwards, we are man and wife — hence the drinks. Make merry while you can my jolly fellows, for who knows what tomorrow might bring?"

A slight chill seemed to enter the stuffy room, and a brief silence ensued. However, Wladek refilled the glasses and soon the party was again in full swing, with songs being sung and tales told.

Martyn, though ostensibly joining in with the party, was also keeping a cold eye on Wladek. Though seemingly outgoing by his usual dour standards, Wladek was still not giving anything away. He was pumping the others and getting them to talk about themselves, turning away any enquiries about his past, and when he spoke, he did so at great length but without saying anything. Martyn had concluded that there was far more to this man than met the eye, and he believed that even Cressida did not know him quite as well as she liked to think. Neither his gestures nor his words gave anything away; nothing was revealed.

He was brought out of his considerations when Wladek began to sing in a rough and rude tone a refrain in a language unknown to the rest.

Dye gitari za stenoyu
Zhalabna zanyli
Sertse pamyatne napyev
Mily eta tyli

(Chorus)
Ekh raz yeshcho raz
Yez cho mno ga mno ga raz
Ekh raz da yeshcho raz
Yez cho mno ga mno ga raz
Veter, polye vassilki
Dalnaya daroga
Sertse noyet at taski
Na dusche trevoga

Pagavari — zhe tv so mnoyu
Padruga semistrunnaya
Fsya dusha palna toboyu
A noch takaya lunnaya

Gdye balit, chto bath'
Galava s pakhmelia
Sevodnya pyom, zafira pyom
Tseluyu nedyelyu[1]

---

[1] The song sung by Wladek in this chapter is, in fact, an old Russian gypsy song called Two Guitars. An approximate translation is as follows.

When Wladek had finished there were spontaneous bursts of applause, followed tediously by Cressida going on at length about the need to retain cultural and ethnic traditions, for they were part of the heritage and extremely relevant to the common people. She also saw fit to mention the fact that there was some French blood in her veins, since her great, great grandmother on her father's side hailed from Rouens from where she had been driven by the Terror (here Frank did some quick calculation and estimated silently that either Cressida had left out a couple of greats, or that she was

---

Two guitars in the next room
Plaintively are sounding
How my heart knows that old tune
Dearest can it be you?

Chorus   Play it once and once again once again and
once again
Yes, once and once again once again and once
again

The wind, the field, the cornflowers
And the winding highway
How my heart aches from despair
And my soul is heavy

Won't you have a talk with me
My guitar my dear one
My whole soul is filled with you
And the moonlit evening

Where's the pain? What's the pain?
How my head is spinning
We drink today, tomorrow too
And the whole week through

considerably older than she said, or that the whole tale was pure hogwash).

She continued to drone on; "It may be for this reason that I always feel some spiritual affinity with the Gallic peoples. Once, at the height of the season, I chanced to be in Paris, and indeed felt truly peaceful, as if it were my historical homeland. I know the language fluently, learning it proved no difficulty; I hold that this all boils down to the fact that I have some French blood in my veins.

"Ah! Timothy, I see that you have discovered my guitar; play *Plaiser D'Amour*, or even *A La Claire Fontaine*. Anything French will do."

"This is a version of the Irish traditional song *She Moved Through the Fair*. Feel free to join in if you know it," said Timothy who then began to play the wistful Celtic melody in open C, before singing the evocative lyrics.

I once had a sweet-heart, I loved her so well
I loved her far better than I ever could tell
Her parents they scorned me for my lack of class
Saying never to drink from the poisonous glass

My young love said to me, my mother won't mind
And my father won't slight you for your lack of kind
And she went away from me and this she did say
It will not be long now till our wedding day

She went away from me and she moved through the fair
Where hand-slapping dealers' loud shouts rent the air
The sunlight around her did sparkle and play
Saying it will not be long now till our wedding day

When dew falls on pasture and moths fill the night
When glow of the embers on hearth throws half-light
I'll slip from the window and we'll run away
And it will not be long love till our wedding day

True to his promise at midnight he rose
But all that he saw was the discarded clothes
The sheets they lay empty 'twas plain for to see
That out of the casement with another went she

I dreamed last night that my true love came in
So gently she came that her feet made no din
And then she went onward, with one star awake
As the swan in the evening glides over the lake

Martyn watched with a pang of envy. Timothy played the guitar rather well and his voice was decidedly lilting. Still, Martyn decided that it was now time to unveil his talent.

"I don't do songs by others as I prefer to write my own material," he stated, sounding rather more pompous than he might have intended. "I don't trouble myself with fancy fingerpicking either as I prefer to let my words do the talking. This song is very much a protest song called *Atlantic Jellyfish*."

Without further ado Martyn began to strum on the guitar making a rhythmic but particularly monotonous *chang-a-chang* sound in the key of A.

I'm making a protest for all I believe in
I'm campaigning for what is right
There's no more in-depth discussion required
So who will be up for the fight?

(Chorus)
Yes who will join me in my revolution?
Will you stand close at my side?
Or will you be spineless – like the Atlantic Jellyfish
Who just ebbs and flows with the tide?

I'm taking a stand for the concerns which matter
Issues which keep me awake in the night
In daytime I'm dreaming of a better tomorrow
My anger is burning, my eyes shining bright

Chorus

The gatepost is clacking, the long breezes blowing
My boot heels are ready to walk the long mile
Down crumbling cart tracks and through silver
*   meadows*
Chasing the rainbows, while cracking a smile

Chorus.

Martyn concluded the song which was followed by polite applause and an emotional outpouring from Cressida.

"Wonderful, truly wonderful," she gushed. "True talent lies in the ability to write one's own songs rather than singing those of others." (Here she glanced sideways at Timothy who was enjoying a rather large glass of the potent beverage.)

"I myself have penned quite a few songs which I believe to be reflective of my inner disposition." She clutched the guitar and produced a capo which she placed at the fifth fret and then began to strum a D chord shape (therefore in the key of G) which consequently made a high-pitched 'rinky-dink' sound. "My song is called *The Nonpareil*," she uttered breathlessly before commencing to sing in a shrill warble.

> *I am the mermaid with jewelled eyes*
> *I can see up to the skies*
> *I can stare straight into the sun*
> *I can do what's never been done*
>
> *What is the sand inside the grain?*
> *What is the hurt beyond the pain?*
> *What is the cry which isn't heard?*
> *What is the age when no one cared?*
>
> *I am the voice behind the dawn*
> *I am the eye inside the storm*
> *I am the key that turns the lock*
> *I am the stick that beats the rock*
>
> *Who will see what lies behind?*
> *Who will follow like the blind?*
> *Who will walk up to my gate?*
> *Who will have the time to wait?*
>
> *I am the salmon in the pool*
> *I am the teacher in the school*
> *I am the force that guides the hand*
> *I am the rain that cleans the land*
>
> *Where is the boy who cannot speak?*
> *Where is the truth that he must seek?*
> *Where is the song that he must sing?*
> *When he's riding on the wing*

I am the clock which plays with time
Take note of my warning chime
My ship is ready to set sail
I am, of course, the Nonpareil

Hearty applause followed the ending of the song, though this may have been due to the potency of the brew or widespread relief rather than general appreciation of Cressida's prowess as a singer-songwriter. She hoped that there would be a call for more of the same, but this did not materialise, so the guitar was placed back in the corner where it had rested for some time prior to the night's proceedings.

Frank stood up abruptly. "As well as novels I frequently write poetry," he announced to the gathering. "This one is called *My Cousin Horace, The Inflatable Doorknob*. Obviously when I write poetry, I do not feel the need to descend to using quaint rhymes, preferring a more experimental style. I am inspired, not by past poets, but by what I see around me in the modern world," he proclaimed, somewhat superfluously. Then he began his recitation.

Flapping and clucking as circumstances allow
No fried egg for breakfast obsolete
Caterpillar in your hair, no square to stand in
But who and what is the entrepreneur?

Have you been rattled by prevailing gusts
Of wind at the window writing in pain?
Lead lights, stained glass petrified
Oh but you knew that all along

On Sundays sitting bellyaching
Nondescript patterns on your wall
Monday afternoon canvas painting
Cold coffee calculations gone askew

The pink and yellow apparel glowing
Brighter than the cat's eyes in moonlight
Sunk deep beneath the tragic bedsheets
Where I lay ofttimes nonchalant

The goat goes mad in the summer heat
Around the house with malevolent stare
Too little too late the chair is rocking
And all is lost in the pigsty crumble

The flag is drooping on the edifice
No scurrying rats are visible now
The temperature rose in the early spring
And the ditches beckoned unto me

Halt you may not cross this bridge
O wretched child of the axiomatic potion
With your hedgerow dens and checked kecks
Coming to just below your knees

With ancient tin in your back pocket
Containing nought but yellow dust
My facetious friend with firelit eyes
And a rusted bicycle at your disposal

Stealing golf clubs from garden sheds
And Christmas cards, ancient, unused
Did you ever return to face the music?
Or bellow at the silver birch trees

With your playing card rictus smile
He's too fond of the booze they said
Late again and so it goes on
A dwindling spiral of eroding plans

I killed a rat with a well-aimed stone
Then thought I heard the badger laugh
I turned around to see only shadows of
Polythene banshees in the cuckoo's dream

Who set the tyres alight that day?
The column of smoke seen miles away
Drew small crowds to gape in wonder
Gathering long-discarded bones

I sat with pen and notebook
Designing a tombstone for no one at all
Building a graveyard amidst the bluebells
And only the enchantress was aware and why

For you are many-faceted
A kaleidoscope vision unfettered
And I, for one, am not dismayed
I see through your gaberdine visage

A jotter contains your flimsy dreams
And songs no one will ever hear
Borrowed phrases and second-hand notions
I could care less but not by much

Unfathomable discourse is your forte
Somnambulist stranger with bloodstained shirt
Ripped open by the ruffian screaming rage
When you hoofed the ball into his belly

This pantomime is beyond your grasp
No substitute for late-night radio
With subversive biscuit and stolen wine
You plot your journey to oblivion

Crumbling cake and cracked camera
And washing hanging on Monday's line
You will not take the ferry today
For you belong on the other side

Fill the balloon with soapy water
Send it bouncing down the hill
Cleansing minds of all complexities
This oscillating scapegoat will never fail

And perambulating discourse slowly weakens
A turbulent stream of banal views
Deceptive in the moment stolen
And soon deposited in the void

O glorious land of the midnight sun
I will dance there unrestrained
Bounced back to darkness by the bulk
But I will return once more, tomorrow

Drinking tea in a dingy café
My conversation is at an all-time-low
My words are empty coloured bubbles
Vacuous, bereft, curtailed, short-winded

The bus stop looms majestically
Smiling down as I stand and wait
I scream at the owl in the adjacent tree
And wag my index finger at the blood-moon

Go now! Go now you cousin embellished
By failed artefacts, twisted heaps
I shall not miss you or your structures
My doorknob relative vanquished forever

Frank stopped, looked across at his audience and sat down with what he imagined was a theatrical flourish. This brought forth a raucous applause, although some unkind onlookers, had any been present, might have construed that this was ascribable to a general relief that it was a relatively short poem rather than any underlying passion for Frank's musings. Either way there was no demand for more of the same.

Cressida's guitar was now retrieved by Timothy who promptly announced that he had also written quite a few songs. (Cressida looked surprised by this. She had always been absorbed in her own creativity that it has never occurred to her that Timothy might have similar impulses.)

This one is called '*Your Road*' he said and then, after taking a generous swig from his glass, proceeded to once again break into song, preceded by a rather melodic introduction as he fingerpicked the tune.

There's a road down which I will not journey
There's nothing there I wish to see
No friend or face to greet me smiling
Nor a home to ever welcome me

There is no joy out there on that road
Just a world of solitude and pain
No sunlight greeting in the morning
Just darker clouds and endless rain

Don't ask me to go on that journey
Don't believe I'll be at your side
It's time to close down expectations
Our paths will never coincide

Your road is laden with the lucky
And wealth that I have never known
And power there just for the asking
For those with hearts of ice and stone

And your road may be good to travel
All dressed up and laughing loud
Waving at the lost and exiled
And many fine words for the crowd

But fine words won't feed hungry children
And poison hides behind a smile
And winning's just a form of loathing
For those who lurk the twisted mile

Don't ask me to go on that journey
Don't believe I'll be at your side
It's time to close down expectations
Our paths will never coincide

There was no doubt that the combination of a surprisingly mellifluous voice, enigmatic lyrics, adept fingerpicking and a sense of atmosphere induced by the party mode ensured that Timothy's contribution was the most impressive and even Wladek joined heartily in the applause. Cressida became somewhat subdued as she felt that her creative turf had been invaded somewhat and she was nonplussed as to how she could restore the status quo. What was more, she couldn't help but wonder whether she had been the inspiration for Timothy's lyrics in some wholly negative way as the song seemed, so far as she was able to discern, to poke criticism at the lifestyles of the privileged. Still she tried to give nothing away and allowed herself another large glass of something red and strong. Likewise, Martyn also resolved to work a good deal harder at his songwriting and perhaps seek to improve his guitar playing to some extent.

*   *   *

And so they went on until all the wine had been drunk and all had fallen or collapsed into slumber — all but one, for Frank sat staring at the wintry sky, the unwholesome look back on his face. He rose unsteadily to his feet, muttering, "I know where he'll be. He never even went to T'osh, he'll be in his vicarage, scrounging for food. Well I know how to deal with the likes of him."

He lurched off into the cellar and returned with the shotgun and cartridges.

Frank had found the going harsh. The constant need to be wary, the running, the hiding, the constant threat of being caught, tried and sentenced to be disembowelled. All this had told, and something had finally come apart. He recalled the long, scathing and acrimonious arguments with the man, his growing loathing of the creature and all he stood for, and in some manner, Frank now saw Padlock as being the root cause of all their troubles. Padlock was a sort of rampant infection that had to be cut away by any means that could be brought to hand. T'osh was now forgotten — it was Padlock above all else that needed to be dealt with.

Frank opened the door and stepped into the frigid night.

"I'll fix him," he said to the sentinel stars. The others, drunk and snoring, slept on.

Chapter 10:

Undisclosed Private Income

Miss Harmony Poffle tossed and turned in her narrow bed, unable to make contact with the world of dreams. Always did her mind return to anxious thoughts of precious Padlock. Was he dead? A prisoner? Why, oh why, had she heard nothing? It was all too heartbreaking for words; and when, in those rare moments that her mind was sufficiently calm to allow the tide of sleep to wash over her, then would the dear, pleasant and pallid features of her beau draw her back to a frantic and frustrated wakefulness.

When this happened then she spent a few envenomed moments thinking about her brother who, at that very moment, was scribbling gibberish into a tome illumined by the guttering of a low-spirited dip candle. Oh, but it was all right for Quartus, closeted in his world of books and insane hypotheses; he cared little for the world, and the world cared little for him in consequence. He had no allegiance to anyone but himself — not, despite his earlier mutterings, to the Black Magician certainly; he was merely a means to get Quartus's gibberish published and, now that it seemed there was an organised resistance to T'osh, Quartus did nothing to aid his erstwhile leader.

Quartus Poffle

Now a great calmness came upon her. For a while she stared at the frosty stars and felt a delicious luxury in lying in bed warm whilst the frost crackled outside. Then that feeling was gone, replaced with one of arctic cold, for she had cast aside the blankets; how dare she enjoy such comfort when the light of her life might be undergoing tortures beyond belief?

She lit the stub of a candle and by its fitful light searched for whatever clothes she could muster. Some of the clothes were pre T'osh and therefore dangerously fashionable (though her substantial frame imposed certain limitations in that direction). Having dressed she put on a sloppy felt hat, a large woollen cape and cowhide boots. Outside, the air was as sharp as razors, that frigid stillness that seems to come from between the stars themselves. For a moment she stood in the yard, sneering at her brother hunched over his work.

As she left the farm, she noticed a red glow in the direction of Ormskirk and, carried by the still, chill air, a faint babble of noise and shouts. She did not know what was going on but felt obscurely relieved that she was not in the town tonight.

Harmony, as will have been gathered, was both a shallow thinking and impulsive person. She had guessed that her *cherished* was in trouble and needed her help, therefore she must go to him. The fact that she did not know where Padlock was at that precise moment was of no importance in the scheme of things. She would go to Padlock's vicarage and there would find some clue as to his whereabouts. This she did not doubt; and even if there were no clue at the tumbledown pile, well, there would be other places to look — yea, even unto the oral cavity of T'osh himself.

Harmony also knew that Padlock felt the same way about her as she did about him, though she could produce no concrete proof, and a cynic could have shown her evidence to the contrary. Still, she knew he loved her the way she loved him and saw, in her coming rescue, the opportunity to whisk Padlock off to some more pleasing land away from the blight of T'osh, where they could pursue their life of connubial bliss. She did not think that Padlock would object too strongly to a departure from this hateful land. Did he not say that the locals were inherently dull; incapable of being the arable land wherein the needs of the healthy society would be planted? A fresh start in a new land would undoubtedly enable her *treasured* to unwind and embrace all the tangible pleasures of life including, she imaginatively assumed, the sensual ones. It was only a matter of time.

*   *   *

Quartus Poffle gazed at the gibbous moon, idly thinking of a monograph he must start shortly concerning the moon's melancholy soul and how broadcasting stations should be set up to radio the works of Poffle to the unhappy satellite in order to cheer it up.

But then, strangely, his mind came back to more immediate matters: his future and his safety in that future. If he had read the signs correctly T'osh's empire would soon be crumbling, and where would that leave him? Would his entrails be spread over several fields, whilst brutish workhands plundered the house? The thought chilled him at first, but the thought of the labourers' stoic inertia cheered him. No, they would do nothing other than what they were told; if not, there was always the quiet bribe.

Oh yes, he was a wealthy man. Good management of the farm together with frugality of taste — eating nothing but corned beef, though of late following this with profuse amounts of melomel — had made him a wealthy man — a golden hoard kept in a metal box in the cellar testified to that.

Perhaps it was the melomel, but now he began to scoff at the magician and his plans. What half-witted stupidities they were! The magician was a joke! What cared Quartus for anything or anyone? *He* could move away from this cesspool to any place that took his fancy — Paris, Venice; any place where men of learning and culture could be found

He began to speak aloud: "In trufe I am dependent on no one and nuffing. I have my wealf and good healf and can always make a living from my writing. Perhaps I could become a lecturer, for is my knowledge not worf imparting to uvvers? I fink vat I will go and count my vast wealf. Vat should keep me busy – tee-hee."

In the cellar he placed the candle on the floor and dragged his great-grandfather's iron chest into the centre of the room. Odd, he thought, how much lighter the chest seemed; must be all the melomel I've drunk, making me more— but then he noticed that the lock had been forced and now in a total panic opened the chest

"Aaaaaaaaaaaaaaaaaaaaaaaaaarrrrggggggghhhhh hhhh!" screamed Poffle. "Who has robbed me? My chest, empty! I will kill vem! My life savings, gone! Ooooohhhhhhhhh! Gone! My gold, my silver! GONE! GONE! GONE! I will murder vem! I will crush vem! Vey are doomed"

Strong words, but they fell onto the chill and empty air — there to be lost — for his only listener was a small rat who had stopped to find out what the commotion was about and soon left in search of nourishment.

Poffle fell to his knees and wept bitter tears.

* * *

T'osh stood upon a hastily erected platform surveying the several hundred faces that were turned up to him. Here one of the faces sported a sneer, there a frown, and a third stared vacantly into space: but though there were surface differences each of the men gave a feeling of malevolence to the chill night air. Any one of the multitude seemed capable of unlimited mayhem and evil, and the miasma of terror that they exhaled was not false, they were the acme of thuggery, T'osh's Praetorian guard, stormtroopers and the first part of T'osh's plan to regain total control.

"At ease, my men, and pay heed, for the words I say are pearls of wisdom. Let each word be carven in the adamantine of your brains.

"This evening marks a new and important stage in our glorious movement; for tonight we begin to consolidate what we have rightfully achieved. It will not be easy. But I say to you that there are those abroad, decaying order of paretic swine though they be, who seek to engineer my downfall."

T'osh surveyed the faces, listening with pleasure to the mutters that echoed through the dismal room. Yes, the faces in the chiaroscuro of the torches were angry with righteous ire; the time was right to channel that anger.

"My dear comrades, there are people abroad who tell that the old days were better, that the regime is a great step backwards. How can they say this, *how*? They whine about hospitals and schools, sanitation and hygiene, balanced diets and life expectancy — PAH! I spit upon such notions. Oh yes, though they talk about such evil things of the past, longing for them as if they were worth having, do they mention the benefits I — no, *we* — the benefits we, brave comrades, have showered upon them? No, never. Some even say that we have not brought benefits, only problems, woe not happiness."

The tension in the room was almost palpable.

"Bring one of the bastards here, we'll soon show him his benefits," shouted someone, and this was greeted with cheers.

"Comrades," said T'osh, motioning for silence. "Comrades. These people are misdirected brethren, and our actions must be governed by our concern for their welfare; why else did we set up our regime? Yes, these brethren must be justly corrected. And how shall we do this? How should we deal with these who speak of liberty . . . equality . . . fraternity?

"BY SPILLING THEIR BLOOD! They will be apprehended; they will be incarcerated . . . they will be . . . buried alive.

"Cease your cheering, dear comrades; let me finish. They are not alone, these evil councillors, and they meet with their nemesis when the time is right. But it is not for this happy work that you are assembled. No, you are the new crusaders; there must be no hesitators, no cowards in your ranks, for together we shall advance along the path to domination, that drear road with its dread destination, evil and injustice. You are the guardians of the revolution.

"Your immediate task, tonight's task, is a glorious one. I have spoken of the filth that takes our name in vain, yet there are others who listen to them; if you catch any of these maggots, then deal with them as is fitting, but your target for tonight is not merely the active dissenters, but those not wholly in favour of me. Go into the highways and byways, seek out the dissidents and spies, seek out the betrayers, the ideologues, the enemies of promise, those who would, by a wink or a nod, a sign or a gesture, indicate their disapproval of our proud and noble venture. Crush them, break their bones, split their skins; let them lie in the roadside as an example. Punish those who hold some trappings of the Western lifestyle; damage those who are not entirely for us; GO FORTH AND MUTILATE! Yaaaarrgghh!"

The scene was now frantic with berserker bloodlust; the doors were being thrown open to let the mob upon the streets. Yet one voice was raised.

"But what if we should injure some innocent party? Surely there is— aaaaaargh." The speaker's skull was crushed by a club.

"Indeeeeeed, fear not that you might smite an innocent, for should there be any mistakes, and with you my dear comrades I do not think there will be any, should chance dictate that an innocent suffer, then he will welcome it, for is he not serving a noble cause?"

There was an explosion and a flash of flame and smoke; T'osh disappeared.

* * *

Any inhabitant of Ormskirk would have done well to be elsewhere that night. Fortified with a repulsive liquor distilled from pea pods that T'osh had the foresight to prepare, the ensemble separated into groups of four or five, to wreck and inflict bloody violence, though these four or five could be augmented from other groups did the need arise. No one was safe that night, and blood flowed freely on the streets. People were dragged from their beds, wailing for mercy, only to be left disfigured in the road. Innocents were thrown through windows, onto spikes, covered in petrol and given a lighted cigarette; they were beaten with fists and feet, clubbed with cudgels and iron bars; hacked with knives and machetes.

Houses were burnt to the ground and nobody checked whether there was anyone inside. Plague-carrying rats were released in the town centre. By the lurid light of burning houses, horrors were carried out, and through the smoky air shriek after shriek rang through the night. Most people hid in the cellars, praying that the sackers would not find them, or worse, set the house on fire, but others were not so lucky as to have a reasonably safe hideaway and took to their heels. Some escaped, but most met a foul fate, being stuffed into the sewers below the town where, since the sanitation services had been idle for months, the rat population had become shockingly enormous; they did not carry the plague but were, in the main, rather hungry. And, caught trying to escape, an old man and a boy were hung on the clock tower. Though the populace were the main sufferers that night, not all of T'osh's forces went unscathed. Some few rifles and shotguns were drawn from hidden recesses and these were used to telling effect until they were silenced — generally by one of T'osh's men managing to ignite the house. Some troopers were the victims of either their own or their colleagues' enthusiasm; one, for instance, setting fire to a house, then finding he could not escape from the

inferno; another being pushed from the tower of an
abandoned church by his colleagues who were all busily
hanging a local upside down in the bell-chamber prior
to giving a few peals of triple bob majors. Another, his
leg crushed by a falling corbel, upon crying, "I've been
betrayed. T'osh has betrayed me!" was hacked at by a
group of his fellow troopers.

Noah Halfmoon was in the thick of the action,
putting to good use his well-honed skills as an arsonist
by ensuring that any house fire he attended would
be guaranteed to ensure the entire building was
completely gutted and beyond redemption. At points
he could be seen dancing a grotesque form of jig
dangerously close to the burning building and making
irregular noises at the back of his throat which suggested
he was in some form of delirious reverie. Meanwhile
Ormskirk was submerged in a nightmare from which
there was apparently no awakening; T'osh's masterplan
was underway.

*　　*　　*

Padlock knew nothing of these events. His lust for
power had put a keen edge on his nervous system and
had turned him insomniac.

Foregoing sleep, he wandered into the dark and
squalid room where in happier times he had composed
sermons of fire and wrath. He pulled at a drawer in
his rotting wooden desk, taking it out and reaching
into the cavity. He withdrew three filthy bags and
caressed them.

Some ten years before he had inherited a store of
gold sovereigns from a deceased uncle. Naturally he had

not spent any of them; but when times were bad, he achieved much innocent pleasure from looking at and feeling the coins. He would run his bloodless fingers through the auriferous mounds and his eyes would shine and his thin lips would compress, and his features would glow and he would sometimes think that this was the true quill, the distilled quintessence of what the lower orders experienced in copulation.

This was not of course the total of Padlock's wealth — oh no, that mighty mint had been divided and was now secreted in various hidden caches — but this was his collection of gold, and gold had a texture and aura that no other substance could boast.

He counted the coins in the flickering light and did not look up from his desk, nor did he look up to the window — which was just as well ... for in the darkness of the weeds and shrubs that grew by the window stood Frank. Glinting dully blue in the starlight was the shotgun, and Frank raised the weapon to his shoulder, aiming along the barrel at Padlock's head.

But he did not fire; like Padlock, he was fascinated by the glint of the gold. Why, that old bag o' bones, he thought, all that money and he would not even provide a decent cup of tea. I'll blow a hole in that head of his — by God, I'll blow the bastard's head clear off!

But still he did not fire.

*　　*　　*

Miss Harmony Poffle, unchilled by the weather, was in militant mood. She held a stout stick in her hand, and she would use it to draw blood, should it prove necessary to save the lovely Reverend Pedaiah Lock.

She was a schoolmistress of the type that had been described in *The Perfect State* as the ideal, giving as little information as possible, whilst enforcing strict discipline. Her methods were less than subtle, and indeed it could be said that to her the idea of sparing the rod and spoiling the child was, by far, too liberal and progressive. Entrusted with the task of teaching (for want of a better word) the village children aged between five and eleven, she had pursued this aim with such a vigour that mothers were often dismayed to see their beloved offspring returning home with cuts and bruises, accompanied by the occasional broken bone or piece of raw and bleeding scalp.

Parental remonstrance had not been successful, for Miss Harmony Poffle was wont to use the rod on parents as well as children. This had all meant that she had an extremely well-muscled right arm, a sullen respect amongst the people and a horribly cheerful boast that she had not killed anyone . . . yet.

As she neared the vicarage, she was elated by the light coming from the downstairs window — Padlock was safe! She ran towards the window to sight her adored; then stopped in horror as she saw Frank aiming his gun at Padlock.

She threw her stick at Frank's head, screaming blue murder. The stick hit Frank in the shoulder, and, in shock and fear, he dropped the gun. Before he could retrieve it the considerable bulk of Miss Harmony Poffle was all over him, kicking and punching, scratching and gouging.

Having felt her head banging the wall a few times Harmony was minded to let go of Frank, who scuttled to the shotgun, picking it up by the barrel.

"Try to hurt my Pedaiah would you? Take that!" she said, aiming a mighty kick to Frank's groin.

"Gnnnnnnnggggggggggggg!" responded Frank, falling to his knees.

Then Harmony was on top of Frank again. John Ambler, roused from bed with the noise and still in his night attire, rushed out of the rectory and joined in the melee.

Frank made a desperate lunge for the gun, grabbed it, but before he could start clubbing his assailants with it, one of the barrels burst into life. Harmony screamed and fainted dead away. John Ambler lost interest in furthering the fight, for he seemed to be engaged in a studious and, so far, detached examination of the bloody ruin that had been his left hand, which now lacked both the entire small finger and most of the ring-finger.

Half-dazed and in great pain Frank pointed the gun at the lighted window and fired. The glass disintegrated, but the angle of fire was too high, the rain of deadly pellets shooting over Padlock's pallid features. With a groan Frank disappeared into the bushes.

Throughout the fight Padlock had merely looked at the combatants without helping; after all his clothes might have been damaged — and that would have cost implications. But when the window was shattered, and the ceiling peppered with shot, a great fury overtook him and he peered out of the window and shouted to Ambler: "You are an oaf, sirrah, you let that fool wreck my window and ceiling. Money does not grow on trees, you know. I'll deduct the cost of repairing the damage from your wages." (Which might have been a trifle difficult to do, since Padlock had not, and had no intention of, paying Ambler a brass farthing.) "Why couldn't you have stood in front of the gun, sirrah? You answer me that, instead of spending your employer's hard-earned cash."

*   *   *

Dawn was blood-red the following morning. In Ormskirk the cold air was thick with the smell of ashes and gore. Bodies were sprawled over the street, some moaned, most lay still. A number of the bodies were dressed in the felt hats, black cloaks and dirty boots of T'osh's troopers, but these had in the main collapsed from drunkenness rather than from any stout defence put up by the townsfolk.

By the glowing embers of a burnt-out cottage, six troopers were finishing off the last of some looted flasks of melomel. They were singing.

> *I banged on the rooftops*
> *I rattled the door*
> *I jumped through the window*
> *And pounded the floor*
>
> *I espied an old man*
> *Aged seventy-eight*
> *I drew out my cudgel*
> *And battered his pate.*
>
> *I drank yet more ale*
> *Then went on my way*
> *I knew there'd be others*
> *With a price yet to pay*

I met a young fellow
All brazen and brash
But his throat was sliced open
With one swooping slash

The bodies are swinging
Or covered with mud
The traitors defeated
The roads red with blood

*   *   *

Martyn was watching the dawn. Despite the carousing of the night before his head was clear.

"Frank's disappeared," said Timothy in the doorway.

"He's probably gone for a walk; don't worry about it."

But then the door burst open and a bedraggled Frank staggered in. "Drink," he croaked, "strong drink."

A draught of melomel inside him, a warm fire before him, Frank told of the events of the previous night.

Martyn listened in fascination and horror. "You tried to . . . kill Padlock . . ."

"Yes, but I failed, damn it."

"But surely . . . I mean, murder?"

"Justifiable in the circumstance."

*   *   *

Later Wladek heard the tale, and Martyn noted that a lustful expression fleetingly crossed the man's face at the mention of Padlock's gold.

Said Wladek: "It now seems that we have two sets of adversaries to deal with: on the one hand, there is the

Black Magician and all his cronies; on the other the unlikely combination of a schoolmistress, a parson and a farm-worker. Strange indeed. But we must not discount the second group out of hand, for they could prove to be dangerous in ways as yet unforeseen. Luckily, we do know where we can find them.

"We must continue to lie low, for I have heard that the Dark One is starting a new campaign to entrench his position, though I do not know of what form this will take, though, fear not, I will discover what it is this very day when I venture into Ormskirk. Expect my return some time after the pubs have shut."

Wladek was perhaps disingenuous when he spoke of going to Ormskirk, for first he went to the home of Quartus Poffle, whom he found in the front room, staring out of the window and in a very agitated state.

"I thought I'd pay you a visit and advise you on the state of your land."

"Bah!"

"Pardon?"

"I don't care about vese fings."

"Is something wrong?"

"My money, my life savings, vey have all been stolen."

"Your life savings?"

"Yes, I have been secretive enough over ve years, but someone has managed to discover my wealf and vey have stolen it. When I find out who it is, I will murder vem. Vey shall die slowly."

"But how will you discover the culprits?"

"Don't worry; I have a good idea who it was. Don't forget vat while I was being held prisoner by vose wretched people vey would have had ample time to ransack vis house and search every nook and cranny. It was one of vem and no mistake."

"Now are you quite sure of this?"

"Of course! Who else came to vis house? Only yourself came to vis house, and you are but a simple drudge wiv no great need of wealf. After all, do we not barter everyfing?"

He paused. "I fink I know who did it: vat Reverend chappie." He weakly punched his left palm with his right fist. "And, my sister has gone off in search off him — she finks she loves him, but he is ve one I most suspect; I do not fink vat anyfing will stop him where money is concerned."

Poffle squinted and leant close to Wladek, saying in a conspiratorial whisper: "Do you know, I will go straight to T'osh, whom I have yet to tell ve story of my capture and period of imprisonment. I know for a fact vat ve Reverend set off to find and kill T'osh; it follows vat if he had been successful, we would have heard somefing. We must conclude vat he wasn't, and he must be either (a), a prisoner, in which case a lighted candle applied to ve soles of his feet will loosen his tongue; or (b), still at large, in which case I will assemble a tough crew of guards loaned by T'osh and search all ve likely haunts, starting off wiv his rotting vicarage. Ven we will see somefing."

"I wish you luck in your mission."

*　*　*

The day was clear and quite pleasant for this chill winter, but there was a vague stench in the air. Really, it was quite strong outside and not much more dilute inside, not after Frank had shattered the window with the shotgun. Though the chiselled appearance of

Padlock's nose gave rise to rumours of its olfactory acuteness, it was but an indifferent organ: which had caused Padlock much sadness and forced him to spend many a fruitless hour in trying to improve the sense; for, if air was free, so too were the smells, carried on that medium — Padlock was missing out on something.

But whatever the limitations of his nose, Padlock had picked out the main constituent of the smell: smoke and ash; a thin miasma that drifted from the general direction of Ormskirk.

Yet this morning he had other things to worry about, mainly the cost of repairing the window. He was standing in the dank shrubbery outside the ruined opening, inspecting the rotting frame to see if it would be possible to replace the window without replacing the frame. He had reluctantly decided that glass rather than oil paper was necessary for the transparency and was now deciding, not without much soul-searching and sighing, that the frame too would have to be replaced. The thought of replacing these objects brought the picture of money to his mind, not the delightful one of having coins tumble through his waxen fingers, but the loathly one of handing the coins over to some deceitful tradesman who would almost certainly overcharge, for everyone knew what these people were like. He thought of the bags of gold — *the bags of gold* — merciful heaven, did — was — last night, when he was counting the money, Frank must have looked through the window . . . looked through the window . . . and seen the gold.

Too stingy to shriek, he merely sighed and swooned onto the chill undergrowth.

* * *

Wladek was renewing his perennial acquaintance with the landlady, Florinda Farrier, in the Stanley Arms. He stayed with her for some time, deep in discussion; then went over to where a weather-beaten peasant with hollow cheeks was sitting before a fire.

"Well, my old friend, how goes it? How are things?" The old man's eyes opened in terror. "Haven't you heard?"

"Heard? Heard what?"

"Of Ormskirk. Of 'im, the Magician. Last night set 'is bully boys out at 'em: streets runnin' with innocent blood . . . old men clubbed. . . babes there were, cast from rooftops . . . children taken for slaves . . . women defiled . . . buildings set a-blazin' an' all the doin' of this 'ere T'osh."

Even Wladek was stunned — at the magnitude of the event, if not its occurrence. That was of course if the old man was not exaggerating. "I have not heard of this, but I will trouble you for further details. And one other thing: do not trifle with me and disclose to me your true nature, for you are surely dissembling."

"Eh? I dunno what you mean."

"You do. See how your glass is trembling in your hand, and do not say that it is with the ague, for I will surely laugh in your face. I say again, I know you. You are a writer, a writer as was so called in the days before the ascendancy of the Dark One, not a scrivener and transcriber of spells as this sorry time coins the word."

The old man summoned as much dignity as he could manage. "I do not imagine that in this enlightened land I will be merely deported. Come, let us away to the torturer."

"Sit, old man; I have no love for the Black Magician and would have him put to the torturers before any man."

"Dangerous words in these days."

"But true, very true."

"Aye, but perhaps spoken less loudly."

Wladek went off for drinks for himself and the old man. When they were seated about the fire again, he asked: "How come you are still in this region? Would have thought that you would have fled a long time since."

"So would I; it seems that old age breeds courage, or at least diminishes the fear of death."

"I can remember you, typing away at the front window of your cottage whenever I went past on messages for my employer, or master as he thinks himself."

"Young Poffle. I have not seen him for some time, though that may have been caused by breaking my walking stick over his head the last time I had the pleasure of a visit from him and was subjected to a lengthy rant about the idleness of the labouring classes. You know, I still live at the old place: course, I've taken up an occupation more in keeping with the times."

"But why stay here at all?"

"The story I will be able to tell of this mad time when the reign of terror is over. God, what a tale it will be.

"But you were asking about the sack of Ormskirk. Well . . . it seems that our leader has become even more paranoid, or fearful that his grip is loosening on the land, and last night started on a campaign of liquidating any dissidents and cowering the ordinary people into terrified inaction. I won't go into the details of what happened last night in Ormskirk, it's pretty awful; whatever you imagine, I can assure you the reality was worse."

"Is it still going on?"

"Yes, his bully-boys have sobered up enough this morning to go roaming about the country, setting fire to anything that looks like it might burn, stealing anything they damn well please, and drinking anything that might contain alcohol. I believe that something big is being planned for Sunday."

"And last night wasn't anything to write home about? What is going to happen?"

"Something bad. Sitting here you pick up lots of information — too damn much; you try separating the wheat from the chaff. So far as I can make out there's going to be some sort of festival held in a field just outside Ormskirk. I believe that some of the dissidents have been imprisoned; they will meet their punishment in that field, for T'osh will be displaying his latest methods of torture and ingenious punishments. That will be for starters, followed by readings from *The Perfect State*, backed up with some entrapments not standard to a normal lecture. Then will come the grand finale, a black mass that will be so . . . huge? . . . gross? that Satan will surely turn up.

"I believe that attendance at this event will be mandatory, with something involving boiling oil for those who fail to attend.

"You see, what he knows is that what most people want is the quiet life. They'd be quite happy to see the back of T'osh but lack the energy to get rid of him. T'osh knows that this lack of enthusiasm can only be muted by ruthless displays of terror and power. Things might get so bad that in a repressive regime like T'osh's the worm will turn of his own accord, but he is going to be a damn sight more reluctant to turn if he knows that at the first sign of dissent four thugs are going to jump on his head.

"Remember too that T'osh was first welcomed as the new leader not so long ago. There's a certain inertia in people that discourages them from thinking that they have erred in some way, that the new boy is an evil toad, no matter how foul his acts. This would mean accepting that they were wrong, that they fell for a pack of lies, and that is abhorrent to many, regardless of the weight of evidence stacking up daily, for it means owning up to their own gullibility and, in some ways, their culpability. There is always the hope that at some ill-defined point in the future things will get better.

"So, this is the situation we have — by the way, forgive me for lecturing — but the thing is so obvious to me, and doubtless to you, but so hidden to the rest. Ah, I fear that this foul regime will go on for ever."

"For ever?"

"Do not be so literal; everything is relative. You know, I can even see the end of this regime brought about without the direct intervention of God. If some charismatic leader appeared to unite the people and bring them out of this madness, the way Moses led the Israelites out of the land of Bondage. For they too were ready to be slaves for ever and ever, just as the people here; yet there arose a leader to unify them, make them one unit of fearful strength and not just x-number of individual rabbits. Yes, if a leader did come . . .

"You know, I even considered myself for the role, but when weighing myself in the balance was found wanting — damn quick, I can tell you. Besides I'm too old, and my present protective camouflage does not give much of a springboard for any campaign: old Abel Renton, farm labourer, sometime drunkard and regular bore.

"By the way, what's yours?"

"No, thank-you, but I must be going."

"Another time then. Barmaid! A pint of porter please — no, make that two." He sighed. "Sometimes my role as drunkard fits me too well." He finished one pint then vigorously started on the other.

Wladek stood up. He put his hand on the old man's shoulders. "Do not worry; I feel sure that the days of T'osh's imperium are numbered."

"Arr, 'appen, mebbe so. Queerer things have 'appened at sea. That they have, that they have," said the man who called himself Abel Renton.

* * *

Twilight: the end of another of the winter days. From a distance, it looked as if a light fog had settled over various parts of the land; but the grey wreathes were smokes from burning barns and houses. Here and there were patches of brilliant flame as if a star had fallen from its canopy.

In many ways, the landscape had a northern beauty, down to the dark clouds scudding over a scarce lighter sky. The burning buildings, in the distance and failing light, could easily have been the campfires of several armies: armies waiting to sit out the fearful Fimbulwinter in relative warmth before scaling the Bifrost bridge and Asgard, ending everything with Ragnarok.[1]

---

[1] In Norse mythology and Asatru (according to the Eddas), **Fimbulwinter** is the immediate prelude to the end of the world, **Ragnarok**. **Bifrost** is the rainbow bridge of the gods from their realm **Asgard** to earth.

But then, it was always easy to concoct gotterdammerung[1] if it was somebody else's house on fire, harder to think of the spiritual value of pain if it was your head that was being jumped upon.

And yet the building burned; and yet the bodies were strewn over hedgerow and lea; and yet T'osh looked out at the crepuscular landscape, sure that the lands he had felt slipping from his grasp would, in but a few days, be handed back to him . . . by those same stupid and brutish serfs who had fallen under his sway.

The fools.

---

[1] a collapse (as of a society or regime) marked by catastrophic violence and disorder

Chapter 11:

All Things Considered

There was a garden at the back of the cottage. Timothy had taken note of its ragged condition and Wladek had explained that he had little time for gardening and Cressida had no inclination for it, being far more interested in meditation and various artistic pursuits. Thus it was that the place was rank and the gross and overwhelming growths unwholesome. Even in winter, with all the plants dead, it was overcrowded, with dry stalks rattling in the icy blasts and mounds of sere leaves and rubbish lying where the wind had tossed them.

Martyn walked through this dead garden, heading for the small pond that lay at its bottom. There had been a frost the night before and the dead growths were limned with frozen skeins that, in this thick light, seemed like encrustations of mould. The melancholy of the garden reinforced Martyn's own gloom. He wrapped his collar closer to his face as the wind carried sleet before it. It was very quiet; only the distant cry of an unidentified bird broke the stillness.

This garden is like the rest of the land, thought Martyn, neglected and maltreated and seemingly not wanting to be helped. Is our mission doomed, as dead as that three-treed break over there? Spring will come back to the garden . . . but will it return to the land?

Martyn's concentration was broken by the repeated cry of the bird which was, now he took more note of it, coming from a much closer distance than he had first perceived. As he neared the pond, he saw that it was glazed with ice and that by the edge of the pool was an exhausted redwing[1]. Martyn was moved to pity and though he knew but little about birds, presumed that the creature wanted water and was tapping on the thick ice for that purpose. Moving carefully so as not to affright the exhausted bird, he picked up a stick, broke the ice and left an area of clear water. The bird hopped to the water and began to drink.

The incident performed some strange chemistry in Martyn's mind, for as he was returning to the cottage, he felt an explosion of sinew and fibre and courage surge through his mind and body. He stopped in his tracks and looked at the curdling sky. "We shall win," he whispered, "we *shall* win."

*　　*　　*

When Martyn returned to the cottage, he found Timothy and Frank seated at the breakfast table, both drinking mint tea for some reason destined to remain a mystery. They

---

[1] **Redwing**

Redwings migrate from Northern Europe, Iceland and Russia to the UK in the winter months. They are like blackbirds and song thrushes in size and can often been seen in mixed flocks with fieldfares. They have a distinct red flank and light-brown eye stripe. They favour berries and fruit-bearing trees.

were — what else? —engaged in argument, with Timothy enthusing about the need for a return to democracy.

"So," he was saying, "once T'osh is overthrown, we need to have a system which ensures that this sort of thing can never happen again. To speak in general, we need something more than universal suffrage, something to ensure that the peasant not only uses his vote, but uses it wisely, and does not succumb to the first rabble-rouser who grabs his ear with shallow and emotive words or is forever encouraging the masses to point the finger of blame at some minority group in order to foster hatred and opprobrium whilst simultaneously practising the dark arts of malversation. T'osh is not unique; there are many abroad who would be ruthless in their pursuit of power given a chance. Regular elections are a must for all at least."

"No good at all," said Frank, shaking his head.

"What do you mean? Surely you are not trying to tell me that you do not believe in regular elections?"

"I believe they exist."

"That wasn't what I meant — and you know it. I am asking you if you approve or disapprove of systems where governments and leaders are chosen by all of the people in elections that are free, fair and secret."

"Let me put it this way; I would be a great believer in universal suffrage if — and this is a very big if indeed — if all the people could be shown to be exercising their powers of reason and choice when making their vote."

"And you don't believe that that is possible?"

"Except in the case of a small minority, no, they are not."

"Do you think they just make a random choice, Frank?"

"Not random, no; but their choice is guided by all manner of irrelevant factors. They vote for *Joe Bluffington-Bilge* because their father always voted for him; or because all their mates at work do; because that's what the papers said to do; because he's a nice man and you can see that he means all he says. He's got nice eyes! He dresses smartly! He always stands his round! He is straight talking! He once was a scrap metal dealer! He's a multi-millionaire so knows what he is talking about. He can drop Latin phrases into his discourse, so he must be a superior intellect. These are the prime factors in determining a voter's decisions, and they almost exclusively ignore the main issues; the economic and social issues are not even known to exist." Timothy's face moulded itself into one of smug satisfaction.

"Interesting," he said, "but what evidence do you have to support this?"

"Bah!" Frank snorted, leaning over the table and staring directly into Timothy's face. "Fool! Do you honestly suppose that I carry documentary evidence for each and every piece of wisdom that I strew before you? Am I supposed to have a copy of the architect's plans for the house in my pocket if I tell you the kitchen is through that door? Should I whip out the latest astrophysical treatises before I can say whether the sun is shining this morning?"

He paused for breath, surprised at his heated reaction. Really, he thought, I must be under a strain, otherwise I would never have allowed a lesser-intellect to upset me so.

"Suffice it to say," he said in a calmer voice, "that I have in the past perused many learned studies, taken in various parts of the western world, and that they tend to conclusively prove that vast numbers of the electorate are wholly innocent of the policies of the party for whom they vote, and in many cases they vote for parties whose ideals are at total variance to their own ideas, feeble though they be; their resultant misery caused by the use of the vote they see as some sort of divine intervention, totally divorced from their use of the franchise.

"Look at the floating voter, and don't try to tell me they're an insignificant minority; there the anile and feeble views have gone together, and all that is left is a sort of jellyfish, free to drift on the currents of whatever the demagogue or, more so these days the advertising agency, may make in political waters.

"I'm not trying to say anything but the obvious, that in a democracy the electorate is not only ill-informed, but guilty of this ignorance through apathy. Who was it that said, 'Politics is only slightly less important than breathing'? — but you try telling that to the average voter. He will look at you as if you were a creature from a different galaxy.

"Here's my argument, then; it is ludicrous to imagine one of the labouring classes being as adept at making political judgements as one of the intelligentsia — such as myself."

"You *may* be right," said Timothy, wearily, thinking that it was typical of Frank to regard himself as worthy of placement in the highest strata of any theoretical system.

"Hang on a minute," said Martyn, "it's quite a while since I read it, but I remember a work done on the psephology of the 1952 US elections. I can't remember the exact figures, but they prove that Frank was at least partially valid. Something like two thirds of the voters — and I can't remember how many people didn't even bother to vote — did not know or did not see any difference between the aims of the two parties. The conclusion reached was that there was little evidence of structured thinking, political or otherwise, based on that evidence. Naturally this is wrong, and I have my own opinions of the solution to the problem, but, as you started the argument Frank, will you give us your solution?"

"Certainly," said Frank, standing up, as if before a crowded auditorium. "To begin with, I must own to the sketchiness of my plan. This is partly due to my opinion that such political trafficking is below that of my artistic calling, but one must help out when one can, and secondly, I claim no true infallibility; there are doubtless improvements and short-cuts to be taken when the scheme is put into actual use; only a fool and a madman refuses to trim his sails slightly before the winds of the time.

"I think that it must be stated as axiomatic that it is both naïf and puerile to assume that members of the unskilled classes can and should be allowed to take as full a part in the political life as, say, a lawyer, surgeon, scientist; those that are in the professions. But it must be allowed that not all the professions as they are currently defined should be included. Clergymen, for example, are ossified relics of feudal times. They should be cast to one side, along with homeopaths, astrologers and palmists, there to play an even lesser role than the labouring masses.

"On both the physical and mental plane there are differences between individuals, and though the environment must play some part in the creation and reinforcing of these differences, the seed, and sometimes the full-grown plant, are there at birth. If two unrelated babies are brought up separately in similar environments, what is found? Why, by the age of five differences can be clearly perceived. Child A may be taller and stronger, whilst Child B may be a more articulate thinker. Because the state must demand of its subjects their best talents, these talents must be recognised and inculcated. Every society needs its doctors, soldiers, artists — the list is endless — and the state must endeavour to find these talents at the earliest possible date, and once the talents are discovered the child must be brought up in such a way so as to bring and develop these aptitudes to the full. Conversely the child must not be distracted by useless information which at most gains the state nil and possibly distracts the pupil; what is the point in teaching a child Shakespeare if his talents lie in the laying of bricks? The notion of an all-round education, a professor knowing how to lay bricks, a sewer worker knowing psychology, though widely held, is both futile and costly."

"But aren't you going to end up with all generals and no privates, a mass of schools — one for bricklayers, one for violinists and so on — a vast bureaucracy of teachers?" responded Martyn, aghast. "Apart from that, I don't know if that isn't the most elitist blether I have ever heard — or, if not elitist, since I don't know whether you are making any value judgements, saying that a violinist is better than a bricklayer, or vice-versa, isn't your society nothing more than a vast and complex bee-hive?"

"It is simply a matter of being practical. If—"

"No!" cried Timothy. "Don't gloss over this horror. Is it not unjust, not to say unthinkably atrocious, to pluck a five-year-old, or a ten-year-old, from his environment and teach him, together with his other victimised colleagues, nothing but bricklaying? That, for the rest of his life, nothing but bricklaying has any meaning for him?"

"This means that the workers will have but the narrowest of all outlooks," said Martyn: "Intelligentsia must have all the best of everything," he continued. "Just give the workers bread and circuses, tabloid newspapers and football, they'll still clean the sewers out as well as ever, but don't give them the opportunity to indulge in the things that make them human. You couldn't do that; one glimpse of what the intelligentsia have, and the workers would be in revolt. And you've got to give the cognoscenti the best of everything simply because it is either part of their work or necessary for them to utilise it so that they can carry on with their work.

"And wouldn't this carry on forever and ever? Once the stratification is complete, then the second generation of the elite would not know of the working classes. The cold-hearted bastards who set up this state would be culpable for this horror, but what about the second generation of the elite, cut off from any contact with the workers? How could they find compassion for those who are, somewhat subjectively, defined as unskilled? It would have been cut out of them by this foul education system of yours. You don't really want to help mankind; you want to bleed out of it everything that makes it worthwhile being human!"

"Look," snarled Frank, "in Ormskirk the milk was delivered to the doorstep every morning — or it was until

T'osh took over. Once a week, every Friday morning, I would rise at some unearthly hour and pay the milkman. Then it was a case of 'Lovely weather lately,' 'Six shillings and fourpence,' 'Thank-you,' 'Good day,' and so on. Are you so childish enough to suppose that either of us could benefit from a deeper relationship — or even desire such a thing? Of course not. He would much rather be in the pub, conversing with his peers about pigeons, sausages or whatever they thought fit to discuss. Do you honestly think that he would — or could — enter into any meaningful discussion concerning the writings of Kafka or, God forbid, Joyce? Never!

"Of course, this is my very point. The rulers must be drawn from the intelligentsia, for who else would be fit to govern? Likewise, they must be the ones to have the most say in the workings of that government. I would propose a system of sliding scales; a master surgeon might have a vote worth ten times the voting power of a humble shepherd. This would be far more practical than the current muddle."

"Your republic is . . . is . . ." Timothy, white lipped with suppressed fury, groped for words, then settled with the feeble, " . . . fraught with danger."

In a dangerously calm voice, he continued: "Suppose . . . suppose that a man surrenders himself entirely to some calling, say that it's music. He surrounds himself with it; all day with bright and complex constructs; all night with soft and mournful airs; all his time is given to the delights of song and melody. At first this would merely temper the bellicose side of his nature, but if he persists in this then this necessary part of his nature will melt away from him totally; he will be left fainthearted and weak.

"Take, on the other hand, the man who cultivates only the physical side of his dual nature. At first the infusing of physical health fills the man with self-confidence and energy. But suppose that he does nothing else but this and refrains from any aspect of culture. Then, supposing that he had the capacity to strain for knowledge, then he is starved of instruction and never encouraged to think for himself by taking part in rational discussion of intellectual pursuits of any kind. His brain is a barren field untilled by instruction, unfertilised with knowledge and the darkness that clouds his sight is never lifted. Such a man will be a despiser of culture and reason. Having no use for words or persuasion he will try to gain his end by the use of brute force. His mind will be fogged by the dull stupor of ignorance; he will not have any inner harmony, nor will he be cognisant of the lack."

"It is a question of combining the practical and philosophical elements of a person's nature," piped a voice from the doorway. It was Cressida, risen from her slumber and managing to catch on to the latter end of the conversation. "The purpose of any education should be to bring these two elements in tune with each other by adjusting the tension of each to the right pitch. Anyone who can bring to the soul this education of blending, in perfect proportions, will be an expert in the field of harmony greater than any who strum the lute, cittern or guitar."

"Oh, go and find some fairies at the bottom of the garden," muttered Timothy, a much-changed man.

Frank was turning a peculiar shade of white.

Martyn paused momentarily, trying to make some sense of Cressida, before realizing that she was just spouting her usual whimsical nonsense, then added his weight to Timothy's argument.

"From what you were saying, it seems that you are trying to justify some sort of corporate state by focussing on the faults and shortcomings of one kind of democracy. After all, there are many countries in the world whose political systems can be described as democratic yet are set up in ways totally dissimilar to those of Western Europe. I accuse you of being a generaliser of the first water.

"You must not overlook the fact that in the western democracies the role of the people has been greatly minimised; there is much evidence to suggest that there are elite groups already well-embedded — economic, military and political — linked by close family and personal ties, who wield the greatest power. Then there is the rise of the mass media which, irrespective of their links with, and subservience to, the elite groups, create hierarchies of their own because of their very nature. More and more people are on the receiving end of opinions they do not hold but which subtly change their opinions whilst having no chance of effectively airing their own original ideas. Those who impose their opinions are absurdly described as journalists, but in reality, are crypto-politicians, despite having no defined constituency, mandate or accountability, but wielding enormous power and influence. The poor man or woman lacks the influence with which he could state his or her opinions to a wider audience.

"Frank, it seems to me that you are saying that the western democracies do not work and ought to be scrapped, but in many ways, they are a rather mild form of the very system you wish to introduce. All the aspects

are there, the hierarchical structure, the lack of movement between the strata, the sacerdotal intelligentsia,
yet you say it does not work whilst advocating an iden-
tical system that will work! Is this a paradox from one
of your novels — or is it just gobbledygook?"

Timothy leapt in; "What is needed is greater emphasis
on meaningful participation and the importance of the
community. People must be allowed to exercise more
control over their lives, especially in the sphere of economic production. Liberal democracy is a sham, with
the power held in the hands of the capitalist classes.
What we need are more trade unions, workers' councils,
cooperative enterprises, a system which does not tend to
dehumanise people. In short, we need more democracy,
not less!"

"Idealistic claptrap," sneered Frank, "you would do
well to read more about the subject, since it is clear that
you have read pitiably little. Come back when you have
more facts, then your opinions might be wiser."

"How about suggesting some titles?" asked Martyn.
"The scribblings of Benito Mussolini or a certain Mr
Mosley might be a starting point."

"The trouble with you," yelled Timothy, waving a
finger in Frank's now alabaster face, "the trouble with
you is that you spend all your time in a room, scribbling
gibberish. You've no idea how ordinary people live their
lives; you simply carry in your head an imaginary
picture of placid, unthinking creatures in need of help
and guidance from such as yourself. Intelligentsia? Ha!
That's a laugh from the start — you get a few books,
memorise them, learn a few stupid arguments, repeat
them, then go around expecting people to be impressed.
Well I'm not! Not one bloody bit! You're a failure as a

human being, but I don't suppose that'll worry you too much. But you're a failure as a philosopher and a raconteur and everything else you think and imagine yourself to be. As a writer, you are a crap artist and that so-called novel of yours would be the greatest laugh on earth if I didn't fall asleep halfway down the first paragraph. Damn you! Caterwauling clown! To hell with you!"

Timothy stormed to his feet, knocking over the chair. He waved his fist in front of Frank, but instead of striking him Timothy strode into the garden.

"Dear me," said Frank, "don't some people take things seriously?"

"Very true indeed," said Cressida, "I once tried to explain to him about the five noble truths and the nine-fold path to enlightenment, but of course it was a waste of time. He would not admit that suffering was inevitable. It is all quite simple, really. The first stage is to look at life from the right viewpoint. Now if it is accepted that suffering is due to selfish desires, then it follows that if—"

"Excuse me," muttered Martyn, heading after Timothy.

*   *   *

Outside the stillness remained. With the dropping of the wind the rattle of the leaves and the clatter of the stems had ceased. But with the silence there had come an intense but dead cold. The sky was still its anonymous self, still the clotted overcast.

The knives of cold cooled Martyn's rage. His breath steamed about him in gelid clouds. Timothy turned as

Martyn placed his hand on his friend's shoulder and Martyn could see that the acrimony and resentment still remained in Timothy's eyes.

"Cold," said Martyn.

"Yes."

"I don't like the look of these clouds. Snow, I reckon."

"Yes."

Martyn sighed, "You'll have to make allowances for Frank; he's had a rough time of it, and, when he has, his cure is to sneer and goad."

"I know — but haven't we all had a rough time?"

Martyn stared at the sky before answering, "Yes . . . yes. We all have, but the thing is that some of us are better than others at taking it."

"I know. I know. It's just that . . . well, whatever you might say, Frank didn't have to . . . that . . . prison cell."

"It must have been a terrible experience," said Martyn, as Timothy turned away. Timothy began to shake uncontrollably. "You don't know — you don't know," he said, "you can't know what it was like."

"No," said Martyn to Timothy's back, "but don't worry my friend; victory will be ours!"

"How do you know? How do you know we're not just wasting our time?"

"I don't. Of course I don't. We might lose everything in the next hour, or we might gain all now. I don't know the future, but neither does T'osh. Hope, man, hope! We're still alive, and the only sure way to lose is to do nothing. Turn around, listen to me. Don't you think that I feel despair from time to time? Why, I felt utter despair just this morning." Here Martyn told the tale of the redwing.

"I don't know if I understand it or not," said Timothy, "but for you to admit of despair and then say that you successfully fought against it — my God, let me shake your hand! There is no force upon this planet that can subdue us. We will win — no doubt about it — victory will be ours."

Martyn's heart glowed with pride and joy; here was a man as loyal as Dancing Jack or Red Joe.

*   *   *

That afternoon a gale of gusting warmish air broke the stillness and melted the ice. It was a dirty wind, dragging with it grit and dust, a damp wind, with the prospect of a storm to come.

By mid-afternoon the storm cloud had arrived, darkening the already short day. Wladek could see tapers and candles in all of the houses save one mouldering pile.

His nose wrinkled at the cloying stench of mould and dust that drifted from the rotting bricks of the festering semi-ruin.

Though he was in unfamiliar territory, he acted with his usual swagger. Coming to the door of the pile he smote it three times with mighty gusto. Plaster and rotten brick fell to the earth by the door. An upstairs window creaked open and a glistening and domed forehead was outlined in a ghastly and glowing manner against the moiling sky.

"What do you want? You of all people?"

"I have come to give you fair warning. Quartus Poffle is currently gathering a number of ruffians and will shortly be on his way here."

"For what possible purpose? Explain yourself, sirrah."

"He believes that while he was being held captive you searched his house and took his riches."

"Nonsense! Nonsense! I did not know that he had any money."

"Be that as it may, Poffle thinks differently, and he is on his way to retrieve it by fair means or foul. They'll probably ransack your house — tear it apart — and will probably do the same to you. That's the message. Good day to you sir."

"Reverend to you!" spat Padlock.

But Padlock said it to the gusting gale, for Wladek had gone.

But not far. As soon as he was out of sight of Padlock he went across the field to his right and into a copse of mostly dead wood. It was extremely gloomy inside this wood and he was extremely grateful for the blazing taper in his hand. Though not a man of weak nerve, the wood startled Wladek. It was not merely the soughing in the trees that seemed to infest the place with all sorts of wispy and invisible presences; no, there was a solid aura about the place. He was glad when the rain started, and the patter of the deluge drowned out those unpleasant half-heard sounds that had been coming from all about him.

He was close to the edge of the copse, near to the vicarage, when he tripped over one of five upright stones, each perhaps two feet high. Wladek could not make out whether there was eroded writing upon them or whether it was just some veining and cracking in the rock.

He picked himself up and went to the ruin of a pigsty that stood half-in and half-out of the wood. There he found a dry corner, in which stood some ancient, rusty, but potentially useful garden tools, and watched the darkened vicarage.

For perhaps five minutes Wladek waited. Then the vicarage's side door opened, and a furtive figure crept out, darting from side to side. Padlock passed within five feet of the concealed Wladek, but he did not see him in the gloom. Watching, Wladek saw the miserly man of God scuttle to the middle of the stones, drop a dark object from his cape to the ground and begin to dig a hole. He worked quickly and quietly. In but a short time a hole was dug, into which Padlock dropped the dark object. He refilled the hole, covering traces of the excavation with dead leaves and wood. When he was done, he looked around the gloomy wood once more, then slunk off.

Wladek wasted no time, and as soon as Padlock was out of sight, he went hurriedly to the site that Padlock had so recently vacated, caring nothing for the clinging mulch that oozed down his clothes. His digging shortly revealed a stout chest, small but heavy, fastened with a mighty padlock.

"How appropriate!" he muttered as he crept out of the wood. It was difficult for Wladek to leave the wood, for he much wanted to see what happened when Poffle arrived; but caution was better than foolhardiness, he thought, and decided to establish a good distance between the crumbling vicarage and himself.

When Wladek was out of the wood, he did not strike across the highways of the land, but chose a more laborious route over the fields and hedges. After scrambling through thorny hedges, muddy fields and treacherous ditches, he found himself once more outside the Stanley Arms. Florinda Farrier appeared instantly, and threw her arms about him, despite his wet and muddy garments, and soon, clad in dry comfortable clothing, he was seated before the glowing fire of an upstairs room, drinking large measures of rum, affectionately served by the alluring and ever-attentive landlady. The contents of Padlock's chest were now safely stored in a room nearby.

* * *

Poffle called upon Padlock less than an hour after the departure of Wladek.

Peering through the grimy glass Padlock saw a number of hulking brutes, possibly a dozen, approaching the vicarage through the gloom. Their leader was rather smaller and weedier than his troops. The last light of the day glimmered upon his spectacles.

He strode up to the door and smote it with his small, pink, flabby fist.

"Open up! I know vat you are in ver. Open up before I am forced to break in."

"What do you want?" asked Padlock, knowing full well what the answer was.

"I have it on good aufority vat you have stolen my money. I demand vat you return it."

Padlock had rehearsed his reply. "Money? What would I know of money? How would I know that you had money? Besides, why should I lust for money sirrah? Doth not the Lord command us not to store up money and treasure on this earth, where the rust corrupts and the moth consumes? Money — what use have I for it? — Do I not look askance upon the frivolous pursuits of men and how they squander their wealth? No sirrah, I fear that you must look elsewhere for your errant riches."

As Padlock had no idea that Poffle was quite so gullible as to accept this statement as truth, he had prepared the second part of his speech and began delivering it, not knowing that Poffle was turning away.

"Of course, if you doubt my word — the word of an agent of the Lord — then you are quite at liberty to examine my humble abode and disabuse yourself of the fantasy about the situation of your wealth."

Poffle had expected that the mere sight of his little army would extract a terrified confession from Padlock; he had not expected this; he was quite bowled over. Entering the house, he failed to notice a grin of triumph across Padlock's face.

"Uh, can we do 'im over now?" asked one of the army.

"Silence! To work!" Poffle bleated.

The twelve (for Padlock's calculation had indeed been accurate) were thorough and no nook or cranny was missed in the search; they tore up ragged carpets, opened ramshackle cupboards and rotting chests; they banged on walls; they thrust heads up chimneys; they stumbled through dark cellars; they crawled through reeking attics — but all to no avail. One even suggested searching out of doors, but to Padlock's relief the idea was overruled.

"I told you. There is no money here."

"Bah! Ven it must have been ve uvvers."

"Who?"

"Vose uvver people who held me prisoner."

"Then you had best search them out sirrah."

"But I don't know where to look."

"I would strongly suspect that they will be holed up in Wladek's cottage."

"Do you mean vat he is in league wiv vem?"

"Oh yes, he seeks to bring down T'osh."

"But he is friendly to T'osh. He . . . he has always played ve part of his right-hand man. I cannot believe what you are saying."

"Please yourself."

"Ven he is a traitor, a double agent?"

"Near enough."

"Ven it was probably he who stole my money. I'll murder him. To fink vat I trusted him. I never liked him vough. He has always been a bit too clever for his own good. Well, I will deal wiv him. My small army will make short work of old peg leg himself and his comrades."

"Are you going right away?"

"Goodness no! We shall bed down here for ve night; it is far too inclement to venture outside. I trust vat you have some food in ve house. Where is my sister? Ah, here she is, bring us some food quickly or my guards will complain."

Harmony, who had said nothing, put on her most sullen expression and left the room, followed by John Ambler, his left hand bandaged with a piece of dirty and bloodied linen.

"I trust you have some wine here — don't worry if it is used in services — we will still drink it. Cheer up Reverend, no harm will befall you if you do as you are told — tee-hee!"

Poffle grinned. Padlock's porcelain features cracked into a frown.

Padlock foresaw problems. It would be in his own interests to have Poffle destroy Wladek, Martyn and the rest. But it would equally be in Poffle's interest to drag him before T'osh and have him accused of trying to murder T'osh, blowing up his statue, conspiring and so on. There was no reason why Poffle shouldn't have his cake and eat it — destroy Wladek and arrest Padlock.

Padlock closed his eyes and shuddered. It required a lot of thought . . .

Chapter 12:

The Set Up

The rain had ceased but black clouds still bounded over the sky, blotting out the frozen silver of the moon, driven by the fierce gust of a boreal gale. Bare branches and hunched bushes were twisted about. It was a night for sitting in inglenooks, hot negus[1] in hand staring at the ghosts made by the flames in the hearth, listening to the booming of the wind in the chimney.

The landscape was a checkerboard of black and silver to Wladek's eye as he forced his way through the gale. Close at hand were the whisperings of the soughing trees; then, hither and yon, the cries of the creatures of the night — stoats, badgers, foxes — going about their business; and, in the far distance, the howling of a pack of wild dogs baying at the moon? But what of the other sounds? Did the wind bring ineffable traces of an incessant wailing?

No matter, he thought, drawing into himself.

The money he was minding for T'osh, the cache of Poffle's wealth, the fortune he had obtained from Padlock — all were now safely ensconced in an upper room of the Stanley Arms.

---

[1] A hot drink of port and lemon juice, usually spiced and sweetened

It felt good.

Yet he realized that he could not blind himself to the risks and dangers his Machiavellian ploys had of necessity created. He knew that overconfidence and smug self-satisfaction would be the doom of him, for Padlock knew very well about his, Wladek's, part in the destruction of T'osh. Probably, no, certainly, Poffle would know of it now also, for Padlock would most certainly talk about everything just to get rid of Poffle and his cronies. Though Wladek was not certain of what Poffle's reaction to the whole thing would be, he felt sure that the noxious land-holder would either run screaming to T'osh with the entire story or would take it into his deranged head to mete out rough justice there and then and hare off after Wladek.

Padlock, Wladek felt sure, was a burnt-out case so far as he posed any risk to Wladek. At that moment he would probably be sick at the thought that Poffle would have in his hands enough information to damn him before T'osh. Padlock's moment of courage — or madness — would have evaporated any reserves of self-reliance he might have possessed and now he would tremble and cower, trying anything and everything to preserve his skin and bones. Or would he? There was, after all, the man's insane lust for power and his paranoid belief that he was a Mosaic prophet. For a moment Wladek began to change the factors in his mental equation of the situation — but no, he thought, Padlock's lust for power was a mere chimera; it would wilt beneath the arid glare of his self-preservation. Padlock would surely keep a low profile, creeping along, trying to find some cranny or slimy crevice where he could hide.

There seemed to be but one danger attendant upon Padlock; if public disaffection vis-a-vis T'osh should ever become really strong, then the populace might search blindly for a new leader — any leader, regardless of whatever personality flaws such a potential overlord might exhibit. That would have to be a time when Padlock would need to be silenced by whatever means necessary.

As usual there was a lot to think about.

* * *

Poffle was not an early riser by nature, thinking that the hours before the sun reached its zenith had been divinely appointed as times when the menial orders went about tasks that would have distressed Poffle's delicate constitution had he been a witness to them. On this morning he woke in the dank and grubby sheets of a strange bed. For moments a panicked dislocation of reality affected him, then he saw the armorial device of auriferous moneybags surrounded by crossed keys, argent, on the headboard and he was calmed; he was in Padlock's bed.

Feeling peeved, he said in a whine, "Breakfast, I want some."

No reply.

"Have you all gone deaf. I want somefing to eat — corned beef will do nicely."

The bedroom door was flung open and one of his cronies shambled in. "Gone," he said in a voice as dead as a firework in a deep pond.

"What on earf do you mean?"

"Gone. All gone. In the night."

Poffle sprang out of bed and hurried to where his henchmen were seated upon the rough floor staring at themselves in cloddish amazement.

For Padlock had been busy. Whilst the men snored in drunken stupor, he had removed their capes, hats, boots, what few possessions might have been in their pockets, leaving them only their stiff shirts and ragged trousers. Nor was that all: every removable object that could have barter value had been removed from the vicarage. What was more, Poffle noticed that one of the men had absented himself from the twelve disciples of Poffle.

"Where is your brover?"

"Brother? . . . brother?" asked the man addressed, as if he had been presented with an abstract philosophical concept and was struggling to make sense of it. "Yes, I have a brother," he continued as if this was only recently acquired information, "Noah is his name. Noah Halfmoon. He was here last night. Last night."

"Yes, I knew vat much already!" responded Poffle tetchily. "Where is he now? Is he still lurking in vis house?"

But he was there no longer. A search of the house and grounds failed to discover the missing man. The man addressed, who called himself Caleb, appeared to have no idea as to his brother's location. "'e goes his own way, 'e does," was his unilluminating conclusion to the discussion.

"Vis is a slight setback," said Poffle, still in high spirits. "We had a Judas in our very midst who may be intent on betraying us. But we must continue in our mission. First we must deal wiv vat Wladek fellow while we have ve advantage of surprise; ven we must track down Padlock and . . . murder him."

There were only moans from the peasants.

"Ven I shall see to it vat you are greatly rewarded. Your names will be mentioned to T'osh — over whom I have no small influence."

This seemed to lift their spirits, and they were raised to even higher levels when Poffle suggested that they should leave the vicarage in a state of even greater disarray than it was in already. Although their lack of footwear necessitated a circumspect gait, they fell to the work with much gusto, trashing everything that could be destroyed. Poffle found a battered tin of paraffin, the contents of which he splattered quite liberally over the wreckage. Soon the place was alight, and tongues of flame raced over the rotting beams and panelling. In minutes, the whole tinderbox was alight; only the crumbling stones did not burn, but even they cracked and puffed into glowing cinders. Standing before the baking heat, Poffle admitted to himself that he had not wished for "fings to go quite vis far," but he had to admit that the flames were quite pretty and was soon with the eleven rustics, performing a grotesque dance around the fire.

From a distance Noah Halfmoon lurked in the woodlands. He saw the flames burning brightly and felt a surge of envy sweep over him, for he loved a conflagration more than any man alive and was somewhat adept at orchestrating a good blaze himself. He briefly considered returning to the scene. But in his heart, he knew he had made the right decision in deserting the posse of thugs so hastily assembled by Poffle. He, Noah Halfmoon, knew that a superior pathway was open to him and that he would soon be upon it.

"Ex . . . act . . . ly," was the terminology he selected to express this conflicting sense of inner turmoil fused with the notion of deferred gratification.

* * *

Wladek rose early and roused his fellows sententiously: "Today we shall be attacked," he said.

"Bah! and pigs'll fly," muttered Frank from under his blanket, "we're safe here. Let me sleep."

Wladek stared at Frank, as if he were making a decision. He kicked Frank, "Get up you fool. I tell you that a mob of peasants will shortly be at our throats. We will fail if we attack them in the open and will have to revert to subterfuge."

He opened a greasy burlap sack from which tumbled a frilly shirt made up of strips of green, red and pink silk, a tall, floppy, yellow hat with a blue riband, and a ghastly pair of pink pantaloons.

"We must spring a trap; and a trap must, as you know, have a bait. This is the bait. We will hide in the trees that surround our abode save for one hero who will be situated at the front gate. Envision it! The ragamuffins hove into view, their minds bent upon spilling the blood of us all in the cottage, and what do they see? Why, this fantastical fellow — they will be so incensed by this flamboyant display of decadence that all they can think of is the destruction of Fran — er — the champion dressed in these clothes. That is the moment, when they transfer their anger, when they are struck mute with rage, that we strike from behind — we will smash them into the earth.

"And who will be dressed in these clothes? Where can we find a hero, a Charlemagne, one who will take the risks this desperate venture entails? I tell you this giant is in this very room."

All the while Wladek had been staring at Frank.

"No way! Oh no, not me. I refuse point blank to get into those clothes. Besides, what if something goes wrong and you don't get to them in time?"

"Fear not. I have planned a device that will ensure that you do not fall into the clutches—"

"The answer's still no."

"Will you get changed?"

"No!"

"GET CHANGED!"

"NO!"

"Are you refusing an order?"

"Yes."

Frank did not see the blow coming. But, like a tall tree in a hurricane, he plummeted to the ground.

* * *

When Frank crawled achingly to the periphery of consciousness his first thought was that someone had been using the top of his head as an atom-bomb testing ground. He felt nauseous, but the cold air calmed his stomach and he deduced he was in the open air someplace. But where? Slowly he opened his eyes — and quickly closed them again. He thought that he had been transported to another planet, so alien was the panorama. He seemed to be seated at a great height, looking over a series of red, purple and green fields set out in a strange patchwork. In the distance rose two hills, or ridges, of a shockingly pink colour. Where was he? Mars? Outside the solar system itself? He tried to move and found that he was constrained in some manner. Reflexively he opened his eyes and again that alien landscape was before him; but this time it quickly resolved itself into a microcosm of outlandish clothing which he was wearing, whilst the normal landscape stretched out before him, cold, still and utterly deserted.

The true nature of his plight returned to him in one shocking moment of realisation. Here he was, a Judas goat, bound and waiting for the tiger.

"You bastards! You can't do this to me. Let me free at once. Let me loose, I say."

The landscape stretched out before him, cold, still and utterly deserted.

Frank wailed in terror, struggling to free himself. Then came the sound of branches being moved aside.

"About time you came back. This stupid joke has gone on long— oh my God!"

A short figure came into the open and stared at Frank in unabashed amazement. He looked slug-like with his pallid, lardy skin, though his spectacles, glinting in the wan sunlight, gave his face a harder, more chitinous appearance. Other, bulkier, figures now came through the break, to stand in a dullard's version of consternation.

"Kill him!" squeaked Poffle. He and his henchmen, muttering withering oaths and curses, trotted to where Frank squirmed.

"It's not my fault! I didn't want to do this. I was set up for it. Don't harm me; I'm a brilliant artist. It'd be a great loss to the world were—"

A silvery, irregular shaped object described a high arc through the pellucid air, to bounce onto the earth some feet from the approaching assailants. For a few seconds nothing happened, then the device exploded, sending ribbons and billows of flame and smoke through the shattered air. The concussion threw Poffle's gang high into the air, though it seemed only to cause superficial injuries, and even Frank found himself buffeted by the fractured air.

Then, through the walls of smoke, Frank saw glimpses of Martyn, Timothy, Wladek and Cressida attacking the floored, erstwhile attackers; Martyn mercilessly smiting one with a stick of ash, all the while chanting, *"I'm making a stand for what I believe in."* Cressida, showing a side to her personality which had hitherto remained veiled, could be observed cruelly kicking Poffle in the groin, then rolling him through some whin and down to the frigid waters of a muddy ditch. Timothy forced two others, by dint of an iron rod, into a clump of gorse where, because of their barefoot condition, they leapt and hopped and whimpered. Meanwhile Wladek had availed himself of a stout walking stick which he used to trounce the burliest of the thugs.

"Kill them! Kill them!" shrieked Frank throughout the fray.

"No!" boomed Wladek, once the fight was over, "Killing them would serve no purpose. We have shown that we, though possessing less clout, by use of intelligence and courage, qualities that T'osh would breed out of the race if he could, can always beat mere brute strength."

He turned to the bedraggled peasants, "Learn this lesson well, you poor deluded fools; shout it from the housetops. The days of T'osh are numbered in this land.

"Drag yourselves back home — but remember that any found in future association with the Father of Lies shall die and die screaming for mercy and surcease from their agonies — and none shall there be found. Be thankful for your lives."

They slowly rose to their feet and limped off, muttering in pain and humiliation.

Wladek turned to a scurrying distant dot on the horizon. "There goes Poffle. Fear not, I have not forgotten the little worm." Without another word he strode off in pursuit.

"This is jolly!" said Cressida clapping her hands. "We must have a celebratory luncheon in honour of this—"

"No need," said Martyn.

"Don't trouble yourself on our account," said Timothy.

"What about me?" rasped Frank.

"Oh, I insist," trilled Cressida, skipping off into the cottage, strangely euphoric after engaging in physical combat.

"How about untying me, you bastards?"

"The thing is," said Frank as he was being released, "the thing is, what exactly was Poffle after? Why did he try this in the first place? And how come Wladek knew all about it? I think that there is more than meets the eye here."

"Isn't there always?" asked Timothy wearily.

"Wheels within wheels," said Martyn.

"Shut up," said Frank, making no attempt at eloquence whatsoever.

* * *

When Poffle reached his cottage, he was weak with his injuries and with sheer exhaustion. He was not an open person and preferred the knife in the back technique rather than some straight dealing. True, he did at times use naked force, but this was hired, and he was generally miles away when the explosion took place.

The humiliation at the hands of the weaklings, the rout of his troops, the injuries inflicted by that damned woman, the terrified flight from the pursuing nemesis of Wladek, all this had driven the slight-framed machinator of devious ploys into an ecstasy of terror.

But — perhaps due to some obscure imbalance of metabolism brought on by the unusual effort — now the terror was flowing away, sloughing off in rotting layers, leaving behind the fearful courage of a cornered rat. He knew that he stood no chance against Wladek, but he knew that he would not crawl — never!

*   *   *

Wladek kicked open the door. Poffle felt a moment's terror, and then the newfound courage replaced it. "What do you want?" he asked imperiously.

"I have come to ask a few questions."

"Have you now? Why should I answer?"

"It will be . . . easier — for you — if you do."

"Ask ven."

"I presume that you have visited Padlock in the recent past. What happened?"

"Yes, but he disappeared. But we burnt his place down. Tee-hee."

"All of them left the building?"

"Yes."

"Including your sister?"

"Vat is what I said."

"No matter — to you at any rate. For me, Padlock presents but a mere bagatelle. But now for you, what plans do you have?"

"Hah! I must see T'osh, to tell him about you, vat you are a foul traitor."

Wladek seized Poffle's scrawny neck. "Suppose I take steps to prevent this?" he asked, squeezing Poffle's throat.

"Are you mad? Take your hands off me! I'll see you swing from a yardarm for this. Get off!"

Wladek's grip tightened still further, but Poffle's cornered courage was still strong. "Are you deaf?" he squeaked, "You will be sacked. Who do you fink you are?"

Wladek released his hold, casting Poffle to the ground.

"Very good. Now get out of here," he croaked.

Wladek laughed as he reached forward and tweaked the glasses off Poffle's nose.

"Give me vose! I can hardly see wivout vem."

Poffle rose from the floor and, with outstretched arms tried to get to Wladek through the grey obscurity that had once been his room. He tripped over a pile of ancient books and fell to the floor once more.

"I want vem back," he wailed.

"Silence. Do you ever venture out of doors without these? Come, speak up."

"No, it would be too dangerous. Give me vem back I say, I say!"

"I think that I shall look after them for some time — the time it needs to overthrow T'osh. Tell you what, I'll give you them back then."

"Noooooooooooooooo," whinged Poffle, as he tried to catch the debatable blue that was Wladek, departing. He fell again and chipped a tooth on the hearthside. Reduced to crawling on all fours, he roamed the room wailing, weeping and shrieking, "I'll murder him! Two-faced traitorous misanfrope! I'll murder him!"

*   *   *

It could never be said of Padlock that he was a good planner. True, if the chance of money came his way, he would grab it with both hands, but this was purely reflexive and no more part of the higher functions than removing one's hand from a flame. Any later explanations of why he did this or that was pure rationalisation meant to deflect anyone from the — true — supposition that all of his life, every single aspect, was devoted to the acquisition of money of any kind.

So it was that when the trio of the vicarage crept away from their recumbent captors, they had no plan as to what they should do once they had put a safe distance between their loutish guests and themselves.

It was a nightmare journey of damp meadows, punishing winds and a grim awareness of lack of sleep.

Well past midnight, with the gibbous moon on the wane towards the horizon, Padlock saw the dark mounds of the ruins of an old church; surely there would be some sheltered corner.

There was not. Whether it was deflection of the winds by the trees that surrounded the ruins, or whether it was some form of Divine Malice did not bother Padlock; all he knew was that every ruined wall and corner seemed singled out for an icy blast. In the end, picking one place at random, he crouched against the masonry.

The others did not appear enthusiastic at the choice of site; but they lacked the intelligence and the energy to argue.

When they were all hunched together, Padlock said, "Here, this is what we will do; as this was my excellent idea, I think that I am entitled to the collection of expropriated cloaks. They will ensure that I, your leader, will get a good night's sleep. Thank-you."

He grabbed the garments and wrapped himself so thoroughly within them that not one particle of his alabaster complexion glimmered in the moonlight. Soon this bundle of rage was emitting a noise midway 'twixt that of a rheumatic donkey and that of a starving hyena. Perceiving that their leader had entered the Gates of Horn, the others began a cold, miserable and sleepless vigil waiting for the dawn.

Sometimes during the small hours, Ambler, his hand still wrapped in the same filthy bandage, began to emit a keening wail that the wind wafted into the chill woods. Harmony either ignored these sounds or failed to hear them at all; she was staring fixedly at the mound beneath which her darling snored.

"Even whilst sleeping he carries with him the aura of saintliness," she whispered softly to Ambler. Ambler, who had just noticed that his damaged hand had turned bright green, could have been excused for not answering.

*   *   *

Harmony raised her head to salute the bright sky into which the sun had recently arrived. To her right crouched the moaning Ambler; to her left, now with shining head exposed, lay her beloved, still sleeping. Every few seconds he would produce strange sounds that set his entire skeletal frame a-shiver. Miss Poffle sat with gaze transfixed at this charismatic, saintly figure, he who had chosen to forego all worldly pleasures and lead a life of strict asceticism, his only trappings those needful for his authority.

"A pity he cannot cultivate the taste for a good woman," she sighed to herself, for she had begun to realise that all her efforts to gain the love and devotion of this man were in vain. Her love went unrequited, for Padlock's world had no room for women; they were to be despised or, if they served some useful purpose, merely to be ignored.

Miss Poffle's musings were suddenly interrupted by the appearance of a figure from out of the trees. Dressed in bottle green garments except for cowhide shoes, he presented a spectacular and not slightly malignant figure. In height, he was in no ways remarkable, but in width he was a source of wonderment; he seemed designed for a planet of greater gravity than the earth, so squat and stocky was he; his shoulders were as broad as oxen yokes, the girth of his body seemed that of an oak tree, his thighs were bigger than the body of such as Padlock. But it was his face that excited most alarm, with its beetling brow, gleaming piggy eyes, blob of a nose, sneering twisted lip, surrounded by curls of metallic hair, supported by a massive neck of corded veins and knotted muscle. One arm was injured and hung in a sling, the other carried a gleaming knife, flecked with specs of rust which, upon closer inspection turned out not to be rust (Harmony did not like to speculate on what the flecks actually were). The injured arm, together with other bandages and a general stiffness of movement suggested most strongly that he had recently been in a fight.

"Wha'r' ya doin' 'ere?" the man asked in a breath that reeked sourly of stale beer.

Harmony answered for them all; "We are harmless and destitute and were simply using this place as a shelter for the night. We mean no harm whatsoever."

"That's as maybe, but I'm appointed guard of this sacred place and have right to kill all who trespass."

"Oh, you needn't be bothering yourself about us; we're just leaving."

"Aaaah," he sighed, running his finger along the blade of his knife, "But I like to draw blood now 'n' again, 'specially now that I happen to be on the lookout for some bastards who got the better of me not long ago."

"But we meant no harm. We will leave directly."

"But how do I know you are not one of those who are trying to overthrow our leader?"

"No! Not us! We are as loyal as any."

"Prove it,"

"You will just have to take my word for it, my good fellow. Anyway, I do not believe that I will listen to any more of this nonsense. Come, we will be away directly."

The man had stopped listening to Harmony. He was looking at the huddled figure of Ambler. "You! Weren't you the peasant whose house T'osh lived in?"

"Him? Nonsense! You must be mistaken."

"No, I ain't, lady; I never forget a face." He prodded Ambler. "He's a deserter, and you and him'll have to come with me and explain all this to the *Father of Us All* himself. Gather up your rags and come with me." So saying, he kicked the bundle of rags.

The bundle of rags gave an ear-piercing wail and out tumbled Padlock in a frightful rage. "Have you no decency, you lumpkin? Are you a barbarian? Are you so low that you could kick a saintly man of the cloth?"

"Yes."

"Then your soul will be consigned to eternal damnation and hellfire I fear."

The man seemed unimpressed by this portentous notification. He studied the ranting clergyman, trying to remember where he had seen him before.

"Any that try to do me harm should do well to be wary of such an act, for the Lord doth protect his own, and the Lord's punishment upon that sinner will be seven and seventy times greater than the original sin. Take heed, I say! Any who try to attack me, then their offending member will be paralysed; any who think ill of my works or of myself, then shall the Lord make them blind. Thou art the enemy of the Lord and he shall wreak vengeance upon your wretched head. Thou shalt wither and rot. The coldness that will spread upwards from thy feet, deny it though you will, this coldness will mean that you—"

"SHUT UP!"

"Thou shalt beg those around thy festering body to remove the demons that torment it. Yet even death will not give you a release, for there in the flames and brimstone—"

"SHUT UP YOU BALLBAGGED, BOLLOCK-BRAINED, PORNOGRAPHIC BASTARD! I know where I've seen you before. In Ormskirk, just before the statue of our leader was blown up, you were skulking around the place with something under your arm. Well, you've got a lot of explaining to do my lad. I imagine that T'osh'll love to examine your innards and drape them over the walls — whether he's used anaesthetic

250

will depend on how cooperative you are with your confession. Come on, all of you!"

Padlock calculated the odds, then commanded his followers, "Get him!"

Harmony went for the man's throat, grasping it as best she could with both her hands. The surprise of the assault, plus Harmony's weight, bore both of them to the ground. Though one of the man's arms was useless, Harmony would surely have been gutted by the knife in the man's good arm had not Ambler joined in the fray, stamping on the man's wrist till he let go of the knife, then kicking him all over, opening old wounds as well as causing fresh injuries. Harmony freed herself, then kicked him savagely in the head. The man went limp.

Padlock came out of the safety of the wall (behind which he had taken shelter when the fight began) and searched through the man's pockets, finding only a few copper coins, which he quickly transferred to his pocket.

He bit his lip in consternation.

"We'd better beat it," said Ambler, "He might have friends who'll be won'drin' what's 'appened to him."

"Quite so, servant; do you presume to think that I had not already thought of that? Quickly then, strip him of his garments; we will exchange them for some provender."

They fell to the task, leaving the still-breathing, softly-moaning thug with just a few scraps of ragged undergarments to protect him from the harsh wind.

"Good. Now as I see it, Poffle and his men will be long gone from the vicarage by now and it will be quite safe to return there. That is what we shall do."

The others were not sure of the worth of this plan, but as Padlock was already marching off, they had little choice but to gather up the garments and follow.

The return to the vicarage was done in silence. Both Padlock's 'lover' and his servant, having had no sleep the night before, now sank into a torpor, and Padlock seemed lost in thought.

He was brought out of this contemplation as they entered the field next to the trees that circled the vicarage. He smelt the tang of burnt wood in the air. Looking up, he saw a smudge of brown smoke in the trees. The significance of this did not strike him at first, but then his companions were woken by a shriek and the sight of their master racing over the fields, wailing,

"*The Lord have mercy on us. What have they done?*"

Tearing through the wood. Padlock ignored the brambles that caught at his trousers, the low branches that slapped his face, and all too soon his maniac running brought him to the still smouldering ruins of his vicarage.

"By the beard of Moses, I will bring terrible justice upon the animals who enacted this atrocity."

At least, he thought to himself, my treasure is still safe.

"You," he said, when his companions caught up with him, "search through the ashes, see if you can find anything of value. I am off into the woods to pray for comfort and the eternal damnation of that demon Poffle."

*   *   *

Inside the wood Padlock calmed himself. True, any loss of revenue was a major disaster, but at least the bulk of his fortune was safe, buried near the stone, safe within the soil. Making sure that he was not seen, and that his companions were busy, he went to where he had buried his loot.

The upturned soil told its own story.

With a wail of utter despair, he cast himself to the ground and began digging in the loose soil with both hands, like a dog in search of a bone. A frantic search quickly revealed that his wealth was gone.

"All is gone. All is lost. What foul hearted demon could have done this to me?"

He put his head in his muddy hands and wept and wept and wept.

Chapter 13:

Philosophies

Martyn was endeavouring to sew a patch on his worn-out jeans; Timothy was oiling and polishing the shotgun; Cressida was writing a poem; Frank was working on his novel; Wladek was reading a dusty tome written in a foreign language; all was quiet in the cottage apart from the crackles and hisses from the coal fire in the grate, in whose ashes some potatoes were baking, a late snack for the company.

"I wonder," said Timothy at last, "what has become of our friend Padlock." Martyn, seeing the hopelessness of his attempted resurrection of his beloved jeans, put down the ancient cloth and replied, "It wouldn't surprise me to find that he has decided to cut his losses and . . . well . . . just bugger off."

Timothy thought this over. "I doubt it, somehow. Our erstwhile comrade's fanaticism provides him with sufficient courage — or foolhardiness — to venture into the most unpleasant of environments. You must remember he thinks God's on his side; this gives him enough nerve to forget his inherent spinelessness, if he feels he's on a crusade against evil. I doubt very much if we have seen the last of him or his cronies."

"His lust for gold shouldn't be forgotten either," added Martyn.

"That is certainly true," said Wladek, looking up from his book. "That reprobate will stop at nothing if there is the possibility of monetary gain in the wind. 'Tis a pity in many ways that we did not make him kiss the clod ere now."

"I nearly did," said Frank.

"And failed," muttered Timothy.

"I tried! —Which is more than can be said for the rest of you."

Frank studied the floor. "No matter. My cause was just; and if a second chance should ever come my way, well, then I shall surely shatter that shining head into a thousand shards. And that deed would surely have already been done but for that wretched sister of Poffle and his other accomplice."

"Enough of this bickering," said Timothy, "I am sure that this creature is still lurking in the vicinity of his dilapidated vicarage and I greatly fear that we will hear from him again — and this before long."

* * *

Cressida had been listening to this conversation, for she had been halted in the composition of her poem by her failure to find a rhyme for the word scissors — a task that Tennyson himself had failed in. For a moment, she thought of something relevant to say; but realising that this was not her forte, said,

"What that man needs is to be enlightened in certain fundamental truths, for he surely walks in darkness as a man bereft of his lantern. Were he to be a Buddhist, he would realise that suffering, sickness, and poverty are inescapable parts of the Wheel of Life.

"Allow me to relate — one of the tales of Prince Gautama, the Sakyamuni, the Buddha himself. He was the son of a wealthy rajah, and he grew up surrounded by opulence: even as a young man such things as poverty or disease were not part of his experience. Then, one day, as he was riding to the royal park, he came across an aged and wrinkled old man, a loathsome sick man, and a dead man."

"A dead man? It sounds a bit random. Why hadn't they buried him?"

"How should I know, Frank? Really, you are very trying sometimes. Anyway, it's beside the point.

"Well, Gautama, being a Hindu and believing in reincarnation, began to wonder how anyone could escape from this eternal cycle of misery and suffering which did not end even in death, for death was the gateway to being reborn and enduring another life of misery."

"That's easily solved," said Timothy, "bribe God to ensure that you're reborn as a prince, or give all this rubbish up and become a follower of Calvin, the jocular funster."

"Don't be so facet— faceic— don't try to be clever. May I continue?"

"—"

"Thank-you. When he was twenty-nine, he left his wife and children to seek an answer to this question. He cut off his hair, put on the saffron robe, took up his begging bowl and joined a couple of monks. Two years later he was no nearer the answer so, with his companions, he began to fast, hoping that this would put a keener edge upon his meditations. For six years he lived on but one grain of rice a day—"

"Hold on," said Martyn. "This can't be true."

"Why not? Surely you do not doubt the word of *The Buddha*?"

"One grain of rice a day! For six years! You try it for six days and see what happens. What about water?"

"Pah! I should have expected such a response from you bunch of unenlightened failures. I'm wasting my time — but don't let it worry you: the Buddhist faith will be none the poorer for lacking the membership of such as yourselves."

"One grain of rice," echoed Timothy.

"For six years," scorned Frank.

Cressida assumed what she fondly believed to be a thinking position and ignored the world.

A knock was heard at the door.

* * *

The place stank. John Ambler was somewhere in the ruins of the vicarage, searching for anything of value; Harmony Poffle could not see him, but could see the glow of his lantern on one of the scorched walls. Harmony had started to search for valuables some time before; but the effort and the stench of the fire's aftermath had quickly changed her mind about the wisdom of the enterprise. Now she stood on the edge of the trees.

Unseen, Ambler shrieked: his hand was troubling him.

"Come away from there, you clod," commanded Harmony, "you'll find nothing of value. Come away, I say."

Ambler approached her. She became conscious of a sound emanating from the depths of the gloomy wood. She felt that she had been hearing it for some time, but had ignored it, putting it down to some obscure cause; possibly the cry of an animal or bird — her ignorance in such matters was great — as it was generally.

"Ambler, do you hear it? What is it?"

"Dunno."

"By the Lord Harry, what is it?" gasped Harmony, for the cry had increased in volume until the woods rang with its strident ululation of despair and horror. It sounded like the cry a canonical saint would make when shown the gates of hell as the reward of his life's work.

Thoughts of her beloved swain being in danger came to her now frenzied mind. "What are you doing there, standing like a dressmaker's dummy? Don't you know that my cherished Pedaiah might be in peril?"

* * *

They found him; face down in the forest's mulch, his muddied hands deep in a small pit. Seeing him thus, Harmony thought him to be in a somewhat serious condition. "Dead," she croaked, falling in a swoon.

* * *

Brought back to consciousness by a sleek and well-fed rat running over her head, Harmony saw that the spark of life had not been extinguished in her beloved. Ambler was ministering to him; he had seated his master on the bole of a fallen tree and was dutifully removing as much filth from the clergyman as could be achieved, given the pitiful state of his hand.

The Reverend Lock looked ghastly, with his porcelain features a terrible grey, his eyes unfocused; his whole appearance was that of a man who had suffered some shock that had temporally unseated his reason.

"My gold," he mumbled, "my gold . . . gone . . . all gone . . . my gold, gone, gone, gone, gone . . . all gone . . . stolen, stolen from me . . . from me . . . MY GOLD" – (here Ambler had to restrain his suddenly violent master) – "gone . . . gone . . . gone . . . gone, gone gonegonegone . . . ruined . . ."

"My darling," said Harmony, "my cinnamon, my honeysuckle, tells me what wrong has been done to you, my fair. I will kill him or her who did this to you. What happened? What is this talk of gold?"

At the mention of gold something resembling the Padlock of old took up residence behind his cold eyes.

"It has always been my heart's desire to go upon a pilgrimage, and I had saved a small — *small*, mark you — amount of gold over the years. I hid it here when Poffle and his gang of hobbledehoys came, for safety's sake. But now it is gone. Who could have taken it?"

"Who else knew of the gold?"

"No one."

"Then someone must have seen you bury it."

"Impossible, I took great pains to make sure there were no witnesses. After Wladek left—"

It seemed as if a thunderbolt had struck him. As thoughts of the visit of Wladek and his strange warning came back to him, Padlock leaped off the bole, standing rigid in the lamplight. So great was his fury that some colour ran into his cheeks.

"WLADEK THE THIEF!" shrieked Padlock to the ebony sky. The other two thought — for a moment — that their leader had lost his marbles.

Turning to them, they could see that there was a feverish glint in Padlock's eye and his face had set in an ugly rictus of frenzied determination.

"We must waste no time. The time is for action. My enemies had best tremble in their beds, for the Lord's vengeance has come.

"Now, we will find somewhere for us to live. Next, you, Ambler, will go into Ormskirk with what possessions we have, to trade them for provender. Then we will seek out Wladek, kill him slowly, retrieve MY GOLD.

"Then we will deal with T'osh: we have waited too long already. I have some intelligence of a secret weapon in the possession of Wladek; this we will obtain and then we shall shortly become unquestioned rulers in this land. There is much to do and no time to waste — come!"

* * *

The little band wandered for many hours until the sky began to lighten in the east. Outlined against the paling sky was Harmony's brother's cottage. Impishly she suggested that they see if the place was empty or not, and, if so, they should commandeer the place. Ambler did not like the idea; but Padlock did not veto the plan, for he was deep in prayer — or rather curses — against the vast number of his enemies, and so did not care for worldly matters at that juncture.

Certainly the ground floor had the air of dereliction, with almost all the furniture turned over. Ambler still did not like it, so Harmony, in irritation, sent Ambler to search the upper floors.

The already nervous Ambler was further discomfited by the state of the upper rooms, which, especially in the thin light, seemed to have been designed and furnished in the school of architecture best described as haunted house. Perhaps the poisons in his bloodstream from his wounded and infected hand were another causative factor. Whatever, Ambler was already highly agitated when he heard certain unpleasantly suggestive sounds coming from the next room. Soft paddings, gentle bumps; something large and boneless was in there.

Trembling, he crept silently to the door — and shrieked as he saw a pallid undefinable creature, fully five and a half feet, blindly weaving its monstrous form towards him. (It was of course Poffle, stripped to the waist and wearing white pyjama trousers, blindly groping his way to the bathroom — but then, the light was bad . . . and it was Poffle after all.)

Padlock was drawn out of his reverie by this frantic shriek close to his ear; it came from a terrified Ambler.

"Speak, sirrah."

"Ga— ga—ga—"

"Out with it—"

"Up there! Up there! Oh, leave this place. Sir, leave it now."

"Up there? What is up there?"

"A monster, master; an 'orrible monster. Move, or we're doomed."

"Quite so. Come."

And so they left.

* * *

It will have been noticed that Padlock was not a credulous man; or rather, it will have been noted that Padlock was not a credulous man except where his own lunacies were concerned. Had Ambler said that the upper floor was given over to, on the left side, offices of the KGB, and on the right side, to offices of the CIA, then Padlock would have been suitably sceptical and would have, in all probability, asked where Ambler had stashed the gin bottle, but Padlock was a firm believer in Yahweh, a smiting God, vindictive and cruel, and that he, Padlock was God's right hand. Since Poffle's visit to the vicarage the main subject of the prayer/curses had been Poffle himself, so when Ambler saw a monster on the second floor Padlock was not unduly surprised. Either the monster was Poffle after he had felt the vengeance of the Lord, or it had been dispatched by the Lord to do unpleasant things to Poffle. Either way, Padlock did not wish to stay to find out.

Proceeding down the road, they came to the cottage where Cressida and Timothy had once resided.

"'Orrible monster, 'orrible monster," moaned Ambler.

"Shut up, you maggot."

"'Orrible monster."

"This residence shall do quite nicely."

"'Orrible monster."

"Harmony, quiet the dolt."

"Arrrrrrrgh."

"Well done. You are but a woman, yet you have your uses."

The house was deserted.

"Just as I thought," said Padlock, "the cowards have completely abandoned the place. It will do us well as a vantage point. All our cloddish enemies are within easy reach, and, if we do not make our presence obvious, none shall know that we are here. A masterly stroke of genius, I would say. Now, let us make ourselves at home, and make use of the wine which, I suspect, remains here about."

Padlock searched the house in the manner of an inquisitive rodent. He found some seven bottles of wine. These he carried to the front room where, jealously guarding the others, he applied his long and dexterous fingers, thin like pallid spiders' legs, to uncork the bottle in his hand. His long, pointed nose circumscribed the opening of the bottle many times.

"Aaahhhh, this is no refined vintage, but will it provide, my comrades, suitable requirements to my needs."

He gulped down a huge draught of the wine.

"I would have thought your ascetic lifestyle would necessitate the exclusion of alcohol. After all, it just about excludes every other pleasure of the flesh." The last Harmony added rather ruefully.

"*Drink no longer water, but use a little wine for thy stomach's sake and thine often infirmities: First letter of Timothy, chapter 5, verse 23,*" recited Padlock.

" '*For the love of money is the root of all evil: which while some coveted after, they have erred from the faith, and pierced themselves through with many sorrows:' First Letter of Timothy, chapter 6, verse 10,*" said John Ambler, but nobody heard him.

Padlock took another mighty drink. His eyes glazed over.

"Ma'am, do you suppose that I enjoy the consumption of these beverages? Well, I can tell you truthfully that I abhor them; I loathe and detest every mouthful — every sordid . . . repugnant mouthful. My whole frame cries out to be . . . to be liberated from these subtle and insidious poisons. Do you know why I drink? Upstarts will say that I like the stuff — pish! Every burning mouthful reminds my soul of another place that is burning, a place where the fires will never go out. I see my eternal misery unless I walk the paths of rectitude. A man who knows of perdition and damnation will steer his ship to the havens of eternal salvation."

"But surely the money spent on alcohol could be better used. Surely the money you spend on drink could be given to the hungry poor, or some such charitable cause?"

"I have yet to spend a single farthing upon alcohol: what I drink is given to me by the Lord so that I may be saved. As for the poor . . . if the Lord wanted them to have money he would have done so; he has not given them money; therefore, he does not want them to have money; thus, my argument. As it is, they must use their abilities, such as they are, to better their lot as best they can, although obviously they should not seek common cause with their fellow men by joining evil organisations, such as trade unions for example. Anything else would be a most shocking violation of the will of the Lord. But having said this, I must point out that the Lord provides. Look at Ambler; he is a poor man, he may lack ability, yet the Lord has seen fit to provide him with vast reserves of health and strength."

Ambler, who was examining the somewhat necrotic condition of his injured hand, merely snivelled. Harmony continued,

"Let me get this straight. Poor people are poor because they lack the initiative to be otherwise."

"True enough."

"They lack resourcefulness and energy."

"Then what of their children?"

"Inheritance. We have been through this before."

"Yes, but I was reminded of something that Timothy said when I was a prisoner: he said that environment plays an important part in determining what a person may or may not become."

"Absolute balderdash."

"I thought so too."

"I feel like being amused by the specious arguments of the fool. Tell me more of what he said."

"Well . . . he said something about the brotherhood of mankind. Yes, that was it; that each individual might have different talents, but all had equal rights, and all should, so far as is possible, have equal opportunities."

"Simplistic fairy stories," said Padlock, starting on the second bottle.

"I know that, Pedaiah, but how could I argue such things to the unenlightened masses?"

"I see." Padlock drank some of the wine, then thought deeply of how best Harmony could promulgate his beliefs — certainties, he corrected himself. Padlock was under no illusions about Harmony. She was a pretty good bouncer but was apparently limited in the mentality department. As she was a member of the female of the species, she was *per se* inferior anyway. Padlock knew that as a man, his extremely logical and chronological thought processes were unattainable to those unfortunate enough to have been born women.

When Padlock began to speak, he did so as if he was addressing an auditorium.

*   *   *

When Sir Francis Galton promulgated his theory of eugenics in the 19th century, he would doubtless have shuddered to think that so obvious a madman as the Reverend Pedaiah Lock would have blindly grasped at the idea.

A common and very substantial criticism of eugenics is that it inevitably leads to measures that are unethical. Firstly, who says what the intended goal should be; secondly, how is this achieved.

Padlock of course had the answer; firstly, Padlock; secondly by any and every means he saw fit. His utopia was being spread out before Harmony, a ghastly landscape made up of mismatching and broken parts of *Plato's Republic* and Huxley's *Brave New World*.

"The Spanish American colonies succeeded in enticing those men who were possessed of courage, enterprise and intellect. As these people left, the mediocre were the only ones left behind, and therefore Spain went into a decline that continues to this present day.

"Unfortunately, the colonists failed to bring their best women with them, being content to mate with the lowly Indian women; the result was a hybrid race lacking in vigour and potency."

"Is this true when whenever people of different races — er — wed?"

Padlock was a textbook case of repressed feelings of inferiority. As such he showed the classic response of vilifying anything that dared to be even slightly different from him. Since racial characteristics are, more or less, the first port of call for such dolts, Padlock had long been a believer in the superiority of races. His was the best (naturally), and he fancied his race to be the Aryan race — despite the fact that the term Aryan refers to a language group and not an ethnic group[1]. Accordingly, his reply was no surprise.

"Generally, the crossing of races nearly related in stock, such as English and the Scandinavians, tends to make for a healthier, adaptable and capable type; whereas crossings between widely differing stock, such as ahem . . . darker peoples . . . that is to say . . . ahem . . . black and white-skinned people certainly tends to produce a much weaker progeny, both physically and mentally."

"There would seem to be truth in what you say."

"It is indisputable; only misguided fools would suggest otherwise. Let me just mention in passing that noble group of men and women under Miles Standish, the Pilgrim Fathers. Escaping from religious persecution, they founded their colony in America. They were willing to undergo unheard of dangers and suffer terrible privations for their beliefs. It naturally follows that the loss of their germ plasm was a serious blow for England. She has still to recover some of these qualities.

"As a direct result of the Pilgrim Fathers America has imposed a limiting quota on the number of immigrants, this to maintain the quality of the national germ plasm, so that it is not deleted by an unwholesome admixture

---

[1] Even in ancient times, the idea of being an "Aryan" was religious, cultural and linguistic, not racial

with that of African or southern European stocks. Of course, such people, inferior as they are, provide an excellent base for cheap labour, and there are a number let in each year for such a purpose. Naturally there is little fear that there be any actual mixing of plasm between the two strata, but the racial characteristics of these lesser races predisposes them to be feckless and lawless pseudo-citizens of limited ability who require continual and extravagant state monitoring. This is not the source of the state's ultimate strength."

"Yes, but how—"

"In the great war, the voluntary enlistment which was maintained in the early years of that conflict meant that the best of best racial types, the ones upon whose shoulders the future and prosperity of the nation depends, were enticed abroad, killed; thereby their collective worth was lost to the state — and to the future, for the majority of these men had not sired fine stock from their loins. Yea, the gold of that generation was lost. Those who remained were all too frequently plodders and idlers, lacking in innovative skills and preferring to rely on collective rather than individual approaches to improve their lot. Most of those who joined trade unions would almost certainly have belonged to this dismal cluster."

"'Appen," said Ambler, whose hand had stopped aching for the time-being, "but could it not be that it were them as were daft enough to go off straight and got killed, while the ones with a head on their shoulders became objectors or stayed away from the frontline for as long as possible?

"Also, now I've got a chance to speak, I reckon as to these people who reckon others to be stupid are just trying to make themselves big in their own eyes and trying to explain why they treat people as slurry."

For a moment Padlock was too amazed to speak. A sneer crossed his lips. "One could expect no more sophisticated opinion from a common labourer, a blockhead, such as yourself. I suggest you read some books ere you care to tilt at your betters."

"Can't read too well."

"Just as I thought."

*   *   *

The day dragged on, Padlock's lunatic notions hanging like a cloud of afflatus over the cottage. At length even Padlock grew weary of his own voice, though naturally believing every word of his rabid utterances and rarely wasting an opportunity to denounce organised labour in any form, as this was clearly most abhorrent to him, for reasons unexplained. Ever one to delegate tasks, he commanded Miss Poffle to gather food, of some sort, from somewhere or other and make some kind of meal, one way or the other: logistics was most certainly not the Reverend's forte.

Thinking about it, he could not definitely remember when last he ate, though it must have been at some time in the past month, else he would have been considerably closer to the grave by now. His frame, which at the best of times could only be generously called underweight, was now even more emaciated than usual, so that he looked more like an aid to an anatomist giving a lecture than a living human being.

"I will do my best to get you food."

"You will do at least your best, ma'am. Now, you, Ambler, go take yourself off to Ormskirk and barter those items provided by Poffle and his men. Be practical, else 'twill be the worse for you."

"Yes Master."

"And don't spend all your time in bookshops."

Padlock's isolated attempts at humour rarely gained any sort of reaction. This was no exception.

*   *   *

There are certain sorts of days that, by some subtly wielded magic, the scenery and the weather drive out feelings of depression. This day was one of them, a pearl of a day for the time of year, and one redolent of the nascent year.

However, all was gloom so far as John Ambler was concerned; there are some sloughs of desponds that hold too firmly for the day to drive out all darkness.

Padlock's command that he be as speedy as possible ignored, Ambler detoured to visit his cottage; he might find surcease from his sorrows there.

Entering the break of trees that fronted his home, his depression lifted. But this was merely because fear and apprehension had replaced it. Every movement, every sound might bode the presence of the *'ounds of 'ell*, but, after a few nervous moments, he reached the glade in which lay his cottage.

Coming to it from the south, he saw only the featureless back wall, but felt that something was amiss. He noted a dead silence hanging in the still air, the air which still smelt faintly of . . . what? Coming to the front of the cottage he did not at first notice anything wrong — a man will detect a small change but miss the large — but was at the front door when he remembered about some guttering he had meant to do — had his wife done the repairs since he left? She had not, but he also saw that there was no roof to the cottage, only a few charred spars. No reaction. He tried to open the front door but discovered that he no longer had a front door; only the hinges, melted out of shape, remained. Still no reaction. Through the architrave in which the door had stood he could see that the cottage was a fire-blackened shell, with all his possessions lying ruined amid the char on the ground.

His mind now took in and collated the three impressions, and the enormity of what had happened struck him. Wailing he fell to the grass. He wept.

"It's 'im, I know it is. T'osh did this. Curse 'im. 'Im as brought us nowt but pain and sorrow. Nothing but pain, sorrow and death. Damn 'im."

"Where on earth 'ave you been?"

Ambler turned in amazement as he heard his wife, Adaline's voice. He embraced her and, after many mutual pledges of undying devotion, she told her tale.

*   *   *

Shortly after Ambler had left T'osh had finally discovered the loss of the dagger. It was not known just how highly T'osh revered the dagger, but his paranoid and megalomaniac reaction to the loss indicated that he esteemed it most highly. He had cursed Wladek, Quartus Poffle and Arthur, his burly henchman. T'osh had long been known to help along his own curses with bits of executive action of his own, so that it was no surprise when Arthur had been found bloodied and bested, covered with gashes and lacerations: everybody had assumed that T'osh had done it.

However, when news of the beating reached T'osh he was not at all pleased; he fell screaming to the floor where he writhed and shrieked for upwards of an hour, hurling obscenities and imprecations to his listeners, gabbling on about a plot to undermine his regime. T'osh was not known for his consistency or lack of erratic episodes, but this was of such a grotesque nature that Adaline Ambler had fled in terror, not returning until sunset, when the cottage was still burning. Though upset at this, she was so pleased that T'osh seemed to have gone that the loss of her home was small ale indeed.

Ambler then related his tale, concluding, "But as for 'im, Padlock," — here he spat, "but as for 'im, I don't care owt. 'E's just as bad as T'osh. I thought 'e were good a' first, but now 'e's as bad as T'osh. This be no time for the likes of us, an' 'e be no good for us, lass: 'e just sponges off the likes of us. If I meets 'im again, I'm like to drive a blade through that bugger's 'ead. All 'e cares about is money; I crippled meself savin' 'is life, but 'e don't care if I live or die."

Adaline agreed that he seemed like a nasty man but thought that plans for the more immediate future were of more importance, for, as far as she knew, when T'osh had left he had not taken the *'ounds of 'ell* with him.

At a safer locale they discussed their plans. Ambler had decided to keep the goods Padlock had given him to barter as payment in lieu of his seemingly eternally deferred wages. But where to stay now that the cottage was destroyed?

"John — those people that you spoke of."

"That Wladek man, aye; and Mart . . . think that were 'is name; . . . an' one called . . . Frank. . . aye . . . that were it."

"Why not go to them?"

"Aye, happen they might take us in. Seems they're decent people; they'll take us in — 'specially since we got summat on the Black Wizard for'm. An' I think I know where they can be found."

*   *   *

And so, they plodded their way over the fields in the thick crepuscular light. Ambler thought to himself that it was a year almost to the day that T'osh had finally recovered from his wounds. He knew exactly what he would do if he was given the second chance and have T'osh, weak from loss of blood, come to his door again: it involved sharp knives and the completion of a partially done job of decapitation.

It always comes to this, he thought, trudging over a muddy field, weak with hunger and injury, motivated only by a burning determination. At any twilight he could have been found here, but before T'osh, night had only been a prelude to the following day; now it was when the foul things crawled out of their burrows. He had always been tired after a day's work, always been hungry, but there had been a cottage to come home to, a meal on the table, and the work had been to some purpose: it kept them in food, warmth and comfort, with enough to put away for the luxuries, even if those luxuries consisted of a week at Blackpool once a year and enough money to pay the repairman when their ancient television set went through one of its traumatic patches. Now, all had gone. There was no hope; the work was as arduous as ever, the profits less, the luxuries nil, the danger ever-present, the hope a commodity as tangible as fog. And *that* was the worst; the total lack of hope, to be in a guarded enclave commanded by lunatics was bad enough; to be in the same enclave with the same leaders for ever and ever was unbearable.

As they went their way, listening to the whoops, howls and croaks of creatures it would have been wise to avoid, Ambler thought of the other unclean creatures whose paths had crossed with his. T'osh, ranting and screaming, thumping his thigh, twisting his lips, spittle flying through the air, shrieking that he was going to throw Ambler to the hounds. There was Padlock, pale and emaciated, yet bloated with distending gasses of self-importance and arrogance. There was Arthur, brutish, mindless and cruel, with all the humanitarian instincts of a hungry tyrannosaur.

"I'll get even," he muttered as he went to the lighted cottage and knocked.

*   *   *

Padlock and Harmony sat before an inadequate fire, which spluttered spasmodically in the dusty grate. Harmony was lucky that she had even this much fire, since her Reverend had forbidden fires in the 'summer' months (February to November). She poked the fire with little hope of achieving anything.

Padlock was still drinking wine, thinking about his lost riches, and, most of all, the sacred dagger. From time to time a heavy tear would run down his gleaming cheek to splatter in the dust.

Harmony too was deep in thought; she too was contemplating a loss, a turn in the wheel that had cast her from the heights to this sinkhole of despair. It seemed such a short time since she was a proud schoolmistress, fearing none, feared by many; and now, in days, she had been debased to destitution, hunger, cold and damp. Her heart had gone out to one who cared little for such things — and oh! that was the worst. She rubbed her hands over her hefty stomach, but this did little to assuage the pangs of hunger; she knew of no nostrum or panacea for the pangs in her heart. A tear rolled down her adipose cheek, plopping in the same dust as her beloved Padlock's had also fallen.

"Where can that dolt have got to?" whined Padlock. "Where can he have gone? Ambler, that illiterate dullard, that agrarian lack-wit, that bloodstained boy, that whoreson rogue, that red-haired rambler, that plough-pushing poltroon. Where is he?"

"I'm sure I don't know."

"I do: he's made off with my property."

"The stolen stuff?"

"Rightfully expropriated, ma'am. He's struck out on his own, like as not."

"What will you do?"

"Why, kill him of course."

"No — I mean, like now. What are we going to do for food?"

"You think too much of matters of the flesh."

"I'm hungry."

"Mortification is good for you. Think of that whilst I drink my wine. You may fetch me my Bible. I'm sure the Good Book has many useful things to say on such matters."

"Doesn't it say something about being fruitful and going forth and multiplying?"

"?"

"You know, every 'man and woman must have children; their duty, as it were."

"?"

"Oh, never mind! I'll fetch your . . . Bible."

Chapter 14:

When Wind is in the Trees

Martyn stared at the fire, at the potatoes baking in the hot ash. He was warm and comfortable and not a little sleepy. The room's homeliness and security, together with the pleasing prospect of tea and jacket potatoes had lulled him into a state of torpor. So deep was this sense of safety that Martyn, who had started off composing a protest song about the ills suffered by the American Indians, was now working on a song telling of the delights of boiled potatoes, boiled cabbage and boiled bacon.

Someone knocked on the front door.

This did not revive Martyn though, for all he knew, the magician himself could be knocking, but sent him yet further into his barren realms of meditation. An event could not be an event for Martyn: it had to be an auger or avatar of something mystical or profound. A pitiful fact was kidnapped out of context and in the confines of Martyn's mind had all sorts of grotesque accretions and additions piled onto it until it turned turtle, capsized by its own superstructure.

Thus, when the sane procedure would have been to answer the door, Martyn ascribed to the sound of the knock a pitiful air, as if the knocker was begging rather than demanding an answer. The second knock seemed to him to be even less hopeful, as if the caller was losing both strength and hope. There was no third knock; instead there was the rustle of something collapsing down the door and a sound, neither scream nor gasp, from a female throat.

Heaven only knows what volumes might have been thought by Martyn as to these last sounds had he not been jerked awake by Wladek's rough shaking.

"'Tis best if you answer the door."

"But it might be enemies," wailed white-faced Cressida, picking up a robust blackthorn stick which stood in the corner. Her *ready for action* stance did seem somewhat at odds with her professed enthusiasm for a nonviolent approach.

"I don't give a half-boiled, decomposing carrot. I'm not waiting here any longer," said Martyn, confused, and unwittingly, letting his aggressiveness master him.

What he found confused him still further. There, on the doorstep, was a crumpled bundle over which crouched a woman. She looked up at Martyn with pleading eyes.

"Help us, please help us — we need your kindness. We are fleeing both Pedaiah Lock and the Magician himself."

Martyn continued to gaze blankly.

"Please, help my husband and me. If you do, I will tell all we know of the Magician and his works."

The rough shaking and pummelling of Wladek finally waked Martyn into action.

"Why are you standing there, you fool? Is it not before your eyes that John Ambler needs aid? Come in woman. Help me with her husband Martyn."

They brought the exhausted form of Ambler into the main room and laid it on a couch which they put before the fire. Oddly enough, Frank said that he had just had an inspiration for his novel and the muse required immediate attention. Cressida was at least ingenuous about it: when the slightly green Frank left the room she glanced at Ambler, at the filth, at the blood, at the suppurating hand, and said that really it was a liberty that such people should trouble decent people with sights that could only induce nausea and vomiting — really, why couldn't they do it elsewhere?

With the departure of Frank and Cressida, the rest took to themselves the task of laying and easing Ambler. Wladek mixed up a strange brew, of which a potent white spirit seemed to be the main ingredient, and made Ambler drink it, saying not only would it set him back on the road to health but would lengthen that road by many a mile.

With John Ambler at rest in a deep, healing sleep, Adaline Ambler, fortified with the baked potatoes, which they were all eating now, told her tale fully and succinctly, pausing only now and again when a question was asked, or some clarification was needed. They increased knowledge greatly by this talk, even though Mrs Ambler's knowledge was mainly second-hand and fragmentary. Still, they had this much already; what new wonders would be cast before their feet when John recovered?

* * *

Frank, driven from the main room by the sight of gore, could not sleep for, like it or not, and at this late hour he did not, the muse had indeed come knocking — or if not a muse, whatever impelled Frank to type on thousands of sheets of paper millions of words describing nothing, and even that nothing was described badly and obscurely.

But at length he forced himself from his bed to the writing desk and began to work: *aut insanit horno aut versus facit* [1] — or, possibly, both.

He looked at the pile of completed papers and began to feel better. Soon the work might be finished, a masterpiece, developing brilliantly the ideas of dos Passos, Borges, Kafka, but most certainly not of Joyce.

Blood On Mud

behold lectears here befare your very eyes magickshone trick of napes jack will see — Si — what goes on off insidle yon head of Knarf – for it is a wisely wisdomful head not fill of lead or bread or things in a shed. Nay not at all for the brain of Knarf is deeper than the deepest sea and taller than the tallest tree – indeedly deedly dee.

Ozymandias trick: circumstances chances merry dances dancers go on off without change of money and the conductor would not let me get on the bus it to where and why should I bother to where the coach goes merry pipers on the green turf where I will rot and fester and be no more of me no more gone without making his mark on the state world what have I done

[1] *Horace Quintus Flaccus: "Either the man is crazy, or he's writing poetry".*

that I should think of it cancel it out better look at the leaf
that fall brown leaf that fall like we to grave wrinkled like
an old mans face old man ready to go down into the
floor and down down down he must fall through the
flawed bored and down to the very foundation garments.

Damn

I cannot go on much longer

$$I will \quad sn—ap$$

$$into \quad v \ e \ r \ y \ s \ m \ a \ l \ l \ bits$$

$$b \quad u \quad t$$

$$sur ely$$

there is hope
for such   as   myself   to end

oppression where it is at its most oppressive think of
what you have been through damn them all if you can't
get revenge then vengeance for the whole world
flames skin melting in the flames suburbs melting in
the flames the flames the flames the crackling of wood
the stink of smoke the screams the screams of the
damned the screams of those who are now having the
foretaste of the flames of hell that await us all for all
eternity oh I can feel the agony of them all the pain the
pain is in my head my ………… head my head hellfire
the pain it's getting…………… worse

my god how long did that last thank god, it's going
now the

throbbing
shaking
aching
forsaken
quaking

281

pulsating
ticking
like a very
large
time
bomb

bang it cannot be but it is coming towards me my god
the glass the blood the agony but it's him Rekaorc free
damn his smoking but alive and next to me free alive
vengeance for his blood no need no need him free but
how was no he could not have but how is he here not
dead am I mad I must think of this think but have I time
to think must

I act?
but
but

I have it where is Nivek Reckaorc is here but Nivek
where could he be?

*does Nivek exist do you do perhaps we simply
imagined his existence reality doesn't exist but*

Think on this, gentle reader, I am God and I created
the world five minutes ago, with all your memories
intact. Sleep well.

. . . but . . . tub . . . but
backwards my thoughts run backwards
sdrawkcab nur sthguoht ym sdrawkcab
my soul
supposing

that a trees branches grew into the earth that a stone
defied gravity's law that an apple exploded that blood
was blue that death came before birth that rain burned
that the sun came

f
a
l
l
i
n
g
from the sky

oh, Rekaorc why does your blood flow backwards in your veins my head is still . . . my brain is being . . . strangled by . . . my thoughts are being strangled by that yellow dandelion walk to the dandelion, pick it up. pluck it. I pull it to pieces but I know no peace

I kill it.

oh Rekaorc I am here to save you from the ruin of time that flows backward drink deep of me and you will have your salvation eat this dandelion and your blood will once more flow forwards here eat it the roots as well you have been saved and so is mine for I can see clearly now that I must learn to be very careful wherever there are yellow dandelions lurking in the vicinity because they try to stop me from thinking and plotting my explosion my watch it cannot lie yet I see that time is flying dying all about and I do nothing nothing but I remember now that the pain is gone that Nivek will be at the church tower create an explosion, come Rekaorc dance with me dance to the tune of the piper me dance that I may see the exhibition of the wheels of time

I pick up at stone. I throw it at Rekoarc. I see him dance wildly, manically, frantically. I throw more stones. I think Rekoarc is good except for the blood in his veins that flows in the wrong direction. Why? I see no

dandelions. I cast more stones. I see Nivek. I think good. I see Nivek look puzzled. We have everything and nothing or nobody is going to stop us from setting the world on fire everyth—but wait I chance to glance at the sky while Rekaorc's dance pounds into my brain
I suddenly realise that the clouds are
turning purple the colour of the robes
of Caesar . . . what does it mean? If
I think that I am changing
and — I'm becoming a lar
ge green and yellow
caterpillar or
so it seem
s to m
e o
h

There came a time when even Frank grew confused as to what exactly was going on in the novel; accordingly, he ceased typing and decided to await the return of his deranged muse before carrying on with any further 'creativity'. As he looked up from his desk he was surprised to see how dark it was, the only light coming from a sun that had already set, yet still lit the western sky with a weakening light. He lit a candle, and in its guttering glow noticed for the first time the decorations on the walls.

The cottage had once been occupied by one of Padlock's more fanatic parishioners, a man who realised that he could not spend his entire life in a church, and so had decided to make his home as like a chapel as possible. He had started his task in this very room, but he had not gotten far with it, having fallen from a

Frank worked feverishly on his novel

stepladder during the course of his labour. At least this was what had been posited when, three months after the event, the desiccated corpse had been found, its skull smashed open.

The magnum opus, that the fanatic had been engaged upon when he met his end, was a mural showing Lucifer being cast from Heaven. Little more than a rough sketch had been completed, but some detail had been lavished upon the face of Lucifer, twisted in unimaginable agony. The completed mural, opposite the first, had been done in the same primitive hand, though a hand that undoubtedly owned much raw power, and this too showed an unhealthy awareness of too much pain. In it, Abel was lying in a cornfield, blood pouring from where his left eye should have been and where remained only a red crater. Somehow the artist had successfully suggested that the victim was alive, though dying, and writhing in agony. In the middle ground was the retreating figure of Cain, holding Abel's bloodied sickle. His face was more than half turned away, but the artist had somehow inputted a hint of devilish delight on Cain's face. And, oddest of all, there seemed to be some unidentifiable figure crouched malevolently in the scrub to the right of the picture. In all, disturbing.

Frank shuddered and turned away, finding little solace in the crepuscular sky.

That damned clergyman! he thought, the memory of his incessant ranting is a keening pain to me. Damn him! I should have killed him — time will show that I was justified; I should have blown his brains out — bag of bones! Blast him!

*   *   *

Though outwardly having no truck with superstition, Padlock was awash in a sea of pseudo-religious twaddle. At this moment he was holding a closed, worn-out Bible, its horizontal spine resting on the top of the table. He closed his eyes and released his grip on the Bible, which fell open at random. His eyes were still closed as he picked a random sentence with his forefinger. Opening his eyes, he read the chosen passage. As he did his unwholesome face lit up with glee.

"I was right: it worked! The *Lord* has allowed it to pass that the scales should drop from His servant's eyes so, that I can read this guiding passage. Job 7, verses IV - VI:

When shall I arise, and the night be gone? And I am full of tossing to and fro until the dawning of the day? My flesh is clothed with worms and clods of dust. My skin is broken and become loathsome. My days are swifter than the weaver's shuttle, and are spent without hope.

"I thank you, *Lord*, that you have shown me the way. I have it: where didst Jonah go but into the belly of the whale? Did not Daniel enter the lion's den? I must strike at the heart of the enemy and drive out the legions of hell that I find there. I must away at once, ere the sands of time diminish the power of my hand and make it weak.

"*Hast thou entered into the treasuries of the snow? Or hast thou seen the treasures of the hall, which I have reserved against the times of trouble? By what way is the light parted which scattereth the east winds upon the earth?*"

* * *

Padlock was by now violently agitated, a condition that his starved metabolism could not long endure. Still, when he burned he blazed. He threw himself up, knocking the chair and table to the floor. He staggered around the room like a drunken man, preaching gibberish in his singsong whine.

> *"Who hath devised a watercourse for the*
> *overflowing waters?*
> *Who put a way for the lightning of thunders? To*
> *cause it to rain on the earth where no man is*
> *To satisfy the desolate and waste ground.*
> *The face of the deep is frozen,*
> *But I shall rise to venture forth*
> *To seek my sacred dagger;*
> *And when I raise my hand, I shall rule Ormskirk."*

Miss Harmony Poffle's repose was somewhat unusually cut short.

"Wake up, woman, chattel of mine, sluggard. Arise: The Lord's work remains outstanding; we must away ere the candle burns too low."

"Ngg!"

"Hath thou perceived the breadth of the earth? Declare if thou knowest all?"

"What's going on?"

"Who can number the clouds in wisdom?"

"Are you mad?"

"Canst thou bind the unicorn with the band in his furrow?"

"Tell me this moment what you are doing."

"Or will he harrow the valleys after you?"

Harmony gave up; she had seen him in moods like this before and knew that no sense would be forthcoming from the Reverend until his erratic energies had burnt themselves out. Sighing, she bade farewell to sleep for the night, dressed, and followed her adored.

Though, later on, clouds covered the moon, the first part of the journey was carried out in brilliant moonlight. There was no doubt that Pedaiah knew where he was going, and there was likewise little doubt that for some unknown reason he was eschewing conventional roads, travelling instead through fields, over hedges, and at least twice along the base of a ditch. At first this was quite exciting, but the mud and the thorns and the nettles soon tarnished the adventures' brightness. Nor was it helped by Pedaiah's extempore squeaking:

> *"All hail, the Reverent Pedaiah Lock!*
> *Who is so good and wise:*
> *Righting wicked evil:*
> *Punishing wicked lies*
> *He never walks in fear*
> *All angers he will face;*
> *And enemies are banished,*
> *To vanish without trace."*

Miss Poffle said nothing, venting her fury on the weather, which seemed to be brewing up a storm. Though he was becoming more and more volatile, Harmony still felt a deep affection for Pedaiah, and viewed the trek as an adventure still. It was like a crusade, she thought vapidly, with Pedaiah well suited in his role as Peter the Hermit. As well as the ecclesiastical overtones, there were the more Gothic elements of a moon-drenched landscape too austere for the more insipid form of romance, but one ably fit to encompass the wider meaning of the word; momentarily she expected to see a Rhine castle appear behind the trees, all turrets and windows like glazed eyes.

Behind the party, stumbling along at a distance of about forty or fifty metres, Noah Halfmoon listened and watched in wonderment. His eyes glowed with the fanaticism of the true convert. His brow was furrowed in concentration as he sought to accurately articulate his emotions. Eventually he located the vocabulary which best mirrored his state of mind.

"Ex . . . act . . . ly," he mumbled repeatedly.

Now the rags of cloud were scudding over the moon, and more substantial clouds were behind, grumbling with ill-contained thunder.

A wind arose, making the trees whisper and twisting Pedaiah's frayed clothes. To Harmony his aspect was wild, a character out of some *sturm und drang* romance.

Then the illusion was shattered; at the same time as large drops of rain began to hiss about them, Pedaiah began to sing again.

> *"Onwards march the soldiers,*
> *Facing mortal danger*
> *Fearing not the wicked hand of an evil stranger:*
> *For as the Lord is on our side,*
> *We can but conquer all.*
> *God bless the Reverend Pedaiah Lock,*
> *Who shall—"*

He stopped in mid-sentence, for he had seen a light flicker behind some writhing trees.

"Forward, my merry men. Food and drink await us, there, at the blessed spot that the *Lord* has seen fit to reveal to us. Some crazed fools will say that it is but an oil lamp, yet they are blind and will not list—"

He stopped his harangue, for Harmony was far ahead, racing for whatever shelter that solitary light could provide.

At that point in time, miles above the wet earth of Ormskirk, there was beginning a process that would have some effect on the climax of the matter of the eradication of the Magician and would be talked about for years. Below, spring was burgeoning, and the storm that was drenching Ormskirk was normal for the time of year, but three great gusts in the jet stream seven miles above the air did not know that. They had braided themselves in such a way that they now dipped down to a height only several thousand feet above the earth. They would shortly return to their chill heights, but for the moment, air, travelling at three hundred miles an hour and with a temperature below that of an Antarctic storm, hovered and mixed with the low storm clouds.

As Harmony sped towards the light, she felt the temperature plummet, until breathing became painful and her skin could be felt cracking. She saw a puddle freeze over; one minute, no, one moment, it was liquid, then — presto! — it was ice. She saw frost form on the trees and race over the ground like a time-lapse film of fungi's progress. She felt the rain change into bullets of hail; then stop. Then come again as a snow storm of such severity that she would have disbelieved any account of it had she not witnessed it; it was a complete white-out, the light was lost to view — even the shrub to the left of her by perhaps five feet disappeared.

"Pedaiah beloved: Here I am!" But she could see nothing. Then a chill, thin hand grasped hers.

"Do not be faint hearted; have faith in the *Lord*." Without another word, he guided her along. Idly she noted that his face was hard to see in the snow, so pallid was it, then wondered how she could see his face at all, since the moon was hidden.

Two steps further and her puzzlement was solved, for she could plainly see the brilliantly lit facade of the Stanley Arms, one of whose rear windows must have provided the light they had seen.

Padlock tried to knock stoutly on the door, but his energies had all been spent, so that all he achieved was a feeble scratching. Harmony gently shoved him aside and thumped the door.

The door opened slightly and Florinda Farrier, the landlady, looked out. She seemed astonished at Pedaiah's appearance — as well she might, for an icicle now depended from his sharp nose.

"We are two travellers, weary, hungry and very cold. We go about the *Lord's* business. Have you rooms and food for us for the night?"

The landlady let them in. She thought that she had seen the man before, reasonably recently and in different context. She was going to give the matter thought but the routine of running the hostelry tossed it from her mind.

The jet-stream winds had now ascended again, but the snow would fall for many hours yet, leaving a blanket so deep that the sun would not be able to clear it away for several days; certainly not before the day of the Dark Festival.

Noah Halfmoon did not seek to enter the tavern. He located a low building in the grounds, possibly once a pigsty, and, after locating a very ancient and long discarded garment and a small heap of mouldy hay, lay in one corner shivering as the snow piled up outside, eventually covering the building entirely and affording some slight, if begrudging, respite from the cold. He resisted the overwhelming desire to deploy his expertise as a notorious arsonist to kindle a few flames from the hay, sensing that this would not be a shrewd move at this point in the proceedings. Although the term *deferred gratification* was alien to his vocabulary there was a primitive understanding that if he bided his time for the moment his day of glory would come soon enough, one way or another.

* * *

Frank was still cursing Padlock when he entered the main room of the cottage to discover that Ambler had recovered and was now being questioned by all the members of the company, save Cressida, who was nowhere to be seen.

"What is puzzling me," said Wladek, "is the matter of the dagger. True I can see that they both want it for themselves because of their natures and their systems of belief. But both want it for more than that; they seem to think that it is somehow decisive in the struggle."

"Stories, masters, stories. 'im as 'as it, will rule, and will by right of law. The people'll back 'im who 'as the dagger, no matter who 'e is."

"Ah, I see," said Wladek, "in some ways the Magician has been his worst enemy. He has heightened the superstition of the people to such an extent that they will back whoever has the dagger. T'osh must wish to show the dagger at the Dark Festival; if he does, then his power is secure, but if it chances that someone else shows the dagger, then he is just as securely overthrown. Go on, tell us more of the Dagger of Ormr."

"The dagger . . . 'im as 'as it rules the people an' 'as just right to do so. Course none's seen the dagger in recent years, but all knows of it, and all knows the tales . . . the tale. . ."

"This story must have some truth in it," opined Timothy, "I recognise many of the names involved."

"Pointless fairy tale. Pish and tush! Nonsense!" The voice from the doorway warned those present that Frank had abandoned his novel for the time being.

Timothy, with an effort, refused to be goaded; Martyn did react. In a voice of infinite politeness, he said: "There is no such thing as a pointless fairy tale: every legend, folktale, even nursery rhyme has some point, either moral or historical. Surely you, as a writer, must know this."

"As a writer I am aware of the fact that there is a great deal of rubbish in print."

"And a damn sight more yet to get into print," said Timothy with an airy wave of his arm in the general direction of the room Frank had just vacated.

"Silence yourselves!" commanded Wladek. "We have more important things to do than indulge ourselves in pointless verbal orotundity. Ambler, let me get this straight: Padlock had the dagger?"

"Well, I never saw it, but 'e kept on singin an' rantin' 'bart it, so I guess he had it."

"Do you have any idea when it was lost?"

"When we saw vic'rage burning down, we, me an' schoolmarm, we saw 'im lying' in this little grave, like, weepin' and sobbin' fit to burst. Said that 'is gold was gone, so I reckon that's when dagger went, with the gold."

"I see," said Wladek, then he leaned back in his chair and assumed a thoughtful look.

"I maintain," said Martyn, "that many of the legends and old tales do have some basis in the truth."

"Ha! Show me your pixies, show me your gnomes, goblins, elves and Billy Goats Gruff," retorted Frank.

"Are you being deliberately difficult? Okay, let's take a literary example. Gulliver's Travels: on the surface it's a fantasy, but look below the surface and what do you get? A savage satire of the times. I'm quite sure that some aspects of your works can be looked at in this light."

"Mmm . . . perhaps." He paused for a moment, then addressed Ambler on a totally different subject. "Would it be true to say that you have made the best of yourself?"

"Eh? 'Ow do ye mean?"

"Do you never feel the need to concern yourself with matters of intellectual and academic interest? Take Joyce for example: have you never felt the need to acquaint yourself with any of his works; for instance, Finnegan's Wake?"

Martyn and Timothy exchanged puzzled glances; Ambler said: "No. Can't really read very well."

"Surely man, you have been to school."

"After a fashion. Generally my father kept me away to 'elp on farm, 'n' when I were in school, marm just beat me all the time."

"But these are feeble excuses! Had the ability and the will been there, surely you would have overcome such trivial setbacks."

"Perhaps, but ye just listen to me, Mr Crafty: in diff'rent circumstances I'd 'a' conquered them differences a damn sight easier. An' bein' flogged an' made to stand int' yard for hours as punishment for gettin' a few sums wrong didn't help me much. Maybe I'm just simple—"

"Surely," simpered Frank.

"Maybe I'm simple, but it do seem funny that some people who live in Ormskirk's posh parts always do better than thems that don't!"

There was silence then, a silence only broken by Wladek donning his heavy coat and opening the front door to the howling snowstorm.

"I have some business to venture," he said, closing the door.

The company sat in mute surprise.

Chapter 15:

On a Knife-edge

As the snow fell about the inn, Harmony Poffle was shovelling a huge meal into her ample abdominal. Her beloved had merely picked at a potato but had drunk an entire bottle of elderflower wine; this latter quantity had been necessary to take the chill off his pale bones, or so he maintained. It had also made him loquacious.

"Why?" asked Harmony, mindless of the gobbets of food churning in her mouth, "Why exactly have we come to this dreary place, and on such a night as this?"

"It is simply a matter of ideology tempered with pragmatism."

"Eh?" said Harmony, inwardly bracing herself for an onslaught of quotes from Ezekiel or some such.

"To begin, this is where it all began; or, to put the matter more nicely to the point, the place where I entered the grand scheme of things, as it were. On reflection, perhaps I should rephrase that preceding sentence. This is where I grandly entered the scheme of things.

"Here, but scant months ago, I was introduced to certain characters who in turn brought me to that first encounter with the Black Magician. My destiny became clear at that point. I came to know — with the *Lord's* help of course — that I must one day come to rule this land and lead its sinful people into the arms of God. The people here were but small catalysts in bringing about my eventual succession to the throne of T'osh. Ah . . . though they are most certainly bound for the eternal fires of damnation, yet I feel some small — very small — gratitude to them, even though they are probably members of a left-wing group such as a trade union, organisations which are ungodly and despicable.

"So, you see why it is, that to this inn we must repair, in order to see our plot through. I feel confident that certain developments will take place shortly."

Harmony was by no means sure that she knew what Pedaiah was talking about. This was no novelty; what was unusual was the smile of triumph that crossed Pedaiah's face, making it seem venal and stupid even to her, when she could see no reason for the smile.

"Ma'am, I know that you are but a woman and needs must prattle on about trivial matters. Knowing this, I have shown great leniency and have let you talk on, consciously thinking of worthier matters but letting each and every word, foolish though they almost all were, sink in. Now Ma'am, think back to some days ago, when you were talking about your brother."

"Quartus? Yes."

"Now can you recall what you were saying about Wladek — that swine — when he worked for your brother."

"Yes, I said that Quartus thought well of Wladek; he was a good worker, his only fault lying in the fact that he seemed to spend more time in the public house, this very one in fact, than he did tilling the fields. But I—"

"What you have said is quite sufficient. Now cast your mind back a few weeks to when you were speaking about your visits to Ormskirk, and you mentioned that you once saw Wladek there."

"Yes, he was with the manageress of this pub, and there seemed to be a disturbing amount of physical contact between the two. I had no doubt that there was some sort of clandestine relationship between the pair, I can tell you. I have no doubt you would have been scandalised by the display of wantonness."

"Now you understand why we are here tonight."

"No . . . I don't."

"Oh Ma'am, I realise that, as a woman, you are significantly inferior to me, yet surely you can see why we have come to this place."

"No."

"No matter, then. Come, let's to bed."

"Yes, let's," she said with undisguised enthusiasm, her very recent condemnation of wantonness having been forgotten.

"I have the key to my room; this is the key to yours."

"Oh!" she said with unconcealed disappointment.

*   *   *

Despite the chill of the room Harmony was soon asleep. Padlock did not even attempt to sleep, but lay fully clothed upon his hard bed, thinking up interminable sermons, though all the time his ears were pricked.

At last there came the sounds that told him the inn was now shut for the night. Shortly afterwards he heard the landlady climb the stairs and enter the bedroom, the one directly below Padlock's room.

Padlock had earlier surveyed the rooms of the first floor and had found little of interest, save a few copper coins that had been dropped down cracks. There were, apart from storage cupboards and the like, four rooms. These too he searched, then made his way up to the third floor. The rooms were derelict and were of no interest to him; the door to the attic was, for, apart from the stout and aged lock on the door, four new and well-oiled padlocks had been added.

The Reverend Pedaiah Lock had long thanked his fierce and merciless God that he had been born into a family that had a relative like his uncle Jedidiah Pencewyse. He had been both a blacksmith and a locksmith in his day, and he counted himself the world's expert on padlocks. He was not that anymore, not merely because he had been in the earth for seven years, but mainly because, prompted by his uncle's teachings, Padlock had far surpassed the knowledge of his mentor.

Bending to the locks, he pulled out lengths of ductile wire from his shabby clothes, and in less than five minutes the padlocks lay unlocked upon the damp linoleum.

The main lock presented more problems, since the tumblers of the lock were far too heavy to yield to the ministrations of his wire. Still, he had all night, and there were more ways than one to skin a cat. He noticed immediately that the lock was nothing special, presumably fixed there when some previous owner had something of not too great a value in the attic. It was not possible for him to disengage the tongue of the lock with the plastic card he kept for such a purpose, but he saw that the lock's fixer had made the incredible error of screwing on the lock with the heads on Padlock's side of the door.

It was hard work, for the screws resisted their extraction, but at last a delighted and exhausted Padlock saw the entire lock fall to the ground with an unnoticed clatter.

Painfully he rose to his feet — and found that the door was jammed, resisting his feeble attempts to open it. Whimpering, he descended to Harmony's room and abruptly awoke her. Quickly she dressed and followed her love, who showed her the problem. She applied her substantial shoulder to the door, which then shivered into fragments.

The attic was in complete darkness, but Padlock thrilled to a faint intimation that he had achieved his goal. His pallid fingers were nervous, making them look like intertwining maggots, as he pulled a candle from his jacket, lit it, and held it high as he entered the attic.

At first Padlock's brain could not register what was in the room. Then he realised what the brightly shining objects were. Falling to the floor in shock, he stared at the mounds of coin, the pyramids of gold and silver; the lines of ornament and jewellery that everywhere filled this Golconda. His own box of valuables seemed paltry compared to some of the objects that lay adjacent to it.

His own box! Frantically he fumbled at the clasps, then dug through the coins and pelf until he held again the sacred dagger. He possessed it again and hid it close to his cold and bony chest.

Padlock's mouth felt dry; his eyes burned; he had never seen so much wealth before; he could have gladly remained in this room until the last trump echoed.

"Look, we can't stay here forever, we must get away while the going is good, taking what we can."

Harmony stood behind Padlock, wearing her outdoor clothes and holding Padlock's moth-eaten duffle coat.

The thought of leaving some of this wealth had not occurred to Padlock, and when it did, it was total anathema; he felt that his heart would break if so much as one insubstantial mote of silver remained in the room. A feeling of frantic urgency swept over him. He ran his hands through his few hairs.

"No, no, no," he gabbled, "we cannot leave all this, no, no, no, no, we can get a horse and cart, load it up, take it all, yes, yes, that's what we'll do, won't take long, yes—"

"Don't be stupid, Pedaiah. Where is your horse? Where is your cart? It's going to be bad enough getting away from this place as it is."

"Nononononononononono, I cannot leave all this, I must take all of it, ALL of it, *ALL OF IT.*" He looked to the rafters of the roof. "*Lord*, oh *Lord* do not desert me now, show me the way."

"Don't be ridiculous, we cannot take it all and that is that."

"We must try. The *Lord* has shown me a way."
"How?"

"We must carry the *whole* of the wealth out through your bedroom window, hide it, then, when it is safe to do so, we must—"

Padlock's ravings were cut short when someone knocked on the front door. The knock was distinctive . . . and familiar: three heavy knocks, a pause, two heavy knocks, a pause, one very heavy knock.

Padlock fell to the ground, assuming the foetal position. Through the thumb stuck firmly in his mouth, he whimpered: "It's him, oh it's him, Wladek. What am I to do? He'll kill me, He'll kill me."

Harmony slapped Padlock hard; this seemed to bring him back to reasonable calmness.

"Look," she said, "I take it that you've got the dagger. Ok, now all we can do is carry away as much as we are able."

They fell to this, putting coins and pelf wherever they could upon their person. Padlock even filled his boots with coin and was busily overcrowding Harmony's already amply filled bra with jewellery when even he decided that they could stay no longer. They fled down to Harmony's room, thankful that the room had a stout bolt upon its door. Thus, temporally secure, they began to knot together sheets and blankets.

*　　*　　*

Wladek and Florinda Farrier were ascending the first flight of stairs.

". . . it being such a bad night we haven't had much custom. Oh yes, we did get some rather odd travellers, the two who are staying the night. They're harmless enough—"

Wladek stiffened; they had ascended the second flight of stairs, and Wladek stared up the stairwell. "God," he gasped, then sped up the final flight.

He stood outside the attic, almost speechless with fury. Finally he turned to Florinda.

"These travellers . . . "

The landlady fidgeted in discomfort. "One was . . . a woman, bit on the large side. Pink-cheeked."

"The other — was he like a skeleton? Nose like a knife?"

"Yes — how did—?"

"I'll kill him."

Wladek and the landlady went to the second floor.

"Where are their rooms?"

"One had that room, the one with the open door; she had that room there."

"Stand aside!" he said, charging the door. Wresting it from its hinges, he was carried headlong into the room. One of its windows was open, trailing a rope of sheets that ended at the snow.

"Damn! Not only do I have to contend with T'osh, I've got to worry about that lunatic. And he's got the dagger, and he's got some money now. Cack and shite!"

*　*　*

The snow continued to fall all that night, ceasing only when dawn tinted the landscape. Even in the most sheltered parts it lay several feet deep; in exposed places it was twelve feet deep — and there had been little drifting, for the gusting wind had suddenly died towards midnight. It would take days to melt, and there might be flooding.

Still, it gave a tranquil appearance to Melling and Maghull, and a gentle one to Ormskirk, where it covered the bloodstains that daily stank on the streets.

*　*　*

Lord of the Universe, Potentate of Potentates, Binder of Demons, Controller of Devils, His Serene Thaumaturge T'osh was in his headquarters, the old Magistrate's building. Hulking toadies, who stood around dully, staring at nothing, saying nothing, surrounded him. There were also a few quislings of some intelligence and no ethics. These were the ones who counselled, as much as he could be counselled, T'osh. It was a lucrative post, but also a dangerous one; more than one of the rotting heads that periodically adorned the spikes around the parish church had belonged to counsellors who had said the wrong thing — or even the right thing.

The fawner who was speaking now to T'osh seemed close to utter panic, as if wondering what the view from the parish church might be like. "Your majesty, I have to inform you that at no point in time have you been so unpopular, nor have the populace been so restless as now."

"Indeed! Think you I do not know this, that you ply my ears with platitudes? Of course I know this, but it will all be different once the Dark Festival is over. Then, the populace will be mine."

"But if something should happen before the festival is over—"

"Contain your childish fears, dolt, nothing will happen, nothing can happen. You!"

"Me, your greatness?" asked a second quisling.

"Indeeeeeeeeeeeeeeeed, who did you think I meant? How has the task I set you progressed?"

The quisling licked his lips. "Your eminence, I regret . . . to inform you that no progress has been made."

"You always say this to me — why? Is it not enough that an object of some slight value has been stolen from me — is that not enough to set you upon the course whereby you regain this object?"

"Master, I did not realise that this knife was of such value; I had not put it high on my list of priorities."

"This knife was used by my grandfather in the Boer War. It does not have any real value, other than that of sentiment, but yes, I feel that I want this knife back now. Yes, attend to it at once. Arrange it with your peers that your workload is spread so that you give all your attention to the matter of the knife."

A third quisling had entered the room. "Oh Master, will this snow affect the timing of the festival?"

"Indeed it will not. Though I seem to be unable, at the moment, to cast a spell to melt it all away in but a few seconds, the snow will have to be cleared by peasants. Go. Obtain them."

"That will be no problem, but we seem to have a lack of shovels."

"Shovels? Why have you need of shovels? They can clear it with their bare hands – 'twill give the sullen brutes a taste of hard work."

The first quisling spoke up again. "Master, do you think they will come to the festival, or will the snow drive them away?"

"They will come. They must come. Circulate the notices to say that anyone found not at the festival, or if discovered at a later date not to have attended, then they shall have their eyeballs removed with spoons prior to being slowly disembowelled."

The meeting was soon ended and T'osh then examined the charge sheet for the prisoners brought to the dungeons in the past twenty-four hours. Those brought in during the course of the previous day should now be heading to the *room where the question is put*. He saw a name, Abel Renton, and a charge, shaking his fist at an image of T'osh while said prisoner was in a state of intoxication. Feelings of violent rage filled his mind; it was unthinkable that there should be dissention, that somebody could question the Perfect State. For a moment he feared for his position, that perhaps he did have feet of clay, but this was soon drowned in a surge of his gigantic ego. He went down to the cellars; already he could hear the screams of the wretch who had defiled his graven image.

* * *

"Snow!" exclaimed Cressida upon looking out of the window. "Snow. A gift from God to purify the polluted, man-stained landscape. Isn't it just wonderful? How it raises my spirits. I am uplifted. Who's for snowballs?"

There was only a minimal response to this monologue; Frank yawned; Timothy scowled; Martyn bit his fingernails; the Amblers continued to sleep.

"I wonder where Wladek has got to," said Timothy.

Said Cressida; "Oh, I wouldn't worry about him. He always knows what he's doing."

"That's why he married you, I suppose?"

"Precisely."

Martyn was looking out across the snow-carpeted fields, his eyes slitted against the intense reflected sunlight. Despite this, he could just make out a dark object making its way with difficulty to the cottage.

"Here he comes now," said Martyn.

* * *

Wladek, at an early age, had decided that if he wanted something he would get it, by fair means if possible, but, if not, by any means necessary. He did not know whether he had mellowed or gone soft in his old age, or whether such random factors as Padlock added to his already complicated scheming, but whatever the cause, his plotting had gone badly awry in this case.

When T'osh had come to power, when Poffle had become his most devoted disciple, then the vague plans he had formulated came to concrete fruition. Playing both ends against the middle he had managed to rob both T'osh and Poffle blind, and both of them had thanked him for it. Oh, it had been a great time; so lucrative, so easy. Padlock had complicated the issue, but Wladek had managed, not only to rob him also, but to get Wladek's own enemy to put the parsimonious parson out of the way for a time.

Thinking on it, there was his fundamental error. At that point he should have cut his losses and ran. Now it was too late, and even when he should have fled he doubted that he could have found it in him to run: damn it all, T'osh was an evil animal who had to be stopped, and while he had a high opinion of himself, he did not think himself some form of superman who could eradicate the powers of the Perfect State in a sweep of his hand — but who else was there to do it?

Certainly he could not trust that company of idiots in the cottage to tie their own shoelaces without aid, let alone bring down a regime. Even with all the lucrative advantages gained by marrying Cressida he regretted tying the knot; she was dreary company and somewhat alarmingly self-absorbed; true, she enjoyed the physical side of their marriage but this was a somewhat intermittent pleasure as her daily routine included improbably long meditation sessions as well as her other ethereal pursuits. Martyn was all squall and posturing, with rare bursts of mindless action, and a maddening habit of croaking out abysmal songs he had written with the aid of a badly played and tuned guitar. Frank was hopeless; he reminded Wladek of nothing so much as an eighteenth-century squire, tossing off occasional verses and being an idiot the rest of the time. Timothy . . . well, he had certainly mellowed with age, honing himself into something, if not perfect, then the only one of the lot he would wish to have at his side at a time of crisis.

And a time of crisis it certainly was, for if T'osh were to be stopped, it would have to be before the climax of the Dark Festival. He had delayed everything for far too long, letting the matter coast while he played the game for any last gleans of profit he might grab. Now, was it too late? His pitiful army . . . well they were all he had.

He had kept them in the sidelines long enough, and in one respect it was good that they had been in the sidelines, doing pointless things and for long stretches of time doing nothing whatsoever: they still looked on it all as a sort of game where if people fell there was no blood, and they were in some way immune to the dangers and perils of the situation. Cannon fodder they may be, but they would go out with joy and enthusiasm; that was the one factor that gave Wladek hope as he trudged through the snow, going over for the hundredth time the plan he had hammered together during the long watches of the previous night. He had no great hope in the plan, but it was the only plan he had. It had to work.

*   *   *

As Wladek approached, Cressida went into the kitchen to prepare a breakfast of lentil soup, bay leaves and a variety of other, unspecified ingredients. As soon as the door opened Wladek was met with a barrage of questions which he declined to answer until he had warmed himself before the fire and had broken his fast. This over, he called all the company around for what he called "A final council of war".

"Our hour approaches," he said, "the hour when we make the final strike against the Magician. Time is not on our side; we must begin the final push this very afternoon. I cannot promise success — I can only hope that you will not let yourselves down with faint hearts.

"You wonder where I have been. Last night I discovered that Padlock has obtained the Sacred Dagger of Ormr. He can, if he knows the value of the dagger, and he does, wreak untold damage, destroying all that our valiant efforts have achieved. However, the maniac will not act right away; if we act now to depose T'osh we can yet destroy the Reverend before he can affect our plans.

"The Magician has set tomorrow as the date of his Dark Festival. I am not sure how he will attain this aim, but if the festival goes ahead as planned, he will regain the loyalty of the peasants once again, and this time for ever."

"What can we do?" asked Martyn.

"Nothing," said Cressida, "we can do nothing; our mission is doomed to failure. The Black Magician will win in the end. It is said in my Tarot cards."

"Screw your bloody cards," roared Timothy. "If you lived in the real world instead of in your silly fey imagination, it's just possible that you'd say something that wasn't absolute tripe every now and again. But until you do so, I would suggest that you keep your unhelpful and ill-informed opinions to yourself."

Cressida turned pale and her eyes flashed with loathing.

"If *I* may be allowed a word," said Frank. "We must not allow ourselves to forget certain basic philosophical truths. Evil is necessary; we must have the duality, for without evil there can be no good. Mightn't we, by this very action against the Black Magician, be reducing the store of good?"

"Ah," said John Ambler, "don't see as what's this to do with Black Magician."

"No," sneered Frank, "you wouldn't."

"Quiet, you maggot," ordered Wladek, his irritation at them all showing through. "Attend to what I say; the most important moments in your lives will soon be upon you, and all you can do is squabble. You all make me nauseous at times.

"Well then, if you're *quite* ready, we'll begin. I said that T'osh will have his victory in little more than twenty-four hours. Therefore, we must stop him before then. It will be difficult, but not impossible. We are but seven and we cannot gain victory if we remain but seven. Though T'osh is heading for his ultimate victory tomorrow, today his popularity is at its lowest ever. I say that we must get people to the festival, aye, thousands of them, but they must have but one thought in their hearts; overthrow T'osh before he achieves the final control. All his henchmen will be at the festival. If we eliminate them as well as T'osh, then not only will his body politic be headless, most, if not all of that very body will be eliminated. A sane government will be dragged into the vacuum that follows, the main nightmare will be over, and Padlock can be dealt with as a minor matter.

"I know the question that is on your lips, how do you motivate the populace? They sat doing nothing when T'osh came to power and in very many cases welcomed his ascension to the throne. Why should they do anything now? That is what we must do today. We must go to as many people as possible and tell them that there is already a vast conspiracy against T'osh, that he or she must attend the festival tomorrow, that he or she must wait for the given signal, that he or she must with the other hordes storm the ramparts of T'osh's empire and hurl him down. It does not matter that we do not have a vast conspiracy, but it is vital to the whole fate of the enterprise that the person you speak to *does* believe it, for each will tell one man or woman, and those two will tell four, and those four will tell eight until you do have the vast collusion at the field of the Dark Festival. Once more than a few people have been convinced then this action will bring about its own momentum, so that, when an unconvinced person has heard the tale from several people, he can do nothing but believe it.

"We must be careful where we tell the tales, and I do not merely warn you to be wary of T'osh's spies. Where do men and women, outside their homes, feel most relaxed and free of tongue? In a tavern, of course, and we must spread the tale in taverns, but not only in taverns, else all is lost; we must tell the tale beneath the clock tower, in shops, as you relieve yourselves in public urinals: everywhere."

Wladek paused for emphasis. Now for the final pep talk, he thought. "It is a dangerous mission; it might be one into the jaws of death; but it is the last and desperate operation to remove the malignancy of the Magician. Though faint hearts that do not come with us can stay here, I will not condemn them; they will do that themselves in later years. But those who are with me to pluck the bright jewel out of the nettle danger will know what it is to be crowned with glory.

"We go now, donned in our peasant's clothes, into the heartland of Ormskirk; there to disseminate our message of hope. Later, in the dusk, we will distribute what leaflets we have left, then we will all rendezvous in the Stanley Arms, for a last night of drink and merriment — for I tell you solemnly that for some it might really be the last night. Any especially promising peasant, bring him along also, for I will arm him with stout cudgel or quarterstaff, and train him in how to handle the angry mob; they will be our field-lieutenants. Remember, once we get into Ormskirk we separate. You are on your own: don't take unnecessary risks, but do not pass up opportunities.

"Come; let the Company of Glory make its mark on history."

All stood, save Cressida, who said that she had only moccasins to wear; these would let in the snow. She did agree to meet the company later in the Stanley Arms once she had managed to construct something less permeable to wrap around her footwear.

They were soaked in instants by the deep and fast-melting snow. All fell over several times, and all were soaked to the skin, but the warm sun and the cloudless blue of the sky cheered them.

Martyn was filled with optimism and a new confidence, an elation-like feeling that had been alien to his moods for many a day, not since he met Red Joe and Dancing Jack for the first time, in that adventure which now seemed to belong to a long-bygone era.

"Well, here we are, out on the road again. I wonder what will happen this time."

Incredibly enough, Frank was feeling uplifted, or rather, the mantle of affected gloom that he generally maintained was not so all encompassing.

"You know, in some ways this road is symbolic of the struggle which mankind inherits," he opined. "The struggle for liberty and freedom, which is constantly denied. In some ways this snowy scene reminds me of a story from Dubliners."

"Dubliners!" gasped Martyn.

"Isn't that by . . .?" whispered Timothy.

"James Joyce. Of course. I was thinking about that story, the one called The Dead, where snow plays a fundamental role in setting the scene."

"But you've never read Joyce," said Martyn.

"Nonsense."

"But you said a few days ago that you had never even heard of him."

"Impossible."

"But—"

"My work, *my* work — is but an extension of Joyce's works, though other writers do influence me. You may have misheard me. I remember making justly disparaging comments about that clueless oaf Lawrence. Now there is someone who I wouldn't claim to have read much of."

"Lawrence? I rather like him,' said Timothy. "I think he maintains a distinct and unique stance on life throughout all his work, and he has a strong notion of the mysteries and complexities which surround human relationships."

"Twaddle: his work is the work of an imbecile; one who is likely to take a trivial, everyday incident — a man breaking ice to allow birds to drink from a frozen pool, for example — and turn it into some hopelessly deep, important and long-winded metaphor. It is all so futile."

Martyn and Timothy exchanged glances and said no more. Frank certainly could be difficult at times, and puzzling.

Their journey took longer than expected because of the snow, but at last they found themselves close to the clock tower in the centre of the town. The place was the usual hodge-podge of contradictions, with fine buildings and shops left to moulder while whatever trade remained was carried out from rickety wooden stalls. The streets were packed with people; all engaged in tasks that the visitors had trouble in understanding. The goods being bartered were likewise strange; a goat's hoof, a bible sawn in half, wooden images, mummified vegetables, rusty knives, untreated leather boots and a very large quantity of a murderous brew apparently distilled from a concoction which included potatoes, cabbages and mushrooms.

They split into pairs, Frank and Wladek, the Amblers, Martyn and Timothy. They had decided upon this method as the safest which would cover enough ground. Alternately one would spread the lie while the other kept in the background, ready to give assistance if need be, but ready to flee if the circumstances warranted it.

Frank and Wladek started in the marketplace and could be seen to have gained a few early victories, before the Amblers left.

"I know that Wladek said that we shouldn't spread the news in just pubs, but neither of the other pairs are working the taverns; what do you say to a quickie in the

Magician's Head over there?" proposed Timothy to Martyn.

"Right on, man."

* * *

It was a regular's pub.

Martyn had never really believed the movie cliché where the man walks into the noisy saloon and all falls silent, but he had evidence of it when he went into the musty gloom of the bar. The old men, seated and hunched, motionless as reptiles, stopped their hurried conversation; the young men stopped playing darts. When the drinks were brought, they were brought sullenly, and the air was tense, motionless.

"Well, here goes," whispered Timothy. "DEATH TO THE MAGICIAN!"

There was not physical change; still the temperature seemed to drop by many degrees.

"Say that again," said one of the young men, edging to the door as he spoke.

"Death to the Magician. He must die. He *will* die."

The young man shot the bolt of the door and drew out a wicked looking knife. Trying to fool us, eh? I know you, you're one of the Magician's men — not that I've seen you around, but that's of little significance — and you're trying to get us to say something against our great leader so as you'll have something to beat us up for or, if you're feeling lenient, stick us in jail. Well it won't work, will it, lads? We . . . we're all for our glorious leader. Three cheers for T'osh."

"I wouldn't start cheering too loud; *They* might hear."

"And what's that to be afeard of? We want to be heard by our glorious leader."

"Not *them*, no, the ones you will have to fear are those thousands who in the very near future are going to overthrow the evil power — start cheering too loud and they might take it into their minds to start right now."

Timothy could see the doubt begin to grow in the young man. He seemed to still think that Timothy was an agent provocateur, but there was now that slight doubt in the back of his mind.

"What's all this nonsense about thousands of people? I don't know of anyone," said one old man at a table.

"You haven't heard about it? Really? The only people I know of who have not heard the news are the lackeys of T'osh; maybe you really are supporters of T'osh. If so, I wouldn't like to be you on that day — in fact, tomorrow."

"You haven't answered my question," persisted the old man.

"Oh, you will have seen the men; it's just that you haven't noticed it. I'm sure that all or some of your neighbours have been behaving oddly, going off at strange hours and coming back with stranger faces. Think about it."

They did . . . and they began to mutter. Thinking on it, every man could recall some member of the community who was not behaving as normal. A rarely came to the pub anymore; B was seen leaving the house at unearthly hours; C, once all openness and jollity now rarely spoke to anyone. Timothy did not have to convince them anymore; they were doing it for themselves.

There was a furious rattling at the bolted door. The young man, after seeing who was outside, let in an excited old man.

"What do you think you're doing, bolting the door when there's still a good half-hour's drinking time?" He did not see Martyn or Timothy. "Have you heard the news? I just got it from one of the stallholders. Seems there's thousands of people going to overthrow the bastard T'osh, and we can join in if— who the hell are you?" he asked of Martyn and Timothy.

"Two people I reckon we have misjudged," said the young man at the door. "Ten minutes ago I was ready to knock the pair of them on the bonce but now I know I was wrong."

The audience was hooked.

"Right," said Martyn, "now you know what is what, here's what you can do to help."

"Yes!"

"Count me in!"

"Death to T'osh!"

"Always remember that he was nearly assassinated a while back; we can do the job properly this time. And settle a few scores with his henchmen, I can bet."

"Right, you know about the Dark Festival tomorrow."

"Too bloody right."

"You want us to boycott it — But T'osh has threatened to take out our eyeballs if we do not attend, not to mention the inevitable disembowelling, of which he is said to be particularly fond."

"I know, that is why you must attend."

"Never!"

"Death first!"

"Listen: the Festival is the only time that we can be sure of having T'osh and his henchmen all in one spot — and the only time that we can safely gather in large numbers. At a suitable moment there will be a signal and we shall arise as one and overwhelm these evil men. Persuade everyone you can to come to this festival, whether you trust them or not. Those you do trust however tell them to bring with them knives and cudgels, sticks and stones — things that break bones and split skin. T'osh and his thugs will all be killed — and even if any escape they will be of such small number that they will never return to bother you."

"I like the sound o' that," said one of the old men. "Deed I do. 'Tis good grafting on a good stock. I'll spread the word, that I will."

"We must go now," said Timothy, "but remember tomorrow, as your grandchildren will surely remember it if — no, when — we will win through. We do not want faint hearts but heroes. Take care who you take into your trust. Don't take risks, but don't miss opportunities."

*　*　*

In a field outside Ormskirk T'osh looked over his cleared festival ground. The site was very large, and the cleared snow had been built into sloping ramparts. On these hundreds of peons lay exhausted, drinking out of stone flasks a fearfully potent ale.

But the cleared area was by no means free from activity, for hordes of men scurried to and fro, building a great wooden stage some thirty or more feet high, supported by massive oaken legs. A large area in front of the stage had been left untouched but, beyond this arena, countless stalls, huts and less readily describable buildings were being hastily constructed from ill-cut laths. Some were very small, little bigger than an outhouse, but many were large, and some were huge.

The exact purpose of the buildings could not always be readily defined, and this mystery was exacerbated by the dumps of grotesque and sometimes lewd objects that littered the spaces between the huts.

At the far end of the field a line of horses stood champing the grass, while the goods they had transported were being unloaded off the wagons. These objects were oddly at variance with the optimum technological level of *the perfect state*, consisting of various pieces of electronics, fireworks, smoke-bombs, and some other weird and inexplicable objects. A large hot air balloon was also being unloaded, its plastic glistening in the sun.

* * *

T'osh studied the landscape. His face was a mask of malevolence with little evidence of humanity, and from this face his beady and pig-like eyes glistened like jewels in slime. His teeth were bared in a rictus of fury and delight. They were discoloured, broken and carious; if there was anybody standing close by, he or she could easily hear the sound of their gnashing.

Indeeeeeeeeeeeeeeeeeeeeeeeeeeeeeeeeeeed, thought T'osh, *I will subdue these peasants once and for all this time. They will writhe in delight and terror and they shall be mine. More than ever before they will be mine, body and soul. Forever. And after that, I shall claim Maghull as my next prize.*

He fingered the great scar on his neck.

Let any who dare stand in my way. Let them: I will unroll their entrails and hang them from the clocktower. I will feed their heads to the crows. I will slice open their filthy throats slowly and with a rusty spade. I will cut portions of their bodies and insert red ants. I will cut off their legs and force them to eat them for food. Indeeeeeeeeeeeeeeed.

T'osh looked at the land about him: everything seemed to be rushing to the glorious culmination that would be the Dark Festival. This would be a day to remember – one way or another.

Chapter 16:

A Song for Everyone

The Stanley Arms was a sombre building at the best of times; one which paradoxically became more sombre when it became filled with people. Empty, it was merely a place of dead air and suspended dust with perhaps the muffled ticking of an out-of-time clock heard faintly from one of the other rooms. Filled with people — or at least when there were people in the pub — the sombreness of the place became positive; no one laughed, no one talked gaily, and people drank their ale as if it were a duty.

This particular evening it was worse than ever, with the freak weather helping not at all. Some, though not all, of the snow had melted, giving the fields an insane appearance as of a chess board, with the exposed fields being the dark chequers. Of itself the weather had been merely odd, but the regulars of the Stanley Arms were a superstitious lot at the best of times, and this was certainly not the best of times, and, as with all superstitious types, the odd event could not portend something good, only something malevolent at the very least. The matter of the Dark Festival looming did nothing to cheer the locals.

At first the evening progressed as had any other, with the more hopeless alcoholics drinking rapidly until they had achieved the necessary stupor, then gazing with a vacant idiocy at the glass, and with the rest of the regulars dividing themselves into the same little groups and saying the same little things they had said during the course of a thousand deadly nights. Strangers, so far as they looked like people from hereabouts, were given a grudging tolerance; but out of the district strangers — had there been any — would have found themselves rapidly helped to the rear of the pub, and from said place cries of pain, misery and despair would have issued.

But then, strangers began to appear and group themselves in one corner of the public house. Not one unusual aspect did they openly show compared to the regulars in the bar, they were dressed in the same dull motley and were as unkempt as any, yet they could have come from another world so far as their posture and aura were concerned. They were well built and hale, or at least as well as they could expect to be having undergone the insane regime for a year, and stood straight and proud, an assertiveness that had long faded from the land. In their eyes was the gleam of purpose, something that had generally been hard to find in that area, but which had, of late, been as easy to find as a passenger pigeon in the Antarctic.

The drink flowed freely, and laughter, real laughter, was heard, a noise as forgotten and rare as the cry of a dinosaur.

*　　*　　*

The group of people, now numbering twenty-three (including six powerfully built females), sent obscure fears through the fibres of all but one of the regulars. That man was Abel Renton, who through the pain of the unhealed scars and injuries, with his one unclosed eye saw something good, even great, in those men and women. He saw them with cudgels and axes in hand, hewing down the evil knotweed that had constricted the land for so long. With nail-less fingers he picked up his drink and silently saluted them, for he had heard some of the mutters that were coming from that corner of the pub.

"I 'ates 'im for sure."

"Aye, the sooner he's gone the better: what's he ever given us, that's what I want to know."

"Nothink for nothink, that's what."

"Naw, look at the things as he 'as gi'n us — plague, early death, poverty — public 'angings, by God."

"It's 'im as wants hangin', an' none too soon either."

"'Angin's too good for 'im — burn 'im, I say, burn 'im."

"Aye, and all his henchmen. Throw them to the fire!"

*   *   *

Then some other people arrived, people to whom Abel Renton had spoken of matters grave, and when he saw them join the band of young men, Abel Renton felt hope, an emotion to him now so alien that he had to analyse the feeling before he could recognise it.

*   *   *

Frank had done quite enough proselytising to last him the rest of several lifetimes, and enough mingling with the common herd to last him for eternity, so when he, with the rest of the High Command, had entered the Stanley Arms, the last thing that Frank had wanted to do was to commingle with yet more filthy specimens of the commonality. Already he felt too unclean for words; a sweaty, grimy coating had oozed over his body, some form of vile exudation from the common man that no number of hot showers would remove.

And so, he left Martyn and the rest and stood in lofty silence at the bar. The single whiskey he was drinking was oily: fine for the herd, but quite unpalatable for the man of discernment. Accordingly, he tried to take it to that thought — and beauty proof — chamber he fondly imagined to be artistic excellence. But he was brought back to grim reality by the noxious exhalations that slunk around the stink of manual work. God, he hated it!

There remained but one course of action left for Frank: goad a native; see a pleb squirm under the scalpel of his wit. One such candidate was but a few feet from him, swathed in bandages, doubtless the result of a common fight, drinking excessively of some local rough ale.

Frank spoke to the man in his usual high-handed manner, and gradually he brought the subject around to artists.

"I, sir, am an artist myself — one of great repute and note."

"Like the one who said, *qualis artifex pereo*[1], I don't doubt."

This set Frank back a bit on several counts, but not for long. Staring at some point beyond Renton's right shoulder, he continued. "I am of course familiar with

---

[1] Thought to be Roman Emperor Nero's last words and usually translated as, "What an artist dies with me".

the man, but I fear that you are trying to distract me, the artist and writer, with some mental trifle, some odd fact picked up I don't know where, presented as some evidence of erudition. I won't have it.

"As a writer of no small genius, I feel it my duty to wipe away the pretensions and falsehoods that have swamped and engulfed my less talented contemporaries. I know that I have a mission, to bring light to the masses, to lead them by the hand into the age of enlightenment and reason, where they can shake off the shackles of custom, decency and hypocrisy. Ah, their minds will be enlightened, their hearts uplifted, their blood freed of age-old bonds."

"Money doesn't come into it, then?"

"Money? *Pfui*! I spit on it. Surely you must realise that such as I work only for art's sake; we are sullied by contact with lucre. My life revolves about my work. Once the Magician is no longer a concern, I will go back to my room, my small, ill-furnished room, and continue my life's work."

"Life's work, eh?"

"Yes, a production of singular genius. It is too long to carry about entire, but I generally carry portions of it with me for the edification of the masses. As my genius has done away with the need for plot, characterisation, structure, pace, grammar and syntax — style, all is style — you may begin it anywhere and read it with joy and delight. Here is a chapter. Read it now. I insist. I'll help you if you have any difficulties with the big words."

"Thankee kindly, Master," said Abel Renton.

Pain

pain pain all is pain nothing exists without pain the
western worlds filled with blood

blood

blood

blood

blood

built on blood

blood

blood

throbbing

pulsating

blood

but cannot have always been the way it is there must
have been a simpler time when this was hot so when
druid sylvan fields of druids

DRUIDS

That's it. druids why did I not think of it before why
because my brain has been captured by the military
and industrial complex and they with their mind poisons
have held me captive flashing lights skin torched
mangled dangled jangled

White robes.

White robes.

Where?

A field. A green field. White robes. A green field. So
much. So good So far . . .

When?

The sun. yellow, yellow sun. The sky. Blue. Blue sky.
Yellow sun Summer. Summer solstice. Yes. men. Five
men. White robes. Blue sky. Yellow sun. Summer solstice.

327

You know who they are. Yes.

Rekaorc smokes. The smoke rises. Grey. Like Nivek's mind. Nivek grey. Jiffily grey. Inside. Outside. Knarf is here. I know the five. Five. past. five. present. five. future. Always in white.

Recognise them. Know them. Destroy them.

Our mission do they pose death knife threat to us me you in white menace no blood but they can will harm us blood spurting! Like when Rekaorc died spurting from torn vessels like the fountains its I used to know when I was a child and Rekaorc was alive was a-live but there he is he did die yes but he is here life is confusing and deadly for the rest of us still here: Knarf thought..

Nivek Rekaorc Knarf — *we must destroy them*.

They pose a threat. They must die. Our mission.

OUR mission.
How?
The knife.
The stab.
Look at Rekaorc. Listen.

knife
life
no hope anywhere
Awe spit on YOU you bLoody bastARd.
I am/I am not/I am not a bastard.
sing. sing.

kill me kill you
jolly childlike things you do

kill you kill me then
let's go home for tea
tee-hee
maybe
I see

Nivek. See Nivek. In his hand. Nivek's hand. Knife. Knife in Nivek's hand. Why is this? What does it mean?

Nivek leaps. Leaps upon Rekaorc. Nivek with knife. Blood appears. Appears on Rekaorc. Knife. Knife has slashed Rekaorc. Nivek's knife. (blood oh. why is it always to be so blood bloody light of fires and flesh melting and doors burning and houses crumbling, and pork chops cooking and I feel hungry but how can I feel hungry while there are books burning and women looking like clocks and there are braver men than these cufflinks learning not to solve their differences with bombs all the bloody time it must stop.)

Stop. Stop. Stop. Stop. Stop. Stop. Stop. They stop.

Tempers cool down sl-ow-ly oh so sl—ow—ly and Nivek begins to cry and hold his head in his hands and the salt tears run fame down his cheeks and fall to the pavement and are absorbed by the stone but Nivek still cries and says I'm sorry I'm sorry to Rekaorc and Rekaorc just sits there and is stunned and is hurt and looks at the blood — that runs down his stonechat cheek and watches it drip onto the pavement where it is absorbed by the stone and he lights a cigarette and the grey smoke rises up and it is grey like Nivek and grey Rhyl like the world in all its aspects and Rekaorc throws away the match he used to light that cigarette from which the grey smoke rises and the match is still lit and the five saddle soap druids who have been in the background move away from the burning yearning match but one is not quick enough and his garments of white turn golden then black as the piercing and cleansing astronomical unit flames blaze up and the druid screams and runs around and the flames still burn and the grey smoke still goes up and the world is as grey as ever it was in addition the burning druid runs off with the others in close pursuit then they are trying to put out the flames and we will never know if they succeeded and do you care? No not much. They were only druids. Relics from a bygone age. Who cares, honestly? Druids planning a summer solstice what care I or anyone else for this kind of tripe and pigwash. Druids in the modern age! What is the world coming to? Witches? Maybe?

Rekaorc brightens up and observes that that got rid of the druids and everyone agrees and would cheer if there was anything to cheer about in this grey pillared world and still the grey smoke hovers in the air like the guilt of the world and we are all guilty and we are all like unto that smoke that grey smoke that still curls and hangs in the grey stocking air like that thing which lies under the bed peeping (I always knew about that although you thought I was asleep.). Druids! I ask you.

(I am Knarf and upon this rock I will build my victory and I say to my companions on with the mission and we go but I cannot see outside my plucked head any more do not want to for the things that are crawling out of my brain the filth the gore the blood stop it go back I will not let you out keep back you are — not part of — me I abjure you go back ye . . . ye stunkard no.

(pull yourself together that's better calm down calm yourself think who you are a in will be yes I you astonishment in a bad way you're cracking up and who wouldn't with the sociopolitical machinations of the industrial military combine gnawing at your snow brain but you're rising above that maybe I'll be a coddled martyr but not before the explosion when their blood will flow and Satan will go down on a postcard tricycle with jack of hearts in a jar of pickles

I must try to remain until the Mission is over or all is lost

Spanish boots of cold heels clean pair though must I always be condemned to suffer? Knarf sleeps.

*　　*　　*

"Well," said Frank after a time, "do you not agree that my style is most effective in hacking away many, if not all, of the pretensions and absurdities which adhere to the corpus of contemporary writing?"

"Hackwork . . . mmm," mumbled Abel Renton.

"My style has no limitations, accepts no superimposed expectations — it is abrasive, wearing away all pretensions."

"Wearing . . . mmm, yes. But there could be an alternative interpretation put upon your . . . ah, work."

"You are wrong; my interpretation is the only one but pray give me your mistaken view and I will correct it for you."

"Well, there are those who might say that should an aspiring and arrogant person with a very small scrip of talent who wishes to become a writer would, in all probability, quickly find that he could not construct plots, create living characters or have sufficient experience of life to write convincingly. This being so, his arrogance would not let him take the decent way out and become a lorry driver or office clerk; instead, he would pursue a different line, saying that his work is revolutionary and brilliant. In other words he would write utter meaningless tripe and try to pass it off as avant-garde, esoteric, call it what you will, and that it would fool a sufficient number of pseudo-intellectuals and bandwagon-jumpers so as to secure your place in any—"

"Silence." hissed a white-faced Frank, as his trembling hands clutched his manuscript. "It is just as well that you are a semiliterate peasant. It allows me to look at your case with some leniency."

Frank's voice cracked; he did not seem to trust himself to say anything further, so he shambled off to another part of the pub.

*　*　*

Cressida had entered the tavern unnoticed some time earlier and was now seated cross-legged upon the grimy floor. Actually, she had tried to sit in the lotus position, had failed, and so achieved this compromise. Her eyes were closed, and she was seemingly deep in contemplation, though in fact at least one part of her mind was still active and listening for the sounds of amaze and wonder from the other members of the convocation at her pose and eastern mystic caste. Oddly, these sounds had yet to be heard, and the only creature who had noticed her had been a somewhat superannuated wolf spider, who had dimly regarded Cressida's big toe sticking through a rent in her squelchy moccasins (her attempt to snow-proof them had not been entirely successful), but who had decided against biting it to see if it was succulent or not.

Beside her stood a number of glasses of fruit juice; she had long avoided alcohol, thinking it poisonous, offensive and generally deleterious to the healthy future of humanity.

After a time, when no sounds of praise for her had been heard, she narrowed her eyes, and like a spider waiting for its prey, sat motionless, but ready to spring. From time to time someone would be luckless or drunk enough to come within range and he would be given a broadside of what Cressida thought. The conscientious author has no right to inflict upon his public the full text of what she said; the following should be sample enough:

"The material world is full of miseries, specifically death, birth, old age and disease. It is also temporary. One who goes to the planet of KRSNAP called GOLOKAVRNDAVANA, has achieved the highest perfection, and naturally does not wish to return to this unhappy place. This spiritual planet is, naturally enough, to be located by all who . . ."

. . . and so on for a fearsome length of time. Few people, even the most drunken, were able to sit passively for any prolonged period whilst this twaddle was being spouted and drifted away, though this did not seem to bother Cressida's narration. Some, on the other hand, trying to allay the incipient boredom, tried in vain to interrupt her monologue and put in alternative arguments. But they too tended to wander off after a time.

After a time, her eyes glazed over and from the cast to her face she seemed to be undergoing some sort of psychodrama or abreaction: an alienist[1], had there been one in the pub, would, almost certainly, have ordered her restrained and would this very moment be putting the ECT electrodes to Cressida's head. Fortunately for Cressida such operatives would have been regarded as far too progressive-minded under the regime of T'osh and their careers (and lives) would have been interesting but short.

* * *

Delegating the running of the tavern to her employees, the progressively enigmatic Florinda Farrier had moved to a quiet part of the bar and was deep in a complex conversation with Wladek. At least it seemed to be about some intricate plan; no one was sure, for if a person approached the vicinity he was met with looks of ice, and, if this did not drive the person away, the temperature of the looks dropped to that of the temperature of liquid helium, and if that failed, as it had just once, then Wladek would wreak physical damage upon the unfortunate.

It was very mysterious.

* * *

---

[1] (Archaic) a psychiatrist who assesses the competence of a defendant in a law court.

Martyn and Timothy were deep in conversation with a small group of the red-faced lads. By this time, it was difficult to determine whether the ruddiness of countenance was due to the nature of their outside employ, or to the truly industrial quantities of ale they had supped.

Timothy had mentioned to Martyn that they had been planning for a victory over the Dark One, but no one had considered what would happen ten seconds after the white flag was flying over the courthouse in Ormskirk. Martyn had not understood what Timothy had meant. Timothy had explained in more detail. The peasants had been under the heel of T'osh for a good while and had been forced to change their ways and adopt a new pattern of life. This new way of life would not evaporate with the dissolution of T'osh, but would remain, a foul miasma, which could mean that the post-victory civil authorities would be no better than the gang of madmen currently in power. Planning the revolution was an absorbing and problematic mission. What to do the day after to guarantee that the social order was back on some kind of 'right track' was an even thornier undertaking, as so many have discovered through the centuries.

One second after victory, said Timothy, they are going to have to pick up the threads of their life as was lived before T'osh and they must be made aware of their heritage, rich and varied, now ploughed under by T'osh's brutality but which, given the right nurture, would grow again and strangle the foul weeds of the Dark One.

So it was that Martyn and Timothy listened avidly to the wealth of tradition that the men and women were re-remembering. Perhaps it was the drink, perhaps it was the trust that these men now placed in the outsiders; whatever it was, the men were holding back nothing concerning their heritage, and were now talking about the Sacred Dagger.

After going on about its history, they mentioned its possible current whereabouts.

"Course," said one, "none can now rightly know what has become of it, whether the magician 'as it still or if others 'ave it."

Timothy said, "From what I know, and from what you said, I do not think it at all likely that the Magician has it any longer. I very much fear that it is with the deranged Reverend Lock."

"Not 'im!"

"I very much fear so," advised Martyn. "Like Timothy I feel that he has it in his possession. At present he does not know its value: oh, he knows that it's old and valuable in the sense that he can get a lot of money for it, but he does not seem to know of its power of rabblerousing — and one hopes that he never will. You see, at the right time and place, if Padlock knows the psychological value of the dagger, then . . ." Martyn's hands shook as he took a good gulp of the strong ale. ". . . I fear the outcome just as much as I fear the possible success of the Dark Carnival."

Martyn surveyed the faces of the twenty-three. Some new factor seemed to have entered the situation. The air of resolve and determination seemed to shimmer for a moment and then, though there was no doubt as to its continued presence, seemed to be slightly tawdry somehow.

"Obviously," said Timothy, "we know better than to believe in some mumbo jumbo about a magic dagger.

It's just an old knife, steel and wood and stones — why, I would rather trust to your sheath knife in your belt in a fight than I would to any magic penknives. Come lad, it's all nonsense; you know it is."

The laughter and the cheers that followed were loud and convincing, but to Martyn and Timothy they were not convincing or loud enough. To boost his spirits Martyn began to sing quietly a song – *Land Locked* he had written a few days earlier when unable to sleep – it was a protest song of sorts, although somewhat opaque to all but the most erudite scholar. It was also long.

> *They're raving on the rooftops*
> *Slinging slates at noon*
> *The caterpillar is crawling*
> *And talking to the moon*
>
> *The corner boy is wide open*
> *And selling mustard pots*
> *and now looks set to separate*
> *The haves and the have nots*
>
> *Where is the leading lantern*
> *That shines from up above?*
> *There's nothing left for me now*
> *in a land locked out of love*
>
> *They're selling bombs upon the high street*
> *To blow us all sky high*
> *But what of those folk unprepared*
> *To lay down here and die*

Tombstones glow in the darkness
With flowers tossed aside
The blue-chinned onetime warrior
Just chose to run and hide

Where is the leading lantern
That shines from up above?
There's nothing left for me now
in a land locked out of love

There were many more verses which Martyn continued
to sing, oblivious to the fact that he had now cleared the
corner of the bar where he stood and was therefore
singing entirely to himself.

* * *

The Amblers were there, too. Long had they been the
mere vassals of T'osh, and though they had escaped some
time back, still they had not celebrated their release by
easing their inhibitions with liberal quantities of drink.
This night they well made up for their deficiencies.

As time moved on the sullen regulars seemed to
become infected with the zeitgeist of the evening. Long
disused muscles were recalled to duty as some of them
began to smile and laugh. One went so far as to take out
some scrannel pipes and played a rude but lively tune
upon it. The notes from this syrinx had scarce begun to
vibrate in the air but Adaline Ambler had leapt upon a
table to perform an erratic, erotic dance which involved,
amongst other things, raising her skirts to well above
the knee: a drunkard's Phyllis and Corydon.

Meanwhile, John Ambler lay slumped in a corner, his mind fuddled with strong ale, one hand still heavily bandaged, singing in a cracked vocal style, some half-remembered Victorian verses he had been forced to learn by heart at school and in which he now found a category of comfort.

The freedom of the dragonfly
Suspended in in my garden
Will never make me shudder
Or cause my heart to harden

The sighting of a butterfly
Upon a fresh mown lawn
Will set my spirit soaring
On a cheerful July morn

The night it has grown darker
The wind blows loud and long
But I still have my courage
And I still have my song

Though battered by life itself
And left in shattered mind
I know one day I will return
To the world I left behind

A realm where none could harm me
And all to me were kind
And once more like the dragonfly
Such peace there shall I find

Towards midnight the drinking was at its height.

"This isn't like Padlock," said Martyn.

"What isn't?" said Timothy.

"Him missing a free booze-up."

"Yeah. Maybe he's here in disguise."

"Maybe, but only if he could get his disguise for free."

"Well, if you're still wondering about whether Padlock knows of the power of the Dagger, you can stop right now. If he's here, he'll have heard all about it."

"Yeah."

"You're really worried about this, aren't you?"

"Too right, it's the one factor we can't control. The one variable that can make so much difference one way or the other. And to be honest, if it came to a regime by T'osh or one by Padlock, I'm not sure which I'd pick."

"Don't pick either," slurred one of the regulars who had lurched over to Timothy and Martyn. "Don't pick either. Put 'em in a field, shoot each other. Let the bastards blow the bastard up. That's what I say!"

Thus saying, he fell in a heap to the floor and said not a word further.

"Hey," said one of the twenty-three, "do you know it's five to midnight? Five minutes more it will be Sunday, and Easter Sunday at that."

"Ahhh," said Timothy, "I had quite lost track of time over these terrible weeks; but that explains why the Festival was planned for that particular day. He plans to redeem mankind, I daresay, with yet more suffering."

"Yes," mused Martyn, "a day that is less than five minutes away from us."

"Oh yes," said Abel Renton, "he plans to wash away original goodness, paving the way for the kingdom of hell. Your sins are forgiven so long as you now go out and commit at least twice as many."

That final half-hour proved to be the most frenetic of the lot. Florinda Farrier, who had finished talking to the no longer visible Wladek, and her employees, were swept off their feet trying to serve the orders. Adaline Ambler continued to dance frenetically and managed to remove most of her clothes before being escorted into an adjoining room (for her own protection) by Abel Renton.

People began to sing.

> We'll kill the Black Magician
> Old T'osh will fight no more.
> We'll bury him 'neath piles of turf,
> Upon some barren shore.
>
> No more will his black magic
> Turn us into slaves
> For all his books and daggers
> Are cast beneath the waves.
>
> He'll get what's coming to him
> O' that ye can be sure
> Into the drains of Ormskirk
> His blood will surely pour
>
> And when the night is over
> and darkness twists to light
> We'll say farewell to evil
> On the new day fiery bright

Cressida was still seated cross-legged.

"Today is Easter day," she said. "Good . . . Good . . . I'll be able to see the Easter bunnies . . . won't that . . . be . . . nice," she said and fell into a deep and uncomfortable slumber. The rest of the pub's clientele also crossed through the gate of horn at no much later time.

*   *   *

The moon, appearing from behind a cloud, beamed down upon the sprawled bodies in the Stanley Arms. Some had made it to the beds in the unoccupied rooms, but most lay sprawled where they had dropped. The normal silence of the closed pub was still there, but its sombre spectre had been laid. No more did the air hang like lead inside the walls. The ticking of the clock was still muffled, but that was only because it was in another room; and the clock now ran on time.

In the moon-bathed lands immediately outside the pub there was silence too, but this was the silence of death. In lands of easeful slumber children would soon be awake and receiving sweets and chocolate eggs; not so in the environs of Ormskirk, where only the thin gruel of terror and persecution would be proffered when the sun rose. Easter, Christmas, and a host of other celebrations had been banned by T'osh, and discovery of any celebration of such a feast would be punished by the removal of one's finger and quite possibly other sections of the anatomy as might be thought appropriate depending on the severity of the transgression.

*   *   *

Padlock was seated motionless on a shabby chair, his elbows resting on the rotting table of the smallest room of the cheapest boarding house in Ormskirk. It was at the top of a crumbling and ancient rooming-house of dubious repute: its reputation and fearfulness were so great that even the Dark Forces had been leery of entering it, so it had remained as it had always been, cheap and nasty; the former, as ever, appealing to the unworldly parson. He had also been affected to some degree by the inhabitants of the other rooms and had become more and more nocturnal; this not only suited his current low-profile image but was necessitated by the need to have all other members of the noisome dwelling sound asleep before he opened the rotting duffle bag that contained some of his possessions.

Taking out the decomposing duffle bag, he watched the reflections of the single candle dance upon the gold that now lay revealed. He ran the coins through his fingers, delighting in the feel of the cool metal and listened in rapture to the symphony the clinking coins produced. Then he took out the dagger and held it in his hand.

Ah, the facets of the jewels in the haft as they bit into the pallid skin of his hands: *oh*, the cool of the metal of the hilt on his index finger and thumb: *eeh*, the quicksilver look of the blade as he went to the window where the moon shone through from a cloudless sky. He thought of some particular throats he would like to slit, and his control, never strong at the best of times, and lately extremely erratic, broke.

He hopped around the filthy room, sending up clouds of desiccating dust, and in his madness croaked this song.

For the LORD will not cast away for ever,
Though he dost cause grief and sorrow:
Let us pour joy into our hearts,
And praise the new tomorrow.

And in the day of the full moon,
Shall rise the noble Reverend,
Brandishing the Sacred Dagger,
Banishing all sinful, evil men

A curse upon the evil T'osh,
Frank, Wladek and Timothy:
For ruler of Ormskirk,
Reverend Pedaiah Lock will surely be.

And when that day arriveth
The people will dance and sing
For they are liberated
As the eagle 'pon the wing

"I'm trying to sleep, if you don't mind," said a petulant voice from a tangled pile of rags. Harmony Poffle then went on to warn her beloved that such displays of arrogance and conceit, not to mention noise, could well arouse unwanted suspicion in any who cared to hear.

Padlock made no further sounds, but he stood still by the window, dagger in hand, an insane grin etched upon his moonlit face.

* * *

T'osh paced the confines of his dark palace like a caged lion. All the night he had been pacing; his face in a rictus of anxiety and excitement. Already he had had three long screaming sessions, and once he had taken to punching the walls until his knuckles were covered in blood. His henchmen had long since learned to avoid him when he was in this mood, but never had he been so bad as this.

Now he was pacing up and down a gelid corridor, lit only by the light of five guttering and dying brands. At first he did this march in silence, but then he began to shriek a song which, although hardly a work of outstanding lyricism, did accurately reflect the frenzied state of his mind.

> *Arrrrrrrgh —*
> *Soon it will be daylight,*
> *Soon we shall begin*
> *To carry out our promise,*
> *To worship death and sin.*
>
> *Arrrrrrrrrgh —*
> *Disease shall cross our landscape,*
> *Blood will stain our land:*
> *I shall see a nation*
> *Eating from my hand.*
>
> *Arrrrrrrrrgh —*
> *I shall show no mercy;*
> *To good men, would-be saints,*
> *Their heads will be removed*
> *And covered with black paint.*

Arrrrrrrrgh —
I will rule supreme,
None shall e'er oppose,
For I will kill my enemies,
And I will cut off various parts of their
anatomies and hang them and feed their rotten
maggot-eaten flesh to starving rats and adders
and Satan look upon me this dark night and let
your darkness carry me upon this mission so that
I shall dominate these people and train them for
thy black kingdom. Amen. Arrrrrrrrrrgggggggh!

*   *   *

For Noah Halfmoon the last few weeks had been spent furtively: living in ditches and dark rooms, lurking in alleys and filthy sties, fearful of discovery, yet always hungry and cold and generally terrified.

Most people in that unhappy land had but one enemy; Halfmoon had three. He had deserted the party, led by Quartus Poffle, who had raided Padlock's redoubt. Not being a man of words, he had difficulty in explaining his actions, had he been in a position to discuss the matter, for he had come under the peculiar and at times fearful charisma of Padlock's insane nature. Like several madmen in the past he radiated a strange sort of power that twisted and perverted ordinary people into believing the most utter rot and doing the most grotesque actions. Halfmoon was the only one affected by the whole onslaught of Padlock's aura: Quartus Poffle was both incensed with Padlock and so full of himself that the mysterious rays merely bounced off his pallid face; the rest of the henchmen were of such simian type that one would have been hard put to discover even a rudimentary consciousness which could be affected by the Padlock effect.

So, it was that early that fearful morning Noah Halfmoon had realised that he had harmed a sacred and holy person and, to compound the sin, was still keeping him captive. Such a sin could have but one atonement, and Noah Halfmoon had crept out of the stilly house, having decided to do away with himself at once. However, he found himself unable to throw himself in the icy waters of a nearby pond, and, after standing on the sedgy edge for a long hour, had gone to ground. Though he had watched with a degree of ambiguity, (for he loved a good blaze), the vicarage go up in smoke, he was ultimately filled with remorse and guilt, but also with the desire to expiate the sin he had committed against the Master by token of some great act to help Padlock.

* * *

During the next few days, days spent in misery and hunger, days in which he tried to imitate the fox going to ground, it penetrated his dull and diffuse mind that not only would Poffle be out for his neck, by virtue of his desertion, so too might Padlock — and T'osh for sure would be after his blood. This thought nearly made him flee for distant lands there and then, but the guilt and the desire for reparation made him remain.

At about this time he found relative safety in a crumbling taxidermist's shop hidden down a filthy alley so ancient that the middle of the pavement still possessed a kennel awash with sloppy human ullage. The taxidermist, a bearded ancient loon who had been in that house for as long as any could remember, had a genuine talent for taxidermy, and before the coming of T'osh had sold his ware to customers for respectable sums of money. After the coming of T'osh he practised his art upon the bodies from the prisons, which he got at a cheap rate from T'osh, who in turn suggested that every household should have one as a keepsake. The taxidermist was best on prisoners who had died from natural causes (heart failure caused by gunshot wounds) and executions; he refused to work with material sent from the torturers. "There was not enough left to make a job of," was his professional opinion. He still stuffed animals, though now the fauna were a bit more exotic: the metre-long South American leech that graced T'osh's outhouse lavatory was his masterpiece

In return for food and shelter, all Halfmoon had to do was to listen to the taxidermist's pet theory which he went on long and loud about. It seemed that the world has been at nuclear war since 1945, and that most people had not heard about it was due to a media cover-up (at least, when the media was allowed in Ormskirk). New Zealand had been radioactive slag since 1952, Sweden had been glowing in the dark from a time not much later, and other countries had gone the same way. It seemed, though, that the Russians were slowly losing, despite the efforts of the Martians in their base in Antarctica.

Being fed both physical and mental trash, it is not surprising that Halfmoon began to see the Reverend Pedaiah Lock as a god-like figure, ordained to rid the land of the evil T'osh and establish a free-thinking, liberal minded, Godly regime based upon the principles of ongoing austerity, regular prayer meetings and the stoning of sinful people.

He took to wandering the lanes around Ormskirk, sometimes sleeping rough and sometimes returning to the taxidermist's residence when he needed warmth, food and shelter. It was during these sojourns that he came to realise that Padlock was indeed alive and well. From time to time he had stood in ditches, fields or cart tracks keeping a look-out for the reverend and these occasional glimpses of his champion had further fuelled his belief in the omnipotence, omniscience and general worthiness of the parsimonious parson.

Thus it was, that upon Easter Sunday, Halfmoon lay upon a rotting bed and declared his undying fealty to Padlock, finding, in his fanaticism, an ability to upload a vocabulary which would normally have eluded him. In a voice which sounded as if sandpaper had been applied to his vocal cords, he murmured the following verses.

Tomorrow I shall find him; I shall be his knight.
We shall rid this country of T'osh's evil might.
The Reverend Pedaiah Lock shall realise his vision
Oh Lord, I pray for only victory in our noble mission.

I have been a sinner; I have done much wrong
Walking the lost highway, where I did not belong
But all is now clearer, my soul shall not be damned
For Pedaiah Lock's the Shepherd and I his willing hand.

In the morning I'll be rising, the hour it will be mine
I'll see the new day dawning, I see the pointing sign
My journey is a short one, This is now my fate
For I must do my life's work, I can no longer wait.

'Ex . . . act . . . ly,' Halfmoon concluded, before drifting off to sleep, his dreams infused with apparitions of a skeletal ecclesiastic who commended Halfmoon's perpetual constancy.

Chapter 17:

The Final Conflict

Once he had a name, but that had long since been driven from his mind with the pain. In the moments when the pain inflicted by the torturers was not too great, strange images would rise from some murky depth of his mind. He supposed that they were memories, though they all seemed alien to his experience, distant, like an episode from a half-remembered book.

At the last session, when the torturer had been doing something unspeakable with an oak branch, and when the pain had become both so intense and so prolonged that it did not matter anymore, he had asked not, "Why am I here?" but "Who am I?" He was certain that the torturer had smiled when he said this, though the tormentor's face had been hidden by the felt mask. The torturer had not said anything but had removed the oak branch and indicated to the two men standing by the rush lights to take him back to the cell. Since then — and how long a time that might be he had no way of guessing, other than that he thought it was a matter of days — he had been left alone in his cell with a flagon of vinegary wine and a mouldy loaf.

He had no time sense in the cell; there were no sounds other than the rhythm of his breath and heartbeat; there was no light other than the fitful glow of a gaslight that flickered over the spout of a naked pipe. He had tried counting the seconds, but he found that the numbers tended to flow into each other like melting wax.

He awoke from an irrelevant dream of autumn fields and woods, dragged from this idyll by the grating of locks. The iron door opened and, framed in an architrave of mould, were the silhouettes of two men. He judged that it was now time for another session with the torturers, and in a strange way he welcomed it; at least there would be some positive input to his brain, not the nothingness of his oblivion in this cell. But the men did not come into the cell and drag him away; instead, one threw a filthy cloak at him, and the other said, "You. Go, you're free."

"Free?" he croaked, wondering if this was some sort of cruel trick. The men made no movement. Ignoring the pain of his wounds, he rose from his filthy pallet and put the cloak around his thin shoulders. The cell whirled as he went to the door, the two men having to hold the former captive lest he fall. There then followed confused impressions of corridors and rooms as he was led along. At one point he could hear frantic screams as if someone was in mortal agony but, as they continued, he discerned them to be the cries of a brain totally unhinged. They died away to a crazed croaking of, so far as he could make, "My festival, *my* festival".

He had become used to the foul exhalations of the subterranean corridors and had resigned himself never again to breathe the wholesome air of the surface, but as the stones of the corridors were replaced with wooden panels, the air became fresher and pungent and poignant with a billion scents he had never forgotten. "Oh God," he whispered as the warm, dead air of the corridors was replaced by the cool, living air of the surface.

The three turned a final corner and there, with oil lamps on either side, stood an oaken door, open, with the night air rushing in. A third guard stood by the door, a hulking brute in bottle-green trousers, his face showing the scars from many recent altercations.

"Go," he rumbled, "and sin no more. Attend the Dark Festival, or it'll be the worse for you, you ballbagged bastard."

With that warning he was cast onto the pavement as the stout door slammed behind him. For many moments he lay supine upon the street, breathing in the air, letting every trace of scent impinge upon his consciousness. From the quality and temperature of the air, from the absence of sound, from the setting moon, he judged it to be near dawn. The dripping mounds of snow confused him, for the trees were in bud or leaf, but this was a minor mystery, for solution at a later date.

Dark Festival? What was it, he thought? How long had he been in that cell and how had life changed on the outside? He looked behind him and saw the spikes that jutted from the wall and at the rotting objects that were impaled upon them. He knew things had become much worse.

The electric streetlights had fallen into disuse, but here and there some form of lantern glimmered. In near agony he rose to his feet and staggered to where some poster had been hung. 'COME TO THE FESTEVALL' it said in makeshift letters. Above was a crude picture of men dancing around a raging bonfire, on top of which, like a fairy on a Christmas tree, writhed a figure marked with the placard, 'CLERGIMAN'. He groaned inwardly and leant against a lamppost for support. A smaller poster had been stuck on the post, bearing the same message, but this time the victim was a person holding an electronic calculator. He was in an iron maiden and the lid was being lowered.

He thought he heard a rustling behind him, but when he turned there was nothing other than the impression of many small glinting objects, which he dismissed as imagination.

There followed a disjointed memory of aimless wandering; when next he was fully conscious, he was wandering down a terraced row of houses, the sky grey with dawn. It was odd, he thought how many houses had their lights lit, how many furtive sounds there were for this early hour. From the pavement he could hear disjoined and fragmentary pieces of conversation. All were about some festival or other that was taking place that day. None were in favour of the event, imbuing it with a horror that was only exceeded by dread of what would follow if a person did not attend.

What was this? There was another blank in his memory. Now he was lying on the grass verge of a minor road leading out of Ormskirk. It was full dawn and the dome of the sun was rising over the trees of a distant coppice. It was all very beautiful, with the sun shining, the birds singing and the smells of spring in the air. Images or memories or both flooded back and he almost remembered his name. Apart from the time in the cell it had been good, very good, while it lasted, but he knew that it was now nearly all over. At least he had been lucky enough to go quietly and calmly and in the open. It might be the last sunrise he would ever see, but it was a magnificent one. A deep calmness filled him.

The rustling came again. He looked back and saw a swarm of brown rats formed in a crescent behind him, and he knew that the glinting objects he had seen in the glow of the lamps had been their hungry eyes.

The rats advanced and covered a kicking, squirming, squealing object that was finally still.

*   *   *

The Reverend Pedaiah Lock had spent (another) sleepless night. This one had been worse than the others, for he had felt himself prodded and goaded by some exterior force. Something had been weighing him, and he knew that whilst he had not been weighed in the balance and found wanting, the scales were poised very nicely, and that if he failed his Master in the near future whatever other good he might do in the course of his miserable span on earth, the brimstone of the pit would be his lot forever.

As he was twisted in the sweat-stained sheets he seemed to hear a voice of power and command telling him, "*Today is your day. You must be present at the dark carnival. Your star is in the ascendant. It is foretold.*"

For the rest of the night Padlock's mind was in an even greater turmoil, but with the coming of dawn he found himself wide awake and with a sort of nervous belligerence filling his thin frame. He opened the ancient window and breathed in the cool air. Far away, across the fields, he fancied that he could hear a series of thin, faint screams, but he paid it no mind.

Ragged shoes, worn coarse grey trousers belted with rope, black shirt with clerical collar, mould-inhabited duffle coat, closely buttoned to hide his religious calling, this was his attire this momentous day.

Then he went to his hoard and for once he ignored the clinking gold but pulled out the sheathed dagger with an ill-disguised lust. Unsheathing it he felt power flow from the blade; he thought he could hear some deep and powerful thrumming come from the earth, like the vibrations from the engines felt on a ship's deck. He put the knife in the coat's one serviceable pocket, making a mental note that the blade should never leave his hand whatever happened. Then he roused from sleep the snoring Miss Harmony Poffle.

*　　*　　*

The brother of Miss Harmony Poffle, Quartus, was at that moment clawing ragged chunks of corned beef, into his unwholesome mouth. He could see the tin only as a cubist blur, as could be attested by the small cuts to his hands where he had caught them on the jagged ends of the tin. He slobbered in his hunger.

He could tell it was day because the ill-defined objects and questionable blurs were brighter, but he could not ascribe other than the most rudimentary names to them. He had spent several fearful days searching for his spare pair of glasses, but had given up hope after a time, and decided to wait it out until somebody called and saved him from this mess. But, so far, nobody had called and supplies of corned beef were running dangerously low.

He groped his way to a chair, sat in it, and tried to rid his fingernails of the detritus of corned beef fragments. This done, he lapsed into a reverie of times gone by. Had T'osh not outlawed the use of the telephone (upon pain of having a red-hot nail driven into the eardrum), there would have been no real problem and he would have been able to obtain a new pair of spectacles. Spectacles were not proscribed in Ormskirk, only discouraged; there were better herbal remedies. Some of the peasants regarded such facial adornments as synonymous with those who were learned, and thus in need of a beating. Perhaps, mused Poffle, some of the things that T'osh said were not the true quill. Still, the new style spectacles, plain metal rims, no fancy ornament, were better than some of the decorated monstrosities of earlier times. He himself could remember—

—T'osh be praised, thought Poffle, dredging up a twenty-year old memory. He had been a boy terrorised by thugs in school. Sometimes they would rag him for no reason, but more often they would attack only when there was a reason. 'Four-eyes' Poffle had an ordinary pair of glasses, but one day he had come home from school to be confronted with a pair of glasses bought by his doting mother, and with the most awful design work possible on the frames – with the pink and blue colours seemingly selected by someone planning a career on the music hall stage. He had gone for an evening walk, had doubled back to the house, hidden the glasses in a trunk kept in the loft. Then he had gone outside again, covered his face with dust, and had tearfully explained to mummy how some corner boys had beaten him and thrown the glasses in a deep pond. Why he himself had not tossed the glasses into the pond rather than secreting them away in this centuried trunk, filled with the junk of generations, was something he could not now remember, though it was something that he gave profound praise for as he wiped away the dust from the top of the chest.

Suddenly the world righted itself and took on concrete form as Poffle looked at the world through the corrective lenses mounted in the hideous, gaudy frame.

Now it was time to get even with that damned Wladek. He would pay; oh, he would pay a terrible price. He would go to Ormskirk and denounce Wladek to T'osh, with a request that at the very least Wladek should be made the more symmetrical by the removal of his right leg.

But, first things first, a decently prepared proper meal of the corned beef.

*   *   *

T'osh welcomed the new day with a high-pitched scream. As he tore his bedclothes into flinders, shrieking, the pain from the scar on his neck increased.

"SATAN IS DEATH SATAN IS OUR LEADER WE WILL SERVE NO OTHER LORD HE IS OURS TO FIGHT FOR WE SHALL BE BROUGHT INTO EVERLASTING LIFE O LUCIFER THOU ART GREAT . . ."

It did no good.

*   *   *

Noah Halfmoon lay on his bed in a state of semi-consciousness; there were cruel folk who, said that his mind rarely, if ever, progressed further than that state. Like turgid waves on a vast and viscous ocean, images of the past welled up from the pelagic depths.

His formative years had been spent with an ancient and near senile relative who practised white magic to no visible effect and seemed to make ends meet by being the receiver of stolen goods from some petty and generally unsuccessful criminals. This experience was shared with his brother, Caleb, who, despite being similar in outlook to Noah in some ways, with an equally plodding disposition, did not share his one overriding passion. Noah had shown no academic prowess, nor had the household been conducive to the nurturing of any latent curiosity and intelligence. The ancient relative had, for the most part, been gin-sodden through the day, and anyway did not give a damn about whether or not Noah went to school; so his early years were largely spent in a wood behind the house, where he would light small fires and watch the flames with delight. This fondness for fires had remained with Halfmoon through adolescence and beyond and about a year ago he had thought the police were after him. But then came T'osh, and whatever peccadillos were in the past, they would safely remain there undisturbed. Although he felt a pang of regret that he had not been present at the burning of Padlock's parochial dwelling-place, he thought that this was a just part punishment for his defiling of the great man.

Deep in his brain thoughts slowly drifted along nocturnal paths, and sometimes they would link up to make an association that was sometimes sage, more often mad. Thus, he reasoned that Padlock would surely be at the Dark Carnival, and that, somehow, Noah Halfmoon would pay his debt to the great one there and then.

Of all the maniacs so far described, Halfmoon was the most dangerous. With T'osh and Padlock one could guess their intentions and actions and, if one was wise, run as quickly as possible in the other direction. With

Noah Halfmoon that was impossible: he had no plan or direction; he could come at you from any angle.

* * *

While the moon was on the wane there was some activity at the Stanley Arms. Wladek and the ever appealing, but now very animated, Florinda Farrier were busy loading a cart with crates taken from an upstairs room. It was very furtive work, judging by the silence in which it was done. At last the wagon was loaded with the last of the boxes and a stout tarpaulin was fastened over it. Wladek brought from a nearby field a hale Percheron[1] and tied it to the wagon's traces.

By now it was fully light, and the sun was nearly clearing the horizon. Florinda, now in a black cape, urged Wladek to speed, but he merely said, "Much is lost, woman, through needless haste."

Finally, the job was finished. Florinda and Wladek were bidding a very fond *au revoir* when a thin screaming came drifting from afar.

"My God, Wladek, what is that?"

"I do not know, but think it best we tend to our own affairs, Florinda Farrier. Be on your way now; you know where we will meet again."

Following a short but passionate embrace she climbed onto the board of the wagon and headed southwards.

Ormskirk lay to the north. Most of the border guards had, apparently, been temporarily relocated to the site

---

[1] A compact heavy breed of carthorse, grey or black in colour

of the Dark Festival to assist in preparations, leaving most minor roads and some major roads unmanned.

Wladek wistfully watched her go down the road until the wagon was only a black speck on the horizon; then he went into the kitchen of the inn. Deciding against further sleep, he made himself a cup of strong black coffee. Seated at the bare table he reviewed his schemes and stratagems over the past year and was pleased with them. He had not planned to be a conspirator — well, not much of a one, anyway — and had been content to skim off the profits of Poffle's farm, but then came this gang of jesters and zealots and the opportunity was far too great to be missed. He did not think that he had hurt anyone who did not deserve to be hurt and indeed, he held it to be unthinkable that the country be left in the power of T'osh. He certainly would not leave Ormskirk while the blood was still flowing through T'osh's veins.

He went into the bar where he moved between slumped bodies until he found a stool to sit on. God, he thought, what a gang of clowns to be saddled with: Cressida, a moon-dancer of the first water; Frank — talentless poseur; Martyn, an impotent idealist, vague and wishy-washy. He could think kindly only upon Timothy, who had started out as the worst of them, but had improved and matured, and had found inner strengths that Wladek certainly had not thought he possessed.

The plans! The stratagems! Wladek shook his head slowly at the memory. Some of the tasks he had set Martyn and the rest had been for his own gain, some to help in the actual downfall of T'osh, though the plans he had carried out in secret were, if anything, more condign, but many of the rest had been simply to keep the fools engaged. From an early stage he had realised that he had to keep the idiots both occupied and out of the hands of T'osh. It had not been easy — no, it had been damned difficult, and, even so, look at the fiascos he had not been able to forestall: the blowing up of the statue, the escape of Padlock, Frank's murderous and wholly unexpected attack upon Padlock. God!

And today, the most important day, when he would have been far safer alone at the Festival, he still had these idiots tagging along. Wladek always admitted to himself that his was a devious imagination; he supposed that his subconscious was even more devious. Bearing this in mind, he strongly suspected that his subconscious had its own good reasons for organising the previous night's celebration; he supposed that it was a half-hearted attempt to get the whole grab-bag of them arrested — after all they would be in T'osh's custody for less than twenty-four hours — so that he could get on with the task of exterminating *King Rodent*.

At about mid-morning, when he deemed the time right, he turned to the kitchen and prepared a hearty breakfast that would sustain and invigorate. The others came into the kitchen and tucked into their steaming plates of food. There seemed to be little evidence of hangovers; they all would be living on adrenalin from now until the death of T'osh.

The meal finished, they dressed themselves in the *fashionable garb* of Ormskirk — cloaks, floppy hats and high boots. But beneath this attire was kept all manner of weaponry — cudgels, knives, sticks, hatchets, axes, two chopped-off pikestaffs, and even a crossbow with seven quarrels[1]. Abel Renton held a light throwing-

---

[1] an arrow having a four-edged head

knife in his scarred hand and muttered, "Just let me get within ten yards of the bastard." He had always been good with the knife, but frequent practice over the past few days had turned him into an adept.

*   *   *

Wladek had loaded the shotgun and had strapped it to his wooden leg. Baggy trousers served the purpose of both concealing the weapon and enabling him to get at it easily. He did not think that he would have much time in which to aim and fire, and he would have to aim with great care, for he had shortened the barrel by many inches. He could never have concealed the weapon had it been its full length, and he doubted whether the scattered shot would have been sufficient to kill T'osh at the probable distance from which he would be firing. No, much better to take the added risk of an extra second of time to aim and send two packages of unscattered shot at the little monster. He reckoned that he could shatter the head of T'osh.

Limping slightly more than usually, he went to his men and gave them stiff tots of brandy.

"This no time for great speeches," he said, "but time for great actions. Let's go and exterminate the rodents who have sullied our fair land. Let's carve our way into the history books."

They began the resolute march to the Field of the Dark Festival.

*   *   *

If T'osh's so-called *Perfect State* had looked to the Dark Ages for their example, then the Dark Festival had looked even further into the past. It hailed from a dim and distant time that is not all that dim and distant, but which is hidden by a tangle of myths and ignorance for most people; the time before the Roman invasion. To most people, and certainly to the inhabitants of Ormskirk, who in general thought that the best use of a book was to prop up the leg of a shaky table, it was a time of dark forests, of airy presences, of strange stones, of druids, of bonfires on lonely hills: a world where magic, dark magic, worked.

*　　*　　*

The site of the Dark Festival was a large plateau some three square miles in area and perhaps thirty feet above the rest of the land; the design of the festival mixed aspects of Neolithic henges and Iron Age hill forts.

At the base of the plateau ran a ring of dykes, much like those of the oppidan at Wheathampstead, that ensured that no wheeled vehicle could pass the barrier, only a man on foot or, at best, one on horseback. There was, of course, a way through, for T'osh had transported most of the Festival gear by heavy lorry in a secret convoy, but that was not general knowledge.

Beyond the dyke, once one mounted to the plateau, the site of the festival could be seen. The ground was elliptical, with a length of slightly under a mile on its longitudinal axis. Like the henges, its boundary was marked by a series of dykes, ditches and ramparts of earth and melting snow. Only at two points did the dykes and ramparts cease: at the longitudinal axes, where the central causeway ran straight through the ground. At these points, the only points of entry, two

3 6 4

gigantic trilithons had been erected and here stood numbers of troopers taking the names and addresses of the visitors.

Just as the site jumbled history, so too did the garb of the troopers: there was one carrying a Celtic spear; there another with a Viking double-headed axe; there a third with a Mesolithic bow. If there could be said to be a norm, then one would have to settle for the typical garb of the Belgae[1] of about the time of Vercingetorix[2], and even then one had to make allowances. But, in general, the dress was of woollen hosen banded with linen strips, short, plain kilt and tunic, and a short mail shirt made of strips of cured leather joined by twine. The sword was the Celtic long sword, though this time made of beryllium-steel, and the shield was a small, round targe.

Inside the field, slightly to the west of one of the foci of the ellipse, a mound had been raised, and upon this stood structures of wood. Nothing stood at the base of the mound; the stalls and shows were at the other end of the field.

Some of the stalls had been made into the shape of dolmens and cromlechs; others were of more conventional make. Some of the huts were tightly locked and troopers would come and drive away any who seemed to become interested in these problematic buildings.

There was of course no technology in this most ancient setting but what was this cable leading away from a wooden box? Why was there an amplifier,

---

[1] An ancient Celtic people who in Roman times inhabited present-day Belgium and France.

[2] Gallic chieftain and hero, executed for leading a revolt against the Romans under Julius Caesar

undoubtedly an amplifier, in the box? It was very curious.

*　　*　　*

Padlock looked at the people going into the Festival, and at the whole festival itself from the branches of a tree. He touched his dagger, saying, "We shall cleanse the temple."

*　　*　　*

Martyn had no difficulty in entering the Festival ground; the guards were merely taking the names of all those who attended so that when the event was over those who had not attended could be punished in a suitable manner. He gave his name as Benny Barwise, after a blues musician he been friendly with, although he had not seen him for more than a year. However, he knew that Benny lived just outside the *Perfect State* in rural Bickerstaffe and would have had the sense to keep well clear of events such as this one.

Inside the Festival the men separated and went their pre-arranged way.

Near to the entrance the stalls were of a reasonably mundane nature and sold goods that were hard to get outside. Hats, cloaks, boots, all manner of clothing had been difficult to procure for the past several months; under one of T'osh's many ill-considered edicts the populace were expected to make their own clothing. Further into the Festival the goods became more exotic, with ointments and unguents, charms, holy piglets, tame crows, wolves' teeth and questionable liquors and many other strange objects on display. One stall sold only juniper wood, which, it attested, was not merely useful for construction, but also cured sickness and kept away the demons. Another stall sold potatoes, not as comestibles but as rheumatism preventatives, and, it was said, were pretty good at curing warts.

Though it was shortly past noon, the ground was already well filled with people and Martyn found himself jostled by the horde. He had difficulty in heading for the mound and found himself forced to follow the crowd as it swirled around the stalls like a tide around jutting rocks. He was almost forced into a dark and fearful cromlech, but managed at the last moment to divert into a side stream. What was particularly wrong about this stall Martyn could not definitely say. Perhaps it was the dwarf, who stood upon the lintel stone, croaking,

"To foretell the future, put an ivy leaf in a bowl of water on New Year's Eve and leave it there until Twelfth Night: if it is still green, the coming year will be happy; if it has developed black spots, there will be illness."

At the next stall, an open circle of stones this time, a fire had been lit, into which broad beans were being thrown. A short, ruddy-faced man mainly in the garb of a La Tene Celt[1] was reading a declaration:

"It has been discovered that the souls of the dead reside inside broad beans, and the perfect State has discovered that if a person sleeps in a bean field he will awake

---

[1] Of or relating to a Celtic culture in Europe from about the 5th to the 1st centuries BC and characterized by a distinctive type of curvilinear decoration.

insane. We have incontrovertible proof of this. Therefore, we are burning all beans. If, after this date, someone is discovered with beans or bean plants he will serve ten years in penal servitude, then will be hanged."

Stocks and pillories were dotted between the stalls, filled with dejected looking people in capes awaiting their fates. He passed a temporary smithy and was surprised by its homeliness amid the horror. But this pleasant feeling was short lived; for in the smithy eight women were having metal masks fitted to their faces. "Suspected gossipers," Martyn was informed by a delighted spectator who was clearly trembling with the anticipation of some sort of floor show. For these unfortunate women the mere allegation was enough to secure their punishment. It was considered to be a bureaucratic excess to actually put them on trial. T'osh had, at one point, made much of the fact that he was dispensing with so much *red tape* which only served to impede the administering of justice. "We can make our own laws, without interference from outsiders", he had proclaimed to widespread approval, feeling it unnecessary to also point out that he alone would be the one deciding what those laws might consist of.

Martyn was nearer the stage on the mound by now and could see someone mounting the wooden boards. The hidden audio equipment worked well enough: everyone in the enclosure could hear, *by magic*, everything the speaker pronounced.

"Oh people of Ormskirk, we are gathered here today in the name of T'osh, who has done so much to improve the land and our lot in life. So I say, eat, drink and be merry; for there is much to do and see. Meanwhile, a feast of entertainment awaits you upon this stage. We will begin on a light note with the dance of the druids."

A group of six men, dressed only in leather aprons and carrying severed heads (which might have been imitation, but were much more likely to be real), began to dance upon the stage to the accompaniment of flutes and an assortment of lutes and other, less identifiable, medieval stringed instruments.

A surge in the crowd dragged Martyn to a stall where a dwarf was shackled. He was whimpering and crying, but this seemed to have no effect upon the men and women who were throwing rotting vegetables and ordure at him. A prize of a mug of strong cask ale for three direct hits upon the dwarf probably explained why most of the people around the stall were riotously drunk. It was not clear why he was being punished.

As he came nearer and nearer the stage, exotics came up to him and showed Martyn their scars and their stumps. One particular maniac, in the tertiary stages of syphilis, tottered up to him in a crazed shuffle and thrust a rotting, greenish-black arm in Martyn's face. The arm was impaled with myriad pointed objects. The owner of the arm twisted several of the objects and tittered that he could "feel 'em scrapin' agin the bones." This particular creature was also notable in that his entire dress consisted of worn female undergarments. After twisting and tweaking a number of the pointed objects the exotic saw that Martyn's only reaction was to turn somewhat grey. He then tottered to other members of the crowd, singing in a voice as cracked and demented as his pitiful mind:

I have so many panties
provided by me aunties
And plenty more big knickers
From other people's sisters

My lingerie collection
Is quite a nice selection
I steal from washing lines
But now they are all MINE

* * *

Noah Halfmoon had come to the Festival and was wandering through its alleys, seeing nothing unusual or appalling in such stalls as the 'Great Felix', who did frightful things to live cats, or the 'Mighty McGurn', a gangling giant whose slavering mouth puked out all sorts of sanctimonious shite, whilst the same time he pawed and fondled the body of a girl, no more than eighteen or nineteen years of age, drugged with alcohol. The devil himself could appear at the festival and Noah Halfmoon would not think it too unusual.

* * *

Napalming the *Surplus Workforce* was the next item on the agenda. Several men, too old or too feeble to carry on with the tilling of the land, were herded into a chicken wire enclosure. A small ballista had been set up on the stage and its catapult drawn back. Three troopers gingerly put three grey metal cylinders into the catapult cup. By this time the men in the enclosure had become somewhat agitated, even to the point of trying to climb the wire, so the chief trooper on the stage let fly the ballista. The enclosure and all inside disappeared, engulfed by bright orange flames and greasy black smoke.

*   *   *

The light of the pyre glinted in Halfmoon's eyes and he remembered the fires he had started in the past. The little fires in the wood, the bigger fires in the wood, the times he set fire to barns and sheds and derelict houses; the three times he had set fire to houses that were not derelict. He had enjoyed them all and would have still done the same even if the police had caught him. Oh, it had been a close-run thing, with the police circling in, but then T'osh had come.

One evening he had been seated in his filthy hovel when there had been thunderous knocking on the front door. He had opened the door to be confronted with three thugs. "I — I — I never done it. It wasn't me," he had blurted out in terror. Then T'osh had stepped out of the darkness. "Indeeeeeeeeeeeeeeeeed, but it *was* you. You are a fire raiser. I have need of your services."

The happy time: He had been doing what he most enjoyed, and he was being paid for it. He could still see the schools and libraries burning, and he had special memories concerning the burning of the main library; T'osh had dictated that the Chief librarian and all his staff be trapped by that fire. And he had done that part, done it well. He could still remember with delight hearing the crackle of the fire as the building burned, and the shrieks of the doomed people trapped in the basement.

And it had all been like that, so good, serving T'osh. But now, had he been part of some monstrous error.

T'osh had attacked Padlock, a man whose boots T'osh was not worthy to lick. And he had been part of it. He must harm T'osh and help Padlock. But how?

* * *

Quartus Poffle continued to trudge towards Ormskirk. His limited diet did not induce much stamina or staying power, so he was hot and tired even before he had completed his first mile. Still, he had a mission.

* * *

Noah Halfmoon did not feel well. His brain was buzzing, and he wished that he could shut it down for the time being. Various matters, previously thought unconnected, now seemed to be linked. Halfmoon had no time for deep thought, and very little time for formal thought; but he was being forced to see everything in a new light.

For example, months back, some of T'osh's Legion II Asmodeus garrison had taken in a cat as a pet. It was not strictly banned; T'osh had said in passing that the Perfect State could not really tolerate pets. Still, it had seemed a minor sin, and Halfmoon had been given the task of looking after the cat. Malkyn had not been much of a cat, but it was one of the few things that had ever shown affection for Halfmoon. He fed it twice a day and gave it as much milk as he could steal from the Commissary. Then one day along came one of T'osh's new henchmen, the Great Felix. He had seemed friendly and had bought Halfmoon some drinks. In the course of conversation Felix had said how much he had disagreed with the anti-pet ideas of T'osh. Halfmoon, warming to the man and his views, had told about Malkyn.

Next day Malkyn was gone. Halfmoon had assumed that it had just wandered off, but what he had seen the Great Felix doing to cats in the stall . . . could this have happened to Malkyn too?

For the first time in his life he felt doubt about the rights of what he had done. He felt that he had made a terrible mistake in siding with T'osh: he was the devil. He should have known that the real man of God was the Reverend Pedaiah Lock.

He knew remorse for the first time in his life, but could find no vent for it, other than to file it away with his tumorous guilt and hope that some means of expiation come along.

He broke away from the crowds, pushing them aside, and headed for the ramparts of the festival site. Sometime before he reached the first rampart, the personality of Noah Halfmoon disintegrated and was sucked down a mental vortex and was reborn in tatters and fractured shards. As he began to run, he grunted out repeatedly two words, "I'm sorry!" By the time he reached the rampart these words had become metamorphosed into "BURN: DESTROY."

He rolled down the rampart slope, bruising himself on the sharp stones of the bottom, and then scaled the muddy ditch slope. Whatever the thing was that ran across the field, it could no longer be called a human being.

How long he would have run, his ruined mind aflame with images of destruction, of flying through the air, blasting and burning things whilst something omnipotent thrummed in the background, it is not easy to say. However, some few hundred yards beyond the ditch he was tripped by something and landed painfully on the ground. Dully, he looked around for what had tripped him. He found numerous cables, some large and thick, some thinner than earthworms, seemingly leading from the Festival site to a grove of ancient trees. The throbbing, which had been in his head, was still there, but it seemed to emanate from the grove. Animal curiosity drove him to the trees.

Peering through he could see large yellow boxes mounted on wheels and small red boxes lying on the ground; the cables all came from these boxes.

Noah Halfmoon sniffed the air: he could smell petrol.

* * *

The man in charge of the generators had committed a minor breach of etiquette in front of one of the Legionnaires and had been given the maintenance and running job. It was not a job he liked: the small, petrol-driven generators were all right; but it was the diesels that were the buggers. He switched off number 4, which was getting low on fuel, and manhandled the large drum close to it. The top of the drum stuck, and he was a few minutes taking the top off, then to top it all, the bleeding stirrup pump seemed to take on a malignant life all of its own. Cursing and swearing, the man did not see Noah Halfmoon creep up on him, armed with an eighteen-inch wrench.

Noah Halfmoon looked about the site. In the large drums, difficult to manhandle in their own right, was the thick oil that was no good for burning. But he searched around and shortly found several two-gallon jerry cans. Opening them he smelt the lovely scent of petrol. He resealed the jerry cans and tied them to a piece of rope, three to each end. Using the spanner as a yoke, he lifted the cans and started back to the festival.

Halfmoon's expiation had begun.

*   *   *

The crowd was, by early evening, sullen and ugly. The brilliant sun, which had melted the last traces of snow, had also burnt the crowd. The air was thick with sweat and the crowd were hot, tired and dirty.

The festival, which had been meant to mark the eternal Perfect State, had gone sour, and Wladek, who was near the stage with Martyn, thought that the fall of T'osh could be brought about with little or no help from him. He was wrong in this, for when a tocsin bell called all and sundry to the stage, and T'osh himself appeared amid a cloud of smoke and sparks, there was no sudden storming of the stage; only a scattered clapping which grew louder until tumultuous; this being effected by several dozen thugs armed with clubs going about the crowds.

A sort of trial had gone on, the conclusion of which was a speech given by an extremely intoxicated juryman, in which it was stated, in a somewhat slurred manner, that so-and-so had been found guilty of:

a) *Saying that T'osh was not all that he was cracked up to be*
b) *Wearing bright clothes*
c) *Trying to 're-invent' electricity.*

Gallows had been hastily erected, and the prisoner had been brought out and the noose put round his neck. At this point T'osh appeared, and began to deliver a lengthy, frantic, and at times hysterical speech, which covered well-trodden grounds and mentioned the need to subvert progress, punish wrongdoers etc.

Meanwhile, the condemned man waited.

Martyn nudged Wladek and hissed, "You have the gun; surely now is the time to finish off the Evil One."

"Not yet! His guards are all around and would be upon us before I took aim. Wait until they are bored by the speech and tired by the sun."

"But how long?"

"Our chance will come."

The condemned man was duly dispatched as previously indicated. His place was soon taken by another who had dared to transgress in some way or other and therefore was considered to require mortification to be closely followed by an early demise. Naturally all of this was 'for his own good' although he remained obstinately hesitant to express his gratitude.

* * *

Quartus Poffle was near total exhaustion. He had gone to Ormskirk only to trudge the extra miles to the festival when told that T'osh would be there. When at last he saw the site of the Festival, he was tempted to break into a run, but his constitution would never have allowed him to take such gross liberties. Besides, he had to think about his ingrown toenails.

As he entered the grounds under the lintel of the trilithon, he saw that the crowd was gathered around the stage and was being addressed by someone who was too far away to identify by sight, but whose voice was clearly that of T'osh. Ah, the magic of T'osh that by some arcane art he could project his voice throughout the entire encampment.

But what was this smell of petrol? Poffle was passing some stalls, and he could see that a bearded and lumpish youth was pouring some liquid — petrol! — from some cans onto some of the stalls.

"What do *you* fink you are doing?"

Halfmoon looked up and saw the loathly Poffle. He suppressed an overwhelming urge to make unkind remarks about Poffle's unusual eyeglasses.

"Ah . . .'tis you again."

"Yes, and I can see vat you are up to no good!"

"Ex . . . act . . . ly"

"What are you up to?"

"I 'ave a job to do, 'n' I intend to do it well."

"Is vat so? What job, my lad, is vis?"

Noah Halfmoon pursed his lips and spoke but one word: "Fire."

Poffle saw that drastic action was needed but realised that he was ill equipped to deal physically with "vis insolent brute" now approaching him intimidatingly. He trotted off in terror, heading for T'osh.

* * *

The two security men, at the bottom of the steps leading to the stage, eyed Padlock and Harmony with suspicion but did not approach them. Padlock had spent a terrible day looking at the evil of the *Perfect State* and was nearly as unhinged as Halfmoon with his cans of petrol. He was trembling, and his bone-china complexion was now so utterly pallid as to give the impression of transparency.

If only he could gain access to the stage, then T'osh would meet his doom as the sacred dagger slid between his ribs. Then would Ormskirk be his by divine right. If only . . .

Padlock closed his eyes and whispered a prayer. *"Oh Lord, look upon your humble servant who seeks only to deal out justice and retribution to evil sinners."*

Unfortunately, one of the guards must have had excellent hearing, for he approached Padlock. "Was that praying I heard, you ballbag?"

As the man approached and came from the shadows cast by the stage, Padlock gasped, for the man's face was a cicatrix, a network of scars, and the club he carried served at times as a walking stick. Then Padlock saw the bottle-green trousers and he recalled that night he, with the minimal help of some godless lost souls, had set upon this thug and trounced him. The man also recognised Padlock.

"Ah-ha, so it is *you*, is it? Well, my jolly boy, you've got some explaining to do. Not that it will do much good."

Padlock, in an excess of cowardice and terror, forgot that he could have sent the man considerably nearer God — or the devil — by a simple blow with the dagger. Instead, he allowed the oafish henchman to grab him by the throat and lift him into the air.

Padlock began to turn blue about the face.

"Wait," he wailed, "you are mistaken. I come in good faith. I—"

Padlock's tongue, rapidly turning black, popped out of his mouth.

He was saved only by the arrival of Quartus Poffle who, near to death with exhaustion, blundered past Miss Harmony Poffle who was fruitlessly searching for a large stone to brain the thug, and fell down, gasping. Padlock was contemptuously cast to the ground.

"I must see T'osh," wheezed Poffle in a voice reedier and feebler than ever. "Great trouble . . . over ver . . . about to happen . . . and warn T'osh . . . bout Wladek . . . up to no good . . . warn . . ."

"What are you saying? Speak up, or I will hit you."

But Poffle could say no more and could do nought but point a pink index finger in the direction of Halfmoon's sabotage. The henchman called over one of his colleagues and, after whispering rapidly, they decided that whatever was happening demanded investigation. They ran off through the crowd, which by this time was so densely packed they made perhaps ten yards in as many minutes.

For several minutes Miss Poffle stood around, doing nothing, looking at the unedifying sight of her brother and her treasured gasp and wheeze in the sunlight. Both seemed to recover enough to try to essay the ladder at the same time. Poffle had gone up three rungs when he felt a pallid claw upon his ankle.

"Oh no you don't," said Padlock.

"I must see T'osh."

"I have a prior appointment."

"Well, you will just have to wait," whined Poffle and started to climb the ladder.

Neither of the antagonists could be described as physically impressive; one was skeletal, pale and fragile; the other short, pasty of complexion and, partly as a result of following his own prognostications for a healthy life (ie:- no exercise, no vegetables, no fresh air), almost totally without physical strength. However, Padlock thought that the time for talking was over and the time for action had come. Taking one of Poffle's ankles in both hands he pulled, slipped, and fell backwards, bringing Poffle down on top of him.

"How dare you," shrieked Poffle, "I'll kill you! I'll murder you!"

But Padlock had extracted himself and was kicking the supine Poffle. Then Padlock fell, when Poffle twisted Padlock's stationary foot; Poffle was all over Padlock, pounding feeble blows that nonetheless caused Padlock to retreat. His pudgy hands gripped Padlock's already weakened throat and began to squeeze.

To one side of the combat was Harmony Poffle, hopping from one foot to another with impotent and confused fury. She felt incapable of interfering in the fray, for she had a certain regard for both combatants. She loved the Reverend dearly, but she did not want her brother to come to harm. But when the Reverend's domed forehead began to turn blue, and then blue-black, she felt she must act or lose whatever love she might find in her barren existence.

"I'm sorry Quartus," she said as she brought a large, flat stone upon her brother's head. There was a dull thud, a groan from her brother as he rolled off Padlock and lay moaning in the grass which was soon adorned with a slight trickle of blood and a pair of garish spectacles which had slipped off their owner's head.

*   *   *

"Firefirefirefirefirefirefire," chanted Noah Halfmoon as he lit a match.

For a moment he looked at the glow, the pretty glow, as it crept along the wood. Then he lit the strip of paper and dropped it at base of one of the huts. There was a crump! — and the hut was engulfed in a mushroom of flame. Three further crumps! — and the whole line of huts was ablaze. A gust of wind sent the flames to the next group of stalls. And then to a third doused row.

"Firefirefirefirefirefirefire," repeated Noah Halfmoon.

*   *   *

Padlock had reached the top of the ladder and stood at the back of the stage. He looked at the little monster on the stage, down on his knees, banging his head against the bare boards, screaming hoarsely his inane, repetitive mantras. Then he saw the flames that were engulfing the stalls.

So too did T'osh.

Padlock drew the dagger from its sheaf and started forwards.

". . . these ragged tongues of rotting decaying flesh shall be consigned to the flames, *the flames*," T'osh was saying. "We will have none of this in the perfect state. No, we will kill them all, punching out their eyes and putting pointed sticks in their anal pass— AAAAAAARRRRRGGGGGGGHHHH! LOOK YOU DOLTS! FIRE — FIRE! — ARSON! My enemies pooooooooooooooooooohhhhhhhhh! Put out the fires. PUT OUT THE FIRES!"

*   *   *

Down below there was confusion and panic. Everyone was alarmed but those at the back of the crowd, those nearest the flames, pushed inwards, crushing those nearer the stage. This caused much milling about and some panic. The situation was not improved by the action of the troopers who, trying to get to the blaze, at first pushed people aside; then, when this did not meet with much success, knocked them to the ground with the pommels and flats of their swords and the butts of their spears.

Martyn was knocked to the ground, but Wladek rolled up his trouser leg and unfastened the shotgun. Putting it to his shoulder he aimed at T'osh, who was standing on the stage, looking at the conflagration with a look that mingled rage, despair, shock and a realisation of defeat.

"Now!" shrieked Martyn.

T'osh turned his head to look at the mob. The shotgun kicked back. Once. Twice.

* * *

T'osh's despair was as plumbless as his anger. As he saw the stalls blaze, he knew that the Dark Festival was a flop. He had no doubt that he would remain ruler of Ormskirk for evermore but, until he consolidated his hold again, his methods of control would have to be even more draconian than the Perfect State advocated. Still, it could not be helped. The people were still his, though, and would forever remain so.

He gazed over the mob and shrieked and put his hand to the scar on his neck. There! there! was one of the rotting pieces of maggot-infested sludge that had defeated him the first time. And next to him, Oh Beelzebub! was a man with—

T'osh's lower chest and stomach disintegrated into fractures of bone, ruptured grey-blue tubes and blood that did not so much trickle as flood out. In that moment he knew terror, pain and despair greater than he had ever inflicted upon his subjects: he knew he was headed straight for Satan.

The force of the shots spun him around and for a moment he saw a maniac skeleton holding the sacred dagger before tottering to the edge of the stage.

"Assassinated! Arrrgggghhhhh, I cannot die. Satan, do not let me die."

Satan, however, for reasons destined to remain undisclosed, elected not to intervene on this occasion. T'osh tried to say something more, but all that came out was a gush of blood. He fell off the stage, twitched for a few moments, then was still.

T'osh was dead.

*　　*　　*

Noah Halfmoon looked up from the blaze and saw T'osh fall off the stage. He did not take much notice of it, but then he saw a figure behind the fallen T'osh. It was he! Padlock.

In one of the locked huts that were now ablaze, retained in case the napalming of the surplus workforce was not as spectacular as hoped for, stood nine hundred gallons of high-octane aviation fuel; at this moment it decided to explode.

*　　*　　*

Padlock had advanced to the front of the stage when T'osh had fallen. His moon-like face was locked in an expression of dazed idiocy. He still held high the sacred dagger. Looking down past the edge of the stage, he could see T'osh twitching, but Padlock had seen the severity of T'osh's wounds. There was no doubt that he was dead.

Padlock could take in the events, but he seemed to be merely a passive observer; he felt no elation at the fact that T'osh had been defeated, nor did he consciously plan to make good use of this moment. Nevertheless, some part of his mind had all systems green, for it commanded Padlock to raise the dagger high, and cry,

"I have the dagger. The sacred dagger. I am your rightful leader. Listen to me."

Heads at the front of the crowd turned and saw the dagger. A reverential whisper went through the crowd and more heads turned. Then, just as the heads at the back of the crowd were turning, everyone, including Padlock, was distracted by a titanic explosion from the stalls.

Flames and debris flew high into the air, as the twilight was made garish by the glow. A wave of heat scorched those at the edge of the crowd. But even as the flames were still clawing into the air, something, it looked like a candle-flame magnified, came running out of the blaze. This something that shrieked and sent out curtains of flame — crashed through the crowd — frantic men and women clawed each other to avoid the torch's path. By the time it reached the ladder to the stage, most of the flames had died, leaving only a blackened, smoking, oozing object that was clawing its way up the ladder. It reached the stage, tottered across to where Padlock stood dumbfounded. It swayed for a moment, Padlock could see monstrous burns and wounds: how could this thing still live?

"My . . . life . . . is . . . yours, ex . . . act . . . ly," the twisted thing said, then collapsed off the stage, to lie, lifeless, by the husk of T'osh.

All the crowd's attention was now on Padlock.

He drew the dagger on high and shrieked, "I have the dagger. I have killed the evil T'osh. I am your rightful ruler. Seize the minions of T'osh."

The crowd moved as one against the stricken troopers and stallholders. They did not stand a chance.

"Kill them! Rend them to pieces," shrieked Padlock.

The crowd did as they were told.

* * *

"What have we done? Christ, what have we done?" moaned Wladek. "I swear I aimed to do good. I swear it." Turning to Martyn, Timothy and Frank he said, "Get out! Get out of it while you can! God knows what we've done . . . and who knows if it can be undone. Get out of it, while you still can."

So saying, Wladek pushed his way through the crowd and was soon lost to sight.

Despite the carnage about them, the trio seemed to think that the whole thing was some sort of academic exercise; perhaps they were in shock. Even so, though they did not show the breakneck speed of Wladek's departure, they still made their way unobtrusively to the edge of the crowd.

"Truly, this is ridiculous," said Martyn, "surely they must know that Padlock did not kill T'osh."

"Possibly, at first; now, I fear, the crowd are believing what they want to believe, that Padlock is a saviour. As a clergyman he appears to be at the opposite end of the spectrum from the Black Magician. Also, alas, he has the dagger."

Timothy lapsed into a gloom-laden silence.

"What shall we do then?" asked Martyn after a time.

"What can we do?" asked Timothy. "Where are those brave lads from the pub last night? You know where they are: listening to Padlock's every word, lapping up his sentiments, swallowing all his proclamations, no matter how ridiculous. You saw what he did to T'osh's men. If he sees us, or remembers us, we are likely to be torn to pieces also."

"In that case," said Frank, "I suggest that our party stages a discreet withdrawal to some place where we can observe the proceedings without putting ourselves in jeopardy; our friend the Reverend is behaving in a somewhat portentous manner."

* * *

Padlock seized the moment.

"People of Ormskirk, I stand before you on this God-given day, having slain the Dark One, and damned his accursed soul to the fires and torments of everlasting damnation. A shadow has passed over the land, bringing sadness, misery, pain, disease, destruction and death.

"But now light has cast away the shadow. The curse is lifted and evil is once more banished by the power of the *Lord*. Know ye this power, for it hath no equal. Know ye the ways of the *Lord*, for they must also be your ways. Tread no path but the path of righteousness: then shall ye gain salvation.

"This land must be purged of all evil.

"Ye shall seek goodness and cleanliness.

"Ye shall not be proud.

"Ye shall not be frivolous.

"Ye shall not fritter away your time at doors and windows and taverns, but shall eschew worldly pleasures, seeking salvation in the hard work of one's calling.

"Cursed shall be the soul of the idler, drunkard or wastrel. Beware of men who speak only of the pleasures of the flesh, for I warn you, ye who seeketh pleasures on this earth truly forfeits the true pleasures of the next world. Ye shall embrace poverty. Ye shall embrace hardship. Ye shall embrace hunger. Ye shall embrace the harsh winter wind, and, aye, ye shall embrace suffering.

"For *blessed* is the man who indulges in hard work. Blessed he who spends but little and lives frugally. But *accursed* shall be the spendthrift, and *accursed* shall be those who transgress: the thief, the idler, the sinner, those who would seek to adopt a collective approach in the workplace by securing a trade union agreement. They shall be dealt with harshly in our land. Their flesh shall be mortified, until the time that the *Lord* looks kindly upon them.

"Have faith, my people. Be not like the lost tribe in the desert. Know ye the way of the *Lord*. I will show you the gateway to the Promised Land; for we have the makings of it here, beneath our feet in this place — the Sacred City — Ormskirk!

"Blessed is he who knows and follows the ways of the Reverend Pedaiah Lock, GOD'S disciple on earth, who hath delivered the multitude from the Black Magician.

"Be ye not faint-hearted, like those of diverse origins known as the mixed multitude, who in the desert didst turn upon Moses and urge a return to Egypt. Nay! Ye of Ormskirk are of pure stock, and capable of adhering to a chosen path. But the path is not an easy one, nor is it smooth. Ye must beware of the temptations that would lead you astray.

"And ye must act, as ye didst just now, casting down the evil followers of T'osh after I had shown the way by disposing of the arch-fiend himself. Your first task now awaits you. We have destroyed the source of the infection yet is there more of them than have been accounted for here. In their barracks at the Court, in the highways and byways, there are men of T'osh who know not of their leader's downfall, nor of the fate of their colleagues who were gathered here. These men cannot be saved; they cannot partake of salvation. They must be weeded out and destroyed.

"Take your cudgels and break heads.

"Take your knives and slash flesh.

"Take your billhooks and hack limbs.

"Take your fire and burn sinful bodies; give them the taste of the hell that is theirs.

"Take your stones and break bones.

"Take no prisoners, show no mercy, spare none.

"Destroy all their works.

"And if you find one of T'osh's men swathed in bandages and scars, and dressed in bottle green trousers, whether he be alive or dead — bring me his head.

"NOW — GO TO IT!"

The crowd rose as one, with a collective shriek that could be heard for miles. The leaders chaired Padlock, and the dagger glinted in the moonlight. The first kill was given to Padlock. When they brought in a bedraggled trooper, Padlock sunk the blade of the sacred dagger into his throat. The dagger seemed to glow brighter after that.

*   *   *

That night, in the town and in the fields, there were scenes of carnage equal to and greater than anything which T'osh had instigated. The night was made horrible by the howls of the pursued and shrieks of the cornered; the night was made lurid by the flames of the burning magistrates court.

They had gone there first and had trapped most of the forces of T'osh, who were in attendance still, totally unaware of the disaster at the Dark Festival. They were herded into some of the unoccupied cells, told that justice would in time be meted out to them in accordance with the word of the *Lord*, and left to think about their fate. They did not have long to think. With Padlock in the van, they went to the occupied cells. There they interrogated the prisoners. Some had been imprisoned for deeds abhorrent to T'osh but quite acceptable to Padlock; these were released and readily joined forces with Padlock's army. Others, however, had committed offences heinous to both T'osh and Padlock, and these were left in their cells with the assurance that they would be released as soon as possible.

"Their souls must be cleansed," said Padlock to the multitude. "Both the men of T'osh and those misguided ones that still repine in the cells, their souls must all be purified, so that the glory of the *Lord* can enter there unto. And what is the best way of clearing dead weeds from fertile fields? How do you cleanse your fields of dead plants, weeds and vermin every year? Surely you know."

They did. They razed the courthouse, the cells, the occupants to the ground.

Then they started on the remnants of the army that had neither been at the Festival nor the courthouse. In the main they were at known posts and their liquidation was no difficult matter. The rest were hunted down without mercy. It may be that some did manage to escape; but if so, they kept a low profile in later years. None boasted of taking part in the annexation of Ormskirk. None proudly showed scars from the days of oppression. There was complete and utter silence from any putative survivor.

Just after midnight Padlock suggested to the throng that they examine their own consciences. Was there any sin that was being hidden from the eyes of the *Lord*? They were also told to dwell upon the actions of their neighbours. Had any suspicion been lodged in their hearts about the actions, beliefs, thriftiness of their neighbours?

The streets of Ormskirk were running red with blood again.

* * *

They had agreed to meet back at the Stanley Arms once T'osh had been eliminated; they had planned a binge that would have paled the one of the night before. They had not anticipated the utter disaster that had befallen the land, but still, like dazed automata, they were returning there. In the distance, towards Ormskirk, they could hear faint cries, and the low clouds that had come along with the night glowed redly.

With Martyn were Timothy, Frank, Abel Renton and a sobbing Cressida, who had turned up from who knew where? No one knew exactly why she was crying, but no one felt like comforting her. At length she stopped whimpering, and started going on about the divine, if somewhat obscure Buddhist prophet, Bhaghatasee Ranjeet Swami. (Cressida's strand of Buddhism was somewhat far from the mainstream and the total number of followers globally was thought not to exceed double figures.)

"It is simple. One must seek that situation from which, having gone, one never comes back. The branches of this tree extend downwards and upwards, nourished by the three modes of material nature. The twigs are the objects of the senses, and this tree also has roots descending, linked to the fructiferous actions of humanistic society.

"Now it follows that one who is free of illusion, fresh prestige, not to—"

"Oh, for Christ's sake, please put a sock in it just for once, you foolish frippet, will you?" yelled Timothy. "We've all been through a lot today and would welcome a bit of peace and quiet."

"Hear, hear," said Frank. "Unless you have something constructive to say, I suggest that you keep your mouth well and truly closed."

"Where are all the men who came with us?" wailed Martyn.

"With Padlock; where else?" sighed Timothy

"Where is Wladek?"

"Why do you ask this, Martyn?" said Abel Renton, "you said that he ran off when he had fired the shots."

"Ha!" croaked Cressida. "Nonsense, he is back there, ready to shed his last drop of blood for freedom. Why do you tell such lies?"

Some few minutes later John Ambler caught up with them. Cressida asked frantic questions about Wladek.

"Aaahhh," said John Ambler, "ah saw 'im go like clappers out ah the Fest'val. Well away now, ah reckon. Done a bunk."

Cressida began to tear her hair. "Oh hateful, hurtful lies! If he was going anywhere, he would have taken me with him. You are just trying to upset me. You all hate me, don't you? You've always hated me. You'll do anything to upset me."

Cressida fell to the ground, where she pounded her fists on the earth. The rest stood in a faintly amused silence.

They let her carry on for a time, then Martyn said, "I doubt if we can do any good standing here."

"Aye," agreed Abel Renton. "The Stanley Arms best be our first stopping place, as earlier agreed. Perhaps we can pick up word of Wladek."

All of them, even the hysterical Cressida, advanced. They had not gone far when they heard sounds of a figure approaching. They were frightened by this, and tried to take cover, but there was nothing to hide behind. A pair of dazzling spectacles were the first thing they noticed, behind which there advanced a puny fellow. An ovine voice bleated at them.

"Wait for me. I am coming wif you. I don't fink vat Padlock will treat me too kindly. I say, slow down a bit: you must know vat exercise is not good for you.

"Did you see vat Halfmoon fellow? Did you see what happened to T'osh? I fink he is dead. Well and truly blasted out of existence. I vouchsafe vat I have never seen anyfink like vat ever in my life. I fink vat we should—"

"Oh God!" howled Timothy, burying his face in his hands.

Chapter 18:

The End of the Matter

At the conclusion of earlier adventures Martyn had always felt a slight air of unreality waft about his person. He felt ten feet tall; he imagined cheering crowds waving flags at him; he heard the strains of a military band march proudly out of some vast deep. But not now, not when the final defeat of T'osh was a fact; now all seemed horribly real and ugly. The pulsing glow on the low clouds to the north and west carried no awe or beauty; they were the frightful crematoriums of all that Martyn held dear. He had replaced one madman with another. In no way could the shrieks that carried messages of misery and agony be translated into paeans of triumphal praise. Instead of the imperial laurel, instead of the purple, were the taste of ashes and the stink of rot.

The lowly hedge side now burgeoning into new life, the gleams of the distant stars that shone in breaks of cloud, those parts of the spring air untainted with the pollution of the carnage that now ravaged Ormskirk, all these and more howled execration at Martyn. Never had he felt so low, never had he despised himself so much. At other times of hardship, he had always managed to find some real or imaginary bright side to bask in; now there was nothing that even the most comforting of self-deceptions could point to as the slimmest glimmer of hope. His tears had dried up in an arid wasteland of misery, and he was of too shallow a character to find enough fibre and courage to be stoic in adversity.

He looked about his fellow wanderers. Words would not come, only a whimper of fury and misery, as he lurched towards Poffle. He had never killed anyone before, but there was a first time for everything. Timothy grabbed him around the waist before Martyn had time to launch his attack. Martyn tried to break free, but he was not as strong as he liked to believe, and Timothy was not as weak as Martyn had imagined.

"No, Martyn," said Timothy, "what will this achieve? Leave it be."

"Aye," said Abel Renton, "we've lived through bad times; we might be havin' to cope with even worse, but we've got to fight that, not each other."

"You bastards!" wailed Martyn. "Quitters! Shirkers! While I sweat and work my guts out trying to liberate you, all you can do — all you can do, you total bast—"

"SHUT UP!" commanded Timothy in a voice of steel.

Still whimpering and muttering, Martyn stormed up the road until he was several yards ahead of the party, and there he remained, oblivious to the rest of the troop and pent in his moiling hell of self-disgust.

"He's been through a lot," said Timothy sadly, "and he thinks he's been through a damn sight more."

In the distance they could hear the sound of gunfire including what sounded to Timothy suspiciously like the sound of an automatic rifle. This was puzzling as such weaponry had long been long proscribed in the *Perfect State*. It sounded very much as if the forces under Padlock were busily consolidating his grip on the land and not necessarily encumbering themselves with prisoners in the process.

"Now," said Timothy, "let's get the hell out of here."

Sometime later Timothy remembered Abel Renton's unanswered question. "Get over it? Will Martyn get over it? Will any of us get over it? Will this land get over it? What malevolent phenomenon have we engendered?"

There was no answer.

*   *   *

Timothy had resolved to write a book. He did not expect to ever see it published, since it was a tract on how he had changed over the past year and what his current outlook on life now was. He knew that it was all in his head, but it was still confused and dimly lit. He hoped to illuminate it with a veritable searchlight by putting it all down in ink.

Some conclusions had already been drawn; he was vastly different from the unhappy idiot of the year before. At that time, he had been dimly aware of a vague general unhappiness; now he could quantify it as a dislike of himself which, had it been examined more carefully, would have turned out to be a vast loathing of all that he had done, all that he was, and all that he stood for. Now, after a transmutation by fire, he rather liked what he had become. Whenever he thought of what he had been he felt embarrassed and ashamed. He wished for a bout of blessed amnesia in much the same way that many mature writers frequently wished that they could erase from the collective memory their youthful efforts.

Looking back, he was still amazed that the snivelling cur of the previous year could ever have become enchanted with Cressida. Surely even the idiotic Timothy could not be in love with such as her. But he had been, that he knew; whether it was a case of any port in a storm, a vacant sounding-board for his foolish and foppish opinions, or the fact that Cressida had decided that Taureans and Scorpions made perfect partners, he neither remembered nor cared.

"Look," whispered Abel Renton, pointing, to a bulky figure that lay at the base of the crossroads by the Stanley Arms. Abel Renton risked a match and in its fitful glow they saw the injured features of Arthur, T'osh's bottle-green-trousers clad henchman that they had worsted several times in the past.

"Dead?" asked Abel Renton.

"I neither know nor care," said Timothy earnestly, "though I do hope. Come on, let's get to the pub; I think this day has gone on forever."

As they approached the Stanley Arms, their view of it was hidden both by the night and an overgrown shaw[1]. Yet they could hear the sounds of revelry coming from within. Timothy, remembering a tale he had heard from an ex-convoy man, counselled caution. The convoy man told the tale of the corvette he had served upon rescuing the survivors of torpedoed merchantmen. One life raft they had identified by listening to the cries coming out of the dark and filthy weather. The corvette crew had thought that the cries were those of misery and despair; but as the ship came nearer the raft, the cries of seeming misery turned into a spirited rendition of "A Lassie From Lancashire": all the time the men had been singing

---

[1] a small wood; thicket; copse

to keep up their spirits and to keep from succumbing to hypothermia. Likewise, said Timothy, in view of the parlous state of the land, they should not simply assume that the sounds were those of a friendly hostelry — could they not be cries of pain, distorted by the wind and the travellers' preconceptions? — but should act with caution.

They did not follow the road but cut through the tangled shaw. After many snares and scratches, with brambles and gorse, they assayed the far side of the shaw, only to have their precautions made ridiculous by the sight of Martyn, standing in the open doorway, scowling and drinking deeply of a bottle of spirits.

They could see, as they crossed the car park, that the door had been forced open and now swung loose on one hinge. The interior was derelict of management and staff, but half-filled with maybe twenty-five men. They were all in the latter stages of drunkenness — some three or four had collapsed — and were drinking from the spirit bottles at an alarming rate.

"Well, this lot don't seem to offer much of a threat," said Timothy, going behind the bar and pulling pints of bitter beer for himself and the others. "A pint for you, Martyn? It will do you more good than that gin you're drinking."

Martyn's eyes were red and puffy as he lurched to the bar. "No, I won't drink with you," he growled. "I don't drink with defeatists."

"Defeatists?" asked a startled Frank. "My word, I—"

"Shut up, shut up, all of you, you're cowards, that's what you are. We defeated T'osh; we need not have let the menace of Padlock be born if we'd taken the decisions I'd suggested. Lickspittles."

Frank screamed and threw his, by now empty, glass at Martyn. Fortunately (or not) it missed. "Your ideas? Great God, man, who the hell was it that had the courage to fire the shot at Padlock? Not you, not you by a long chalk. You were all set to call me demented."

Martyn took a mighty drink from his bottle and lurched into the lounge. His slurred voice could be heard, but not many of his words could be made out, only something about "more heroical men than all of them, manning the barricades, bound for glory." Finally, one of the near-comatose drunks was heard to shout something along the lines of "Piss off, Hereward the bleedin' Wake!" after which he clocked him one and Martyn was heard no more.

"He'll get over it," said Timothy, "if he remembers anything about it, that is. Defeat is never an easy thing to take. I'm a fine one to talk, though; up to a year ago I'd have been as bad — or worse."

"Aye," said Abel Renton, getting up for another round of drinks. After he returned, with a tray of full glasses, he seemed to notice something by the wrecked front door. It was an envelope, bulky with papers, and had originally been nailed prominently to the front door but had been inadvertently torn down when the door had been breached.

It was addressed to Timothy.

He opened the envelope, finding inside two crumpled pieces of cheap paper and a long letter written on fine paper.

He smoothed out the first of the scraps and read out:

The artist: Frank Grogan.

I. I, artist. I. I, recorder of events. But not just that. It must be more. I am more. I am not a camera; I am an artist. Not a scribe of the mundane. But a recorder of the meaning of things. Can I record the meaning of things? Yes. I am an artist. I am genius. Take this ant upon the wall. It is not merely an ant. It is the antithesis of what could be on the wall but is not. I, I must record not only what is but what could be but is not. More, I, artist, must detail why the ant is there. It is not enough to say that it is an ant. I must say why it is not a centipede. Not a stain of blood and urine. Not nothing. I must state how the ant is affected by the existentialism of Jean Paul Sartre. I, the genius, must decide on all aspects of my work. I, the artist. I must not fear to portray the truth as it is. I must not flinch. I must not portray anything but that which is of significant to me, the sculptor of the written word. I must not squander my talent. I must—

The writings evidently continued on a further sheet that was not in the envelope.

"What tosh, what balderdash," opined Frank.

"But surely you wrote it?" said an amazed Timothy.

"I? I write that drivel? Pah! Only an unfortunate fool could turn out such rubbish."

"But it is in your handwriting, and you have signed it."

"Of what relevance is that? I tell you solemnly that I could never write such trash. The mind behind that composition must be both feeble and demented. I tell you . . ."

Frank continued unheeded for some time. Timothy meanwhile read the second piece of paper.

"Well, I recognise this: it's a free-form poem Martyn showed me a couple of months back. He said that he had woken in the middle of the night and was inspired to write this poem in about thirty seconds. He lost it, or it disappeared a couple of days later. He was furious about it. It's written in red ink; Martyn seemed to think that it was important somehow.

battered bodies bleeding in the gutters
round where the bikers go
plastic towers all burning
and the loner who goes past can't give a damn
heroes of the modern man go out to fight and die
while women wait at home and fritter their lives away
can't the women see that dignity cannot be found
in filthy lands of barren graves
dotted with the untouched smarties
of unborn children

can't men see that dignity and life cannot be found
on the death carts of Verdun
so I will sit here amid the flowers
and watch the river flow
till the bikers and the loners and the bombers
throw bloodstained bombs at me
and I too must die
and yet I welcome the end
I embrace it
wholeheartedly
for my epitaph will echo
down the generations

Timothy opened the thick wad of banker's paper, recognising the firm but small hand of Wladek's writing upon it. He knew that there would be an explanation for many of the mysteries of the past few months contained within its pages, yet he felt a reluctance to read it out, for he sensed that the words would not be kind. So, he prevaricated, pulling another round of drinks, lighting one of his infrequent cigars that he obtained from a spilled canister of them that lay upon the bar.

However, Martyn arrived shortly afterwards, his nose swollen and caked in dried blood, as militant as ever and as drunk as Timothy had ever seen a person. Martyn's abuse and vitriolic invective, unfair and peevish, was difficult to ignore or even forgive, coming as it did from somebody suffering under a burden of pain so great that Timothy did not even like to think about, but laid on so thick that it rankled even the normally placid Timothy into snarling;

"I have a note from Wladek. Do you want to hear it?"

"Hear it? Hear that double-dealing bastard? What slith— self-serving rubbish does he have to say to justify himself, thash . . . that's . . . what I want to know?"

"All right, then," said Timothy and read out the following.

Dear Friends,

By the time that you are reading this I will be well away, and the monster will be dead; or if he is not dead, we shall all be.

I was born thirty-nine years ago in the province of Latskonia. You will not have heard of it and, suffice it so say, that it is the poorest part of a certain south-east European country, which, like most of its provinces, tottered between utter bankruptcy and bare scraping through. Yet Latskonia had a fierce nationalistic past; it had, throughout a period of three hundred and fifty years been a major supplier of salt to the Mediterranean countries. It had been a flower amongst the provinces, a source of the nation's wealth and pride. . . at least until 1836 when the supply of salt ran out.

Latskonia, which had gained a certain amount of self-determination, became the recipient of the scorn and contempt of the rest of the country. Curiously enough, it did not lose any of its independence; rather it gained almost total self-determination, but this was due to the rest of the country ignoring and loathing the province. We fell back, we declined, we reverted to a bare subsistence farming. Do you know that the first steam-powered factory was not built in Latskonia until 1909? Do you know that there are no railway tracks in Latskonia, and that until 1937 there had not been one motorised vehicle within the province? That infant mortality still runs at over sixty percent?

That was the country into which I was born; and yet it was a country that was beginning to change with an unbelievable rapidity, due to a chance discovery. In 1952 a Spanish geologist was taking a walking tour in the Hdraska peaks when he discovered why the peasants avoided the 'cursed' (Hdraska means just that in Latskonia) peaks, why they never stayed on the slopes longer than they had to. The mountains were radioactive: To the geologist he had come across a uranium lode of such concentration and density that it was actually harmful to stay on the peaks. Normally, uranium lode is so diffuse that it is less radioactive than the radon-bearing rocks of ordinary granite, but this was so concentrated that if the peaks had been only a few kilometres closer, they would have started a meltdown process of the entire range!

Cursed be the day that Elka Swalbalti was whelped from the filthy womb of some raddled whore. He was twelve years older than I and could appreciate just what the finding of the lode meant to Latskonia. We were more or less independent of the hated mother country, and the mineral rights to the Hdraska peaks were the tickets we wanted to admit us to the twentieth century. The government of the mother country was having ideological differences with a certain super-power and both of them had forgotten all about us. With the aid of a certain other power, Elka Swalbalti achieved a more or less a priori independence, backed with the covert and overt help of this superpower on the understanding of a holding interest in the newly formed Hdraska Peaks Development Corporation.

And that was the country in which I was raised. The superpower mined the peaks and gave enough money to Swalbalti to turn Latskonia into a decent country. Any but Swalbalti would have done it:

Not he though. He modernised the army, built the palaces for he and his cronies, and became boss of a regime that makes T'osh's seem liberal in comparison.

The blood that is upon Swalbalti's hand! My mother, gunned down in the street; my father, I still do not know what became of him when the police took him away, my sister — but no, of that I will not speak, but only hope that there is in reality a hell, so that Swalbalti can burn in it for ever.

On the twenty-seventh of July 1974, I had my chance to strike back. Swalbalti was touring his country in triumph after some cosmetic improvement in his countrymen's ways of life. He was staying at the Carcyzc Palace, a converted twelfth century castle that day, and I, with thirty-seven other brave Latskonians were going to storm the castle and kill Swalbalti. I had long been a member of the Free Latskonia party and here, we thought, was the blow for freedom we had been waiting for. At the dark of the moon we set out (little did we know that our party had long been infiltrated and shortly after we had left our party headquarters the police massacred the other members left behind.)

It was far too easy to get to the Carcyzc; that should have alerted us to the danger. We breached the wall, cleared a swath through the minefield without encountering a single guard. Then, as we were crossing the lawn in front of the castle, all hell broke loose. By the light of flares and star shells we were cut down by a withering hail of fire from the guards who had been expecting us all along. Most perished in the first salvo; I was spared, but, and I am not ashamed to say this, became completely panic-stricken, running to and fro so that only the merest luck saved me from the guards' bullets and brought me to the perimeter wall. There my luck ran out. I had come to the wall, but a different part of the wall from the part scaled earlier. My one thought was to scale the wall; no thought did I give to any mines. Scant feet from the wall I heard and felt what to me was a deafening explosion. I was tossed high into the air and was somersaulted over the wall.

Consciousness departed for a few moments, and when it returned it was because of the agony in my leg. Flickering light from the star shells reached where I lay and I could see that my boots and trousers had been ripped away by the explosion: worse, so too had all the *toes of my right foot, together with the heel and most of the calf of my leg.*

I felt sick. I was going to die. Yet though this was uppermost in my mind, still there was a determination that if death was to be my lot it would at least be as far away from the damned Carcyzc Castle as possible. Hopping, crawling, bleeding profusely, I shambled into a break of trees and into a gypsy encampment. I have vague recollections of kind, mild faces, outlined in warming campfire glow; and of one aged, moustached, mahogany-toned face, staring down at me and saying something to a young man who held an axe.

There, memory ends, returning only days later, when I cried out at the sight of the stump of my leg bound in poultice and bandage.

I stayed with those kind people — people who risked their lives shielding a posted fugitive — for nearly a year, and they taught me many things, not least of which was how to survive and surmount my injury. One of them even made me an artificial leg which, though crude, I will always prefer over some computer-designed, soulless object of plastic.

My hatred of Swabalti increased; yet it was an impotent thing. I learnt of the massacres and the horrors that my countrymen were undergoing, yet what could I do? — one man, unarmed, un-moneyed. I resolved that the Free Latskonia party would rise from the ashes. I had learned that the rise to power of Swabalti had been masterminded in part by the secret machinations of the wealthy Poffle family. In Latskonia the various Poffle branches had been liquidated later on by Swabalti in his never-ending greed, but that there were some other branches of the family abroad. I resolved to deprive the scum of their wealth.

I succeeded with the Poffles of Norway, of America, of Peru, and late in 1977 arrived in England to rob the last of the English Poffle line, the foolish and foppish Quartus. (His sister, Harmony, I felt able to discount. She has little money.)

The money I had already obtained had been put to good use. Swabalti was dead, the ruling coalition of scum was tottering, and Latskonia was almost free again. Therefore, I could indulge in a little fun, a little artistry with the last of the Poffles. And so I started as a labourer for the foolish Poffle. Almost at once he gave me charge of the running of his financial affairs, so that the interest from certain of his shares poured into my Swiss accounts while I engineered deals and stratagems that would deprive him of his wealth.

I confess I made a grave error as regards T'osh and his power and importance.

At this date it seems an easy mistake to have made, to misjudge the issue, to think of T'osh as a sort of minor irritation, that common sense and decency would prevail. Alas! — how wrong I was:

I should have seen in T'osh the same seeds of destruction that flowered so horribly and foully in the rank garden of Swabalti. And then, to compound my folly, when he was on his way to power, I sat back smugly, thinking, well, this is your fight, mine is that of resistance to Swabalti. As if that could ever mean anything but the howling of a coward who does not wish to know? One must strive for right wherever and however one can; it is not enough to say that it is another's fight. If you are there, if you can help, you do help the good.

Belatedly I realised this, and had started some plans of my own to bring about the man's downfall — by this time the canker had bitten too deep to allow for any simple solution, such as merely killing T'osh outright — when I heard of some freedom fighters who had come to the region and whose express purposes coincided with mine. My spirits soared—

And then I met you all.

I do not recollect what I had expected. Certainly not supermen, but surely more than the fops and dilettantes I beheld. Martyn, all attitude and affectation, talking and singing overblown nonsense and believing it; Frank, a man of no talent, continually belittling others in a desperate and pathetic attempt to boost his own ego; Timothy, weak and foolish, but the only one of you who showed basic strength and decency, though this was buried deep because of the foolishness and inanity of Cressida.

Padlock . . . well, if you despise him, enough said about the man.

And when you came, what plan did you have? None. You seemed to think that pious words could bring about the downfall; that all that was required of you was to march in the general direction of T'osh and he would keel over. Fools! Worse was to follow: when you did start planning and devising half-formed schemes, some stupid, some suicidal, I had to stop you from ruining my own plans and even send you on safe and pointless missions just to keep you occupied.

One thing, and one thing only, stopped me from giving up in despair. She was the owner of the Stanley

Arms, who you knew as Florinda Farrier, but I knew as Svetlina Hrwrothy. She too had been on the raid on Carcyzc Castle, and she too had escaped. She had lived in Scotland for some years before returning to Latskonia, and so had been able to pass muster as a native who had spent many years abroad. If I may risk being sentimental, we were made for each other, and we were still united in our resolution to free Latskonia from its durance vile.

We shortly became partners in every sense of the word; our mission now began in earnest.

Infiltration into the ranks of T'osh was easy, and I saw the wealth that be was amassing. Perhaps cold-bloodedly I stayed the final overthrow of T'osh until he had maximised his wealth and had more or less given the key of his treasury to me, for me to walk in and take it at any time.

So too was my plan of obtaining Poffle's wealth going well. At about this time plans to obtain the wealth of Cressida and her parents were bearing fruit. Without a doubt she is one of the most mind-numbingly tedious people I have ever encountered. If any think that I have not suffered for my country, let them look to my marriage to Cressida. Her parents, though I met them but a few times, were thoroughly obnoxious, clearly in the habit of detesting anyone they regarded as being from the lower orders. I have no qualms in defrauding them. All three probably think that they are still rich: let them look to their accountant?

Padlock I did feel guilty about, for he is so utterly pathetic that words fail me, and I do have the odd qualm about shooting a fish in the barrel. Still, the money was there, and it would be put to far better a *purpose than gathering dust or clinking between the Reverend's bony fingers.*

It is now nearly dawn and I have been writing for several hours. I do not mean to write this as either a justification or an apology. I did what I had to for my country. I do think, however, that an explanation of my actions was called for. I do not too much mind being called a rogue because of things I have done; I do not wish to be called a rogue for things of which I am innocent. You will probably hate me for the strong things I said about you, yet in your heart you know I speak the truth . . . but perhaps it is a limited truth and confined to the past. You have been through the fire: have you been tempered by it or merely scarred? Martyn, have you now grasped the essential point — that men should be judged by how they behave, not how they ought to behave? Frank, have you, at last, benefited from the experience of living, a quality that was as missing from your life as it was from your writing? Cressida, have you, finally and at long last, found out that the universe is not geared to your every whim? And Timothy, you have already shown that you have learned much; always remember that there is always more to learn. I enclosed two sheets of paper containing evidence of what two of you were like before the test of fire.

You may see me again, but it is unlikely. By the time that you read this we will have won the war. The inn is well stocked with food and drink. Make use of it. Please also return to the wretched Poffle his glasses which are at the bottom of this pack, wrapped in a red cotton handkerchief.

Wladek.

Timothy drank some beer to cool his parched throat. "There's another sheet," he said.

In great haste.

Who would have thought it? I do not know whether we have lost the war or won a battle. I cannot stay. Urgent matters abroad. You must continue the fight. Bring down Padlock. You can do it. You must do it. Alone. Do not waiver. Your cause is just, you will succeed if you persevere. You are only sure to lose when you do not begin.

Martyn seemed to have calmed down and sobered up.

"Sorry," he muttered, "sorry about . . . before."

"Forget it," said Timothy. "What do you think about this letter?"

Martyn managed a wan smile. "A strange business if ever there was one. I have to say that I have my doubts about the veracity of the story we have just heard."

"Gone," whispered Cressida.

"Indeed," responded Timothy (to Martyn). "I can't help wondering if the mysterious Wladek has played us all down the line over the last couple of months."

"I think that is beyond much doubt," responded Martyn.

"*The Chronicles of Wladek* I assume. Arrogant bastard, if you ask me," muttered Frank. "I'm not surprised that him and his paramour have skedaddled. I would have said something about showing clean pairs of heels but, in reality, I suppose they have shown a clean *trio* of heels between them." He smirked at his own attempt at humour. None of the others did.

"Deserted," sobbed Cressida.

"Wladek had his good points," said Martyn.

"Penniless," wailed Cressida.

"And some bad ones," said Frank, his fingers once more examining the bruise that still prominently mottled the side of his head.

"So vat's where my money went," wailed Poffle in despair (despite having been reunited with his original, less flamboyant spectacles which now seemed scant recompense).

"Oh, woe is me?" howled Cressida.

"We'd've achieved sod all without him and his help," said Timothy.

"That's certainly right," said Martyn.

"I shall surely die in the workhouse," wailed Cressida.

"We achieved very little, anyway," grunted Frank.

"All my hard-earned cash gone to vat one-legged labourer and vat harlot. I'll murder vem," blathered Poffle.

"It may or may not be true," said Abel Renton as the doors of the Stanley Arms let in a number of burly, cudgel-carrying thugs. "Perhaps he is genuinely heading back to his homeland to fight the good fight, with the love of his life, or indeed purchasing a tavern, or some similar emporium, in a far-flung location with a view to running a profitable enterprise. I expect we will never really know."

"Waaaaaaaaahhhhhhhh!" howled Cressida.

* * *

If the streets of Ormskirk did not run with blood it was only because most of it had dried during the night and lay like a sticky varnish over the cobbles. It was a dawn much like any other dawn under the heel of T'osh.

*   *   *

Padlock awoke with a start, feeling a total disorientation of the senses. He had gone to sleep the night before in a large and comfortable chair — he must have, he was still there. The fire, which had blazed earlier on, was now ash and sullen embers. An empty glass lay by the fire: it had contained white spirit, to "take the chill out of his bones".

He was still rather tired this morning but realised that he would have to move quickly if he was to consolidate his victory; all could come apart quite easily.

"Miss Poffle?" he screeched, "Miss Poffle, where are you? We cannot let the grass grow under our feet when we are about the Lord's work."

When Miss Poffle arrived a few seconds later, she was in an agitated state, saying that there was a small but vocal group of businessmen and local notables at the door, demanding that they see Padlock.

"Demand?" whined Padlock. "Demand? Only the *Lord* demands anything of the Reverend Pedaiah Septimus Lock."

With eyes that were chips of ice he looked upon the deputation.

"I care not for anything that you may wish to call your business. But list: spread the word that at the hour before the noon there will be a meeting in the town hall.

All must attend. Go to it at once my brethren; God be with you."

They had never before objected to any of T'osh's orders; and though they were not completely brainwashed, and though they knew they had a new leader, still they did not think it prudent to say anything at this juncture.

* * *

And so it was that the little town hall was filled with people later that morning. To an objective witness there seemed little difference between one of T'osh's rallies and Padlock's inaugural. In the grey light the faces seemed to be made of dough, ready to be kneaded into whatever image the fashioner wanted. The air was charged with a sullen violence, a static electricity that waited to be discharged at whatever target came into view. If anything, this meeting was yet darker and more awesome than earlier meetings, for T'osh, though he wanted dominance over body and mind, would not have objected to a few rebellious thoughts whining away at the back of a person's mind, provided that the person was too cowed to do anything about it: but at this meeting Padlock wanted body, soul and mind, to blot out any thoughts that disagreed with his arid and bleak philosophy; to turn the populace into a ghastly set of robots without hopes or dreams — other than those he himself had.

Miss Poffle came onto the stage, with a number of waxed-paper spills, and lit the four fat candles set around a lectern; these four candles providing the only artificial illumination in the hall. Padlock strutted onto the stage, dressed in tight-fitting clothes of funereal aspect. At first his fearful head glowed palely, like the coating of a wet maggot; but, as he approached the light of the candles, his skin took on an orange, then a hellfire-red glow.

His eyes were deep in socketed shadow as he looked around the crowded room. His normal whining tones held notes of hysteria as he spoke.

"My dearly beloved brethren . . . I am but a servant of the *Lord*, ordained to do his work upon the earth. I will not detain you for long, for I know that you will have much praying to do, both for this day and for the days that you were held under the thumb of . . . him. I say, the work of the *Lord* is pressing and voluminous. All that I have called you here today for is to give you the following instructions and simple rules.

"All the prisoners of T'osh have been released and have been given pardons;

"Any disciple of T'osh, if there are any still alive that is, and any who say kind things of he who is gone, shall be imprisoned for an indefinite period;

"All black rats must be burnt: any who make contact with the black rat, or are bitten by the rat, or are surprised by the rat, or who tread upon the rat shall do this: they shall wear sack cloth and ashes for seven nights after this, bathing each day in a barrel containing sulphur and pitch: thus shall they be cleansed of the black rat, symbol of T'osh, familiar of T'osh, disciple of T'osh;

"Any who seek to worship the black rat, or talk to the black rat, or give the black rat succour and comfort, or

prevent the destruction of the black rat will be cast into the same furnace that the rat is cast;

"Any who would seek to practise sorcery, witchcraft, demonology, Satanism, necromancy, oneiromancy, chiromancy, rhabdomancy or any of the black arts will be burnt on pyres of blessed wood;

"Any whose body is not constituted with two arms and two legs, and upon each hand there be four fingers and one thumb and upon each foot five toes, and any who are deemed not to be wholesome in body or mind shall be deemed to be the children of Satan and shall be burnt;

"Any who seek to write books about ungodly matters or make conversation about ungodly matters, any who wouldst seek to live in an ungodly manner, they shall be put on trial and, if they cannot prove their innocence, then shall they be burnt at the stake;

"Any woman or man found possessing a black cat without good reason shall be liable to be accused of witchcraft and shall be given the usual tests and if these tests do not show that the person is innocent, then shall they be burnt at the stake;

"All Sunday services shall be restored immediately: attendance at all the services is mandatory, and any who do not attend and fail to show good cause for this dereliction shall be deemed to be in league with the devil and, if they do not prove their innocence, shall be burnt at the stake;

"Donations to mysel— the church will be welcomed — and expected;

"All must aspire to the living of an austere lifestyle, eschewing pleasure and frivolity, working hard and long at one's allotted task in life;

"We shall maintain our exclusion and isolation from the corrupt influences of the outside world. For this world is sinful and ungodly. We will be self-sufficient in our simple needs and shall not trade with the neighbouring lands. None shall come from those lands and seek to live in our Godly land unless they submit to our pious ways and have useful skills and a readiness to be hired at low cost.

"Any who wouldst attempt to enter our hallowed realm by illicitly crossing the border will be dealt a suitably harsh and prolonged punishment for they have not earned the right to dwell in our veritable Eden.

"None shall join a trade union or consider communicating with fellow employees with the intention of forming such an organisation for they are consumed with greed and malevolence and are thus despised by the Lord.

"An unmarried woman will submit to her father's authority – for she is his property until such time as she is married to the man who will be selected by the father according to certain criteria as will be defined by myself at a later date.

"Once she is married, a woman will submit to her husband's authority – for the Lord has decreed that the man is master of the household.

"Any woman showing signs of unwillingness to accept these sacred and statutory requirements will be flogged publicly in the centre of Ormskirk on either a Thursday or Saturday afternoon.

"A statue of myself shall be erected as soon as possible in the centre of Ormskirk; any who would show disrespect for this noble work will, should they fail to show their innocence, be burnt at the stake.

"What is it woman?" These last few words were whispered to Miss Poffle, who had been tugging at his sleeve for some moments.

"I say—"

Say it quickly, woman; cannot you see that I am busy in the work of the Lord?"

"Yes, but could I respectfully suggest that if you wish them to accept and welcome your rule, as indeed they themselves wish to do, a little less emphasis on the more punitive aspects of your constitution might not go amiss."

For the first time Padlock looked at the crowd, and saw that their sullen, malleable faces were beginning to look slightly hostile; it seemed to find a focus at the podium upon which the Reverend Pedaiah Septimus Lock D.D. now stood.

"Ahem," he said the to the audience, "my apologies for the break in my speech, but my deaconess had some important points that had to be brought to my immediate attention.

"I think at this time, since I said that I would not keep you, I will not go into any more of the new rules of living; suffice it to say that in a very short while a modest book will be produced, propounding on the themes I have mentioned and introducing some others. This book shall be given to every inhabitant of Ormskirk — free of charge.

"The body of T'osh shall this day be buried in un-consecrated ground outside of the boundaries of Ormskirk. Today shall be a day of rejoicing and celebration. All inns shall be open from noontide today until midnight and all their provender and drink shall be free of charge. Eat drink and—"

But the rest of Padlock's speech was drowned in cheers and shouts and singing – "For He's a Jolly Good Fellow" — and in the hubbub of a mass shuffling to the exits, for the noontide had arrived.

* * *

Any trumpets blown or heard for T'osh would definitely have to come from the other side, though which mariner of supernatural creatures would be giving the putative fanfare was a matter for personal debate.

A driving rain, fuelled by a cold wind from the east, had started shortly after noon, and in a cheerless copse to the north of Ormskirk six men were cursing silently the weather as they dug a deep trench. The soughing of the wind in the trees, the drip of the rain, the sharp liquid sounds their tools made in the soggy earth were the only noises in that thicket. The rain was so heavy that the bottom of the pit had long since been transformed from glutinous mud into a pool of dark water some several inches deep.

When the trench was deep enough the men climbed out and one of them, with obvious distaste, picked up a dirty, bulky sack and threw it in the hole where it made a distinct splash. Five men began to refill the trench while the sixth fitted a crude headstone to the top of the grave. Its inscription ran:

> *Here doth lie the body of T'osh,*
> *Dark and evil — the Black Magician:*
> *Slain by the hands of Pedaiah Lock*
> *The Lord's ordained physician.*

Padlock fastened a sable mantle about his throat and forced his thin frame into the driving rain. The cloak was new; he had discarded his duffle coat; that was one of the problems of being in power, you simply had to spend money sometimes. At least in this case, he thought, the end justifies the means.

The rain was so heavy that before he had gone many yards the thin hairs that grew sparsely upon his pate had become wet and entangled, so that they writhed down his temple and ears like worms in agony. The wind chill factor, enhanced by the sheen of rain over his pallid face, froze the skin but did not penetrate to the core of the parson, where a glowing furnace of inspiration roared and spat live coals.

He had not only achieved his object but, with the aid of Miss Poffle, was rapidly consolidating his hold upon the land; though best not say *his* hold, rather the hold of the Lord, for Padlock's role, as he saw it, was a mere stewardship for his Master.

One thing that did disquiet the weak and hard to find rational parts of his brain was the readiness with which he had been accepted by the long-suffering hordes. It was not as if he were offering pie in the sky and a land of hope and glory. He was offering more austerity of a type that made T'osh seem liberal in some ways. He reasoned that at some unspecified point in the future, were he to take his foot off the severity pedal, even slightly, there would be immense gratitude from the peasantry who would see it as a reward for their suffering. The insane parts of Padlock's brain held, of course, that the commonality knew what was best for them, and that what was best for them was Padlock. They looked up to Padlock as a paragon of virtue, asceticism, the antithesis of all that T'osh stood for. Padlock's maniac brain-cells knew that the populace looked up to him and, after all, what better master, after a hated Messiah of Satan, than a self-professed prophet of the Lord?

The sane brain-cells concluded that the amnesia of the populace was indeed a pleasing aspect which could serve any leader well. Add to this a fear and loathing of outsiders, a susceptibility to bigotry masquerading as finely-spun eloquence and a stoic sense that things might improve at some unspecified point in the future, once there had been enough austerity, and you had the perfect recipe for a benign dictatorship, reasoned Padlock. He concluded that some people just like to be kicked about quite a lot of the time and then forgot about the matter. If, at some indeterminate later point, they were 'rewarded' with some slight relaxation of the punitive laws, or a very modest increase in their living standards, their gratitude would be boundless.

Padlock firmly intended to maintain a firm grip on the running of the land, and he meant it to come to pass that the state was run exactly as he had planned, with great emphasis placed on certain aspects of Calvinist doctrine, together with some ideas added by himself. Now it just might happen that as a spin-off of this, his coffers could begin to weigh more heavily. But, if this became so, all to the good! Was he not entitled to it? — Had he not freed the land forever of the tyranny of T'osh?

The house he had chosen, both for residence and temporary headquarters, lay some distance from the town hall, so that he was thoroughly soaked and chilled when he reached the security of the demesne. Harmony Poffle had preceded Padlock to the house and had built a blazing fire in one of the hearths. Padlock warmed himself in front of it. For a moment he felt annoyance and his mouth puckered up into a moue — the coal: the expense: — but then smoothed itself into one of his rare smiles: he was rich, he was powerful; surely he could afford some slight extravagance?

Calling to Miss Poffle he said: "Verily and in truth has the wheel turned. Who, under the sight of the Lord, would ever have imagined that I, the Very Reverend Pedaiah Septimus Bartholomew Lock, D.D., ICA, would slaughter the disciple of Lucifer and become the seneschal of the Lord, the most potent and serene ruler of Ormskirk, not to mention Melling and Aughton? These lands are now mine to do with as I wish, and indeed I shall mete out a stern justice to *any* who would oppose me. Veritas, I am now a man of position and substance, and — in vino veritas, tee-hee — I think that a small celebratory glass of wine may well be in order. The elderberry, I think."

Harmony Poffle returned a few moments later with a huge bottle — almost a carboy — of wine.

"Ah, excellent: I think that we shall partake of a small glass. Yes, we shall indeed."

"Oh yes: You have given up so much in your valiant, selfless struggle. It's high time you returned to a normal life again and learn to sample those pleasures which you have hitherto been forced to forego."

"Ah yes, perhaps you a right. Another glass would do no harm, I fancy."

"You must consider your own needs."

"Indeed. Perhaps just another drop of this excellent wine."

"Perhaps take a wife?"

"Ah."

"Maybe produce an heir to the throne, if I may make use of such language."

"—!"

"Oh well . . . enjoy the wine."

"Yes, I think I will have another glass, sirrah —sorry, ma'am."

However, deep in the recesses of Padlock's mind, he had come to realise that Harmony Poffle, despite being a mere woman, had been instrumental in his ascendancy; her counsel was frequently practical; her advice timely and shrewd; her occasional strong-arm approach useful. She had revealed an instinctive ability to manage the expectations of the population. How would he ensure her loyalty in the future? Some consolidation of their partnership, possibly even marriage, might prove necessary. He sighed and finished his glass which was promptly refilled by the ever-supportive Miss Poffle. Difficult decisions could wait until tomorrow.

* * *

At about the time that Padlock was drinking his wine, a poignant farewell was being made at the Stanley Arms. The comrades were seated around one of the few unwrecked tables. Their gloom had in no ways decreased.

There could have been much trouble when the thugs entered the Stanley Arms the previous night. Certainly, they were no better than T'osh's strong arm lads — and Martyn had thought that two or three of the gang were T'osh's men, having undergone either a record change of loyalties or adopting some protective camouflage — and their leader had been a crazed loon far worse than any of T'osh's henchmen; a cleric of even less sanity than Padlock. He had raved about the evils of drink to the labourers, who luckily were too comatose by this time to do anything, and had asked why they were not at home, reading and memorising the good book. Whilst he had been spouting this tripe, the thugs had been amusing themselves by wrecking the place but, once the priest had finished his rant and had gone into the outer darkness where there was much lamentation and gnashing of teeth, the thugs had followed rather sheepishly the example of the holy man.

Perhaps this was the cause of the despairing bitterness found this day in the labourer, Abel Renton. Halfway through lighting his pipe he muttered: "First this T'osh with his bag o' tricks; and now this damned vicar who's mad as a hatter. Sod this for a bowl of candles; I'm off out of it"

He finished off his drink, muttering all the while about the fickleness and wretchedness of mankind and his disillusionment with much of everything, then limped slowly out of the back door, never to return.

* * *

The Amblers decided that it would be both futile and perilous to remain in the vicinity, given their role in the sequence of recent events. Moreover, their farm was unproductive at the best of times and their months-long abandonment of the daily chores had done nothing to improve the situation. Though they owned, now, virtually nothing other than the clothes they stood in, John Ambler was almost cheerful as he wished them a fond farewell. In his limited vocabulary he tried to explain that he had in some way been transformed by the experiences he had undergone; his horizons were no longer bounded solely by the next furrow.

Shortly afterwards they set their feet upon the road leading away from Ormskirk, determined to start a new light-filled and joyous life. Perhaps they did, though they must have changed their names; for even after the most diligent search and investigation, no trace of their current whereabouts has been discovered.

* * *

For Quartus Poffle it was his moment of "trufe". His natural inclinations were to get the hell away and keep as wide a berth as possible between himself and Padlock. However, for once in his life he had to face facts, the main one being that he was totally ill-equipped to face the outside world.

To anticipate the story, he went back to his cottage and penned a letter of appeasement to Padlock, congratulating him on his success and offering his services as a well-respected member of the community. Padlock, upon receipt of the letter, perused it intently then dispatched it unceremoniously into the fireplace. However, perhaps because he was beginning to realise just how dependent upon Miss Poffle he and his affairs had become, he did little else but burn the letter; he did not show any interest in the affairs of Mr Poffle, but neither did he incline towards thoughts of bloody revenge.

Life then, for Poffle, continued much as before. He employed a new labourer to run the farm. This person, although cloddish in demeanour, turned out to be industrious enough and kept the farm afloat, delighting in venturing to the Stanley Arms in the evenings and telling his 'story' to whoever cared to listen – for he, Caleb, was no less a personage than the brother of the renowned 'martyr' Noah Halfmoon.

Poffle spent much of his time penning articles for obscure scientific journals, all of which were returned with letters that began, 'I am sorry to inform you that your paper has been referred to our board of referees and . . .' The rest of the time he spent eating colossal quantities of corned beef and drinking titan draughts of melomel and elderflower wine. Perhaps this last factor made his essays more outlandish than they would have otherwise been.

It is believed that at the time of writing he is penning two essays, one on why the sense of smell does not exist, that it is a perverse creation of the mind of man, and the other that the earth is shaped rather like a banana, and that it's roundness, like that of the full moon, is an optical illusion.

* * *

Timothy knew that he would soon have to leave the region of Ormskirk, yet he was loath to do so, and tried to string out the process as long as he possibly could. He was part of this land, it had shaped and developed him; it was a comfortable place. In time, though, he rightly saw that he was retreating back, that the land had become womb-like. Yet the alternative — the dingy rooms, the scruffy desks, the awful bore of accountancy — seemed far worse. The awful dead round of one examination after another . . .

. . . no, he decided, that was not a viable option either.

He stood up. "There is more to life . . . and I intend to find it out. I have decided to wander the globe in search of . . . well, who can really say? Perhaps I will search for some form of truth . . . or maybe I am simply searching for myself. I intend to share my fate with the poor and oppressed peoples of the world. I shall throw in my lot with the common people in their struggle against injustice, tyranny, ignorance, poverty, disease, malnutrition, colonialism and multi-nationalism. And then — who knows? — I may just decide to return here, equipped with all the knowledge and skills needed and, when that day comes then Reverend Lock had just better watch himself, that's all I can say.

"Goodbye, my friends — my comrades in adversity. I hope that we will meet again, one day. Rest assured that when my tired eyes look upon the setting sun casting its beams upon the silvered waves of some distant ocean; or when I wander through the rot of some rain forest couched at the base of some nameless valley, chasing the rainbow's end; or, when the gentle winds of summer drift over the grit of some ragged, time-forsaken plain; then, oh then, my friends, shall my lined and weather-beaten face, haunted with the sight of untold squalor, soften in fond memories of the heroes I knew in this struggle."

Well, thought Timothy, as he went through the doorway, I've got the claptrap down to a fine art at least.

"A gormless, fey bugger, if ever there was one," muttered Frank darkly.

Before Martyn could reply in Timothy's defence, a frightful shriek rent the air:

"Timoooooootheeeeeeeeeeeeeeeeeeee!"

"God in heaven?" cried Martyn. "What the hell was that?"

"I rather think that it was our Cressida, who does not seem to be quite so deep in meditation as we may have thought."

Through the open door they could see Timothy turn and look to one of the upper windows of the inn.

"What?"

"Well, I wondered if . . . well, you see with all the money gone, stolen by that horrid man, and I was thinking that . . . well, I was thinking if . . ."

"If what?"

"Well, to put it bluntly, you haven't got a girlfriend, and, to put it frankly, I do not have a husband anymore, well . . . I am prepared to let bygones be bygones and forgive you for your various hurtful insults and take you back again — although you will have to make a greater effort to understand me, through my poetry and things.

"Also, I plan to study homeopathy in greater depth and will need to enrol on a full-time course for five years so will need your support during that time but I also will help out with a candle-making business which I intend to start up. Obviously, once I qualify as a homeopath, I will generate an income and we will be moderately prosperous."

"Indeed?"

"Yes, I rather think that you will have begun to see the error of your ways and, like many a good woman before me, I am ready to forgive and forget, and to appreciate you. Well . . . I mean, what do you say to that?"

"Well a kind offer certainly. I would like to take this opportunity to apologise for all the various epithets which I have hurled in your direction over the last few months – they were uncalled for and discourteous. I am no longer that sort of person. As regards your offer, however, I think that, on balance, taking all things into account, I would prefer to be whipped to death with red-hot barbed wire."

Without a further word Timothy turned to face the road ahead and strode purposefully away from the inn and indeed the entire location. It is said that he journeyed to Europe and, after some time, became actively involved in environmental concerns in either France or Germany, possibly both.

* * *

Martyn and Frank were still seated at the table some while later. They had been silent for some time, not because they had nothing to say, but because the frantic shrieks, sobs, howls, and wails that reverberated through the inn, but originating in a certain upstairs room, had precluded any conversation. After a time the noises became less intense, eventually ceasing altogether.

"Well this is a peculiar aftermath and that's for sure," said Martyn.

"As regards Cressida . . .?" replied Frank, portentously.

"What of her?"

"She's not bad-looking, when all is said and done."

"Possibly so."

"She has good, sturdy thighs."

"That is certainly true," responded Martyn, briefly recalling the memory of the voluptuous *woman on the altar*.

"Her rump is well-rounded but firm."

"I would not dispute that fact. Despite her unusual eating habits. Nonetheless—"

"Her décolletage is somewhat alluring."

"I haven't given it a great deal of thought but I suppose you're correct. Could you explain—"

"You would also be forced to agree that her face is, at the very least, quite acceptable, her teeth of good quality, her hair excellent, her skin extremely smooth and soft to the touch, and her person lacking in unwholesome bodily odours."

"I cannot say that I have found all this out by personal experiment, but I dare say that you are right on all counts. Yet—"

"Indeed, one is forced to conclude that she has many excellent qualities, including good breeding; and were it not for the tediousness of her conversation and her inability to cook, she would make an excellent spouse."

"Perhaps," said Martyn, not quite sure to what haven the conversation was drifting, but not liking the drift anyway, "but I don't see—"

"You can cook," said Frank, bluntly.

"Yes, but—"

"Well then, the solution is obvious: in order to tie up all the loose ends, you must marry Cressida."

Great goats and monkeys thought Martyn. For a moment he supposed that he had gone mad, then realised that it was Frank who was round the bend. Still, he could hardly believe what he had just heard. Clearly Frank saw them all as characters in some novel and now thought the time had come to write the final chapter. The more he thought about it, the more his head began to spin and the more increasingly numb his brain felt. (The minor complication of Cressida already being married did not occur to him at this stage.) Suddenly the stench of whisky was too much for him, and, as he rose from his seat, muttering something like, "Get stuffed you total pranny," waves of nausea lashed against him. He had barely made it to the nearest toilet when he vomited long and hard.

He returned to Frank sometime later, and found the latter still seated at the table, a full tumbler of whisky in his hand.

"What about you, anyway? What are you going to do, Frank? I'm assuming that you do not have any forthcoming nuptials on the horizon planned for yourself."

"I am not a simpleton; I know full well that Ormskirk is by no means a healthy place for me at this moment in time. However, despite this, I have resolved to return there. I shall settle once more in my room. Once there, I shall have very little reason to venture from it into the outside world. I have only my novel to think about; and once the final draft of this is completed and ready for publication, I then intend to start upon my next masterpiece."

"Oh. And what will that one be about?"

"Very briefly it will be about a zealot who, by superior methods of bluff and persuasion, managed to take control of a rural community. Once he is in power, he tries to turn back the clock, reverting to a feudal system of government, and bringing back the spectres of black magic, ignorance, disease, famine, illiteracy and so forth. Perhaps the plot is familiar?"

Martyn did not answer; he was wondering just how important a role Frank was building for himself in the novel.

* * *

Later that day a red-eyed Cressida announced that she had decided to stay at the Stanley Arms for some unspecified time while she tearfully tried to repair her shattered dreams. She mentioned various hare-brained schemes and plans, together with a few impossible — and, were they not so pathetic, laughable — dreams, which no one took seriously, and which grew more outlandish and improbable as the afternoon progressed and her steady intake of a rough, locally produced gin was maintained – her oft-stated abhorrence of the demon drink seemed to have been set to one side on this day at least. In addition to the candle-making enterprise referred to earlier these included:

o   Designing and selling her own range of jewellery
o   Busking with guitar singing her own compositions
o   Lecturing on the subject of astral projection
o   Trapeze artiste
o   Landscape gardener
o   Flamenco dancer
o   Toad whisperer
o   Trepanning consultant

Martyn considered that it was most probable she would eventually return to mummy and daddy in the role of the prodigal daughter seeking forgiveness and a sojourn to a French finishing school, or some such; though if Wladek's summary of their reduced financial circumstances was accurate this might prove to be more of a challenge than Cressida would anticipate.

*   *   *

But Martyn was wrong. Cressida fell into a deep, gin-induced sleep. When she awoke several hours later it was as if she had undergone a complete personality transplant – perhaps the gin had been influential. Clear-eyed and purposeful she made a start by tidying up her surroundings and the bar of the inn. Glasses were rinsed, tables mopped, and detritus swept from the floor; in the process a couple of near-comatose characters were persuaded to be on their way, which surprisingly they did without question, Cressida's voice projecting an undeniable air of authority. Then she cleaned and tidied herself up, disposing of some of her more ostentatious garb and dressing herself in a conventional outfit which, she hoped, would meet the strictures of the *Padlockian* regime whilst still looking presentable to anyone unfamiliar with the anticipated, but as yet unspecified, *dress-code* of the area.

After a couple of hours, the place was as transformed as Cressida. Low lamps had been lit, the bar was gleaming and the portraits on the wall, now dusted and straightened, seemed to exude a timeless sense of continuity and warmth. It was a place where anyone could drop in and feel immediately reassured, especially once seated by the roaring fire with a tot of whisky to hand. Was it time to travel a different road? Time to draw a line under the recent past and start again? She stood behind the bar and began to consider her future very carefully indeed . . .

*   *   *

Evening was staining the sky when Frank and Martyn left, perhaps for the last time, the Stanley Arms. They trudged, as they had so many times before, the road to Ormskirk. Martyn could have chosen a safer and more direct route home, but he felt in need of intelligent conversation and jovial company. Unfortunately, he was forced by circumstance to make do with Frank.

"Well, we've certainly had our share of adventures," suggested Martyn as a conversation opener.

"Possibly," said Frank, foully murdering the opportunity.

"I daresay that we've learned something valuable from it all."

"Doubtful."

"Really, I am quite sure that Kafka would disagree."

"Who?"

"Oh God." muttered Martyn.

"Who, I said?"

"Kafka. Franz Kafka," said Martyn, desperately hoping that he had mispronounced the name the first time.

"Who's he? Sounds like a Polish railway worker, if you ask me."

Martyn found himself entirely at a loss for words. Although it was tempting to point out to Frank that the name Franz Kafka was probably somewhat rare amongst railway workers, including Polish ones, he felt rather disinclined to pursue this line of argument as, not for the first time in recent months, he suspected that Frank was indulging in some sort of whimsical little parlour game.

*   *   *

As they neared Ormskirk they could see, for the first time in many months, its lights reflected on the low clouds; under the rule of T'osh the only lights available had been torches, rush lights and the frowned upon lantern. Now, at least temporarily, someone had turned back on the electricity. Soon sounds of revelry and strains of music played on scrannel instruments were heard. The streets were full of drunken people in festive mood. Banners, flags, decorations, crude wall slogans — all proclaimed the victory and glorious execution of

T'osh at the hand of 'Bold Pedaiah Lock.' One large banner carried an illustration of a malevolent character with glowing eyes and fiery hair, clearly in agony, with a large dagger buried in his chest. In the background stood a saintly, if skeletal, parson, who bore only the most superficial resemblance to Padlock: the artist evidently being of a generous disposition.

"Good luck to them," snarled Frank, "if that's the kind of bastard they desire to govern them, then they are bloody welcome to him."

"Aye — but I wonder if they'll be so ecstatic in six months' time?"

"Before I go to my garret — sorry, my room, I do desire to partake of a few jars of ale. I think it would be propitious to repair to a tavern before we go our separate ways."

"Why not indeed?"

Martyn was postponing his return to Maghull and the inevitability of having to resume his previous life. It would not be easy. Crossing the border was not a problem – he knew of many byways and cart tracks which would remain unguarded despite the efforts of the new regime, which at this stage lacked the personnel to effectively police the borders. There was even a long-disused tunnel, which few knew about, if all else failed. But it was the prospect of returning to normality after having endured the surrealism of the last few months which he found singularly unappealing. So, a pint with Frank was a welcome diversion.

*   *   *

They entered the crowded rooms of the Goat's Head (which would soon, no doubt, be due a change of name in order to more accurately reflect the objectives of the new regime), where they tried not to listen to the conversation, for it was all about the glorious deeds of Padlock, a character now raised to mythic stature.

Once they had purchased a large jug of strong ale they found a relatively quiet corner and discussed the lost years of their youth, when days were unspoiled, perfect jewels washed clean of pain and shame by the river of time. Martyn felt his eyes dampen and even Frank showed some emotion.

They did not notice it at first, but as they eased themselves into their situation and relaxed, the sound grew nearer, and they recognised the sound of an accordion, pipes and mandolin. They looked up and saw, over the heads of the customers, some fantastic shape leap into the air, then fall back, then leap again. The men drew back, and Martyn and Frank had a clear and uninterrupted view of the strange sight. The three musicians were formed in a loose horseshoe around a frightfully tall and thin figure, dressed all in patchwork, with a conical hat and hobnailed boots. In a trice this figure would dance from a crouched position to high into the air; so high, in fact, that the bells on the top of his hat would be jingled by the rafters.

Martyn shouted over the din, "Dancing Jack! What on earth—?"

"Ah, now that's a question, that's a question," said Dancing Jack coming across to Martyn and Frank.

"But I—"

"Truth to tell, I came here to do a job, and then found that the job had already been done, so to speak. Ha ha!"

"What job?"

"Why the overthrow of this blaggard T'osh — our old adversary. I really must meet this Pedaiah Lock, sound my warmest approval, and express my admiration for his valiant deed. Knifed the swine, eh? Ha ha!"

"Cack!" interjected Frank.

"What did you say?" asked Jack, nervously retying his polka dot bandanna.

"Cack and balderdash."

"He means that you are in possession of only half the tale. Allow me to tell the whole story — the true story."

"Pray do so."

Martyn related the whole story concerning T'osh, Padlock, Wladek, Timothy, Cressida, himself, Frank, Quartus Poffle, Harmony Poffle, John and Adaline Ambler, Abel Renton, Florinda Farrier, Noah Halfmoon, and various henchmen and supporting players. Jack sat silent and open-mouthed the whole time, his long, thin fingers, playing with the edges of his motley. When Martyn had finished, he asked of Frank if he had been told the truth, especially of the nature of Padlock. Frank solemnly confirmed all the details.

"Now that's a totally different bag o' boiled rats than I had heard. Ha! Of course, you are quite right; there is no more to be accomplished here at the moment. So! You, Frank, are away to complete your novel, and you, Martyn, to hie back to Maghull to begin again."

"True enough."

"But what will *you* do?" asked Martyn.

"Well now, I have no long-term plans as such. I think that I will stay in this hostelry until the towels go up, and then make my way back to the Stanley Arms, where you say this Cressida, this poor misguided Cressida, is eating out her heart. I am intrigued by Frank's description of her, ahem, attributes. I shall offer whatever solace and comfort I can give to this wretched and bereft damsel. She may prove useful one way or another, and no doubt will make a happy man very old, or somesuch — heh heh! Either way, I shall enchant her with my lute." He gave a theatrically lascivious and knowing wink to the two companions and went his way.

*   *   *

Anyone passing the Stanley Arms much later that day might have been surprised to hear Cressida merrily trilling *The Nonpareil* whilst accompanying herself on guitar and Dancing Jack providing further accompaniment on his lute. She had found herself somewhat enchanted with his quirky, carefree Bohemian personality and Jack was certainly taken with her in a variety of ways. It is entirely possible that her recent experiences had chastened her in some way; she now appeared rather less self-referential than previously and seemed willing to start anew, making the best of the situation in which she found herself. Jack, meanwhile, began to wonder if it was time to consider alternatives to his troubadour lifestyle which, in truth, had become a little wearisome. Here, in this tavern, undeniable warmth and companionship were to be found.

The new regime did not, as some might have anticipated, seek to close down licensed premises.

Harmony Poffle advised Padlock that this would only foster resentment and provoke an illicit, and potentially rebellious, drinking-den culture. Whilst many activities were officially proscribed she advised that the proverbial 'blind-eye' might be deployed when such doings were quite harmless; it was far more productive, at least for the time being, to concentrate on the other more dangerous and unacceptable pursuits which threatened to undermine the absolute authority of the monocratic Reverend. The jails in Ormskirk were soon full once more.

It is not certain quite how they organised it, but before long Cressida and Jack were established as joint proprietors of the Stanley Arms and, seemingly, running a successful tavern in which high-quality ale, and live music played an important part. Jack's creativity in the kitchen also ensured that wholesome food was available on the premises. Guests could, if they so desired (and many did) take advantage of other, more furtively available, services which included tarot and palm readings, classes in meditation and quite a few other things into the bargain. Cressida and Jack had devised a variety of strategies in the event of a raid by the 'morality police' (some were certainly known to be receptive to a bribe). So far, they remain undisturbed, seemingly able to operate just below the radar and maintaining a low-key operation. It would be churlish to wish them other than well in their daring enterprise.

* * *

There was a long pause between the conversations, both the companions staring into their drink.

Martyn looked at Frank. "I've a question to put to you."

"What might that be?"

"Do the recent events tend to confirm or undermine your belief in universal causality?"

"What?"

"Do you still consider that every event is itself caused by earlier events? Do you consider that no event is caused purely by chance or accident?"

"What nonsense! What point are you trying to make, man?"

"I happen to recall you going on about — at length — a doctrine of determinism which would hold true for every single happening in the entire universe. Just as the leaf that falls from the tree is caused to fall by the breeze that is in its turn caused by a depression in the north Atlantic and so on, so too is this madman's impulsive slaughter of a frog. Freedom in this sense does not exist. Are you with me?"

"Listen: I strongly doubt that I ever put forth such a ludicrous argument. If I did, then it was solely for the purpose of debate. Yet again you have illuminated — in three-dimensional technicolour, I might add — your own stark, naive gullibility. You people to me signify nought. Nothing! Less than nothing! You are all wage slaves. You lack true idealism. To such as me, money is nothing. Look at this wallet!" He took out an ancient leather wallet and surreptitiously looked over its meagre contents — "See how I cast it into the all-consuming fires of hell. I care not a jot." The empty wallet was cast into the nearly dead grate, where it began to slowly smoulder.

"Furthermore, your lives are so nondescript. You are exactly like the grey, one-dimensional characters featured in the dismal scribblings of such hacks as D H Lawrence and Franz Kafka: full of blustery self-importance, but lacking all colour, personality, depth of feeling. Your lives are like toilet urinals, spattered with chewing gum and awash with vomit and piss: on the one hand trivial and insignificant, but on the other, somehow, obnoxious and foul. Your stench is symptomatic of a decadent, obtuse, and perverse society.

"I neither feel the need — nor do I wish — to continue this debate."

Frank was back to his old self again.

*　　*　　*

"Last orders!" came the call from behind the bar; it was now long after midnight.

"I'll get these in," said Martyn.

"Fair enough, I'll have a bottle of brown ale," said Frank.

"Double round?" asked Martyn.

"Ah, go on then," replied Frank, covertly searching through his spare wallet for the necessary funds.

*　　*　　*

Outside the rain now fell heavily and unremittingly, drubbing the dark streets of Ormskirk and the adjacent villages and hamlets. It pounded the clocktower in the town centre; the roof of the Stanley Arms; the cottage windows of Quartus Poffle; the charred remains of Padlock's vicarage; the ruins of John and Adaline

Ambler's farmhouse; and the open fields and hedgerows in which small, nervous creatures took furtive shelter from the deluge. It soaked the surroundings of the Goose and Goslings tavern in Melling where anxious barmaid Celeste Phlegg was still serving customers in the dimly lit rooms in which a secretive, late-night drinking session was just commencing. It rattled down on the houses, lodgings and hovels of assorted hobbledehoys, ne'er-do-wells, sycophants, lickspittles, turncoats, gobshites, poltroons, head-the-balls, cranks, hacks, blowhards, shysters, tricksters, swindlers, sophists, footpads, poachers, wide-boys, dissemblers and petty criminals just as it fell with equal implacability on the dwellings of the decent, the wise, the erudite, the creative, the gentle and the generous. Brooks and streams burst their banks, garden ponds overflowed, and the neglected drainage system struggled to cope with the surge, so that those still attempting to make their way home through the streets of Ormskirk soon found themselves ankle-deep in gurgling water; their progress additionally hindered by their rough and extremely permeable garments soon becoming sodden and heavy. Some, including the new leader, saw this torrent as a divine manifestation, proclaiming it to be the *Lord's cleansing rain*. Others construed it as yet more evidence of an *ancient curse* hanging over the town. The more phlegmatic merely declared that it was *bleeding soaking* and wondered if the roads would be impassable in the morning, as the rain continued to fall remorselessly throughout the long, dark night.

*　*　*

The rain fell too on the cheerless copse to the north of Ormskirk, saturating the woodland, waterlogging the adjacent fields and hammering urgently on the gravestone of T'osh, the Black Magician and one-time omnipotent ruler of Ormskirk.

There came no reply.

Sic Semper Tyrannis.

About the Author

Richard Raftery was born in Warwick at the dawn of the Rock n' Roll era, before moving to Melling in Lancashire at the age of three where his grandfather had been the village blacksmith. After leaving school at sixteen he worked in a number of occupations including tax office clerk, labourer and weaver before entering teaching. He later became a trade union official. In addition to *The Return of the Black Magician* he is the author of two collections of poetry – *Smart Boy Wanted* and *Too Big for This Town*.